...d...ning author **Louisa George** has been an ...vid rea...er whole life. In between chapters she's ...aged to train as a nurse, marry her doctor hero and ...e two sons. Now she writes chapters of her own ... ...e medical romance, contemporary romance and ...en's fiction genres. Louisa's books have variously ...nominated for the coveted RITA® Award and the ...w Zealand Koru Award, and have been translated into ...ve languages. She lives in Auckland, New Zealand.

...e **Kincheloe** has been writing stories for as long as ...remember, and somehow they always become ...nces. A Kentucky girl at heart, she now lives in ...see, with her husband, children, and a growing ...gerie of pets. Visit her on Twitter: @AllieKAuthor.

NURSE'S ONE-NIGHT BABY SURPRISE

LOUISA GEORGE

REUNITED WITH DOCTOR DEVEREAUX

ALLIE KINCHELOE

MILLS & BOON

First Published in Great Britain 2021
by Mills & Boon, an imprint of HarperCollins*Publishers*
1 London Bridge Street, London, SE1 9GF

Nurse's One-Night Baby Surprise © 2021 by Louisa George

Reunited with Doctor Devereaux © 2021 by Allie Kincheloe

ISBN: 978-0-263-29762-1

MIX
Paper from
responsible sources
FSC® C007454

NURSE'S ONE-NIGHT BABY SURPRISE

LOUISA GEORGE

MILLS & BOON

CHAPTER ONE

'PLEASE, DON'T MAKE me go to school. *Please.*' Fraser blinked fast at the woman in the passenger seat next to him as she stared out at the whitewashed stone buildings with their grey-blue slate roofs and the sign 'Welcome to Bowness High School'. 'I've got a tummy ache.' He moaned and rubbed his belly, looking for sympathy.

But she clearly wasn't doling any out today. She frowned, rolled her heavily mascaraed eyes and pulled her ponytail tight. 'No, you haven't. You're fine.'

'Please, don't make me go. Please, Lily.' He tugged on her arm and made sad eyes at her. 'Can you write me a sick note?'

She glared at him. 'Isn't that supposed to be *your* job?'

'I need a responsible person to do it for me,' he teased. 'Know any?'

'Stop it, Dad.' A reluctant smile finally...*finally* curved her lips and she play-punched his arm. 'Honestly, you're worse than me. You have to go. It's work. You've signed a contract and everything. Stop messing about.'

'Made you smile, though.' That would be enough to see him through what he knew were going to be difficult days ahead. Just as the last few months...years, really, had been.

She threw him a look that would have frozen hell. 'Only out of pity.'

'You used to laugh at my jokes.'

'Back when they were funny. Like, when I was six or something.'

Now she was fifteen going on twenty-five. Wearing non-regulation mascara and lip gloss that he'd refused to fight about this morning and a skirt that he was sure hadn't been so short when they'd bought it a couple of weeks ago. He'd decided to let it go for today. *Pick your battles.* First day, new term, new school.

New start.

He remembered her first smile, her first tooth, her first day at nursery as if it were all yesterday. Where had that time gone? How had he ended up with this stroppy, beautiful, fierce teenager when only minutes ago she had been a tiny scrap that had fitted into the crook of his arm?

They'd always been a team and he'd always made her laugh. She'd loved his jokes almost as much as he loved her, but now she blamed him for everything that made her unhappy. He met her eyes—so dark like her mother's—and saw the pain there. And the fear too. He had to make sure she was going to be okay. *That* was his job.

Until five years ago he'd shared that job with his ex. They'd co-parented as best they could with shared custody, living just streets apart, short-term lovers who'd become long-term friends. He'd been the bad cop to Ellen's good cop. Funny, sweet, warm-hearted Ellen who had died, leaving both him and Lily bereft and him to parent on his own, clumsily navigating first their daughter's deep grief and then teenage hormones. And now, in his daughter's eyes, he was just all round bad.

He patted her hand. 'Seriously, Lily, are you okay with this?'

She looked out at the sleet melting on contact with the heated windscreen, her smile dissolving into the sulky expression that had been ever-present on her lips since that icy five-hour drive north had brought them here to the Lake District, where her mother had grown up, leaving their London life behind. That expression had remained all through Christmas and New Year, particularly when they'd been to buy the uniform she was wearing now. Lily didn't want to try. She didn't want a new life, she'd been perfectly content with the old one.

And that was why they'd had to move.

She slid her hand from under his and twisted the handles of her expensive new backpack. If he was honest, she looked about as fed up as he'd ever seen her.

'No.' She shrugged. 'I'm not okay about it and you know that already. But here we are anyway. I don't really get a say in it, do I?'

His heart squeezed. If only Ellen were here, she'd know how to do this. But, then, if Ellen were here, he wouldn't have upped sticks and moved away from all Lily knew. Out of desperation he'd thought of this place. Grasping at flimsy straws, he'd also wondered whether Lily's godmother might have moved back here at some point too…cavalry to enlist to help him. Although he wasn't sure she'd want to help after their last meeting five years ago.

Guilt rattled again. Had it been wise to move Lily so far from everything she knew? From the place where she had memories of her mother?

'It's going to be fun, Lily-Bee, if we just try. A fresh start for us both. It's what we need. Trust me.'

Another dark look. This one said, *I did trust you. Once. But now? Not so much.* 'A freezing start, more like. And boring. B-o-oring.'

'Not once you've made friends.'

'Duh. I have friends, Dad. Lots of them. Back in Clapham.'

They hadn't been friends, they'd been…the only word to describe them was *delinquents*. He knew that made him sound a lot older than his thirty-four years. He'd watched helplessly as she'd changed from a happy little girl into a tearaway teenager who had refused to listen, refused to meet him halfway and refused to conform to even the lightest of rules. He'd been at a total loss as to what to do. So much for being the cool outreach doctor who understood teenagers.

But only a few moments ago he'd finally managed to get a smile from her and he wasn't going to spoil it by raking over those old arguments again. 'With your winning personality and the amazing talents you inherited from me, you'll soon make lots more.'

Just one. One nice one. One that isn't into drugs and drinking. One who actually attends school. Please.

He laughed, trying to show her he was joking, about the talents anyway.

She rolled her eyes. 'Yeah, Dad. Whatever.'

'They have an excellent drama programme.'

'I stopped wanting to be an actress in year three.'

'The science programme has won national awards.'

'I don't want to be a scientist either.'

'What do you want, Lily-Bee?'

'Not to be here.' Her nostrils flared and she glared at him. He wasn't sure if it was because he'd called her by her childhood nickname or because she was here in the car, staring at her future…or both.

'You never know, you might change your mind. Give it a chance.'

Give us a chance.

They'd been all out of chances in London. Next stop for her had been the juvenile detention centre. The local police had had his number on speed dial.

Silence.

He dredged up another smile and his cheerful sing-song Dad voice. 'Right, best get going. I'll see you this afternoon and we can drive home together after my clinic's finished.'

Her eyes narrowed. 'I can walk.'

'It's January. The forecast's for snow. It'll be cold and you're not wearing walking clothes.' He held back the criticism as he looked at the short skirt and school shirt open one button too many, unsure how his city girl would fit into the country school. But it was too late now. They were here and he was determined they'd make the best of it. 'Anyway, it'll be a good chance to chat about our first day at school.'

'You're only going to be here for a couple of hours later. I have to put up with it all day. Every day. Until I die of total boredom.'

'Or you could embrace the delights of rural living in a beautiful place.' Behind the school buildings rugged snow-topped mountains provided a breathtaking backdrop. Or would have, if visibility hadn't been impeded by the low-hanging clouds heavy with sleet. He cleared his throat, deepened his voice and threw his arm out as if he was on stage, delivering an important soliloquy. '"I wandered lonely as a cloud…"'

'Stop it, Dad. Maybe you should be the one doing drama, not me.' Another eye-roll, followed by a tut. 'Promise you won't be embarrassing at school? Like, if you see me in the corridor, don't even acknowledge you know me?'

'Is there no end to the ways you can spear my heart?'

he said, trying to put a smile in his voice but remembering how everything his mum had said and done had almost killed him with embarrassment when he'd been Lily's age. It didn't mean her words didn't hurt, though. 'Everyone's going to know eventually, Lily. It's a small school. We have the same surnames. It won't take a genius to work out we're related.'

'Please, just let me have a few precious hours where I'm not the "hot" doctor's daughter?'

She made quotation marks with her fingers and pulled an *I can't believe I just said that about my dad* face, and he tried hard not to laugh.

Hot? To a bunch of teenagers? *Great.* No wonder she was embarrassed. 'Okay. You won't know I'm there. I promise, I'll keep a very low profile.'

'Good. See you later, yeah?'

'Absolutely.' He leaned in to ruffle her hair the way he'd always done, but she was opening the door and swivelling out of her seat, completely oblivious. Out of reach. 'Good luck for your first day, Lily-Bee.'

A bitter laugh came from her throat. 'Believe me, I'm going to need it.'

Me too, he thought. *More than you'll ever know.*

'He hit me first.' The boy pressed an ice pack to his swollen jaw and shivered. He was holding back tears, trying so hard to be the tough guy. 'It was self-defence, miss. Honest.'

'Hey, I wasn't there and I'm not going to judge, Alfie. You don't have to explain anything to me. Save that for your interview with the head teacher.' Briana made her voice as soothing as possible. She had other ways of finding out what had happened without asking direct questions he could avoid. She needed to gain his trust first, which was going to take gentle handling and a bit of time, but she didn't have that luxury right now with a queue of kids waiting and a doctor gone AWOL right on clinic opening. Typical. They couldn't seem to get anyone to staff this clinic for longer than a term.

She gave Alfie a smile. 'I just need to know what kind of injury you have, where it hurts and if you need an X-ray and painkillers.'

Having ascertained his bruised jaw wasn't fractured, she did a quick assessment of the rest of him. His hair was matted with mud, his black uniform trousers were torn and ragged at the knee, his school bag looked as if it had been dragged through cow dung. His hands were red and raw, fingernails ingrained with dirt, no doubt from where he'd landed after the punch to his chin. Great start to the term for this poor lad. He shrugged a scraggy shoulder. 'I'm fine.'

He wasn't fine, and his bottom lip was starting to wobble as the shock of the fight wore off.

Briana looked at the boy's reddened knuckles. 'Any pain in your hands?'

He made a sound she thought might be 'yes', then said, 'He said I was stupid. He said my sister's stupid too and told me what he was going to do with her down by the lake.' His face creased into an expression of pure disgust. 'I told him she's not a slut. That I'd punch his lights out if he said any more.'

'She must be proud to have a brother like you to stick up for her.'

No eye contact, head down, he spoke into his chest. 'She thinks I'm stupid too.'

'I bet she doesn't.'

'They both do. Just because they're two years older than me. That's not my fault, is it? Worse thing is, she loves him.' The boy shook his head in disbelief. 'How can she love someone who says things like that about her and hits her kid brother?'

Oh. Briana hadn't been expecting that.

'She doesn't know any better, Alfie. She's far too young and doesn't know what real love is. She thinks she does, but she's got a lot of growing up to do.'

You get drawn in, you fall too hard and too quickly, get taken in by their manipulation and before you know it, you're trapped.

Briana shoved her memories back. This was not the time to relive her own mistakes. 'Do you want me to have a word with her?'

He rolled his eyes. 'Tell her not to go out with Lewis Parker? Good luck with that, miss. She won't listen.'

'I won't actually say that, because you're right, she's not going to want to hear that from me. But I can have a gentle chat about relationship boundaries and expectations.' She smiled. 'Of course, I won't put it like that either. Lecturing people tends to put them off, right?'

'Right.' He nodded and his shoulders seemed to relax a little.

She tried a different tack. 'Lewis sounds like an annoying toddler. All that carrying on, trying to get attention.'

'Yeah.' His eyes brightened. 'Like my little sister. She won't shut up sometimes. She just makes a noise to get what she wants.'

'And how do you get her to stop?'

'Mum says if we ignore her, she'll just get bored.'

'And does she?'

'Yeah. I s'pose.' His expression became serious. 'You think I should do that with Lewis? Like, ignore him?'

'Do you think you can? It might help avoid a fight if

you don't let him get to you.' Because they both knew Alfie was the one who'd hit out first. Trying to defend his sister, playing the tough guy. Saving face and family honour, even though he'd been provoked, because why else would a thirteen-year-old try his luck with someone two years older and a whole lot bigger? 'Often, ignoring them is the first thing you can do. But there are lots of other things too.'

She made a mental note to speak to Lewis Parker's form tutor as soon as she got the chance. Arming the victim as well as addressing the bad behaviour—or the underlying causes of the bad behaviour—often worked. What was going on in Lewis's life that made him need to bully others?

A sharp rap on the door had her turning round. It was Andrea, one of the school administrators. 'Sorry to interrupt, Briana, but I didn't know how long you were going to be—'

'I'm going, miss. Got to see Mr Wilson.' Alfie put the ice pack down and shouldered his school bag. The bruise on his chin was dark and swollen and he did not look happy about the prospect of seeing the head teacher.

'Okay, Alfie. Come back tomorrow morning so I can have a look at those bruises.' And check on his well-being. Arm him with more strategies.

With kids like Alfie, the best way of helping his emotional needs was to disguise it as dealing with his physical ones. Crafty, but it worked.

Andrea smiled as the boy dashed out of the door. 'The new doctor's here. I've done a walk-round to show him the layout and explained how the clinic works, but he's going to need the full Briana Barclay orientation.'

'As much as I know after only being here for a term.'

'You know more than him, that's always a start, right?

Oh…' Andrea leaned closer and lowered her voice. 'Prepare yourself. He is hot, hot, hot.'

'Who? The new doctor that should have been here an hour ago? No one's hot when they can't be relied on to be on time.'

'To be fair, he said the email had confirmed a two-thirty start.' Andrea shrugged. 'Maybe he got it wrong? Can't have beauty *and* brains, right?'

'I don't care how good looking he is, if he isn't here on time to see the students they'll leave. It's hard enough to get them to attend appointments. They won't wait. They get the jitters, second-guess themselves and leave.'

'Did I mention he was hot?' Andrea fanned her face. Her cheeks were reddening, her eyes bright and dancing behind her reading glasses. She looked like a teenager swooning instead of a motherly fifty-something woman who should know better.

Bri laughed as she stalked into the waiting room with Andrea in her wake. 'Right, where is he? Let's get this over with. I have far more important things to do than mollycoddle a man—'

Oh, God. No.

'Bri…' Andrea was grinning and her eyes were wide, as if to say, *Ta-da! I present to you the hot new doctor.* 'This is Fraser Moore. Our new adolescent health specialist. All the way from London.'

He was standing in the middle of the room, filling it with his enigmatic presence and good-natured smile that she knew were just masking the real Fraser Moore. And, yes, she could see how Andrea might think him hot with his wide, haunting dark eyes. The short dark hair that was well groomed in a stylish city-boy look. The tan-coloured chinos and pale blue merino sweater that skimmed his rugged body. Oh, yes…she could see that someone who didn't know him would think him off-the-scale gorgeous, as she had done once upon a deluded time. Even the girls in the waiting room were staring at him as if a famous actor had just walked in.

But Bri knew better. She knew all about Fraser Moore.

Behind him a group of giggling girls burst into the waiting room. One of them stopped short, stared first at her then Fraser, her mouth gaping. She was about fifteen years old, hair pulled back into a long ponytail, dark eyes. She looked so familiar but Bri hadn't seen her around the school before.

Fraser's eyes widened and he looked guilty as hell, enough that Bri iintsinctively knew who this girl was.

Lily? Sweet, sweet Lily. Her heart lifted and hurt at the same time. All grown up with that teenager-going-on-twenty coquettishness.

All those missed years and missed chances.

Emotions hit her in the chest like bullets. Pain, sadness, rage, love. Bri's heart pounded, white noise filled her ears. She had no chance to gather herself and take stock. No chance to breathe. To try to drag on an expression that wasn't one of pure shock.

They lived here in the Lake District now?

Why? Fraser was a confirmed and devoted city man. When he'd visited years ago with Ellen and baby Lily he'd made it clear he couldn't breathe in all this space. Hated the crap public transport, the lack of buzz. The inward-looking parochialism of it all. So why here and why now?

And still Andrea was talking in her sugar-sweet voice, oblivious to the fact that the only hot things in the room right now were the daggers zipping between Bri and the man she'd hoped she'd never see again. 'Dr Fraser, this is our lovely school nurse, Briana Barclay.'

Briana closed her eyes and tried to stop her body from shaking. 'Fraser? What the actual hell are you doing here?'

The man who'd stolen the last few years of the most precious and dear friendship of her life. Who had prevented her from seeing her dying best friend in her last months of need. The man who'd blanked her and ghosted her. And now he was here to…what? To cause her pain? All over again?

Like hell he would.

CHAPTER TWO

'Bri. Hi,' said Fraser, unsure how to act with someone who'd prefer it if he lived on the other side of the world. Or, in truth, didn't exist at all. And didn't even try to hide it. Hell, he hadn't exactly been expecting to see her either. He'd wondered if she might have moved back to the area but working with her in a school hadn't been remotely on his radar.

His presence here was going to take some explaining. Heart thumping hard against his chest wall, he tried for a smile. 'Surprise?'

She shook her head as her cheeks flushed, matching the silk blouse she was wearing. Red for danger. But he didn't need a sign to tell him he was on dodgy ground, her look said it all. As frosty as the mountains every morning since he'd been here. Her mouth flattened as her blue eyes narrowed. 'Please don't tell me you're living here now?'

'Um. I think I can hear my phone ringing. Got to go.' The administrator woman left the room and Fraser yearned to escape too. *Coward.* But there was no going back now.

'You remember Lily?' He beckoned to his daughter, who had just walked in and was staring at him as if he had two heads. He could feel the daggers in his back

from her too. 'Lily, this is Briana. Your godmother. Not
sure if you remember—'

'Duh. Briana's my middle name. Of course I remember her.' But Lily didn't look at all happy about meeting
up with her godmother. In fact, she looked horrified.

'Oh, Lily, I can't believe how grown up you are.' Despite Lily's antagonistic expression Bri gave her a genuine smile and put her arms out, he imagined, for a hug,
the way she'd done when Lily had been a little girl. Back
then Lily would have toddled into her godmother's arms
and hugged hard. They'd forged a strong bond in those
early years as Lily grew up. Briana had been a regular
visitor at Ellen's house and a keen babysitter when she
could get time off work, but then Ellen had got sick and
everything had gone to hell. Any bond between Lily and
her godmother had been broken years ago.

Lily didn't move. 'Huh.'

Fraser hoped it was meant to be a 'hi' but had come
out weirdly. He felt a need to explain everything to both
of them, but not in front of the gawping audience. 'It's
been a while since you saw each other.'

'Probably seven years, if you count all the time Ellen
was sick and you didn't exactly encourage visiting,' Briana said, the smile fading back to the grim line, her arms
dropping. 'Five years since…' She swallowed and blinked
fast.

She didn't need to extrapolate. They both remembered
the gut-wrenching heartache of the funeral, the way Briana had clamped her mouth shut but had said so much
with her eyes. That somehow it had been his fault.

It had been a brain tumour. Not his fault, but he'd always wondered if he'd done the right things to ease Ellen's pain and the pain of those who loved her. He'd tried
to protect his daughter from it all, but knew he hadn't,

and wondered too whether the way he'd dealt with her mother's illness and death was the cause of Lily's subsequent issues.

Lily glared at him before giving a minute shake of her head. 'I'm going home. See you later.'

His heart squeezed. 'But we said we'd drive home together.'

'And now I'm going to get the bus.' Her eyes widened as they flicked to the teenagers sitting on the waiting-room chairs. *Shut up. Don't embarrass me.*

He'd already done her enough damage by breathing the same air here, let alone having a stand-up confrontation with Briana.

'Lily, I'd love to catch up when you're free. I'm here most days, just pop down. Any time. Or maybe we could have a coffee sometime?' A mixture of emotions zipped across Briana's face. Her long blonde hair had been tied up in a messy bun and she had loose curls wisping round her face. She tucked one behind her ear as she pressed her lips together in a tight smile. She may have been shocked at finding them here, but there was hope in her gaze. She wanted a connection with Lily even after all these years.

It was a chink in her armour, and it gave him a little hope too. For the first time in a long time maybe he didn't have to do this all on his own. But that all depended on Lily, and he couldn't describe her reaction to all this as remotely positive.

'Uh, maybe.' Lily scuffed her shoe on the floor, not meeting Briana's eyes. Then she turned away from them both and walked to the door. 'I'm out of here.'

His heart hurt. But then it always did where his daughter was concerned.

The smile disappeared and Briana turned to him, her expression one of bitter pity.

'Still in the running for father of the month, I see?'

He breathed out deeply, wondering how much to confess and, deciding this wasn't the time or the place, he just went with, 'It's definitely a challenge.'

She rubbed her palms down her thighs, skimming fingers over her black trousers. 'Right. I have to go. We have students to see.'

'Could we talk? Later?'

'You and me? No way.' She grimaced and stepped back as if he'd struck her. 'But I would like to see Lily. We have a lot of catching up to do.'

He needed to explain why he'd acted the way he had back then. 'Bri. Please. I think we need to clear the air—'

'No, Fraser.' She looked as if she was about to explode, but she took a deep breath and gestured to the waiting room. 'I have a job to do.'

'As do I.' He backed off. This wasn't the time or place to talk through the past. 'But I haven't a clue where to start. Andrea said you'd show me around. I'm pretty sure some of the processes will be different from London. I don't want to stuff up on my first day.'

'You already have.' She sighed and shook her head, the red on her cheeks less intense but the glittering anger in her eyes still very much in situ. But she nodded. 'Follow me.'

They crossed the busy waiting area to a door that said 'Clinic Two' on it. She opened it, went in, waiting for him to follow her, and then closed the door, all professional and aloof. 'This is your clinic room. On the desk is a file of information on local providers, but if you've used the EMIS system before you'll know how to find specialists in the area. If you'd arrived a decent amount of time before clinic started, I could have shown you properly. Now you'll have to whizz through the best way you can.

'It's the first day of term so I'm not expecting much more than what we have waiting out there, but you never know what's going to come in through the door. Any problems, call me. Extension 556 on the internal phone. Clinic One.'

'Briana, I'm sorry.'

'For what exactly? Being late? Being here at all? Putting yourself in between me and my best friend when she was *dying*?' She swallowed then held a trembling hand up just as he was about to explain. 'I don't have time for this, Fraser.'

'The email said two-thirty.'

'Then it was wrong.'

And with that she slammed the door behind her.

So, that hadn't gone as well as he'd hoped.

Nausea ate at him during each consultation throughout the afternoon.

Had he made a massive error of judgement by bringing Lily here? Hell, he'd been wondering that ever since they'd packed the car with their belongings and headed north. But being a parent was all about protecting, guiding and keeping your kids safe.

He'd hoped Bri might have been accepting, welcoming even, but he should have known better. She'd been hurt and angry and she blamed him. Well, hell, she had good cause to. If only she'd let him explain, but that needed time and probably some alcohol to ease the way.

After he finished typing up the last patient's notes he pulled on his winter coat and wandered through to the waiting room.

It was empty. The place smelled of gym shoes and the overwhelming cloying sweetness of cheap body spray that teenagers were so keen to cover themselves in. Posters clung to the walls, curling at the edges, with myriad health messages about pregnancy testing, sexually transmitted disease, anti-bullying.

Nothing to help parents with teenagers who wouldn't talk or listen.

And no Briana Barclay to be seen. He wasn't sure whether to knock on her door, wait or just leave, but suddenly her door swung open and she walked out, carrying a large pile of papers and folders. The second she caught sight of him she frowned and stopped.

He decided it was going to take time to smooth things out between them, so he found her a smile, hoping it looked genuine. 'I'll be off, then.'

'How did you go?'

'Slowly. It's hard with only fifteen-minute appointments. I'm used to longer. I like to be thorough.'

'We can make them longer.' A curt nod. 'What do you need?'

'Twenty at least? Let's see how that goes. I know it's luxury to want that much but I do think we get better outcomes if we give our clients the time they need.'

'Anything I need to know about?'

That it wasn't all *my fault. That I need some help. That the last few years have been so bloody hard.*

And with no siblings or parents able or willing to help, Bri might be his only salvation. For Lily's sake. *And Ellen's.*

'Mostly straightforward. Things of note—one kid wanting to bulk up, asking for...' he made quote marks in the air with his fingers '..."legit steroids".' He laughed. 'I put him right about that and suggested a personal weight training plan I've used in the past with good results. A gender identity consultation, which I think is going to take a few more sessions to ascertain appropriate pathways—'

'The nearest gender identity clinic is in Leeds.'

'Yes, I scoped that out. I don't know if we're at the referral stage yet, so I suggested some websites they can look at, some questions to think about and booked another appointment next week. I'm hoping one of the parents might come in too at some point so we can have a family chat. Everything else was straightforward.'

'Good. Sounds like you managed.'

'I did. Do you schedule pastoral team meetings so we can discuss cases in more depth?'

'Yes. I should have given you this.' She pulled out a file from the pile of papers in her hands and gave it to him. 'Proper orientation information. Hours we work, multi-disciplinary meeting timetables, that kind of thing. We talk with the counsellors and pastoral care staff once a month. It's all in there. Oh, and I owe you an apology.'

Interesting. Hope rose in his chest. 'Yes?'

'Looks like Andrea inadvertently told you to come at two-thirty. Should have been an hour earlier.' She turned and made her way to the door, her back straight and her shoulders taut. Her body thrummed with annoyance and he could tell she was hurrying to get away from him.

That was an apology? He wasn't going to argue the toss, but in his world apologies started or ended with *I'm sorry.*

Not exactly the kind of step in the right direction he was hoping for, but it was a start. He owed her an apology too. 'Briana, I didn't know you were going to be working here.'

She whirled round to look at him. Her eyes were large and a startling, glittering blue. Close up he could see hues of gold in there too. He'd never noticed that before. But, then, she'd been his ex-girlfriend's best friend. Very off limits, which meant he hadn't gone looking too hard.

Her lips were full and she'd put gloss on, making them shimmer. His eyes seemed to be drawn there. Weird. And totally inappropriate, smack-bang in the middle of an argument with a work colleague and kind of old friend, who hated him.

He dragged his gaze back to her eyes.

He knew from the years of her friendship with Ellen that Briana was fiercely loyal, often outrageously funny and loved deeply, but she was far from those now and the tone of her words was dark. 'Really, Fraser? I find it odd that you just turn up on my patch. It can't possibly be a coincidence. If I remember rightly, you're not a big fan of the great outdoors. You prefer bars and clubs and music, not mountains and lakes and birdsong.'

'People change. Parenting tends to curb the late nights and loud music, as does holding down a demanding job.'

'People don't change that much.' Her eyes narrowed. 'It's not as if you have any relatives here. What's the real story?'

Even though she had every right to be angry with him her words were like shrapnel piercing him. Everything he'd done had been to protect Lily and Ellen and he knew he'd hurt Briana in the process, but he'd made a promise and he wasn't going to apologise for that.

'We needed to get out of London. I hoped fresh air and climbing mountains might help so when I saw the job advert for Oakdale Medical Centre with two afternoons a week doing outreach it seemed like the perfect opportunity.' And yet here it was, far from perfect right now.

'But you knew I grew up here, went to school here with Ellen. Surely there was a chance I might be here?'

'To be honest, I had no idea where you were. We got

Lily's birthday and Christmas cards from Australia a few years ago. And then…we didn't know where you'd gone.' The presents and cards had trickled to a stop and Briana had slipped from Lily's mind. Fraser's, too, until recently.

'I was in Australia, yes. Four and a bit years. I should have sent her more, I know.' Bri shook her head in a way that didn't invite further questioning.

'I did email you about this job. Three times. I asked whether you knew anything about it. I asked if you were okay with us coming here and if we could try to patch things up for Lily's sake. You never replied.' He shrugged, watching as his words hit home, her expression softening as he explained. 'I figured you'd either decided never to speak to us again, or I'd landed in your junk email box or—'

'I…I changed my email address.' She blinked fast and looked suddenly embarrassed. Good, it was a relief to have the heat shift from him for a change. Their friendship breakdown hadn't all been his fault, although he knew he was definitely the main culprit.

'And you didn't think to let me…let Lily know?'

She looked down, biting her bottom lip. 'I was going to.'

'Well, I've saved you the bother.'

'I was going to.' She met his gaze. 'Lily's my goddaughter and I want to be there for her.'

Five years too late.

'By changing your email address.'

She closed her eyes. 'I had my reasons.'

'Which were?'

'Private.' She folded her arms across her chest in a gesture that was pure panic, as if she was protecting herself and turning her thoughts inward. She was guarded and so unlike the Briana he remembered from years ago.

Sure, he'd expected her outburst. That was how she was. She'd worn her heart on her sleeve back then. She didn't generally tiptoe around and she believed wholeheartedly in being honest—he knew that to his cost.

There'd always been tension between them, a spark of…something. Irritation, maybe. Jealousy, perhaps, that he'd been Ellen's man. He'd always felt she was judging him, that he wasn't good enough for her friend. But he hadn't walked away from Ellen, and he'd made sure he was accessible and reliable and a damned good father.

He wasn't sure what had caused Briana's sudden shutdown and he didn't like the way it made her so guarded, but she clearly wasn't going to tell him anything more. She turned away, rubbing her arms. They'd reached an impasse.

She bent and straightened the files on the reception desk, not looking at him, but her hands were shaking, and he wasn't sure whether it was the shock of seeing him and Lily or for the reason she'd changed her email address.

'I tried, Briana. I didn't want it to happen this way.'

'I've heard that before too.' She shook her head in a gesture reminiscent of his teenage daughter, as if to say, *Whatever.* 'You still haven't explained why you upped sticks and moved here, precisely. Ellen's dad died a couple of years ago and her mum's been gone a long time. Why not go to your mother's if you needed to move?'

'Mum moved to Portugal a few years ago. She did come and help out for a while after Ellen died, but Lily was too much for her. She's retired now and finally living a life she enjoys, rather than scraping by like she had to when she brought me up. I couldn't ask her for more help.' It wasn't as if she'd ever relished playing mother to him anyway and, in fact, blamed him for his father leaving her. So he was on his own. As usual.

Bri's eyebrows rose. 'So, you have no other connection to the Lake District as far as I know. Surely there must have been other GP jobs you could have taken somewhere else in England?'

'Full time but flexible with a side serving of adolescent outreach? Far away from London? Not many. I jumped at the first opportunity. And, well…' Confession time. 'I did hope you and Lily might connect at some point.'

'Why?'

He tried for a smile, but wasn't sure he managed it as the truth of his words hit him square in the chest. 'Desperation?'

'Typical, Fraser.' Her arms folded tight across her chest. 'The only time you'd even consider me is when you're desperate.'

Frustration bubbled up. 'Are you deliberately misinterpreting me? That's not what I meant—'

The door banged open and the administrator stood there, red-faced and breathing hard. 'Sorry to interrupt, but there's been an incident at football training and they need help.'

Fraser's words stuck in his throat. He glanced at Briana. She was still shaking with anger. Her eyes sparked and glittered and he was drawn to look at her again.

She was so striking, beautiful, in fact, yet he'd never noticed before.

The school administrator looked from one to the other, eyebrows raised and a curious look on her face, as if she'd caught them snogging behind the bike sheds or something.

Not bloody likely.

She held the door open. 'I mean…they need help. Like *now*.'

CHAPTER THREE

WAS IT BAD that a boy in pain was a welcome distraction from Fraser Moore?

Probably. But right now Briana was grateful for the respite from all the feelings he instilled in her.

She grabbed the first-aid kit, ran through the school corridors and out towards the sports fields, where a huddle of boys was crowded around dark shapes on the ground. It was dark outside and the freezing northerly bit her cheeks and sheared deep into her bones. She wished she'd had the foresight to grab her coat.

There'd been no more time to talk, but she'd felt Fraser behind her every step and now he was pushing his way through to the boy—no, *boys*, three of them, on the frosted ground. Moans filled the air.

He knelt down on the frozen playing field, looking from one kid to another and then another, no doubt assessing who need the most urgent attention. He went first to a boy lying prone. Eyes closed. Not moving.

'Hey, there.' Fraser's voice was calm and friendly and belied the rush of urgency that must have been spinning inside him at seeing an unmoving child splayed on the earth. 'I'm the new doctor. Can someone tell me what happened?'

'Ball in the air. Head clash.' A teenager holding his

hand to a split lip pointed to the unconscious boy, then to himself and lastly to another kid moaning on the ground, clutching his leg. 'Bad landing.'

Bri looked at the chaos, assessed the damage and fished her phone from her pocket. 'Has anyone called an ambulance?'

'Er…' The boys looked at each other. 'We told Mrs Walker.'

Andrea. And she'd come to get them. 'Right. Good call.' Bri watched as Fraser did an airways assessment on the unconscious boy, who was, thankfully, breathing independently and starting to move his head. His eyes flickered open, then closed again as he told them his name was Connor.

Bri exchanged glances with Fraser and he said, 'Glasgow Coma scale twelve.'

Not life-threatening, but definitely worrying—and at risk of hypothermia if they stayed here much longer.

'On it.' She made the call to the ambulance service, then focused on the moaning teenager who was clutching his lower leg. Josh Parker, Briana recognised him—always in the sick bay with some sort of sporting injury. 'It hurts.'

'I'm sure it does. Can I take a look?' She peeled the boy's hands away from his leg and squinted, not seeing well in the dark. 'Can someone shine a light here, please?'

One of the kids whipped out a phone, swiped for the flashlight then recoiled. 'Ugh. Is that the bone sticking out?'

Yes, the bone is right there. A nasty compound fracture. 'This is going to need more than just a bandage. I'll dial in to ambulance HQ again and ask for reinforcements.' She tried to make light of it so as not to spook the already anxious-looking kids. 'You guys don't do things by halves.'

When she finished the second phone call she heard split lip boy—Henry, in the school blue and white football strip—talking to Fraser in a wobbly voice. 'We were both running for the ball, jumping up at the same time and…we hit our heads. He was out cold.' The kid swallowed, his voice breaking. 'It was an accident. All of it.'

'It…was.' Josh was rolling on the ground in pain, shivering from shock and cold.

'It's okay, no one's in trouble.' She stroked Josh's hair out of his eyes and handed him a tissue from the first-aid kit, then wrapped him in her cardigan.

Next, she took a look at Henry's lip, cleaning it the best she could with some saline and gauze. 'I don't think it needs stitches. Make sure you give it a good rinse out when you get home just to wash all the dirt out. Might hurt to eat for the next day or two, but I've heard how much teenage boys eat and I don't think a little cut is going to put you off, right?' She winked and gave him some sterile swabs to press on to the lip to stem the bleeding. 'You want me to call your parents?' Bri took the names and numbers and made more calls, the cold now starting to seep into her bones.

'We need to keep everyone warm. It's freezing,' Fraser said as he looked at her with concern. 'You're shivering.'

'I'm fine.' She didn't want him to think she couldn't cope.

Even though the cloudy night sky had started to dump sleet on them, Fraser peeled off his thick coat and wrapped it over his patient's skinny frame. Moving Connor would have been too dangerous in case there was a neck injury, but they had to keep him warm somehow, and still.

Briana watched as Fraser moved languidly and confidently and, for one split second—definitely not more—she felt a frisson of something familiar firing back into life deep inside her. She couldn't take her eyes away from the half-smile on his lips as he reassured Connor, the deft way he supported the boy's head. Kind eyes that drew you in.

No.

She wasn't going to start mooning over Fraser again. *Been there, done that.*

She refused to allow it. No way. Definitely not. For so many reasons. Her anger at him, of course. But mainly because back when she'd had her inconvenient crush on him all those years ago he'd barely even acknowledged she'd existed. She certainly wasn't going to start chasing that particular line of thought again.

She cleared her throat and ignored the annoying fluttering in her belly. 'Can someone grab a couple of blankets from the sick bay?' At least they had plenty of hands to help.

Soon enough she had them all wrapped up warmly, except Henry, who refused the blanket and hovered over Connor, concern etched deep in his features, along with guilt. 'Is he going to be okay?'

Connor was starting to come round. His eyes were open and Fraser was getting the boy to squeeze his hands, assessing strength and sensation, and looking for any weaknesses. He moved to the boy's feet, ran his fingers over the ankle bones. It looked as if there was no serious neck or back injury that affected his limbs but they both knew he would need a thorough hospital assessment after a head-clash that had knocked him out cold.

'I'm sure he will be, mate.' Fraser looked up at Henry and smiled. 'Look, I need someone I can trust to go out to the front of the school and direct the ambulance round to us. Can you do that?'

The boy nodded slowly. 'Sure.'

'Great. They won't be long.'

'Good call.' Bri nodded as Henry walked away. 'He needs to feel useful.'

'I know. I've been in the same situation. You get embroiled in something that ends up hurting someone else. You feel like hell, even if it isn't your fault.' His eyes caught her gaze and she wondered if he was trying to tell her something.

She turned away, not wanting to hear it.

The parents and the ambulances all seemed to arrive at the same time in a blur of sirens and headlights. While Briana spoke to the parents Fraser assisted the ambulance staff with Connor, log-rolling him onto a stretcher and keeping his neck stabilised.

Josh's leg was immobilised by an inflatable splint, he was given pain relief before his journey to hospital and his mum went with him in the second ambulance.

Briana was right, Henry's lip didn't need stitches, but Fraser wrote a prescription for antibiotics in case the wound started to look infected—a possible complication owing to the prevalence of mud on the boy—and made Henry's parents promise to make an appointment at the Oakdale Medical Centre if they were worried.

One by one the other team members and their parents left and Fraser spent a couple of minutes talking to the paramedics.

He looked genuinely concerned about Connor's head injury and the long-term implications of concussion, and Briana was impressed with the way that they'd handled the situation as a team. Nothing like a medical emergency to smooth things over and make them forget—or at least put aside—their differences.

For now.

But Briana hadn't forgotten how Fraser could be. She would never forget that he'd put a barrier between her and her best friend. Or forgive him.

There was nothing more for her to do here and she could have just left but that seemed churlish and rude after what they just shared. She decided to stay, if only to thank him for his help.

He was taking his time, so it wasn't exactly her fault if she let her eyes wander across that broad chest. *Hmm.* He'd changed from the last time she'd seen him, although admittedly that had been at a funeral. He'd been thin then. Eaten up with the stress of looking after Ellen and his daughter. No doubt made worse by Briana's railing at him…but he'd deserved it.

Five years on, he'd filled out, added muscle where muscle looked very nice on a man: arms, butt, thighs. Eyes that mirrored his emotions.

He wanted to patch things up for Lily's sake and that had to be good.

Her *goddaughter.* Guilt rippled through her. She should have stayed in London, should have helped, forced herself into their world. But Hurricane Tony had happened and she'd been blinded by her feelings for him, eaten up with grief at Ellen's death, and angry at Fraser. She'd needed space to deal with all the overwhelming emotion that had threatened to almost drown her and Lily had somehow got lost in the mix.

Although not in Fraser's world. He'd taken care of his little girl, always put her first. So what had happened to make him uproot her and take her away from everything she knew?

She needed to befriend Lily, take her godmother duties seriously and be an advocate for her. Not ogle him inappropriately. He'd been her best friend's man and that was a line not to be crossed.

'That was certainly a bit of excitement for my first day.' They'd fallen into step with each other, walking to the staff car park. He headed towards an old battered Volvo that looked like it had seen better days. Interesting. She'd imagined the city boy to have something a lot more flash than that.

She zapped the automatic lock on her little silver runabout. 'Thank you for the help. I'll see you on Wednesday.'

But he didn't look like he was in a hurry to leave. Instead of opening his car door, he stopped, turned to look at her and said, 'I'm sorry about the way Lily reacted.'

He did indeed look genuinely sorry. And, yes, having watched him kneel on the icy ground, not caring about his chinos or about getting his hands dirty, or about anything except the injured child in front of him, she had to admit he was climbing back up the hot scales. For Briana, hotness levels were definitely linked to compassion levels and closely aligned to sense of humour levels. Not so much the physical—although he had that in spades—but how a man made her feel.

Fraser Moore made her feel too many things. 'I take it you didn't tell her I was here?'

'I didn't want to get her hopes up in case you weren't. She's not usually like that...' He paused. Ran fingers through his sleet-damp hair. 'Actually, she is. She's changed, Bri. From that sweet little girl into someone I don't recognise.'

'Kids grow up, it's not always a smooth ride and you

know that. You have to give her some leeway to find her own path. Loosen the reins.'

'I did. It didn't work out. I tightened them and that didn't work either. Now we're here and she's worse. She says I'm punishing her when I'm just trying to help.'

'Moving her away from her friends and everything, she knows isn't punishing her? Controlling her?'

'*Loving* her. Protecting her. There is a difference.'

'Yes, I've heard it called that too. So many times. *"But he loves me... Even though he won't let me see my friends... But he cares for me."* That's not how you love someone, Fraser. You set them free. You support them. You—'

His eyes were dark now. 'Let them get a criminal record?'

Whoa. She hadn't been expecting that. 'What do you mean?'

He let out a long sigh and she could see he was choosing his words. 'Lily was caught shoplifting with a bunch of her so-called friends. Just some cheap make-up, but enough to be taken to the police station. I managed to convince them not to press charges and paid the store a lot of money to make it all go away.'

'It happens, Fraser. It's not right, but it happens. She's just being a kid, pushing boundaries.'

His eyes closed for a moment, then, 'There were other things too. One of her friends has been charged with possession of drugs. Another for dealing. At fifteen, Bri. No matter what I said or did, it didn't seem to make a difference. I couldn't stop her seeing these people unless I locked her up. Which, for the record, I did not do. Even when I grounded her, she'd climb out of the window at night and hang out with them. Brought back by the police in the early hours. Not just once. I don't know if she ever took drugs and I doubt she'd ever tell me. She's already on a police caution, Briana.' He looked distraught. 'What next?'

Oh, God. Poor Fraser. Poor Lily.

'I didn't realise it was so bad.'

'How could you know?' He shook his head. The unsaid *you weren't there* hung between them. 'I'm not controlling her, I'm protecting her, taking her out of harm's way.'

The threat of a criminal record must have been a very big wake-up call. She was starting to understand what had driven him to bring his daughter all this way away from everything she knew. A fresh start. Lily deserved that after what she'd been through in her short life. Losing a mother would have been so hard. And for her best friend's sake Bri need to help.

Help Lily. Her goddaughter. Make up for all that lost time. Yes. She could do that.

And if that meant spending more time with Fraser, then so be it. She'd just have to put up with him.

Admiring his body hadn't meant anything.

Even with all this new information and the way he'd looked when he'd talked about his daughter—with such pain and raw love and compassion aplenty—he still most definitely wasn't her kind of hot.

CHAPTER FOUR

'YOU DIDN'T THINK to mention my godmother works at my new school? Some advance warning would have been nice.'

Lily was sitting at the dinner table in their kitchen/dining room, simultaneously growling at her father whilst hugging Jasper, their Old English sheepdog, the only bribery Fraser had resorted to in an attempt to smooth the house move.

'We can get a dog.'

So, of course, she'd chosen the biggest, clumsiest, smelliest, fur-shedding dog she could find. One that broke china with a swift whack of its tail, made muddy prints and drool trails across the slate floor tiles on a daily basis and who thought it was a human, so tried to sit with them at the dinner table. Every. Day.

But Lily loved him. That was something.

It was just a shame the love didn't extend as far as mopping up the trails or replacing the china, but there it was.

Fraser stirred the bolognaise sauce and tried not to rise to another argument. 'I didn't know Briana worked there. I didn't know she's a school nurse. But...' he did concede, because he believed in honesty '...I did know she grew up near here, like your mum. So we may possibly have bumped into her at some point. Look, I emailed her about us moving here and she didn't reply, so I assumed she was still in Australia. I didn't see the point in saying anything to you if we weren't going to see her. What's the problem with her being here?'

Lily grimaced. 'You have spies everywhere, right? Here in cosy little Oakdale, where you can't turn around without bumping into someone who knows your business. And now at school too. I can't have any privacy. Not to mention the fact you had the big reunion showdown in front of everyone.'

'Ah. Yes. Sorry about that. It didn't exactly go the way I'd imagined it might. How was school? Have you made any friends yet?'

'I was trying to, you know. I was hanging out with a couple of girls from one of my classes and one of them had a headache, so we went to the sick bay for painkillers. But—well, you know the rest.' She glared at him. 'Bit hard to make friends with your father arguing with the school nurse right in front of you.'

His gut tightened. 'I'm sorry, Lily.'

'Really?' She buried her nose into Jasper's fur. 'My lovely boy. You're the only one who understands me.'

The dog looked up at her with those killer big eyes and put his paw on her knee.

'I love you.' She nuzzled Jasper's head and the pang of affection and despair in Fraser's chest almost stopped his breath.

When had she last said that to him? Certainly not this side of the Great Move North. Probably not for a year, or two. The damned shame of it all was that she desperately craved affection and attention, but she didn't want it from him.

* * *

Dinner was a sombre affair that involved Lily moving food around her plate and Fraser trying to make jokes that she didn't laugh at. Just as they finished there was a knock on the door and they both looked up. Lily shrugged. 'Won't be for me.'

Fraser went through to the hall and opened the door. A blast of freezing air and thick snowflakes blew in as he peered out. To his surprise, Briana was standing there, her blonde hair in loose curls around her shoulders and flecked with snowflakes. She had a pale blue scarf wrapped round her neck above a navy corduroy jacket, figure-hugging jeans and boots. She looked ten years younger than she had in her work clothes—back to the young woman he remembered. And a little nervous. His gut did a weird jig, tightening again but for a very different reason.

It really needed to stop doing that.

She smiled. 'Hey.'

'This is a surprise.' He stepped back to let her in, strangely relieved and intrigued that she was here.

'Is this convenient?' She walked into the hallway and popped a large handbag on the floor while she shook the snow from her jacket. 'I've come to see Lily.'

Of course she had. His ego took a hit on that. *Idiot.*

Why he'd thought she was here to see him he couldn't say. And why he felt deflated was even more of a mystery. He walked her through to the lounge where Lily was lying on her back next to Jasper on the floor, her legs propped up on the sofa as she talked animatedly on the phone.

'As soon as I can. I promise. I've checked the train timeta— Oh.' She twisted upright when she saw Fraser and then Briana, her eyes rolling. 'Later,' Lily said into the phone and hurriedly slipped it into her pocket.

'Hi, Lily.' Briana waved. No big hugging gesture. He assumed she'd learnt the first time. But she didn't look abashed, just friendly. Casual. 'Just wondered how you're settling in?'

Lily shrugged.

Bri nodded. 'It's a pretty relaxed school and, between you and me, it's the best place for Wi-Fi signal in the area.'

Lily's eyes widened. 'It's rubbish here.'

'Same at my house. It's all the mountains.' Bri shrugged. 'My movie streaming is so slow I get that swirling circle of doom on my screen every time.'

Lily shot her a look that suggested she couldn't imagine Bri knowing what streaming was. Then she looked back at her phone as if it was the answer to all of her woes.

'Well, as long as you're okay. First days are always daunting.' Briana watched her, then slowly took a large book out of her bag. 'Before I forget, I've brought some photos to show you guys. Thought you might like to see what Ellen got up to growing up around here.'

'Er…' Lily's eyes darted to her dad and then back to Briana. She looked like a caged animal searching for an escape route. 'It's just…I have…er, homework.'

Fraser frowned. Homework she hadn't mentioned yet?

'Hey, no problem. I wasn't going to stay. Just thought I'd drop them off for you to have a look later.' Briana put the album on the coffee table, her smile fading a little, and he could see her work to bring it back to full wattage as she bent and patted Jasper, who promptly drooled on her shoes. She grimaced then looked at Lily. 'He's gorgeous. What's his name?'

'Jasper. But Dad calls him a pain in the ar—'

'Lily.' He growled, but Briana laughed. 'He's the most handsome boy I've ever seen.'

'Yes. He is.' A little hitch in Lily's voice and for a second her eyes softened, then she turned and walked to the door. 'Homework.'

Bri nodded. 'Have they got you working on your first day? That's just mean.'

'Yep.'

Exasperated with Lily's monosyllabic responses, Fraser took up Briana's cause. 'Lily. Come and have a look at the photos.'

But his daughter had disappeared with exaggerated thuds up the ancient narrow steps of their stone cottage, followed by the swish swish of her faithful Jasper climbing the stairs behind her.

Fraser found himself apologising for his daughter. Again. 'I'm so sorry, Bri. I'll call her back down. She can't be rude like that.'

Briana blinked. 'It's fine. I don't expect her to want to spend time with me. I'm pretty much a stranger in her life. Making her come down isn't going to be pleasant for any of us.'

'She needs to learn her manners.'

She raised her palm. 'Hey, I totally believe you'll have taught her how to behave properly, Fraser. Don't worry.'

'I have talked about you. She does remember you.'

'It's okay. Honestly. It's a lot for her to take in.' She started to walk towards the door. 'I just thought I'd pop by. It's going to take time for her to get used to me again.'

He felt bad that she'd come all that way only to have the full-on rude Lily reception, and he wanted to make amends for…everything. 'Wait, Bri. Do you want stay for a drink? Glass of wine?'

She shook her head. 'I should go.'

'I remember you like a glass of red.' He held up a bottle of merlot to tempt her. 'It'll be nice to have adult company for a change…someone who isn't going to flounce off in a strop or tell me I'm embarrassing every time I open my mouth.'

'Picked the wrong woman here, then.' She laughed, although he wasn't sure if he imagined the hint of bitterness there too.

He shrugged, feigning nonchalance even though the thought of having a glass of wine with someone was off-the-scale good. 'I'll take my chances.'

'I've been working on my flouncing. I've reached expert level.' Her eyebrows rose wryly. 'But, for the record, you're not embarrassing *every* time you open your mouth.'

He liked the sparring. 'There's a relief.'

'Just ninety-nine-point-nine percent of the time,' she threw at him with a chuckle.

But she didn't leave.

He took a couple of glasses from the oak dresser and waggled them in front of her. 'I think we need to clear the air. From a work perspective, if nothing else.'

She thought about it for a moment and he wondered what was going on in her head. Her eyes darted from the glass to him and then back. Eventually she shrugged. 'Okay. We need to talk from a Lily perspective too. I promised both you and Ellen that I'd be there for her, and I haven't been.'

'The promises we keep, eh? Get you into trouble if you're not careful.'

Her back stiffened. 'Fraser, I'm not ready to go over that yet.'

He wasn't sure he'd ever be ready but he needed to explain. 'Bri, we can't ignore it.'

'Not today, please.' She rubbed her head. 'It's all a bit much, to be honest. Seeing you and Lily brought so many memories back. I'm still processing.'

'Okay. Another time. Sit, please. I think that seat is dog-hair-free, but I can't be sure.' His heart thumped as he indicated for her to sit on the sofa. That old ground would have to wait. He'd have to reassure her that he hadn't wanted to lie. That he hadn't been playing mind-games. But that was for another time.

He poured two glasses of wine, unsure what they were going to talk about if they weren't ready to talk about the elephant in the room. 'Sorry about the drool.'

Awkward.

'Oh?' She followed his gaze to her shoes where a sticky spill oozed over her laces. 'Not a problem.'

'Occupational hazard when you've got a dog like that. Big dog, big mess.'

Just like Fraser's attempt at conversation.

This was not going well. Searching for some common ground that wasn't going to erupt in an argument, he picked up the photo album. 'I bet there are some photos in here I haven't seen before.'

'These are from when Ellen and I met at nursery, right up until we left here to go do our nurse training together and I think there might be some of that night we met you at the hospital Christmas ball.' She gestured for him to come and sit next to her as she showed him pictures of two small girls—one dark haired, one blonde, playing at a beach, at a park, in the school concert. On the Windermere ferry, eating ice creams, on the top of a mountain. Girls growing up together, sharing secrets and having fun. Then photos of older girls with straightened hair and make-up, wearing ballgowns.

His heart tripped as he looked at Ellen, so full of life and with so much to look forward to.

Briana ran her fingertip across the photo. 'Imagine… if we hadn't been at that ball, you and I wouldn't even know each other. Lily wouldn't even exist.'

Another photo, this time of Ellen and Briana inside the ball venue, holding glasses of bubbly up to the camera. Then a picture he hadn't even known was being taken of Ellen, Briana and himself. Briana grinning at the camera, he and Ellen grinning at each other under a sprig of plastic mistletoe.

It had been lust at first sight. He, a medical student on a rare night off and letting off steam with his friends, and Ellen, a beautiful, bright student nurse—they'd bumped into each other at the bar, shared some hilarious, lecherous conversation and a few jokes, danced until their feet ached and then spent the night…

He wasn't sure what had happened to Briana after the music ended, he'd been so wrapped up in Ellen.

'Shame the band was so bad,' he said, just to break the heavy silence as they lost themselves in their memories.

'We were just excited to be glammed up and going out after spending weeks studying.' She quickly turned the page to find more photos of them, this time the girls on another rare day off sightseeing in Covent Garden. She peered closer. 'What the hell were we wearing? Oh, God. Look at us.' She slammed her palm over the print. 'No! Forget that! Do not look at us.'

'It can't be anything I haven't seen before.' He snatched the book from her and held it high above his head so she couldn't grab it from him.

She reached out to get it, but didn't manage. Although

she put up a good fight, stretching, giggling, groaning. 'Don't you dare laugh, Fraser Moore. I took my clothing choices very seriously at eighteen.'

'I'm not going to be responsible for my reactions.' Intrigued, he turned his back on her and opened the album, relieved that the atmosphere had morphed into something almost friendly. *Almost*, given the elephant she refused to talk about. 'Let me see. Oh, yes. Ah. I see what you mean. Got to love the naughty noughties.' He couldn't stop the laughter escaping even though her cheeks burned. But she was laughing too, her eyes dancing and bright. Her smile radiant.

Something caught in his chest as he watched her. How had he never realised how pretty she was? How... *attractive*?

She reached and laughed and her gaze caught with his. As she looked at him his body prickled hotly.

No. She'd always been off limits. Still was. This weird feeling inside him was just a giddy relief that they could manage a semblance of communication.

Possibly, also, because he was sharing some time with a level-headed grown-up.

She reached for the album. 'Please, Fraser. I am dying here. I'd forgotten that was in there. You can see my—'

The door swung open and Lily flounced in, eyes narrowed in suspicion. 'I thought I heard...laughing.'

It sounded like an accusation. As if laughter wasn't allowed. Okay, so it had been missing for a long time, but he ached for more of it, to see his daughter's rare smile.

Briana pointed to the photograph, the laughter less but the humour still in her voice. Her cheeks had bloomed hot pink and he wondered if she'd felt that zip of electricity too. 'Oh, Lily. This probably should be X-rated, but what the hell? You're old enough not to be scarred for life. Have a look and learn from our mistakes. Whoever thought thong knickers and low-rise jeans were a good fashion statement?'

Lily leaned in to look, a faint smile playing at the corners of her mouth, but she pressed her lips together as if willing herself not to laugh.

Poor Lily. Wouldn't allow herself to be seen to be having fun.

Still laughing, Briana put the album on the coffee table, open at the offending picture. 'Those were the days, eh?'

He chanced another look at Briana. When she forgot to be cross with him she was enchanting, disarming.

But she was looking at Lily now. 'Let that be a lesson to you, Lily. Don't be fooled by trendy ideas.'

Lily looked shocked, but also surprised. She laughed. Actually laughed. 'Don't worry. I actually do have fashion sense.'

'Unlike us, back then. We didn't have a clue. You know, you look so much like her. Especially when you laugh.' Bri touched her heart with her palm and her voice cracked as she spoke. 'You have her eyes. All dark and sparkly.'

'My mum's?' Lily blinked. Swallowed.

'Yes. You have Ellen's eyes and smile. She was so pretty and funny. Sometimes a bit ditzy. Not exactly the most organised of people.'

Chaos, Fraser was about to add, *delightful chaos*, but decided to keep his mouth shut. Besides, he wasn't sure he could force words out of his lumpy throat. He rubbed at the pain in his chest as if it might go away with a bit of pressure. Truth was, the pressure had often been intense, and the pain always remained.

'We were always running out of milk.' Lily smiled at

the memory, clearly enchanted to be talking about her mum. 'I used to make her write lists or she'd just forget things.'

'You and me both.' Bri laughed. 'She was so not a list person. But she was such fun to be around no one cared.'

'She was.' Lily glanced at the photo album. Then slid sideways onto one of the armchairs, her long legs dangling over the arm, and casually flicked the album to face her. Then she glanced at it. And away again. Trying not to show interest when she was clearly intrigued.

'There's a photo of her when she was about your age. Peas in a pod.' Briana pushed the book closer to Lily.

Lily flicked the album open at the beginning and slowly looked through the photos. Briana gave her a gentle commentary explaining when and where they had all been taken, going over Ellen's life in much more detail than he probably could. He'd learned a lot about his ex over the years, but as their romantic relationship had been a flash of lust that had fizzled out just as quickly, they hadn't done the whole needing to learn every little thing about each other. They'd probably have never seen each other again had Ellen not discovered she was pregnant.

They'd agreed to co-parent, that a romantic relationship wasn't what either of them wanted, but they'd both adored Lily and the three of them had developed a tight bond, an unconventional family that had lived only streets apart and that had worked. Until Ellen had become too sick to look after herself, never mind her daughter, so she'd moved in with him and he'd ended up as carer to both females in his life.

When Bri closed the book, Lily jumped up. It was hard to read his daughter's expression. For a few minutes she'd been engrossed in the stories but she didn't look comfortable now. She edged towards the door.

His stomach tensed. Dealing with his teenager was like walking a tightrope. One false move and he was spiralling into despair. But he knew he just had to keep holding on.

Briana looked at him worriedly, eyebrows raised in a silent question… *Is she okay?*

He stood too and managed to halt Lily with his words. 'You okay, Lily-Bee?'

'Dad, please.' His daughter shook her head as she turned to look at him, her tone acid. 'Just Lily is fine. I'm not five any more. I'm going to bed.'

He wasn't going to have an argument with an audience, so he acquiesced. 'Okay. I'll come up in a few minutes to say goodnight.'

'No need.'

'In a few minutes.' He tried to keep his voice level while also indicating to his daughter he would definitely be up to say goodnight. Like always. He could see the pain the photos had caused her, and he was going to make sure she was okay, whether she wanted him to or not.

She absentmindedly patted her pocket where she kept her phone. 'Can you make it a bit longer? Just got to double check my maths.'

He knew she was stretching the truth, but he let it go for the sake of keeping the peace.

Briana stood and picked the album up. 'Goodnight, Lily.'

'Yeah.' His daughter nodded then disappeared upstairs again.

Bri's gaze followed Lily to the door and she said, 'Do you want to go up to her? Make sure she's okay?'

'I will in a little while. I've learned to leave her for a few minutes when she's upset or overwhelmed, otherwise she feels crowded.' He shrugged. 'There was a time when she'd come to me for comfort, not push me away.'

'She'll come back to you, Fraser.' Bri shot him a sympathetic look as she walked out into the hallway. 'I'm sorry if I've upset her.'

'Not at all. She looked like she was enjoying seeing pictures of her mum. It's not something we do enough of. Certainly not recently. With the help of the hospice Ellen wrote a little diary about her life and I know Lily treasures it, but it's lovely for someone else to tell her stories about her mum. And it's good for her to have an adult on her side other than me.' He hesitated, unsure where to go to from here. 'That is, if you're happy to be on her side?'

'That's what I signed up for, right? As a godmother? I know I haven't been the best recently, but I want to make it up to her.'

He glanced upwards, imagining a grumpy Lily flopped on her bed. 'I can't promise it'll be easy.'

'I'm up for a challenge.' Briana flexed a bicep and laughed. His eyes were drawn to her mouth. Her lips were more sensual than he'd first noticed. Great mouth. Gorgeous eyes. Kind. Funny. She was the whole package.

He pulled open the front door and let her step in front of him out into the icy dark night. As she passed he got a whiff of her scent. Something fresh that reminded him of the little potted garden he'd tried to grow in London. Freesia or some sort of flower.

He was acutely aware of her. Feeling off balance by her being here. There was so much unsaid, so much anger and mistrust bubbling under the surface that they needed to deal with and yet there was an undercurrent of something else too...something he was trying hard not to notice.

The last thing Fraser wanted was to get involved in

anything deeper with Briana—or any woman, for that matter, if he was going to be spending time with them. Like this. Mushing over photo albums, trying to make his daughter happy. Together. 'Thank you for bringing the photos. It was hard fought for, but you did get a smile.'

Bri turned to look up at him and beamed. 'More than once, so I'm happy with that. It's a start.'

'It is.' He had a sudden urge to run his thumb over that mouth. Followed by his tongue. He swallowed. *So inappropriate.* 'Right, then. I'll see you next week. Clinic.'

'Yes.' She blinked up at him and he was sure—as much as a man who hadn't dated properly since the beginning of the century could be sure—that there was a flash of heat in her eyes as she said, 'Oh, and we need to plan our sex—'

'Our what?' Heat rippled through him, singeing his nerve endings in a powerful sting of desire.

Whoa. It was unexpected, unbidden. Unwanted.

What the hell was wrong with him?

'Sex education lessons.' Her eyes widened and her cheeks burned red. 'They're part of our contract. We give each year group age-appropriate sessions about boundaries, relationships and the developing body through puberty and beyond.'

Plan our sex. He couldn't get rid of an image of her lying on his bed, naked and satisfied. Or the wonder of what she would taste like. 'Oh. Yes. Of course. Do we... do it...' He swallowed again knowing he was making a total ass of himself. 'I mean...them...the lessons... together?'

'No. We split them up. We cover more ground that way.' Her lips twitched and eventually she laughed. More at him than with him he realised as she said, 'Fraser Moore, did you just think I was offering you sex?'

'Not at all. That would be ridiculous.' And yet…not so much. In fact, he took in her amazing body, long legs and perfect curves and thought it would be pretty damned stupendous.

Her expression changed from fun to confusion and then to rebuttal. 'Yes, it would. Don't you forget it.'

How could he? The thought of having sex with Briana had never entered his head for the whole time he'd known her.

But, right now, it was all he could think about.

CHAPTER FIVE

I MUST NOT think about Fraser's mouth.

I must not think about Fraser's mouth.

I must not...

Fraser's mouth. Perfect lips. Great teeth. Gorgeous smile. She'd been drawn to it. Watching him speak. And then…as they'd stood in the doorway, *wanting* that mouth on her.

It was happening all over again, despite everything. She'd wrestled her attraction to him under control years ago, or so she'd thought. There was no point wanting him. But, *man*, that mouth. His laugh. The sadness in his eyes that had twisted her heart.

A knock on the front door made her jump and had her heart slamming against her ribcage. *Tut-tut. Guilty minds.* 'Coming!'

Her ex-next-door neighbour and old friend, Beth, was standing on the doorstep of Bri's cottage in Lower Oakdale, her breath wisping out into the cool, crisp late-afternoon air as she spoke. 'Ready?'

'Totally.' Briana pulled on her trusty navy jacket, dragged on a matching bobble hat and locked the door behind her. 'I need a good walk and I'm so ready for a catch-up. It's been too long.'

'Like four years? More?' Beth grinned then glanced

down at the leads in her hand that were starting to wind around her legs. 'I have a friend for you, if I can manage to untangle myself. Didn't want you to feel left out doing walkies without a dog.'

Ah. Bri looked at the large dog drooling onto her doorstep. There couldn't be many Old English sheepdogs around here. She bent down to ruffle his fur. 'Jasper?'

Beth frowned. 'You've met?'

'Indeed we have. He's messy, so watch out.'

'Tell me about it. But he's also adorable. I'm looking after him because his owners are busy.' Her friend sank her hand into Jasper's thick fur and then snuggled the other cute puppy bouncing up and down like the Energizer Bunny. One ear was floppy and the other stuck up to attention. He was just about the cutest thing Briana had ever seen. Beth laughed as he jumped and tried to lick her face. 'Okay. Okay. Don't be jealous. You have to share me. This is Boy. He's just learning how things are and he's a little excitable.'

'In that case, I'll take Jasper and make sure I keep my shoes out of drooling distance.' Bri took the Old English sheepdog's lead and fell into step with Beth.

Her friend grinned at her as they crunched through snow crystals that were turning to ice in the freezing dusk. 'Okay, spill the beans. I want to know everything about your Australia trip.'

Oh, no, you don't. 'Hot. Snakes. Spiders. Red dust.' She counted them off on her gloved fingers.

'Four years and that's all you've got to say?'

How to be honest about what had happened without telling the whole sordid, sorry story? 'Let's just say that going all that way with Tony wasn't my finest decision.'

'Why? I thought he was The One?'

'Er… No.'

Beth frowned. 'Did he break it off and break your heart too? Is that why you came home?'

'*I* broke it off. But far too late. To be honest, he wasn't the man I thought he was. He was…' The man she'd turned to when she'd been in despair over her friend's death, when she'd finally admitted her feelings for Fraser were completely one-sided. Briana took a deep breath and confided some of it to her friend. 'Turns out he was a bully. He felt he owned me, had a right to tell me what to do…'

Beth's eyes widened as she looked at Briana. 'I'm guessing that would not have gone down well.'

'It took a while for me to figure it out. He was very subtle. But as soon as I extricated myself from him, I wanted to put as much distance between us as I could. So I came home.' Briana shivered and it wasn't all because of the icy temperature. 'Tell me about your love life, Beth. Mine's woeful.'

At that, her friend's mouth split into a wide grin and her eyes became sort of shiny and soft. 'I'm back with Alex.'

'That's a surprise.' The two of them had split up years ago.

As they trudged through Oakdale village Beth regaled her with the tale of their break-up and romantic Christmas reunion and Briana listened with envy. So far her own love life had been sadly depressing. There were lucky ones, she knew…people like Beth and Alex…but it just wasn't going to happen for her. She never wanted to risk her heart and her life again with a man. Never give anyone the chance to abuse and control her. And the thought of filtering through the bad ones just to find the possibility of a good one made her feel sick.

Beth sighed. 'I'm sorry things didn't work out with Tony. But you've been back here for months and we haven't seen you. Don't hide away. It's time to start over, right? You need to get yourself back out again, Bri.'

'I just don't know if I've got it in me to trust a man again. Use them for sex, maybe.' She laughed and Beth did too.

'Atta girl. Scratch that itch.'

They were walking past Oakdale Medical Centre and she couldn't stop herself craning her neck to see if Fraser was there. Late Saturday afternoon? She didn't think so, but a girl could look, right?

Even if Fraser Moore was the last person she'd trust, he was definitely good eye candy.

And good at scratching an itch?

She was shocked that she'd even thought that.

The screechy whine of brakes had both women turning their heads. Caught in a slick of black ice, a car was descending the hill at speed. Directly towards them, and out of control.

There was barely a moment to think. Limestone wall behind them. House to left. Grass verge to right.

'Watch it!' Bri put her arm out and pushed her friend to the right, her heart thumping as her head whirred with dreadful possibilities. The dogs yelped. The car got faster. Closer. The yellow headlights pinned her against the wall.

This was it. This was the end. All breath stalled in Bri's lungs. She was frozen to the spot.

'Bri!' Beth shouted, as something tugged Briana sideways. Jasper? Beth? Ellen's ghost? Her dead friend was the last thing she thought of as she sprawled over the verge, hitting her head against the tarmac just as the car barrelled towards her, skimming her legs so closely she felt the shiver of air as it screamed past her into the wall with an almighty crash and grinding of metal.

She closed her eyes and let out a long sigh. She was alive.

Within moments there was a flurry of activity all round her. People came running out of their houses to investigate the noise. Bri sat up unsteadily, checking herself for damage then immediately thought about the people in the car.

The bonnet was concertinaed in a mess of bare metal. Smoke billowed from the grille at the front. An elderly lady sat in the driver's seat, looking stunned. She had blood dripping from a head wound but she was talking to Beth's boyfriend Alex and another doctor Bri knew from living around here, Joe Thompson.

And Fraser was there too—having materialised seemingly out of nowhere. He ran over to her. 'Bri? Are you okay?'

I am now. That was her first instinctive reaction. Swiftly followed by giving herself a very determined stern talking-to. She would not be okay just because a man was around. She would be okay because *she* decided she would be.

He knelt next to her and smiled. 'If you're going to have an accident, it's always best to do it near a medical clinic. Are you okay?'

'Go see to the people in the car. I'm fine.' She waved him away, noticing her hand was shaking.

'It's Mrs Wilkinson from the post office. She's a bit battered and bruised and definitely shocked but she's okay. Alex is there with Joe and Rose and they've called an ambulance as a precaution.' His eyes scanned her face and he gently pushed back her hair. 'I'm more concerned about you. You look pale. Anywhere else hurt?'

He was concerned about her. *First time ever.*

Her head was throbbing, but she was intact. At least physically. Although her body was prickling at Fraser's touch.

'I hit my head as I fell.' She patted down her body and her hand squelched against something wet and sticky on her jacket hem. She remembered being pulled down and thinking of Ellen. And if that wasn't enough to halt her soppy thoughts about Fraser, she didn't know what was. 'I think Jasper saved my life.'

'The Drool Meister does have his benefits after all.' Fraser smiled and just kept on looking at her. She couldn't drag her eyes away from his. It felt as if they were somehow connected, not physically but something else. On some other astral plane, or in other parallel life. That there was something bigger happening between them. Something important.

The knock to the head had clearly shaken something loose in there because she really, really wanted to slide into his arms and stay there yet he barely knew she existed. Not in *that* way anyway.

Beth wandered over and bent to look at Briana's head. 'Ouch. So, you two have met, then?'

'Weird story, but yes…we know each other from London.'

He stole my chance to spend the last two precious years of Ellen's life with her, she reminded herself before she got too carried away with his gooey eyes and gorgeous smile. With Fraser she'd started to let her guard down in ways she didn't want to allow.

'That looks nasty.' He pointed to her head.

'I'm fine.' She pressed her fingers to her forehead, and they came away damp. Red. 'I think I need to clean up a bit. My house isn't far away.'

'The medical centre's closer. Let's go there and I can have a proper look. It's too dark to see here. You might need stitches.'

No. Yes. No.

Before she knew it he was hauling her up, wrapping his arm around her waist as if she needed help walking and marching her up the road to the medical centre.

For fear of having a rerun of those silly flutters and longing glances that stoked an unwanted heat inside her, she refused to look him in the eye as he cleaned her wound. His closeness was unsettling. She liked the way he smelled of fresh snow mixed with the sharp tang of aftershave and something distinctly sexy. Liked the way he touched her with care and consideration, as if she was worth something.

Had Tony ever touched her like that? At first, yes. But things had changed. Things had changed between Ellen and Fraser too. Things always changed. And never for the better.

After he'd patched her up and washed his hands Fraser smiled. 'You look a lot more human now.'

'Urgh. What was I like before? Zombie, probably, with all that blood on my face.'

'Zombie? The least scary zombie I've ever seen.' The corners of his eyes crinkled as he laughed and she noticed tiny lines there. He'd had a rough few years. She imagined him dealing with a grief-stricken ten-year-old. Nursing a woman who wasn't his wife or lover through a devastating illness.

He put out his arm to help her up, but she shook her head, not wanting to be so close to him again. Not when her emotions were clearly all over the place. 'Thanks. I'm okay now. I'll head on home.'

'Everyone's gone to the pub. Fancy a drink?'

'Alcohol, with a head injury?' She shot him a cautious look.

'I meant just a lemonade or soda.' He slid his hand over hers, making her belly dissolve in a fizz of desire. 'I want to make sure you're okay. That was a nasty bump to the head.'

'I'm fine.' She tugged her hand away, shocked at the way her body yearned towards him. The way her insides melted into liquid at his touch.

Fraser Moore was not good for her resolve. But he was very good for her libido.

'Wait.' He reached out to double-check the cut on her head. Or so she thought. But he paused, fingertips on her temple, then they trailed down to her mouth. His thumb smudged across her lips, making her breath come fast and hard. Thoughts fuelled by pure desire swirled in her head. *Touch. Mouth. Taste. Kiss.*

He came closer. His breath warm on the side of her face. For a moment she thought he was going to kiss her. Wanted him to. Ached for that soft pressure of his lips on hers. His head tipped and he tilted her chin up, looking at her with such heat it made her tremble.

She swallowed, about to reiterate her refusal—because it would be the most foolish thing she could do—just as Beth breezed into the room, making them jump apart. 'There you both are! Alex has taken the dogs back to ours. Joe got us seats by the fire and there's a bottle of shiraz open. Come on.'

And so she wasn't allowed to refuse as her friend grabbed one arm and Fraser took the other and they walked her round to the Queen's Head pub.

'You know, you can go home if you want. We're just concerned about you,' Fraser whispered a few minutes later as he brought her over a glass of lemonade then sat next to her. She was acutely aware of the press of his thigh against hers. Aware of the deep timbre of his laugh. The way his hand rested on his lap and the pleasure-pain longing for those fingers to slide over to her thigh. To feel them on her face again. To breathe him in. To kiss him.

She was going mad.

She edged away from him and from his heat. When he asked her a question, she tried hard not to look at him. Gave him one-word answers, anything not to spend more time under the gaze of those sexy eyes. Desperately searching for a distraction, she turned and spoke to the woman sitting across from her.

Rose had a healthy winter sun glow with white ski-goggle patches round her eyes. 'Apologies for the panda look.' She laughed. 'We got back from skiing yesterday. It was awesome. Bluebird skies every day. So, do you live in Oakdale?'

Bri nodded. 'I grew up next door to Beth and her mum. Then I went off to London to do my nursing training, stayed there for about ten years. Then did a stint over-seas.' She wasn't going to go over that again, once was enough for today. 'Came back here in September.'

'I haven't seen you around.'

'I've been keeping a low profile.'

Rose nodded as if she understood. 'I'm glad Beth persuaded you to come for a drink. It's a lovely community here. Everyone knows each other and they've all been so helpful with our wedding preparations.'

'You're getting married? You and Joe?' Bri remembered Joe's first wife and the car crash that had killed her. She was glad he'd found happiness again. 'I'm so pleased for you.'

Rose smiled and looked the happiest Briana had seen anyone look in a long time. 'Ten weeks today and counting. I'm driving Joe mad with all the organising. The hen do is a month before. Oh!' She clapped her hands. 'You must come to the hen night. Please. Say yes.'

'Oh, no, I couldn't.'

'You'd be doing me a favour actually. Everyone knows Joe. His mum's bringing some of her friends and I'm going to be very outnumbered.' Rose winked conspiratorially. 'I'm looking for cavalry to be on my side and any friend of Beth's is definitely worth getting to know.'

Beth nudged Briana's ribs. 'Come on. It's a hen night. Booze, brides and bawdy games. What's not to like?'

It sounded fun and it had been a long time since she'd had any. Bri breathed out and smiled. 'Okay, yes. I'd love to.'

'Give me your number.' Rose tapped the details into her phone. 'So, what prompted you to come back to Oakdale?'

I escaped and needed to find solace in the familiar.

'It's a beautiful place. When I saw the advert for the school nurse job, I just jumped at it.'

'Based where?'

'The team office is at Bowness Community Clinic. I cover a few primary schools across this area, but mainly I'm at the high school.'

'We run the adolescent outreach together,' Fraser interjected, and Bri's back stiffened at the sound of his voice oozing into the conversation. Along with it came the slam of lust she was trying hard to ignore. She turned her back to him. Swallowed deeply and tried to focus elsewhere.

Rose nodded. 'I think we're looking at that school for Katy when she's older. Oh, I don't want her to grow up, she's so lovely at eight. What's she going to be like at fifteen?'

'Yes, Fraser. Any tips for growing a good teenager?' Briana couldn't help throwing at Fraser.

I missed those lovely years because of you, she thought as a spark of anger mixed with the crazy desire inside her. *You stole my chance to be her friend. And now I can't get those years back. Precious moments. Lost. Because of you.*

And despite all that she wanted to kiss him.

So, it was official. She was all kinds of mixed up with him.

When she looked back at Rose the woman had a curious expression on her face.

'Let's just say that fifteen is…interesting. Give me eight any day,' Fraser said, collecting up the empty glasses. 'Anyone want another drink?'

At the cries of *yes* all round he looked at Bri. 'Fancy giving me a hand?'

The way he was looking at her and the tone of his voice gave her no option. 'Sure.'

When they reached the bar, he put the glassware down and turned to her. 'What's going on, Bri? You've either been ignoring me or throwing daggers at me all evening.'

'How's Lily?'

He blinked at the swift change in topic. 'She's much the same. Doesn't want to be here. Right now, she's baby-sitting Joe's daughter Katy.'

'That's good, right? Gets her out of the house.'

His jaw clenched. 'I much prefer it if I can see where she is.'

Her ire rose by a count of a thousand. 'You can't control her every move.'

'I'm keeping her safe.' He shook his head. 'I thought we'd been over this? I thought we were good?'

'We are far from good.' She couldn't help it. Even though she knew Fraser wasn't the type of guy to do the things Tony had done—not at all—just talking about her ex had resurrected all the emotions, the fear and loneliness and panic. Not to mention the reminder of her friend's death and the anger she still had for Fraser about that. 'You know, I'm not sure this move is working out for you and your daughter. She's clearly miserable and feels isolated. Why don't you just go back to London?'

'Let's go outside.' Fraser touched her arm. 'Talk.'

'No!' she roared, just as the noise in the room seemed to ebb. Eyes turned to look their way. She shrugged out of his reach.

Even to her the things in her head didn't make sense. How could she want to scream at him and kiss him at the same time?

'Briana.' He glanced over to the table filled with their friends and then back at her. 'Let's take this outside. Please, before we become the main act of the evening.'

Everyone was looking at them.

He was right, they had things to say and they certainly didn't need an audience. She couldn't live here and work with him and have this tumult of emotions overwhelming her. Hell, it wouldn't help her and it certainly wouldn't help her relationship with Lily. So, with words ready to tumble from her mouth and her heart beating like an out-of-control train, she slid out the door and waited for him to follow.

CHAPTER SIX

FRASER STORMED ROUND to the side of the pub and called to her back, 'Okay, Bri. Let's have it out, once and for all. Get it out. Tell me what you think. Be honest. Don't hold back.'

Her chin tilted, haughtily. Her hands hit her hips. Primed to attack. 'I have nothing to say to you, Fraser Moore.'

'Yes, you do.'

Her eyes sparked hotly. 'Nothing polite, that is.'

'Just say it.' He prepared himself for a tongue-lashing and knew he deserved it. 'I hurt you. Right? You're furious with me and have been for years. You're also angry with yourself for not being the person you wanted to be for Lily. And you want to kiss me.'

Her eyes widened in rage. She blinked. 'I do not.'

'Two out of three isn't bad.' Interesting that she picked out the kiss on his list rather than the other things.

He was riling her on purpose, because if she didn't say something now she'd keep it all bottled up, keep throwing daggers at him in front of their friends and they'd never move on.

But she did want to kiss him. He saw the heat in her eyes and knew it wasn't all anger. And he wanted to kiss her. Despite everything.

That was the weird thing. The angrier she got the more he wanted her. But they couldn't go on like this...flirting one minute, arguing the next. It was like being on a roller-coaster. He wanted to get off. But he also wanted to stay on for the wild ride.

Go figure.

She inhaled deeply. So did he. Because he didn't want more home truths thrown at him and he didn't want to relive what had happened five years ago, but it was as inevitable as his next breath.

'You should have let me see her.' Her eyes glittered as she glared at him. A look passed between them that made his skin tighten. An undeniable connection accepting there was anger and hurt and yet desire and need there too. It powered her words. 'I thought I'd done something wrong, hurt her in some way, and that was why she didn't answer my texts or calls. Why she sent messages through you. I used to stay awake for hours, staring into the dark, wondering what the hell I'd done to her. I thought... Actually, I didn't know *what* to think except that she must hate me for some reason.'

'She didn't hate you, Bri. She loved you.'

'Oh, yeah?' Her hands balled into fists. 'So why couldn't I see her? Why wouldn't you let me in? Let me know what was happening? I could have done more to help than leaving hot dinners on your doorstep and messages you rarely answered. I'm a nurse, Fraser, and I couldn't help my best friend. I could have cared for her. Something. Anything. Been her advocate. I just wanted to be there for her. So much. So badly.'

'She didn't want anyone apart from me and the medical team to see her like that. I tried to protect Lily from the worst of it.' And, honestly, he'd forgotten about the dinners... They'd magically appeared outside his front door and he'd heated them up and eaten them without thinking where they'd come from. He'd decided it had been a neighbour, or one of Lily's teachers, but it had been Briana. Trying to be involved. Caring. Loving her friend.

Now she was just angry. 'You were the gatekeeper between Ellen and the outside world, you could have let me in. Just for five bloody minutes. You could have fought for me.'

'And she would have hated me for it.' He imagined being in Bri's shoes and not being allowed to see a beloved friend. He would have fought this hard too. 'I didn't handle it well, I admit. But I was doing what she asked me to do. It wasn't anything more than that.'

'It was *everything*.' She was so fired up, her expression animated. Magnificent. Brave. Loyal. 'I will never forgive you for not letting me spend the last dying months with my friend. Never.'

Gatekeeper. It sounded as if she thought he'd had more control over the situation than he'd had. 'I tried,' he growled. Wanting her to *hear* him. To listen. 'I reasoned with her. I begged her, for Lily's sake, if not for mine, to let other people in. But she made me promise. You don't think I wanted help? That I didn't want to share some of it with someone?'

'But she told me about the diagnosis when she first got it and we talked about it. We cried together.' Bri's bottom lip wobbled. 'Then she stopped answering my calls and it felt as if she just didn't want me around. I…I didn't understand.'

He hauled in oxygen as he relived those first unsure dreadful months of weird symptoms and diagnoses, then the horrific prognosis that had eventuated in two long years of battling. 'She was scared. She grew insular and had mood swings, forgetfulness, started lashing out. Headaches had her bedridden for days. Seizures exhausted her and made her zone out for hours afterwards. Her hair fell out in clumps.

'She couldn't bear to look at herself, never mind anyone else look at her. I watched her fade right in front of me. She wanted to lock down at home with her unconventional family, insisting on keeping everyone else at bay. Trust me, I'd have given anything...*anything*...not to have to face all that on my own. Not to have to explain it to a nine-year-old. I would have given anything to have someone to talk to in those long dark nights when I was working out how to maintain a job and look after a child. I had to help my little girl through her grief while trying to work my way through mine.'

The words were rushing out of him like river rapids. Something about Briana's probing and pushing had cracked the dam he'd erected to protect himself. It was the most honest he'd ever been. And the most vulnerable. It was also the most he'd ever said to anyone about that painful, sad time.

'Now I'm here, trying to protect Lily all over again, and all you can do is hurl insults and insinuations at me as if I hurt you on purpose. As if I'm trying to punish my daughter. Who even thinks like that?'

She closed her eyes.

It hit him then. *Briana thinks like that. Why?* Someone else had hurt her. On purpose. His stomach felt as if it was in freefall and the only thing he wanted to do was haul her against his chest and hold her. And then find the person who had made her think like this and lay into them. With his fists. 'What happened, Bri?'

'This is not about me.' She turned away. 'This is all on you.'

She would never listen. 'You know what? I'm done here. It doesn't seem to matter how much I say it, you won't accept it, but I didn't mean to hurt you, Briana. I really didn't. It wasn't about you, it was about Ellen. And Lily.'

He saw the way his words smacked into her like bullets, the pain in her crumpled features as he relived his bare existence of five years ago. He wasn't going to badmouth decisions Ellen had made in her final months, even if he hadn't entirely agreed with them all.

He couldn't take it back. Couldn't pretend, either, that he'd coped, and managed just fine, the way he'd told everyone at the funeral and in those dreadful months afterwards.

He turned and walked away, unable to control the fast rise and fall of his chest. He didn't want her to see him scarred and raw, the same way Ellen hadn't wanted anyone to see her so vulnerable. He got it. He understood. But Briana didn't seem to.

She just wanted to make him pay. And he was. Every day.

He crunched through the snow back towards the pub, but felt a grab at his arm from behind. When he turned around Briana was standing there, eyes wide and huge, the cut on her head marring an otherwise beautiful face. Regardless of the fact he'd put an end to the conversation, she clearly hadn't finished with him yet.

'I'm sorry, Fraser. I was so angry at everyone and everything for such a long time and it's like you just turned on a tap and all the hurt came gushing out of me,' she said, her expression one of agony as she echoed the feeling he'd had—that once they'd started talking it had opened floodgates of emotion. That was why he generally preferred to keep his mouth shut on the subject of

Ellen. 'I hate that you and Lily went through that. And I...well, I...' Briana's voice trailed off as she considered her next words.

He sensed her starting to hold back now. Unsure. Stepping into new ground. He saw in her the same tautness that bound his body, one of honour and duty and loyalty that meant he couldn't touch her hair or her skin or her mouth.

And, God, how he wanted to touch her mouth.

She inhaled deeply then sighed. 'Bloody cancer. And then...after...' Her lip wobbled. 'I was so angry and hurt I ran away to lick my own wounds instead of staying around and helping you with Lily when you needed me most. I just grabbed the lifeline that Tony offered and left. I was so raw and hurt so badly. And I feel so damned...' her eyes filled with tears '...*guilty* about it all. I should have been the godmother I promised to be. I should have stayed.'

'You have no reason to feel guilty, Bri. None at all. You did everything you could, everything that was asked of you, and you deserved to make choices about your life without taking anyone else into account. But I get it. The guilt. The helplessness. I'm a medic too. I should have had the answers, right? I'm sorry you were hurt. I really am. I should have said something sooner. Reached out. Something... But I didn't. I was busy with everything else. But I will not spend the rest of my life looking back at the mistakes I made. I refuse to be eaten up by the guilt or grief. I did what I thought was right at the time. I was looking after Ellen. And now I have to stay strong for Lily. And...'

He didn't want to sound selfish but, hell, sometimes you just needed to be. 'You know, for me too. I'm thirty-four, Bri. I have a lot of years left in me and I'm going to make them good ones. Ellen died five years ago and afterwards I tried to make a life. It didn't work out as I hoped so now I'm making another one.'

'I know how that feels. But a life without Ellen feels… less. I knew her for so long…a whole lot longer than you.'

'It's not a competition, Bri.' He felt his shoulders sag. 'Neither of us won. We both loved her. We both lost her.'

'I miss her.' She wrapped her arms round her chest. 'I don't know if I'll ever get used to her not being here. On the end of the phone, laughing at some silly story about Lily. Or something about you.' She gave him a wary smile then put her hand over his. Her eyes roamed his face and settled on his mouth. Embers of need flared into life. But the connection wasn't just physical, it was deeper than that. It was the weaving of needs and fears and vulnerability, it was a shared history—however complicated.

There was so much more he wanted to know about the last few years of her life. 'Tell me what happened to you.'

'No.' Her mouth flattened. 'Like you, I want to move forward. No point looking backwards for the rest of my life, right?'

'He hurt you.'

She nodded. 'He did.'

But she wasn't going to say any more, he could see. She took a long deep breath as if trying to find some equilibrium and he wasn't sure if it was because of his story or hers that she refused to tell, or the intense connection that had brought them to this point. Bearing their souls. The keeper of secrets.

He wasn't the keeper of hers. She didn't trust him enough to tell him what had happened.

Yet.

He made a promise to himself. Whatever happened, he wanted to be her friend at least, gain her trust so she could speak about her past without fear or the shame he saw in her eyes.

So maybe holding hands and spilling his guts wasn't the best move he'd ever made. Besides, he didn't do this. Didn't do relationships, because he didn't have time or space in his head for someone other than his daughter. Until recently, when all of his time and all of his head-space had been filled with Briana. And he definitely didn't do anything deeper than a fling, especially with someone who was going to stay around for Lily.

He swallowed as their gazes clashed. Pools of deep blue, honest and glittering and drawing him in deeper and deeper. Mesmerising him. 'Sounds like we both had a crappy few years.'

'Sure did. But now I'd like to help.' She squeezed his hand and ran her thumb across his palm.

He ignored the nerve-endings firing off pure lust as her cool skin smoothed over his. At least he tried to, but all he could think about was sliding his mouth over those perfect lips. It had been so damned long since he'd held a woman. So long he couldn't even remember. Seven years? Brief flings before Ellen had got sick and his life had become utterly focused on her and Lily.

He wanted Briana. He wanted to know what she tasted like, how she sounded when she came. He wanted to explore every inch of her. But what would happen then? He couldn't offer her anything. He didn't do relationships or commitment. He didn't have a blueprint for functional, only dysfunctional. 'I don't know, Bri. If every conversation is going to end up in a shouting match I don't think I can do it. I don't want to do it.'

'What if it ends like this?' She reached up and cupped his face. He registered her intention as need rippled through him. He tensed, holding back and back and back, but something deep inside him snapped.

It was the final crack, the dam breaking.

And, sure, there were a million reasons why they shouldn't take the next step, but he'd spent five years fighting and he was done with that. When her lips met his he groaned. His hands slid into her hair and he drew her closer, a gentle exploration at first, a learning of tastes and angles and shapes. The feel of her, her scent.

But it wasn't enough. He hauled her closer, wanting more of her. He wanted everything. And everything went into that kiss. All the anger and frustration and the out-of-nowhere need that invaded his thoughts and his dreams. She was the only person who knew what he'd been through and the way he felt.

The only woman he wanted right now.

She moaned as his tongue slipped into her mouth. He pulled her against him, relishing the feel of her in his arms, the sweet lemonade taste and the press of her soft body against his, unable to get enough of her.

He didn't want to question the sense of this, although his brain registered the complication. He shut it down. Maybe one kiss was all they'd need.

Yeah. He ran his palms down her back as he angled his mouth on hers, drunk on the taste of her. One kiss would never be enough.

And the flicker of a thought slid into his brain.

Maybe Briana was his fresh start.

CHAPTER SEVEN

'I WANT YOU,' Briana murmured into Fraser's mouth, shocked at the urgency she felt and the way his kiss made her want more. Want him everywhere. To scratch that itch that was getting harder to ignore or deny. The rage she'd felt before had exploded into wild, crazy desire, cracking open something carnal and base and freeing. He made her feel so angry, so flustered, so desperate. So damned hot.

He pulled her closer and she could feel how much he wanted her too.

'Briana—' He froze.

From somewhere in the darkness came voices, people laughing and chatting.

No. No. No. Don't stop.

She put a fingertip to his lips, making sure he didn't say a single thing that might make her change her mind. It had been so long since she'd taken control and taken what she wanted, and she was totally going to do this now. With Fraser.

How she'd wanted this all those years ago. She'd put all those wishes in a box and closed the lid but now the box was open and she was going to take it all.

'My place. Closer…' She grabbed his hand and led him down narrow back streets, threading through the snowy village to her cottage, almost running in the rush to have him.

They barely made it through the door before his mouth was on hers again and he pressed her against the wall, covering her throat with delicious rough kisses that made her skin burn with pleasure. He tugged off her coat and threw her hat on the floor then stepped away just for a moment to look at her.

'God, Briana you are amazing. This is all I've been thinking about doing for days.' He slid his mouth over hers, his kiss hot and greedy as his hand cupped her buttocks. He pulled her closer. Their gasps came faster and harder, greedy to taste and explore each other. He palmed her breast over her clothes. There was too much fabric between them. She wanted him naked, to slide her skin against his.

'Upstairs…' she managed on a desperate breath, then she was pulling him up to her bedroom.

The moment she closed her bedroom door he pulled off her jumper and T-shirt in one swift move then laid her on the bed. In the soft glow of a sidelight she could see his beautiful face, the need in his eyes that fuelled hers.

'Do you think they're all still waiting for their drinks?' He laughed as he reached round and unclipped her bra then ran feathery strokes across her nipples that made her curl into him, wanting his mouth there too.

'I'm sure they can manage to sort themselves out.' She snatched wet kisses in between shucking off his layers of clothes. Winter clothes were too thick and cumbersome and took too much time to come off. As she flicked his T-shirt to the carpet she took in the dips and planes of his body. God knew when the man had time to work out but it was clear he did. She ran her palms over the hard, defined pec muscles. 'Meanwhile, I want you to sort me out, Fraser Moore.'

This man who'd cracked her resolve by pushing her. By expecting her to be honest and nothing less. Who had stood there and taken her truth and not belittled it. He'd explained what had happened and why. But he hadn't told her she was being ridiculous, that she was whining, that she didn't deserve to feel like that.

This man who she'd shouted at in a way she'd never spoken to anyone before. Who had then apologised for what he'd done when he'd been going through the worst thing anyone could have to endure. And he was still fighting, for his daughter if not for himself, making changes and choices that were difficult but right. Despite what Bri had assumed to the contrary.

Now the only thing she wanted was to feel his arms around her. To feel his heat.

'I'm going to have some serious explaining to do tomorrow.' He palmed her breast, rubbing and stroking until she thought she would lose control completely, then his mouth found her nipple and he sucked it in.

'Oh, my God. That feels so good.' She writhed against him. 'Don't you dare explain this.' She laughed as she tugged down the zipper on his jeans and palmed his erection. *Oh, man.* 'Let's get you out of these.'

'My pleasure.' He laughed as their arms tangled in the rush to relieve him of his jeans and boxers.

Oh, man.

She took hold of him and stroked. He was so hard and so big and she wanted—ached—so much for him. He took her hand away and placed both her arms above her head, pinning her on the bed, then straddled her. 'I want to kiss you everywhere.'

She couldn't move.

Unwelcome memories rushed into her head. *'Stay there. Do not move until I say so.'*

Panic wove through her. She took a breath, opened her eyes, forcing herself to look at him.

It's Fraser. It's okay. It's Fraser.

It's Fraser...finally.

But suddenly feeling vulnerable, and not wanting to feel like that ever again, she snatched her hands back, her heart thrumming hard against her ribcage. 'Let go. Now. Let me go.'

His body went completely still, his expression shocked and confused. He rubbed his forehead as he rocked backwards away from her. 'Geez, Bri. I'm sorry. I thought you wanted—'

'It's...' She willed her heart rate to slow. Battled the unease that stemmed from her past and not from this man.

Sex Ed for Beginners. Be honest about your boundaries. Tell him what you want and don't want. Be in control of your own body.

'You thought right, Fraser.' Saying his name anchored her. She was here in her bed with a gorgeous man. A man who wanted her, liked her, respected her. 'I asked you here. I want you here. I just don't like being held down.'

He stroked her cheek with the backs of his fingers. 'No. Of course. I'm sorry, I was just playing.'

'I know.' She closed her eyes, expecting him to ask her for more details. Expecting him to leave.

But he didn't. He lay down next to her and wrapped his arms around her, spooning her and whispering against her neck, 'Whatever you want. Or don't want. I'm okay with it, Bri.'

She closed her eyes, glad he couldn't see the flush rising on her face. Being honest was harder than she'd expected. 'I don't like feeling trapped, that's all. I want to do this, Fraser. Honestly, more than anything. You're incredible. But I like...being in control.'

'Now, that I can work with.' She felt his grin against her neck.

'Don't get the wrong message here, big guy.' She chuckled. 'I just mean I don't like being out of control. No holding me down.'

'I get it. I think.' He stroked down to her hipbone and turned her to face him, all serious and genuinely concerned. 'Your pace. Your call.'

Her heart squeezed at his gentleness and she took his hand and ran her tongue along his palm. She watched as he squirmed, closing his eyes as his breathing quickened again. 'I call for more kisses. Then...' she made sure she captured his gaze '...we'll see where that takes us.'

'To wherever you want to go, Briana.' He cupped her face and kissed her so gently, so thoroughly and for so long that her momentary fear became a dim memory. She lost herself in his caresses, the gentle exploration of his fingers, in his exquisite taste.

She forgot everything except his touch, his next kiss. Wherever he stroked her skin she wanted his mouth there too. She learned what made him flinch with desire as she brushed her fingertips down his belly. Learned the feel of him, the shape of him, the dips and valleys of his body. The tight, well-honed muscles. Learned he'd take things at her pace, but that her pace suddenly wasn't fast enough for even her and that she wanted him the way she'd never wanted a man before. Learned also that he truly did want to give her pleasure and not just take it for himself.

Learned that what she said, he would do and that gave her courage.

So when he asked, 'What do you want?' she laughed. And then told him.

'I want you to kiss me all over.'

'Mind-reader.' He sucked in her nipple, sending shivers of anticipation and pleasure through her. 'Lucky me.'

She lay there, almost completely naked and, okay, feeling just a little bit vulnerable but knowing she was completely safe and very turned on—and she knew that didn't make sense. But where Fraser was concerned none of her reactions made sense.

By all accounts she hated him.

But he made her feel so utterly sexy and wanted. It was a battle of emotions and a battle of wills. And right now she felt as if she was winning. She was utterly in control and wanting so very desperately to scratch that itch Beth had talked about.

Beth. Sitting in the pub with the others, waiting for another drink.

Briana giggled.

Fraser slicked kisses down her abdomen, wriggled off her panties and then slid his hand between her thighs. His fingers found her centre and she arched, moaning with pleasure as he seemed to instinctively know what she wanted, the right pressure, the right rhythm.

Then his mouth was on her and her fingers were in his hair. As he kissed her most intimate places she felt wound up tighter and tighter until she could barely think. She gave herself up to the sensations, to him. Desperate. Wanting. Needing. 'Oh, God. Fraser. Don't stop. Don't…'

Then she spiralled out and up and into a million pieces, slumping back against the pillows, her body rippling and yet wanting more. Wanting all of him.

'Fraser.' She barely recognised her own voice it was so thick with sex. 'That was amazing.'

'You think we've finished?' He kissed his way back up, taking a long and delicious detour over her breasts. She was grateful he wasn't asking her permission or waiting for her say-so because she couldn't think past wanting him inside her, never mind find words to actually voice it.

His erection pressed against her thigh, still hard. Harder. She took him in her hands and stroked. Fraser's eyes fluttered closed on a sharp inhalation. 'This is not going to be so memorable if you keep doing that. Or maybe memorable for all the wrong reasons.' He laughed then kissed her hard, pressing her into the duvet. Her back against soft linen, her front pressed hard against solid muscle.

She stroked him faster. He stayed her hand.

'I need to be inside you.' His voice was halting and as desperate as she felt. 'Condom?'

'I'm a sex educator. Of course I have condoms.' She reached out and dragged her work bag across the floor and grinned as she offered it to him.

His eyes grew wild as he looked at the hundreds of condoms in there. Different coloured packets, ribbed, flavoured. So much choice.

'So many?' His eyes danced with laughter and surprise.

'Be prepared, right? That's what I teach them.'

He peered inside the bag again. 'Um. Do you have a preference?'

You. She giggled. 'Do a lucky dip.'

He laughed as he plunged his hand into the bag and brought out a random foil packet. 'Ah. So we have ribs and dots…' He squinted. 'For added pleasure and sensation. Lucky me.'

She smiled and reached to pull his mouth to hers. 'Lucky me.'

He ripped open the foil and sheathed, his smile fun and yet serious. 'I am so glad you decided to rage at me in the pub car park.'

'So am I.' Her voice was husky and cracked, the way she felt with him. Cracked open and raw and sexy and wanted. She'd reached up and kissed him, tired of the push and pull, wanting to take action. Finally. Taking something for herself.

Things got serious then as he gazed at her as if he could see everything she wanted, everything she was thinking and feeling. And as if he understood, accepted her for who she was and who she wanted to be.

He ran his thumb over her top lip. 'Are you sure about this?'

'More than anything. But, wait…' She edged out from underneath him and pushed him back on the bed. Then she climbed onto him, straddling him. Taking his erection into her hand, positioning it at her entrance. 'That's so much better—'

Her words caught at the tight press as she lowered herself over him. Shocked at how he filled her, the pleasure-pain thrill. The thrill too of watching his face—the pure ecstasy in his features, the tremble in his limbs. Knowing she made him feel so good. Knowing she was in control. Taking this for herself. One night with Fraser.

'Oh, God.' He gripped her hips as she picked up a rhythm. His eyes fixed on hers as he thrust and she rode, a sexy smile on his lips as he leaned up and snaked his hands into her hair and pulled her to him. 'You are amazing, Briana. Tell me what you want.'

'This. You. All of it.' She wanted all of him. Skin to skin. Lips to lips. Pressing all of her against the length of him.

He flipped her onto her back and thrust deeper into

her, his fingers sliding between where they joined. And still he looked at her as if she was the only woman on earth. His mouth found hers and he kissed her with a reverence she'd never experienced before and could only lose herself in. Then his rhythm quickened and the kiss became a desperate, greedy clash of teeth and spit and moans. She bucked against his hand, a delicious tension spiralling once again inside her.

He groaned her name, thrusting harder and faster and took her with him, sensation after sensation rippling through her, in her, over her. And she didn't ever want it to stop.

It took Fraser more than a few minutes to come back to reality.

He was in bed with Briana. Not sweet eighteen-year-old Briana all excited about moving to London with her best friend. Not angry Briana who hated him, or his daughter's godmother, or Ellen's best friend.

This Briana was more complex, more nuanced. Someone who'd lived through darkness—although she wasn't ready to tell him about it yet. Someone who was unbelievably sexy and sensual.

It had been damned fine sex and his head was still adjusting. His body was still in *wanting* her mode.

But…what now?

He hadn't thought past having her. Hadn't thought at all, just touched and kissed and rubbed and… God, it had been good.

But…what now?

Her blonde hair was fanned out on the pillow, the soft glow of the sidelight illuminating perfect skin, hooded post-sex eyes. A very sexy smile. His heart clenched to look at her. Not just because he knew it had been a mistake but because he didn't want it to be one.

He stroked her thigh. 'Well, that was unexpected.'

'I don't…can't remember doing anything like that before…so…*desperate*…' She laughed. 'Ever.'

He settled next to her, propped himself up on his elbow, his chin in his palm, already aching to be inside her again and knowing that would definitely be a mistake. 'How long is it since you had sex?'

She shrugged a shoulder and laughed. 'Too long. You?'

'Same.'

She rolled onto her side to face him and ran her finger across his collarbone. 'Have you dated much since Ellen?'

'The odd fling before she got sick. Pretty hard to do anything more than temporary when you're dealing with all that. Then they both moved in with me full time and that completely put a stop to any kind of anything.' His eyes shuttered closed briefly as he pushed back the memories. 'I haven't had a serious girlfriend since Ellen. Lily wouldn't cope with someone else in my life and I have to put her first.'

'So…' Bri's smile dipped. 'That's…definitely a reason not to do this again.' She paused, her eyes roaming his face, searching for something. He didn't know if she'd found it when she said, 'Right? This isn't going to happen again.'

He hadn't been expecting that. He tried to read her. Tried to work out what this feeling in his chest was. Was she willing to just walk away after this? Was he?

He put some light into his voice. 'Are you regretting this already, Briana?'

'No. Not regret.' She bit her lip. 'It was good, very good.'

'But life's complicated enough, right?' He jumped in.

He wasn't sure what he saw flickering across those beautiful features, but she nodded. 'Something like that.'

He felt a need to explain. 'It's hard enough, just the two of us. Adding someone else into the mix would be chaos. To be honest, I've had enough chaos to last me a lifetime.' Was it unfair to put all the emphasis on Lily? When he had a feeling that his reluctance about having a relationship boiled down to the fact he didn't want to invest emotions in someone who might leave. Or stamp on his heart the way his father had done to his mother. The way his mother had done to him. Even Ellen had left him. Why put your heart on the line only to be left hurting at the end?

Bri ran fingertips over his collarbone. 'I'd hope I wouldn't be the chaos-maker, in another parallel world where we did decide to do this again. But it's okay. I understand. I don't need a relationship either, but I hope you'll still let me see Lily. I want to get through to her. Be there for her.'

'Of course.' He kissed her, because he couldn't not. And who knew when he'd ever do it again? He wanted this to count, to remember it. For her to remember him. 'We can't let this…what happened be a barrier to working well together or to your relationship with Lily.' He smoothed her hair back from her face, smudged his thumb across her cheek.

'Good. Thank you.'

'There's more, though. Isn't there?' He'd felt the tension slide back into her.

'I just don't want a relationship right now. I've not long got out of a difficult one.'

'Difficult how?'

'Enough to put me off relationships for a long time. He

did things, said things that rocked me. It's taken me some time to work through all of that. Hence the wobble I had.'

Shame rippled through him. 'I would never hurt you, Bri. Never.'

'I know. At least, you'd try not to.' She smiled and something in his gut uncurled. 'And the surprise of it all is that, despite what I've been thinking, you are a good man, Fraser Moore.'

He laughed. 'If you talk to Lily you might believe something different.'

'She's struggling to find her way too. Just make sure you teach her her worth and to speak up for herself any time she feels uncomfortable.'

'Trust me, my daughter is not one to hesitate about speaking up.'

'I wish I'd grown up like that. Might have saved me a bit of heartache.'

Which of course made him want to know so much more than she was telling him. 'I know I'm not supposed to ask questions, Bri. So I won't. It's your past and it's private. But if you ever want to talk about it, I'm here.'

'Thanks.' She put her hand over his heart. 'I know.'

'Not every guy is the same as him. Some of us are actually okay.'

'You're more than okay, Fraser.' She slid out of the sheets and he got the message it was time for him to leave.

He reached for his discarded clothes and dressed almost as quickly as she'd undressed him and with a lot less excitement. 'From now on we'll stay firmly in the friend zone. I promise I won't venture out of that box again.'

She slipped her arms into a silk kimono-style robe, tied it across her waist and settled back onto the bed. 'Friend zone? Okay. Yes. I can do that.'

Until an hour ago they'd been close to enemies. Someone to mistrust. Someone to blame. Someone to have damned fine sex with. And now he was just plain confused.

She was quite serious. 'It's probably best if we don't see each other outside work. At least not in the short term.'

'When Lily's your goddaughter? How's that going to work?'

'I'll arrange to see her away from you. Girl time, you know? I bet she'd be glad for some of that.'

'Good plan.' It should have felt like a lucky escape from what might have been a complicated scenario. She was making it so easy for him to walk away, but he had a strange tight feeling in his chest.

He sat opposite her and despite what they'd just agreed he wanted to take his clothes off, slip his hands underneath that silk robe and stroke her skin. To kiss her again and more. To hear her story. Maybe spend the night... Yeah, definitely parallel universe wishing. Instead, he was forcing himself to build the barriers back up. She was off limits. They both knew it was the right thing to do. He patted his pockets to locate his phone. 'Any idea what time it is?'

'Ten fifty-three.'

'What?' He jerked up. 'I've got to get back.'

'Lily?'

'Of course Lily. Always Lily.'

The smile had gone but she put her hands on his chest and pushed. 'Go.'

But he grabbed her hand and kissed the knuckles. 'Thanks, Bri.'

'Hey, big guy, I scratched an itch.' She winked. 'The thanks are all mine.'

CHAPTER EIGHT

Six weeks later...

TWO BLUE LINES.

Bri sat on the loo and stared at the white plastic stick in her hand. Her mouth went dry and her throat felt raw. Tears pricked at her eyes, but she blinked them back. She was not going to cry over this.

Oh, God.

Pregnant.

Not that she was surprised. Her period was late, her boobs were sore. She knew the signs. She was a medical professional after all. She knew that condoms weren't one hundred percent effective. That was what she told her students. Every. Single. Day.

She wafted her hand in front of her eyes to dry the mascara that was getting decidedly runny. Why had she decided to do this right before the hen night?

Another stupid decision. But she'd been too cowardly to do the test earlier, preferring to live in wilful ignorance and not face up to the truth, but then Beth had turned up with a bottle of wine and Briana had panicked. Should she drink alcohol? Could she be…?

Yes, she was.

Pregnant.

This hadn't been part of her plan. What the hell was she going to do?

She sniffed as a tear ran down her cheek. Okay, maybe she was going to cry. Just a little bit.

'Hey! Bri!' Beth hammered on the bathroom door. 'The minibus is going to be here in a few minutes, and I need to use the loo before we leave.'

Damn.

'I'm just finishing up.' Bri fisted away the rogue tears. She took a deep breath. Then another. Then she slid the test back into its box, stuffed it into the cupboard under her sink and washed her hands.

How was she going to explain away why she wasn't touching alcohol on a hen night? Headache? Antibiotics? Yes. She rifled through her medicine cabinet and found a tub of old flucloxacillin capsules and stuffed it into her handbag as proof, in case anyone asked. Because she sure as hell couldn't tell them she was pregnant before she'd had time to think about what she was going to do. Or before she told Fraser… The thought of that made her feel nauseous.

After their amazing sex she'd watched him retreat emotionally. Seen the relief when she'd casually suggested they not do it again. She'd been so confused about the way she was feeling…scared even by how *much* she was feeling. Losing herself.

Neither of them wanted a baby right now. Hell, she'd never even thought about having a baby…that was what grown-up, organised people in a relationship did. The thought was terrifying.

Another knock on the door, this time more urgent. 'Bri! Please. I'm bursting.'

'Okay. Sorry.'

Another deep breath. *Glad rags on, game face primed.*

She ran her finger under her eyes then looked in the mirror at the black trails down her cheeks. *Ugh.*

'Just tarting up the mascara. One minute.'

She threw the door open and Beth gasped. 'Wow. You look amazing.' She stuffed something soft and silky into Bri's open hand. 'Put this on. Quick!'

It was a white sash with the words *Team Bride* inked in glittery silver letters. Bri sagged a little inside but slid the sash over her head, wishing with all of her heart that she could rewind her life. Back to when?

Before sex with Fraser?

Saying yes to the hen party invitation?

Returning to Oakdale?

Before Tony?

She shivered. *Well, girl, you can certainly pick them.*

Fraser and Tony were worlds apart, chalk and cheese in looks and personalities. But neither were suitable. Neither was right for her. One was too much of a bully. The other was too…everything.

Pregnant.

Be careful what you wish for.

She'd had her one time with Fraser but what the hell would he say now? She put her hand to her belly and felt panic ripple through her. The last few weeks had been difficult. Despite what they'd agreed, the sex had loomed between them. Awkward didn't come close to explaining it.

Lily had been elusive. Always busy when Briana suggested coffees or catch-ups. Not interested in girl time… or at least not girl time with Briana. Her goddaughter was a hard nut to crack and Bri hoped it wasn't too late to fix things between them.

And now she was expecting Fraser's child.

She thought of the girls who came to her clinic and the

options she talked through with them. The leaflets she gave them, the phone calls she made. But they were teenagers and she was a grown-up. She had the wherewithal to take care of herself and anyone else who came along.

She was strong—terrified, but strong.

'Hey, daydreamer, you okay?' A grinning Beth grabbed her arm and tugged her towards the front door.

'Sorry. Yes. I was miles away. I'm fine.'

Far from fine. Very far.

Pregnant.

She thought of Lily and the lost girl she'd become. Of Fraser's words… *'My daughter comes first. Life's complicated enough. I've had enough chaos to last me a lifetime.'*

Would he even want to be involved? What the hell was she going to do?

A honk outside had Beth running to the door. 'Right. It's here. Come on, Briana. For goodness' sake, smile! This is where the fun starts!'

Bri heard the minibus before she saw it. Raucous laughter, giggles and loud pumping music. Fun? Maybe for the rest of Team Bride. But Briana couldn't wait for the day to end.

Fraser hadn't realised he'd been looking out for her until he saw her across the crowded pub and he instantly relaxed and perked up at the same time.

She was with the hen party, all laughing and drinking, taking up most of the back half of the room. As the stag group wandered over, the noise intensified with shrieks of both delight and horror at the two groups meeting.

In the middle of the chaos Briana lifted her head and caught his eye, held his gaze for a moment and then abruptly turned away.

Pretty much the way things had been going for the last few weeks. Conversation had been tense. Not worse than before, but different. Trying to work alongside her had driven him to distraction—half because he wanted to kiss her, half because he didn't know how to act around her.

At least when they'd been angry with each other he'd known how to feel. Now everything was muddied. His body prickled with need every time he looked at her. He couldn't get the image of her naked body out of his head every time he looked at her. Couldn't forget the way she tasted, the soft moans. Working out a teaching programme with her on sex education had been…interesting.

His mind may have decided one thing, but his body had another idea altogether.

Time to clear the air.

Again.

He sauntered over, trying to ignore the catch in his chest as he took in her tousled hair, the short black dress that hugged her body and the high-heeled shoes that matched the silver writing on her sash. She was radiant as she laughed at something Rose said to her but there was something different about her too, a light in her eyes, a softness he'd never noticed before. It suited her. He had to shout be heard over the loud music and chatter. 'Hey, Bri. This is weird, right? The hen and stag meeting up in the same pub?'

'It was bound to happen.' She shrugged, the softness replaced by something that made her untouchable and the light in her eyes extinguished by increments the closer he got to her. 'Kendal's a small place.'

'Having fun?'

'Great. Yes. Fun.' Not smiling, she lifted her glass and drained it. 'Cheers.'

Okay. 'You want another drink?'

'I'm fine, thanks. We're going soon. A pub crawl isn't a crawl if we stay in one place.'

There it was. The guardedness she'd worn since the night they'd had sex. Whether it was the booze or he'd reached the end of his tether he wasn't sure, but something made him speak up. 'Look, what's going on? There's a weird vibe, right?'

'I don't know what you mean.' She blinked quickly. 'How's Lily?'

That came out of left field, but he was glad she'd asked. 'Not great, to be honest. I think you were right the other day when you told me to go back to London. She's not settling here. She's not happy.'

'But…I thought…' Bri's eyes widened. Then she nodded and her arm curled protectively across her belly, like a barrier. 'I see. Right. Okay.'

'I mean…nothing's planned or anything. But I hate seeing her like this. She's all I've got, you know? Maybe I did the wrong thing by moving her up here.'

Bri pressed her lips together. The colour had drained from her face. 'But London? It's so far away.'

And yet you told me to go.

'Look, Bri, I think we need to talk.'

Her eyes filled and she blinked quickly.

His stomach clenched and he suddenly felt the most sober he'd been his whole life. Was she about to cry? 'What's wrong, Bri? What's the matter?'

Her expression flattened and she shook her head. 'Nothing.'

'Yes, there is. What is it?' Was it because he'd said he'd considered moving back to London? But then…she'd made it clear she didn't want anything more. He had a sudden unpleasant thought. 'He's not back, is he?'

She frowned. 'Who?'

'The guy. The one who hurt you.' His hands curled into fists in an unbidden and instinctive act of protection. He shook them loose before she called him out on being a Neanderthal.

'Tony? I hope not.' Her back stiffened and she walked him away from the rest of the group. 'What do you know about that?'

'Only what you told me.' *Or didn't tell me.* 'I've been thinking about it.'

'Well, don't.'

It wasn't as if he was going to forget the look on her face as he'd held her arms above her head. 'If it's not him, what is it?'

'Please, Fraser. Shut up. This is not the place to have this conversation.'

His heart thudded. What did she mean? 'What conversation?'

Her eyes fluttered closed. 'Nothing. Look—'

What conversation? What was wrong? What had happened?

'Can I call you? Tomorrow? Morning?'

A swaying Beth was tugging on Briana's arm. 'Come on, chatterbox. We have more pubs to go to and more games to play.'

'Okay.' Bri shot him a look then grinned at her friend. Only someone who knew her as well as he did, someone who'd seen beyond her guard, would know she was digging very deep to find that smile. 'Right, then…what's next on Rose's dare list?'

Beth squinted at a piece of paper in her hand. 'Um… She's kissed a bald man's head, so now she has to…oh, yes. Drink a shot without using her hands.'

'Okay. Let's go.'

Bri didn't even turn back to look at him. She just

swished out of the bar with the rest of the women, leaving him with a rather drunk Joe who was trying to throw a dart at the dart board and missing not just the outer rings but the whole board altogether.

Fraser looked back at the door swinging on its hinges and wondered what the hell had got Briana so riled up.

She could be damned well sure he was going to talk to her tomorrow.

Tomorrow came far too quickly in the form of a knock on her door at five-thirteen a.m.

Before she even answered, Briana knew who it was going to be. But, far from the drunken mess she was expecting, he looked very sober indeed.

He was still wearing his smart shirt and chinos from last night under his thick coat. His hair was damp, his nose and the tips of his ears were red from the cold, but he looked just about as gorgeous as she'd ever seen him.

Her heart lifted and melted a little at his wary smile. Which made everything feel worse. 'Fraser. You said you'd call me in the morning.'

'It's morning now. I've been walking around the village for two hours, trying to work out what it is you need to talk to me about. And none of what I've conjured up in my head is good. You said your guy wasn't back, so are you sick?'

'What? No. What made you think that?' Then the penny dropped. He'd nursed Ellen, so of course his thoughts might go straight to that.

He nodded, obviously relieved, but his face was still pale as he walked into her hallway and closed the door against the icy blast whipping round their legs. He followed her into the kitchen where she flicked the kettle on, popped teabags into two mugs and tried to find the right words to say.

But he beat her to it.

'So you're pregnant, then?' he said in a tone that suggested he was joking and that he very much hoped she wasn't.

'Yes.'

His eyes closed and he sighed out a long breath. He looked as if this was the worst possible news he could ever receive. Her heart crumpled in on itself.

'Okay.' He ran his hand over his hair. Opened his eyes. And she saw a struggle there. Confusion. A little panic and yet something fiercely protective. 'Condom failure?'

'It happens. Should have picked a different one, eh?' She wished she'd stayed on the Pill after Tony. Wished Fraser had picked the strawberry- or chocolate-flavoured one. Any of the hundreds in that bag except the one he'd fished out.

But she didn't wish she'd never had sex with Fraser because that brief happiness had been wonderful.

'So much for lucky dip. And you're going to keep it? Or…?' He swallowed. 'Only I know it's your decision and I'll support whatever that is. But, for the record, I'd look after you both, financially, obviously. And…whatever else you need.'

It occurred to her that this was a rerun of his past. *Déjà vu.*

He hadn't loved Ellen, although they'd briefly been smitten in that intense hot flash of young infatuation that was doomed never to last. But they'd worked out a co-parenting schedule and he'd supported the mother of his child and taken good care of Lily.

But this was different. At least, it was for Briana.

She sighed. 'I haven't really thought past the fact I

had some blue lines on a stick yesterday. But, yes, I'm going to keep it.' She knew without a shadow of a doubt that she was going to love and protect this child growing inside her, regardless of what Fraser Moore wanted. 'I know this isn't what you want or need.'

'It's done, Briana. It's not as if I haven't been here before. You'd think I'd have learned the first time.'

There wasn't a flicker of emotion in his face now he was processing it. No congratulations. No *Isn't this wonderful. Our baby.*

'But I never had a dad around and I always swore I'd do everything I could for my kids if I ever had any. And now look… I have two. Give me a little time to talk to Lily. It's not been easy the last few weeks. She's refusing to talk to me because I won't let her go to London for next week's half-term.'

'Are you still thinking of moving back there?' Why had she put that thought in his head? She'd been so angry and frustrated and guilty, and wanting him…awash with out-of-control emotions but long-distance parenting would be so hard.

He scuffed his hand through his hair. 'I don't know, Bri. I feel as if the ground keeps shifting under my feet just as things get onto an even keel.'

'I've only just had a positive pregnancy test, Fraser. We both know anything could happen from here. We can wait until twelve weeks before we say anything to anyone. Should probably wait, actually. No point in upsetting Lily or rashly changing plans if nothing comes of it.'

'I don't like keeping secrets from her, but I can wait until we're sure.' His eyes dipped to her belly. 'Tell me what you need. I'd like to come to the scans.'

'Of course. I'll let you know as soon as I book one.'

It was all going too fast. She hadn't the space or time or inclination to be a mother. But here she was.

It wasn't exactly what she'd wanted. It was a shock. But they'd have to live with it. And somehow work it out together.

Apart.

CHAPTER NINE

THREE DAYS INTO half-term and Fraser's blood pressure was spiralling out of control.

Briana's bombshell news had knocked him completely sideways.

How were they going to navigate this? Especially if he went back to London.

A baby changed everything.

It felt as if he was living in a Groundhog Day of his own making.

The biggest difference between this time and the last was that he'd had no long-term spark with Ellen. Hadn't had that ache in his chest when he looked at her—sure, he'd loved her as a friend, but he hadn't had that *can't stop thinking about you* craving like he had with Briana.

He'd have to wrangle the craving under control. He'd have to focus on the baby and not on the mother. On the practicalities of the situation and not on the way Bri brought out emotions in him that he wanted to hide from.

He glanced around his kitchen, imagining the high-chair stage all over again and realising he'd have to baby-proof it. Just as he'd seen the light at the end of a particularly challenging child-rearing tunnel.

And teenagers should come with a government health warning, he mused as he cleared up the kitchen after last night's dinner. Lily's job. Not done before she'd headed off to babysit Katy up the road and he'd gone to the Ambleside climbing wall with Alex.

He looked at the dog bowls on the floor. Empty. Jasper hadn't been fed. Also Lily's job, and a condition of getting the pet in the first place. As he walked to the dog food cupboard Jasper wound through his legs, almost tripping him up.

'Watch it, mate.' Fraser slopped food and water into the bowls. 'Thank your lucky stars you don't have to worry about anyone but yourself, Jasper, my boy. It's a dog's life all right. Sometimes I really, *really* want to be you.'

As he straightened up his phone pinged with a text message from Briana.

All okay for the scan this afternoon? Should I meet you there? Penrith Maternity Hospital. Two o'clock.

A sharp stab of pain slid under his ribcage. The kind of pain that was bound up with love and protection and a solemn promise. Briana had pulled strings and got an early gestation scan at the maternity unit. Not routine, but she'd wanted to double-check everything was fine and he'd agreed.

Keeping his distance was probably in order, but nothing would stop him going to this scan. Not even the flash of heat at the thought of spending time with Miss Off Limits.

He sent a message back.

I'll be there.

Now all he had to do was find an excuse to tell Lily about where he was spending the afternoon. So much for always being honest. But he'd promised Bri he'd wait before he said anything about the baby to his daughter, so he'd wait. Already things were getting more complicated.

Somehow, he'd managed to get through the last days of his half-term break on autopilot, cooking, hiking the hills around their village with Lily, trying to distract her from her never-ending pleas to go to London and hoping she'd fall in love with The Lakes and start to settle, and save them another upheaval. But she'd been more than a little twitchy.

Jasper pawed at his leg and made puppy eyes at him. Fraser sighed and grabbed the lead and poop bags and pulled on his coat. 'Okay, let's go get Lily. We can take her on a walk too. Maybe with you in tow she might actually smile.'

They trudged up the road to Joe and Rose's house. Rose tugged the door open. 'Hey, Fraser. Hey Jasper!' She bent and nuzzled the dog's fur. 'How's things?'

'Not bad.' *If only she knew.* 'We've come for Lily.'

'Lily?' Rose straightened and frowned. 'She's not here.'

'Oh. Maybe she's back at home and we somehow missed her. What time did she leave?'

The frown turned to concern. She put her hand on his arm. 'Fraser, Lily hasn't been here since last week.'

'What?' His heart stumbled. Something was wrong with this scenario. Very wrong. 'But she told me last night she was babysitting Katy. Staying over like last weekend for the hen and stag parties.'

'No. Sorry.' Rose pulled her brightly coloured crocheted wrap tightly across her body and shivered, her expression reflecting the worry whirling in his chest. 'Where is she?'

'That's exactly what I want to know.' It was too early to panic. Wasn't it?

He ran back to the house and up to her bedroom, checking for clues. Bed not slept in. He pulled open the wardrobe door, scanned around. New backpack gone. Some of her clothes too. No note. No clues to follow.

He sent her a text message.

Lily. Where are you?

And then another.

Please let me know you're safe. I'm not angry. I just want to know you're okay.

Nothing.

He called but her phone just rang out.

Should he phone the police? And say what? *My tearaway daughter has torn away again?*

She'd packed bags, it had been intentional… The police would just tell him to wait. He decided to give it an hour or so and see if she responded to his calls.

He drove around the village and then out into the snow-covered hills, wondering if she'd decided to go for a walk. But without Jasper? That wasn't Lily.

He texted her again. Called her once. Twice. Twenty times.

Nothing.

Nothing for three and a half hours while he lost the plot. He paced. He ran. He searched her room again for any hints as to where she'd gone, knowing the truth in his gut but not wanting to believe she'd actually done it. The too-familiar emotions of helplessness and anger rolled through him. This was his fault. He should never have brought her here when her life was so far away.

He'd pushed her to this.

At twelve forty-five his phone rang. A landline number. London.

'Hello?' He knew he sounded gruff, tried not to, but desperation made him panic. 'Lily? Lily, is that you?'

'It's Police Officer Singh from the Metropolitan police. I have a Lily Moore here to speak to you. Hold the line.'

'Okay. Thanks. But what—?' The police. What the hell had happened? He closed his eyes and remembered all the promises he'd made to Ellen to keep their baby safe. His imagination ran riot with myriad scenarios and none of them were good. He held his breath... There was a muffled sound then, 'Daddy?'

'Lily?' His heart went into meltdown. She sounded scared and so far away. 'Oh, my God. Are you okay?'

'Not really.' Her voice was meek and wobbly. 'Can you come and get me?'

The anger melted away and he knew he'd go to the ends of the earth for his daughter. Although he'd gone way beyond the end of his tether. She'd lied. She'd sneaked out of their home. Other parents would think about leaving her to face the consequences. 'Where are you?'

'Clapham.'

As he'd thought. 'I'm coming right now.'

'I'm...' he heard the sob and it just about broke him '...at the police station.'

'I know. I know, Lily-Bee.' He closed his eyes. 'I'm on my way. Don't say or do anything until I get there, okay?'

'No. Please. Come soon.'

'I'm on my way, baby.' His voice caught. He almost

slid on the icy path as he ran outside, coat hanging off one arm. He jumped into the car and sped down the road. At the T-junction at the end of the village he pulled up short and more dread slithered into his gut as he remembered the scan. Two o'clock. He'd never get to London and back and make it in time. He had a choice to make. A choice that whatever he did would hurt someone he didn't want to hurt.

Turn right for Penrith to go to watch the scan of his new baby. Turn left to London to save his daughter.

He wasn't coming.

That was the truth of it. When it had gone way past her appointment time and he hadn't materialised Briana had managed to swap slots with the next patient, but she couldn't delay it any more. The sonographer was tapping her watch and was clearly not going to let Briana's *traffic* excuse make her clinic run late.

Panic threaded through her as she turned her phone off and settled onto the examination couch. What if something bad had happened to him? What if he'd decided he didn't want to be involved and just wasn't man enough to tell her?

She didn't know whether she should be worried or angry. But all she knew was that she felt something. She felt something for Fraser Moore. Which was even more distressing.

He wouldn't say yes and then not turn up without a reason. There had to be a reason. Surely?

Then all thoughts about him dissolved when the sonographer said, 'I can see the heartbeat. Look, right here.'

Briana turned to look at the screen and saw the little

glowing blob. Her heart almost drowned in a surge of love. 'Oh. Wow. It's real.'

'There's not a lot to see at this stage, but do you want a picture?'

She wanted a damn baby-of-the-year award because this tiny little dot was so beautiful and so clever to have got this far already. She wiped her eyes, felt the dampness on her cheeks. She hadn't realised she was crying. But, *oh*. Who knew you could feel like this for someone you'd never even met? 'Yes…' she managed. 'Yes, please.'

'One for Dad too?'

Briana thought about the panicked look in Fraser's eyes when the pregnancy truth had dawned on him and realised that, no matter how much she told herself it didn't matter that he wasn't happy, it did matter. She wanted Fraser to want this baby. 'Yes, one for Dad. Is everything okay? Can I tell him it's all okay?'

'Everything is perfect.'

The scan was followed by her first maternity appointment with a lovely midwife who briefly walked her through the next nine months and handed her more leaflets than she could fit into her handbag. Bloods were taken. An appointment for another scan in a few weeks. Information about antenatal classes. A book about pregnancy.

In every picture the women were smiling.

Now the glow of seeing their baby was dimming a little and the reality of their situation was dawning, Bri didn't feel much like smiling. Fraser had stood her up. Stood their baby up.

And, boy, was she going to let him have it when she saw him next. To hell with being polite and keeping the peace.

Maybe next time she'd bring Beth to the scan instead…at least girlfriends didn't let you down.

By the time she stepped out into fresh air she'd been at the hospital for two hours. Exhausted and emotional, she made her way to a café, ordered a cup of tea and some cake and pulled out her phone.

She had two missed calls. A voice message: 'It's Fraser.' He sounded out of breath and there were loud background traffic sounds, the screech and whine of lorry brakes. 'I'm sorry I missed the scan, Bri. I really am. But Lily…she ran away. I'm on my way to London to bring her home.'

She imagined his heart would have been breaking and her own heart clutched at the thought of the hurt and panic he would have been going through when he'd left that message.

Bri inhaled as she listened to his message again.

He'd put Lily before his new baby, and she didn't blame him, not at all. How could she blame him when he'd had to choose a runaway over a scan? It would have been an unforgiving choice for him. But she still wanted to shout at him. She'd needed him there. Wanted him there. And he could have called her sooner and let her know he was okay and to go ahead and not wait.

She sent him a text message.

I got your message. I hope Lily's okay. I hope you're okay too.

She didn't mention the scan because she was so confused about the way she was feeling. But she got no reply. Not for a long time. Not for eight hours. Eight hours of checking her phone over and over. Wondering where he was and what he was doing and why he hadn't been in touch again. Thinking worst-case scenarios. She was starting to imagine what it must have been like for Fraser when he'd discovered Lily was missing. Terrifying. Of course he'd run to her. Just as he would run to any other child of his who needed him.

That was part of his appeal. He was a devoted father.

Then, just as she was settling down to sleep, with her hand nestled over her non-existent baby bump, her phone beeped.

We're home. I'm sorry. Can we talk?

She wasn't sure she could have a sensible conversation at this time of night with all her emotions rattling round her. She sent a message back.

You need to spend some time with Lily.

A pause. Then a reply.

I've just spent six hours with her, most of them in the car where we couldn't hide from each other. Trust me, I'm all talked out with her for a while. I want to hear about the scan. How did it go? Is everything okay? Are you okay? Are we okay?

Her heart tripped a little. She replied.

Embryo is high in the uterus. Heartbeat is good and strong. All looks fine.

She sent him the digital picture on her phone…and almost immediately he replied.

Bri, wow. It's real. Beautiful. A new life. He's got your eyes.

She couldn't help but laugh at that. There were no discernible features at this early stage, just a blob that looked a little like a beating black hole where she would pour every ounce of her love…was already doing so. She sent another message.

Let's hope she's got my brains. And my timekeeping skills.

He replied.

Hey, I've got good brains. I'll work on the timekeeping. I promise.

Before she could think of anything witty to reply her phone beeped again.

I know you're angry and I'm sorry. We need to talk. Or I need to talk even if you don't want to. Please.

She knew she was starting to soften towards him again, despite everything. He'd had a day from hell but still wanted to talk to her about their baby. He was concerned and contrite and he thought their little blob was beautiful, the same way she did, and suddenly he was the only person she wanted to talk to about this.

Before she could stop herself, she sent another message.

Tomorrow morning? I'm not at work until lunchtime.

Immediately he sent one back.

Ten work for you? Come up here. I'll make us some brunch. Thanks again for the picture. x

A kiss.

Which made her think about his mouth and the way he tasted. The strength in his arms as he'd held her. The way she felt undone and cracked open when he was around. The way she felt as if she could say anything and he'd hold it, hear her. But, yes, his timekeeping skills needed work.

She sent him her affirmative reply and threw her phone onto the nightstand, resolutely determined not to think about him any more.

Which lasted a whole ten seconds...

When he opened the door and saw Briana standing there—even though he was expecting her—Fraser's heart tightened. His skin did too. Something fluttered in his chest that felt a lot like relief. Not just that she was giving him a chance to make amends, but more. His life was a mess and about to get a whole lot messier, but having Briana here made it all seem more bearable.

She smiled up at him and his first, most natural instinct was to reach for a hug but he reminded himself that that was not possible. They were walking a tenuous line here and he had to respect that.

'Where is she?' she whispered, as she hung her coat up in the hallway and walked through to the kitchen, and he was immediately grateful she was concerned about Lily and not scolding him about missing the scan.

He followed the sweet, subtle scent of flowers that was so familiar and intimate. 'Lily is in her bedroom. She's grounded and sulking. I would have met you somewhere else for coffee, but I felt I needed to stay here to make sure she was okay. You're going to have to put up with my paltry cooking skills.'

Her eyes darted over to the pans simmering on the stovetop. 'You didn't have to cook.'

'I did. I have a lot of making up to do.'

'You must have been out of your mind with worry.' Her eyes softened and she looked genuinely concerned for him. 'Tell me what happened.'

He poured tea into mugs, plated up the scrambled eggs and toast and brought them over to the table. 'She said she was babysitting Katy. Staying over at Joe's like she did last weekend. I texted her in the evening and said goodnight, like I always do. She sent me a reply with two kisses.' His heart tightened. 'You know what? I was so pleased, so grateful for those two little exes. I thought I was making a breakthrough. Instead…'

He hauled in a breath, reliving one of his worst nightmares. He still didn't know how he got to London without crashing his car. 'She was on a bloody train. Or already at the night club. Or…God knows where. With God knows who.'

'She took a risk saying she was at Joe's, hoping you wouldn't check.' Bri started on the food.

'I guess she assumed that if or when I found out she'd have been long gone. Besides, I don't usually check on something like that. It's her babysitting job and I want her to be responsible for it, but it turns out my daughter's all about the risks. She didn't give two thoughts about lying and blithely met up with her friends. Went to a night club where a fight broke out and she was somehow embroiled. I'm not sure of the details but she was collected up with the rest of them and hauled to the police station. She swears she didn't do anything wrong.'

He laughed bitterly. 'Apart from lying to me, underage drinking, you know…'

Bri looked at him and gave him a sympathetic smile. 'She's safe now, Fraser, and that's all that matters in the end.'

'I should have known this was going to happen when she kept complaining about not being allowed to go to London. But I was distracted.'

By you. By our news. And now he was going to have to divide his attention between two children when he couldn't even keep one safe. Here? Or in London?

'I should have read between the lines. She could have been hurt, Bri.'

'I know.' She reached across the table and patted his hand reassuringly. 'But she wasn't.'

'She says she feels trapped here.'

He saw Briana bristle at that, and he knew it stemmed from that guy and that thing in her past she wouldn't talk about. But she nodded and smiled again. 'Maybe I could talk to her? It's about time I stumped up and did the god-mother thing properly.'

'I don't know if she'd be ready to listen.'

'I'll listen to her. She needs to feel heard.'

'Sure. Anything. If you think that might help. You know, this is not how I want things to be. Not how Ellen and I planned. Towards…the end…' he swallowed '…we talked about how I should raise Lily. What kind of parent I should be and we both agreed we wanted a light-handed approach. A confidant, a friend, someone who'd listen and take her opinions and feelings into account. And I've tried so hard to be all that. But when it involves breaking the law, I have to draw a line.' He scuffed his hand through his hair. 'By not being that friend or confi-dant, I feel like I'm not just letting Lily down, but Ellen too. God, I even brought her up here when we'd agreed the city would be a good place to grow up, full of opportunities.'

'Don't beat yourself up about that, Fraser. You weren't to know how things would pan out in London.'

'I would be very grateful if you could try and talk to her. Maybe tomorrow? She'd respond better to you. A woman. A friend.'

She tapped her fingers on the table and thought for a moment. 'I might just have a plan. Leave it with me.'

'And I'll talk to her again later. See if I can break through.' He drank some tea, hoping it would ease the nausea in his gut, and then filled Bri in on the rest of the trip. The police issuing yet another caution and warning Lily it was her last one. The long trip back where he'd struggled to get her to open up. The desolate atmosphere that coated everything.

Bri put her knife and fork down and smiled. 'You have to eat something, Fraser.'

'Later.' He pushed his plate away. 'I'm just not feeling it right now.'

'In that case, can I—?' she stabbed at his toast. 'I'm starving.'

He liked her enthusiasm for food and the fact she was here, helping him hatch plans to keep communication flowing between him and Lily. It was the first time in years he'd felt he'd had someone to lean on. More, a friend who understood what Lily needed. *A friend.* That felt good. He liked her. Not just lusted after her, liked her. That felt even better.

He watched her demolish the toast and smiled. 'That's a good sign.'

'Is it? I remember Ellen throwing up all the time in the first few weeks. I'm not looking forward to that bit.'

'You might get lucky.' His heart tightened at the thought of Ellen's early pregnancy days when she'd lived in the shared student accommodation with Briana, before she'd moved into the flat he'd found for her and his baby. 'We had no idea what the hell we were doing. This time round I'll have more of a clue. Although this trouble with Lily isn't exactly a good advert for my parenting skills.'

He wasn't sure what he saw flickering across Briana's eyes but she inhaled a shaky breath.

'Bri, are you happy about it?' He hadn't even asked her. God, he was so wrapped up in himself he hadn't been there for her.

She blinked. 'I was in shock at first, I won't lie. It will drastically change my life, obviously. But I'll cope.'

'Which isn't exactly a ringing endorsement. You said you don't want to be trapped. This baby will inevitably…' he dug for the right words '…anchor you in a lot of ways.'

'I don't want to be trapped in a relationship. That's very different from having a child. I want to be able to make my own decisions, be my own woman. I want to call the shots in my own life. And, yes, Fraser, I do want this child. I am thrilled.' Her eyes widened. 'At least now I've got used to the idea.' She laughed and he felt the air between them settle. She was starting to open up.

'Not exactly what we'd planned, eh?'

She gave him a rueful smile. 'The key to life is being flexible. Sometimes you have to admit you've taken the wrong path and reroute.'

'Is that why you came back from Australia? You rerouted?'

For a second she looked like a rabbit caught in headlights but then she nodded. 'Yes.'

He waited. Looked away, trying not to spook her, but

silently willing her to elaborate a little on what had happened to her.

She looked down at her hands. 'I thought he loved me, but it turned out he just wanted to own me. I couldn't do anything without his permission.'

'What?' The brief calm he'd felt was replaced by anger. 'Did he hurt you? Hit you?'

'Not badly. But sometimes he was rough.' Her neck flushed red and she rubbed at her wrist where, Fraser imagined, she'd been tugged, pulled or gripped by a coward and a bully. 'He was manipulative. Cut me off from friends and family. Isolated me. Trapped me.' She wrung her hands together. 'I can't believe I let him do that. But he did it slowly and made it sound like it was all for my own good and that he was protecting me and that he loved me so much, that no one would love me the way he did. And I believed him.'

She looked desolate but incredulous, as if she was talking about someone else, not herself. He could barely control his rage. 'He sounds like a monster.'

She nodded slowly and grimaced. 'One day I found myself asking his permission to go to the mall to buy some shoes and I realised my world had become so small and I couldn't get out. He'd trapped me emotionally, physically...'

'I can't imagine anyone doing that. I'm so sorry, Bri.' Everything slotted into place then. Her determination to be in control of her own destiny, to do her own thing, and the panic when he had held her down.

His gut tightened in shame and guilt along with the anger. And something else too. A fierce need to protect her, to take a stand on her behalf. To make her believe how amazing she was. His heart twisted and he wanted to pull her to him but knew another guy tugging at her would be the last thing she wanted or needed.

'No wonder you want to be in control, Bri. You deserve so much better. If you could see yourself the way I see you, you'd know you are worth a million Tonys. More. You're brilliant. Beautiful. Kind. Clever. Funny.'

Her eyes filled with tears. She blinked them away and laughed, but it was on a choked sob, then she straightened up and looked him in the eye. 'Too right I am. And don't you ever forget it, Fraser Moore.'

His smile came from his heart. 'I have no doubt you'll keep reminding me.'

'Don't worry, I will. Right, I'll clear up.' Stuffing his last piece of toast into her mouth, she pushed her chair back and picked up the plates. More, he imagined, to break the heavy atmosphere than a need to do dishes.

He jumped up and grabbed the mugs, racing over to the sink before she got there. 'Don't. Please. It's my mess.'

'It's my mess too.' She elbowed him away from the sink, her eyes snagging his, and they both knew they weren't talking about the washing-up at all.

He smiled at her, wanting to make everything better. 'We can work it out.'

She sighed and smiled too, her cheeks flushing a delightful pink. 'I'll wash, you dry.'

They got into a rhythm of wash-dry-put-away, working together. Sneaking glances. Smiles. And a momentary sense of peace settled over him. This felt so desperately domestic. Shared. *Good.*

How could the simple act of doing the dishes with someone feel so good? All he knew was that he liked being around her. Even with all this tension. It wasn't just about the baby and having to forge some kind of friendship. The sexual energy between them, fed by memories of that one perfect time, coated everything they said, every look, every smile.

Her movements were so sensual. He watched as she bent to the cupboard to put the detergent away. Acutely aware of the slide of her skirt fabric over her bottom.

He felt himself go hard at the memories of her naked body and thrust his hands into the hot sudsy water to give himself something else to think about.

She straightened and frowned, looking at his hands. 'Hey. That's my job.'

'We're switching.' He leaned across her for a dirty pan as she reached across him for the dish towel, her fingertips skimming across his belly.

With just that slight touch his nerve endings fired into life, his body rippling with sensation.

He looked at her, remembering the way she'd gripped his shoulder when she'd come. The softness of her skin, the taste of her. He felt as if his life was on a constant knife-edge as he'd learned how to navigate his daughter, and now this woman had come into their lives and he was learning her too. Overriding his feelings around her and focusing on the baby was proving to be one of the hardest things he'd ever done.

He turned to face her. So she would hear him. He didn't want to ever see that panicked expression on her face again, or the worry of telling him something that made her feel vulnerable. Didn't want to let her down again. Although he knew he probably would.

But he didn't want to, and that had to count for something. 'I am so sorry I missed the scan, Bri. The minute I got Lily's call I just went into action mode and then I couldn't phone until I stopped at a service station. I feel terrible about leaving you to go on your own. I should have messaged sooner.'

She hugged the dish towel against her belly. 'It's okay.'

'It's not. This is my baby too.'

She smiled and her words echoed his thoughts. 'It's not going to be easy.'

'I'm the king of not easy parenting.' He flexed his biceps and she laughed, squeezing his muscle and raising her eyebrows.

'We'll see about that, Fraser Moore.'

He smiled with relief that she was laughing. 'Are we okay?'

'I am.' She grinned. 'But I'm not sure you'll ever be okay.'

She flicked the dish towel at him and he jerked back. He flicked washing-up suds at her and she screeched, flicking back at him with the towel, chasing him round the table and laughing.

'Hey! Truce?' He put his arms out for a hug, not expecting, but hoping, she'd step right in. She looked at him dubiously. 'Come on, Bri. It's just a hug between friends. Where's the harm?'

'Okay. One hug.' She gave him an eye-roll that would have matched Lily's for condescension then slid into his arms, wrapping her arms around his waist. He held her close. For comfort. For relief. For the pure pleasure of having someone to share this all with. 'I promise I'll be at the next scan. I'll be the best dad I can be.'

'I know you will.'

He rested his chin on her head. 'A baby. Wow.'

'Wow. Yes. A baby.' She edged back and smiled up at him, her eyes misting with heat as she held his gaze for a second. Two. Three. Neither of them spoke. Everything seemed to stop then: his breath; time. All thought. The electricity between them buzzed and zinged and all he saw was a beautiful, sexy woman with an amazing mouth that tasted very fine. And he knew they'd agreed, but it felt as if an invisible thread was tugging them closer and closer. He cupped her face. 'Briana…'

'Fraser…' She tipped her head towards him but a choking, horrified voice from behind made him leap away from her.

'What the hell are you doing?'

CHAPTER TEN

LILY WAS STANDING in the middle of the room, hands on her hips, her face blotchy from crying, mascara streaks on her cheeks. She looked young and vulnerable and utterly shocked. Horrified even.

They'd been making so much noise with their silly game they hadn't heard her come downstairs.

Oh, God, this was not what was meant to happen. None of this.

Briana cleared her throat and tried to stop the hammering in her chest that made her feel light-headed. Maybe, with the teeniest bit of luck, Lily hadn't overheard their conversation.

'I'm giving your father a hug because he's had a rough few days.' She opened her arms wide. 'I've got plenty to spare. You want one too?'

Lily glowered and ignored Bri's gesture. 'What *baby*? What *scan*?' She looked from Fraser to Briana and back again, her eyes dark and bruised with emotion. Her bottom lip wobbled as the words sank in. 'Oh. My. God. You're pregnant? Dad? Is Briana pregnant?'

Clearly, luck was not on Bri's side today. This year. *This life.*

Next to her, Fraser opened his palms in a conciliatory

gesture, his expression flat and giving no emotion away. 'Yes. Briana and I are having a baby.'

'Well, wow.' His daughter inhaled a staggered breath, eyes wide and glittering. 'Don't expect me to congratulate you.'

Bri stepped forward, unsure how to navigate this. Even as a nurse who dealt with kids all day, every day, she felt so out of her depth. 'We didn't want you to find out like this.'

'Tough luck on that front.' Lily shook her head in disappointment.

Fraser gave Bri a small smile of support. 'We wanted it to be confirmed before we said anything.'

'We?' Lily spat the words out. '*We've* only been in this stupid, boring place a few weeks and you're already getting it on with Briana? You're together now, is that it?'

'No.' Briana was definite about that. 'We're not together. It's not like that.' Even to her, it sounded weak and ridiculous.

'I just saw you,' Lily slammed back. 'It looked like you were kissing. You're always going on at me about being honest and yet here you are. Lying.'

'I am not lying.' Now Fraser looked about as torn apart as Briana felt as he added, 'I just haven't been able to tell you yet. Briana only had the scan yesterday. I'm sorry you found out like this, but Bri and the baby are going to be part of our lives from now on.'

'Just great.' Lily threw Bri one last savage look. 'A baby? At your age? And you tell me to be responsible.' She disappeared up the stairs, thumping at every step.

Fraser ran to the door and called out, desperation in his voice, 'Lily! Please.'

They heard the slam of a door, the sag of bed springs. Something hitting the floor.

Fraser's eyes closed and he looked close to broken. There was a long moment of silence. Briana truly did not know what to say except that she knew he was hurting. That Lily was too, and she was desperately sorry for them both.

And also that she wasn't sure she could cope with this kind of drama every day when the baby came along. It was going to be hard enough getting to grips with co-parenting as it was.

Fraser rubbed his hand over his forehead. 'At least we don't have to worry about how we're going to tell her our news.'

'I am so sorry.' Bri sighed. 'That wasn't how I imagined it going. Do you want to go up to her? Should I?'

'No. Leave her for a few minutes. Let her calm down. Then I'll go up. I think it should be just me for now. But you were right when you said I won't be getting that father of the year award.'

'You just scooped her up from a police station after she broke not just the law but your family rules. She's been your only focus for the last fifteen years. We can't expect her to welcome a baby with open arms, especially when she hasn't got used to the idea of me being around. Emotions are running high. Maybe she'll be better about it when she's thought it through.'

'You think?' His expression told her he wasn't holding out much hope for that.

'Maybe she'll enjoy having a brother or sister around.' She coughed. 'Having said that, my brother never paid me much attention. I was more of an irritant to be ignored than someone to play games with.'

'You have a brother?' His eyebrows rose. 'I didn't know that.'

'He's five years older than me. An accountant, like my

dad was. Lives in Reading. We're not close.' Like Fraser, she was short on a supply of people to help her with her parenting journey. No parents alive and a brother far away, although she had her friends here and it was a tight, supportive community. And there'd be Fraser, of course, doing his co-parenting bit the way he had with Ellen…if he stayed here. And she would be fine and everything, but it just wasn't how Briana had expected her life to pan out.

After Tony, she'd vowed no men, so kids hadn't been part of the picture. Before Tony, she'd assumed she'd get married at some point, have a couple of kids, everyone living under the same roof. But things were different now and with an angry half-sister to her child in tow. None of it was how she'd envisioned her life.

Fraser walked back to the kitchen sink and started scrubbing at a pan. Hard. 'I always wanted a sibling. It was always just me and my mum, but she worked so hard, such long hours—she had a homeware store in Cheshire town centre. I only ever got the exhausted version. No… it was more than that…'

'What do you mean?'

He shot her a wary look. 'I think she blamed me for my father leaving and was always emotionally cold compared to my friends' mums, as if she was just going through the motions. The minute I left home she declared herself free. Like I'd been a brick round her neck. I don't know…' He shrugged, but Bri could see the hurt in his eyes. 'I always wondered what it would be like to have a dad around too, doing guy things, like my friends had.'

'Where was your dad?'

'Don't know. Never met him.' He started to wipe down the sink then moved on to the counter, rubbing over and over at something only he could see. 'She said he'd dumped her when she'd told him she was pregnant. Never heard from him again. I couldn't ever forgive him for that. How could he abandon a pregnant woman? How could he not want to be involved with his child? Coward.'

Hence Fraser's need to be involved with his own off-spring. Bri sighed. 'My mum stayed at home and looked after us and the house. My dad was very traditional. Strict. Domineering. All that *Don't speak until you're spoken to* stuff. *Do as I say. Don't answer back.*' She laughed wryly as it dawned on her. 'Then I ended up with not only his duplicate, but a much worse version.'

Fraser stopped scrubbing and looked at her, his eyes were so dark, pain simmered in his gaze. 'I want to hurt that man, Briana.'

'He's not worth your anger.' Her heart squeezed for this guy who was so torn and going through such difficult times but still had space for worrying about things that had happened to her.

Thank goodness she hadn't kissed him. Because that was exactly what she'd been thinking as he'd held her. That she wanted to take him to bed and let him kiss her all over.

This was a big mess. Fraser Moore was one hot guy in every sense of the word and the more time she spent with him the more she fell just a bit deeper under his spell.

What were they going to do? About the baby? About Lily? About these emotions that tumbled between them? And about the raw attraction they both felt and hid from and didn't want to admit? Especially when they were going to have to see so much more of each other.

An unwelcome thought struck her. Would he meet someone else and fall in love? Have a 'proper' family? Would she be edged out?

He hadn't edged Ellen out.

Her heart hurt. It was all so complicated.

She suddenly remembered something Lily had said and couldn't help laughing. 'What did she mean by "at your age"? I'm only thirty-three. It's a good age to have a baby.'

'To a fifteen-year-old anything over twenty is ancient.' He smiled. 'You'll have more clue with a baby than I did at eighteen. And you're a nurse too.'

'I don't know about that. It's a lot easier to teach parenting than to live it.'

'Don't I know it.' He wrung out the cloth and put it on the drying rack.

'Oh, God.' She slumped into a dining chair and put her head in her hands. 'This is a nightmare.'

She felt him kneel by her side, his warm hand palming her shoulders, turning her to him. 'Hey, Briana. It's going to be okay.'

She shook her head. 'I think it's all gone to hell, to be honest.'

She covered her face, said more than a few choice words, then let emotion take over.

He stroked her back but when she made a snorting noise he pulled her hands away from her face. 'Briana Barclay, are you laughing?'

'Kind of laughing-crying, I think. Or crying-laughing. Is that a thing? I'm so confused about everything I can't decide whether to laugh or cry, so I'm doing both at the same time.' She pressed her lips together and tried to stop but couldn't, because the whole situation was actually absurd. 'Lily's right. We were totally and utterly irresponsible. Fine sex educators we are.'

'We were failed by a duff condom. Don't we tell all our students this could happen?' He stroked the backs of his fingers down her cheek. 'It was good, though.'

She felt a giggle burst from her chest and stopped fighting it. 'The sex was amazing, Fraser.'

'Best damned sex of my life. But was it worth all this?'

Worth the heartache and confusion? Worth the nausea that would likely soon start to creep up on her every morning?

She took a chance and took his hand, placed it on her belly. The only bond between them that truly mattered was right there, beneath their fingertips. Worth *this*? She knew without a shadow of a doubt that this baby was worth anything and everything. 'It has to be.'

He stroked his palm over her stomach. 'It will be.'

She truly wanted to believe he meant it. Now, at this moment, when his daughter was safe upstairs. But if he was in London and Bri was here with his other child…?

He stood and helped her up, opening his arms, inviting her in for another hug and… Oh, what the hell, it wasn't as if anything else could go wrong today. It was just a friendly gesture and she needed someone to lean on right now. She slipped her arms around his waist, relishing the feel of his strong body.

She laid her head on his shoulder and wasn't sure whether she was going to laugh some more or cry. Or both. But at least they were on the same side for once. He'd told Lily that Briana and the baby were going to be part of their lives. He'd said it out loud. That was worth something.

Now all they had to do was work out…how.

Warmth crept into Briana's chest as he hugged her close. She'd grown nothing but coldness for him for years, but the thaw was definitely happening.

She just hoped she wasn't going to drown in the meltwater.

* * *

'Still not sure why you want to borrow my puppy, but here you go.' Beth stepped over the threshold of Briana's house and handed Boy's lead to her, clearly confused. 'Care to explain?'

Bri bent and fussed over the dog. 'Good boy. Yes. Yes. We're going for walkies. It's a long story.'

Beth's eyes narrowed. 'I'm an excellent listener and I have all evening.'

Luckily, Briana's phone beeped and she tugged it from her pocket. A text from Fraser, right on time.

She's just left. Walking down towards the village.

She sent him a thumbs-up emoji then turned to Beth. 'Sorry, I have to go. Thanks again for Boy. I'll return him as soon as we're done.'

'Done doing what?' Her friend's voice was imbued with teasing and interest.

Being a godmother. 'Something I should have done a long time ago.' She ushered Beth out, waited until she'd steered her car down the road, then locked the door behind her and set off towards the village on foot. She wasn't sure she was doing the right thing, but she had to talk to her goddaughter.

As for Fraser…well, she'd decided to keep him at arm's length as much as possible. The hug had been wonderful. And that was the problem. She couldn't allow herself to get all heated up around him when they'd agreed neither of them wanted any kind of relationship. It would muddle everything and make long-term negotiations over the baby more difficult.

It didn't take long for her to see Lily coming down the road, wrapped up against the freezing temperatures, being dragged along by her faithful furry companion and staring at her phone. Briana walked quickly towards her before Lily saw her and made a detour. 'Hello, Lily.'

Lily blinked and looked up. It took her a second to process but Bri saw exactly when it did. The girl's eyes darkened and her mouth flattened. 'This is why I hate this place. You can't get any privacy.'

But Bri was prepared for Lily's reaction. 'I know. I used to think that too. But when my mum got sick everyone rallied round and helped. Left food for me so I didn't have to think about cooking. People are nice here, Lily.'

'Very *friendly.*' The girl glanced at Briana's tummy and shook her head in distaste.

Even though Briana was prepared for it, it didn't stop her cheeks heating. 'I'm not going to tell you it was planned, because it wasn't. It just…happened and now we have to deal with it. You see, adults make some interesting choices too. Not all of them good.'

Lily shrugged. 'Like dragging your daughter to live in Oakdale?'

'Oh, Lily, we don't have some sort of handbook for being a parent. Your dad does what he thinks is best for you.'

Lily harrumphed. 'Did he tell you to say that?'

'Of course not. No one tells me what to do and say, Lily. I am my own person.'

The girl's eyebrows rose and Bri thought there may have been a glimmer of admiration there but then Lily said, 'Are you two getting married now? Or what?'

'No!' Bri willed her beating heart down to a more manageable rhythm. 'We're working the details out. But me and your dad…we're not *together.*'

'You're not even going out with each other? But you're having his baby.'

'No.' Maybe this hadn't been such a good idea after all. 'I mean…yes. It's a bit of a mess, to be honest.' Lily deserved honesty and at almost sixteen she could handle the truth. 'We're having to work things out as we go along. But whatever happens, you will always be so, so important to your dad. Always.'

'Right. Yeah. Sure.' Lily's eyes grew wide and there was a wealth of judgement there that Briana felt keenly. 'Are you here checking up on me so you can report back to him?'

Bri tugged gently on the lead and brought Boy to heel, trying to act as if this hadn't been a planned meeting, even though there'd been a lot of work behind the scenes to make it look like an accidental encounter. 'Not at all. I promised Beth I'd take Boy out because both she and Alex are working late and this little fella needs to work off some energy.'

Lily frowned. 'She usually asks me.'

Shoot. Briana thought quickly. 'We were chatting the other day and I offered, that's all. Which way are you going?'

Her goddaughter shot her a look that Bri interpreted as, *Any way you're not going.*

But Briana ignored it, and laughed at the dogs jumping at each other, barking and chasing as much as their leads allowed. And even though she felt completely out of her comfort zone she was going to follow through on her plan. 'Aw, look. They're so happy to be playing together. Maybe we should take them up to Oakdale Top and let them off their leads to have a run.'

'No, thanks.' Lily turned and pulled Jasper closer. 'Come on, we're going home.'

Drastic times call for drastic measures. Bri took a

breath and called to Lily's back, 'I'm not surprised you ran away.'

Lily froze in her tracks then slowly turned round to glare at Bri. 'Because you think my dad's unreasonable and stupid, too.'

'No.' Feigning uninterest, Bri sauntered towards her. 'I think it's genetic.'

Lily's frown deepened. 'What?'

'Your mum ran away too.'

'When?' A flicker of interest, pretending not be interested at all.

'She was thirteen. She dragged me along too.' Briana started to walk slowly up the hill away from the village, bringing Lily along with her story, as she'd intended. 'That did not go down well in my house, or hers. Not at all.'

'Why did you run away?'

'The fun fair had rolled into Kendal as it did once a year. Our parents said they'd take us, like always, but we didn't want to go with them and come home early like little kids. We thought we were all grown up and wanted to go on our own and stay until it ended. Maybe even work there, do a few weeks on tour with them. I can't even imagine what we were thinking…so naïve. So we planned a pretend sleepover at Ellen's house, then when everyone had gone to bed, we slapped on make-up and sneaked out the window with packed bags, unsure where we were going to spend the night but determined not to come home until we'd had our adventure. We got a taxi into Kendal—which cost a fortune.'

'Tell me about it.' Lily had the good grace to look sheepish.

Briana smiled. 'We got to the fair quite late and it was brilliant. Such fun. We rode the Waltzers and dodgems and ate candy floss. We flirted with the guys who ran the rides. They weren't teenagers like we'd thought but proper grown-up men and we were in awe of them. We told them we were sixteen and they gave us some vodka to drink. Then some more, and suddenly I'd had a lot and I didn't feel great.

'One of the men...' she took a breath, reliving the panic and fear of that night and that stupid decision '...started to put his hands in places I didn't want to be touched. And when I looked around there was no one else there but us four. It was dark and we were alone with these guys we didn't know, and I remembered stories about young girls being kidnapped and I got very scared. And he wanted... well, you can imagine what he wanted, and I started to cry, then I was sick over his shoes. That put him off.'

She glanced at Lily, who was listening intently. 'Thank God for Ellen, who pulled me away and told them where to go. Then suddenly both our mums appeared, shouting at the men and threatening to report them to the police. Turned out the taxi driver knew my mum and had rung her, asking whether it was okay that we were going to the fun fair so late and on our own.'

'You escaped then?' Lily was wide-eyed.

'I've never been so scared in my life, or so grateful to see our mums.' Bri smiled and nodded. 'I was grateful to the taxi driver too, and that I lived in a place where people look out for each other.' Bri stopped talking then, not wanting to sound too preachy.

Lily's eyes sparkled as all this sank in. 'Were you grounded too?'

'Yes. But I was kind of glad, really. I deserved it and didn't want to venture out for a while after that. And it turned out the fun fair wasn't as fun as I'd thought it would be.'

'London is, though.'

Bri glanced at her as they hiked up the hill. 'It can be. But not when you're breaking the rules. Juvenile detention can get old very quickly.'

'I didn't do anything wrong.' Lily swallowed and looked away, the hard act softening and letting a little bit of vulnerability through, even if she didn't want to. They both knew she'd done a lot of things wrong, but it was okay, she was young and had a lot of learning to do. 'Were you scared?'

'When the fists started flying. Yes. I thought I was going to get hit.'

'It would have been so frightening.' Bri thought for a moment, wondering why Lily had put herself in that situation and for who. 'Do you miss your friends?'

Lily's eyes glistened. 'Mmm…'

'A particular friend?'

Her goddaughter bent to nuzzle Jasper's fur and gave the smallest of nods.

Bingo. 'Does this person have a name?'

A long pause. Lily chewed her lip. Looked away and then down at her boots. 'Jerome.'

'Is he…um…?' *What would Ellen do? She'd just ask outright. Surely?* 'Your boyfriend?'

'No.' The denial was too quick. He wasn't Lily's boyfriend, but she wanted him to be.

Oh, poor Lily. In love and lonely up here. 'How about you invite him up here for a weekend?'

That received a look that said, *Kill me now.* 'To Boringsville? He'd hate it.'

'How do you know? He might be a secret fan of mountains and lakes.'

'He likes good music, dancing, that kind of thing. Not hills and trees.' They'd reached the summit and they were both a little out of breath. The dogs chased and ran across the snowy slope.

Lily was finally talking and Bri felt heady with the breakthrough. 'If he likes you, he'd come and stay, right? He'd want to be with you, whether it's about dancing and music or trees and mountains, or anything else *you* might be interested in.'

'I guess.' Lily shrugged.

Briana scanned the vista in front of them. The sun was setting over snow-capped mountains, coating them in smudged oranges and reds. Lights twinkled in the houses in the valley below. Snow glittered on the fences and grass. It was achingly beautiful. But she could see how a teenager might not see the beauty in it. Not yet. Maybe only when they came back to it after years away and breathed it in, tucking the majesty of it all into their heart and chest, let it slip between the muscle and sinew and into the bloodstream and feel it beat through them.

She loved it here and could see why Fraser might have thought it would help his daughter. And it still might. Lily just had to be open to the opportunities here.

Briana looked at an outcrop of limestone on their left. 'Have you explored those caves over there?'

'No.' Lily followed her gaze.

'There are glow-worms in there. It's amazing. Magical. Tiny microcosms of life, glittering in the dark. You'll have to take Jerome to see them.' She laughed. 'I bet you don't get many glow-worms in Clapham.'

'No.' Lily snorted. 'We have some pretty cool vintage shops, though, and a good market.'

'Oh, yes, London's great for shopping, I'll give you that. But we do have great markets in Keswick and Kendal.' Bri thought for a moment. 'I know! My friend Phil runs the outward-bound centre in Bowness. He does canoeing, caving and bush skills. I could ask him for mate's rates if you like, so it doesn't cost too much. Are there many caves in London?' A chill breeze was whipping round them and Briana huddled closer to Lily so they could hear each other's words.

Lily smiled and shuffled an inch towards Bri. 'No, but it sounds cool.'

'And there's mountain biking. Movies if it's raining. The climbing wall. There's heaps to keep him busy. And, of course, there's you. More incentive to come here than anything else, right?' Briana took a chance and, smiling, tucked a stray strand of Lily's hair back behind her ear, the way she had back when Lily had been six years old. 'Ask him up for the weekend.'

'Dad won't let me.' But her eyes were brighter. She was thinking about it.

'Have you asked him?'

'I'm grounded. I can't do anything.'

'Give it a try. Tell him how sorry you are about London—you are sorry, aren't you?'

Lily nodded, her eyes glittering with tears. 'Yes.'

'You know he loves you. Very much. He just wants you to be safe. And happy.' She tried to be tactful. 'Drugs and stealing and fighting won't make you happy, Lily. They'll give you a buzz that's here and gone in a heartbeat and leave you craving more excitement and more buzz, and it won't ever seem enough. And they won't make you happy in your bones.'

Lily's eyes rolled as if she'd heard this a million times already.

Well, tough. Briana was her godmother and it was her duty to say it too. But she took the hint and turned the conversation back to the boy. 'Good relationships make you happy, you know? When you feel as if you're on the same wavelength as someone and you make each other laugh and you can be totally honest.' Bri's heart twinged, wishing she was able to walk her own talk with Fraser. She felt so connected to him and that scared her more than anything. 'And if Jerome likes you, he'll want to make you happy too. Invite him up.'

Lily thought some more and then her mouth curved into a full, open, excited smile. 'Maybe…'

Bri grinned too, feeling as if she'd finally done something good.

It wasn't exactly a yes. But it was a whole lot better than a no.

CHAPTER ELEVEN

FRASER WAS GLAD when half-term came to an end and he wasn't forced to bear the heavy atmosphere of a sulking daughter all day. He was also unbelievably buzzed to see Briana.

Because of the baby, he tried to convince himself.

But he hadn't realised that working alongside someone who was carrying his child wasn't easy. He tried not to panic as she was jostled by kids rushing along the busy school corridor, or to fuss when she was almost hit by an errant basketball when she crossed the outdoor court. He tried not to stare at her belly, still not able to believe this was all real.

Mostly, he reined in his desire to just spend time with her. Because he'd come to realise that spending time with Briana made him want to spend more time with her—and not in a hands-off fraternal way—and he knew if he blurred that line, they'd all get hurt in the long run.

But here they were, back in the school clinic, and his heart did its customary flip when she smiled at him. He was trying to concentrate on a pastoral care meeting about a troubled truant but all he wanted to do was gaze at the way the winter sun caught strands of copper in her otherwise blonde hair. He'd never noticed that before.

'I'm doing a home visit after our outreach clinic,'

Bri said. 'The mum rang saying Marco has been having stomach pains on and off for a few weeks but is refusing to go to the doctor. I'm just going to go and assess the situation. See if the abdomen pain is real or just an excuse to stay off school.'

'I'll come with you.' Fraser jumped in. 'I can expedite any referrals if necessary.'

Her eyebrows knitted. 'I think I can handle this on my own, thanks, Dr Moore.'

He could see he'd irritated her for some reason, but he didn't care. 'In London, we tried not to go on home visits alone to people we hadn't met before. Safety comes first. Always.'

Amira, the school counsellor, nodded in agreement. 'I think that's wise, Bri. You don't know what you're going to come up against these days.'

Briana visibly bristled. 'I'm quite confident I'll be okay. I've done lots of home visits with no problems.'

'Then you can show me the ropes,' Fraser said. 'Introduce me to some of the local clients.'

Bri frowned at him then closed her notebook and nodded. 'We'll leave here at four-thirty. I'm sorry, I have to run, clinic starts in two minutes.'

Four hours later they were sitting in Bri's car, driving back from the home visit. She hadn't said much since the meeting and he knew it was because he'd insisted he go with her. So he started with an apology. 'Hey, about earlier... I didn't mean you couldn't handle the situation. You were awesome in there.'

'I don't like being undermined in my job and I thought two of us going would be over the top for a stomach ache.' She steered the car carefully along a winding country road and kept her eyes facing forward. 'As it was, I'm glad you came. Marco really opened up to you while you played that video game.'

'My misspent youth finally came in useful. It's a good ploy to get kids talking without staring at them across a desk and making them feel uncomfortable. I'm glad we managed to talk about what's really happening beyond the stomach ache excuse. Poor kid's being bullied and is too scared to tell anyone.'

'Hopefully, he'll attend the meeting with the head of Year Ten and get back on track with his schoolwork. But as he's another of Lewis Parker's bullying victims we really need to address that.' Bri idled the car as they waited for traffic lights to change to green. 'I've already spoken to Mr Wilson about it, but we need to do some more anti-bullying workshops and specifically with young Lewis. Who knows what's going on at home?'

Her shoulders relaxed a little and she smiled tightly. 'How's Lily?'

'I would say, on balance, she's a little brighter.'

Bri breathed out slowly and nodded. 'Good. I thought I may have gone a bit overboard with the lecturing.'

'I can't imagine you lecturing anyone.'

'It's funny, I manage fine with the kids at school but as soon as it's personal I get all tongue-tied and second-guess myself.'

'Welcome to my world.' He laughed, glad that she'd thought Lily was *personal*. 'I don't know what else you said or did, but she's asked if some guy called Jerome can come up and stay at the weekend.'

Bri hit the steering wheel and whooped. 'Please tell me you said yes.'

'On condition she pays for the petrol it took to drive to London and back, doesn't lie to me again, completes her homework on time and does her chores without being asked.'

'You are a hard taskmaster, Fraser Moore.'

'A pushover, more like. But she's been so remorseful about running away, and we made a deal she has to stick to and prove she's trying hard.' He'd been thrilled seeing his daughter's excited face when he'd agreed to the visit. 'God knows what we'll do with him for two days up here in winter—'

'*You* won't do anything except provide a free taxi service and food. Lots of food. And then support Lily when Jerome has gone back to London. She'll either be delighted with how it went or distraught. Either way, you have to be there for her. Not to give advice, just to listen.'

'I'm trying.' It was all very trying, but he had to make it work.

'The truth is, your daughter is lonely and hurting.'

'I know. And it's my fault for bringing her here.' His gut tightened. 'I'm so grateful you're helping me.'

She threw him a scornful frown. 'Fraser, I didn't do this for you, I did it for me and for Lily. I want to spend time with her. I want to get to know her and have a…I don't know, a friendship with her.'

'Hopefully one of us will.'

'You're her father, not her friend. In the end, you have to be the parent and sometimes that's hard.' She smiled at him before looking back at the road ahead. 'You've gone through some very emotional things together. She loves you, Fraser.'

'And I love her so much I don't know what to do with it all. So it comes across as overbearing.'

'I hope…' Briana put a hand on her tummy. 'Oh, nothing.'

'What?'

They pulled up outside her cottage. Bri switched off the engine, inhaled deeply and said on a sigh, 'Forget I said anything, I need to shut up before I start to sound needy or something.'

'You're not. How are you feeling?'

'Rough. Nauseous. Jittery. A bit sore. But it'll pass.'

He'd been too focused on himself and Lily and mooning over Briana's beauty instead of thinking about how she was coping. *Selfish idiot*. 'What do you need, Bri? What can I do to help?'

She waved her hand at him. 'I'll be fine. Honestly. I'm tired and hormonal and starting to believe my own rhetoric.'

His heart hammered. 'Come on, Bri. Please, open up and tell me what's on your mind. We can't do this if we're frightened of what the other person's going to say or how they're going to react. It worked well for Ellen and me because we were totally honest and open. About everything.'

But, he did admit to himself, it had worked because there hadn't been this tsunami of longing hanging over them every time they'd been together. And, he also admitted, he didn't want Briana to be honest and open about any future relationships she may have with other guys, because he couldn't *think* about her with another man.

But Briana nodded. 'Okay. I'm worried that my child—'

'*Our* child.'

She sighed. '*Our* child will be one of those sad little kids who lugs a suitcase across the country to see a parent. Half-term holidays. One weekend in four. It'll be heartbreaking for us both. I haven't had the baby yet, and already I can't bear to think of being separated from it.'

'Then we'll have an arrangement like Ellen and I had. One week with you, one week with me.'

'London and the Lakes? Really? What about schooling?' Briana blinked rapidly, her hand on her chest, over her heart. 'That's not going to work.'

'No. You're right.' If he stayed here he'd break Lily's heart, if he moved back to London things between him and his new baby would be rocky from the start. Never mind things between him and Briana. 'It's difficult, I agree. I've made no firm decisions about moving back to London. We just need to be honest and open and clear about our expectations and intentions.'

She nodded. 'It sounds so transactional. Like a business agreement.'

'It has to be.' It was the only way he was going to survive this. 'Ellen may not have told you, but we drew up a contract just to make everything clear. That way, we both knew what was expected.'

'It's a baby, Fraser. Not some kind of product or a service.'

'Do you have a better solution? Because, trust me, things could get messy further down the track when you meet someone else and you decide to get married or move away.'

She shook her head quickly. 'I won't.'

'How do you know? We can't see into the future. We can't make those sorts of promises. You might meet someone and fall in love and move across the world, not just the country. Or I might. And then what will happen to access and custody? We have to protect ourselves. And our child.' His heart squeezed at the thought of that tiny thing growing inside Briana, and her possessive protection of it, and simultaneously seized at the thought of her having a future that didn't include him. 'We have to have things in writing. I can't promise it's going to be easy, but I do promise I will help in every way I can and that you can always talk to me.'

She nodded. 'You should know I'm not always going to agree with the things you do or say when it comes to raising our child.'

'I have no doubt we'll have a lot to work out and I'll be there every step of the way.' He thought for a moment and realised he was looking forward to sparring with her even if, somehow, he'd have to work out a way of existing and not wanting to touch her or kiss her.

She finally smiled. 'In which case, we need to think of some names. That's the fun part, right? Hell knows, I could do with some fun right now. Any ideas?'

She casually put her hand over his and he felt the rush of heat that happened every time he touched her. She blinked up at him through thick, dark lashes and he saw the bloom of pink on her cheeks. The last time he'd seen that she'd been coming down from an orgasmic high he'd given her. And, *man*, he really needed to kiss her. That would at least expunge this ache that never seemed to dim no matter what he said or did. And, at the same time, cause a whole lot more problems. But they were already so deep in complications he didn't think a few more would make much of a difference.

No.

He wouldn't initiate anything. But the longer they sat looking at each other the more the tension ratcheted up. Kiss or not kiss? Speak or not speak? Truth or denial?

Just to break the silence he said, 'Josie for a girl. After my mum. Vincent for a boy. Or Pep. I like Pep.'

'Pep? Vincent?' She looked confused. 'Unusual names.'

'Not if you're a football fan.'

Her eyes widened in horror. 'I am not naming my son after a football player.'

'You would if you knew how brilliant they are. Imagine the kudos of being named after the captain of the best football team in the entire world.'

'Vincent is kind of growing on me.' She smiled, but she didn't move her hand. 'How about Adele for a girl?'

'After the singer?' He shook his head. 'In that case, what about Lady Gaga? Or Madonna?'

'Maybe we could go for something a little less... unique?' She laughed, then she looked at him and her expression softened and she stopped laughing and bit her lip.

His eyes were drawn to her mouth, but he forced his gaze back to her eyes. There was so much emotion in there...he could see the simmering attraction, the confusion, and the struggle. Mostly, he could see the heat he knew was mirrored in his face.

If they had been two normal people about to get things on, it would have been the perfect time to lean in and kiss her, but because their situation was far from normal he swallowed and exhaled.

But it didn't have the required effect of switching off his libido. Or his feelings. Because thinking up baby names conjured up happy families and they weren't going to do that.

Even though he wanted to.

Yes. He wanted to. He wanted her. Despite all the problems that would entail. Despite the fact she didn't want to. Despite that committing to something scared the heck out of him. He wanted Briana in his life in a more committed way than co-parenting.

Which made him more of an idiot than he'd realised.

He was going crazy.

'Are we having fun yet?' His voice was all gravel and growl.

Her eyes misted. 'Getting closer.'

I wish. That thought rattled him. No matter how much he tried to keep away from her, he just couldn't. 'Briana, what do you want from me?'

'I told you. I want you to care for and about our child.'

'But this?' He looked down at their hands. Somehow they'd gone from her palm covering his hand to inter-twined fingers. Her thumb ran gentle circles over his skin. 'What about *this*?'

She quickly slid her hand away and held it against her chest. 'I don't know.'

'Me neither.'

'I should go.' She shook her head, turned to get out of the car again, but he put his hand on her shoulder. 'Don't run away, Bri. It's all still going to be there even if you pretend it isn't. We have to talk about it.'

'Do we?' Her voice was raw with emotion. 'Can't we just hope it all just goes away?'

'You ever get tired of doing that?'

She glanced back at him, her expression telling him to back right off, so there was no reason for him to stroke her arm and coax her back. But he did.

Her expression also told him she was as rattled as he was about the potent connection between them that had him searching her out, aching to see her, wanting to kiss her.

He nodded as she turned back to him. She was stay-ing, at least for now. He took her hand again. 'This is some kind of intense stuff, right?'

'It's ridiculous, to be honest. I can't believe I'm even acting like this.' She breathed out heavily and sat back in her seat. For a moment he thought she was going to change the subject, but she eventually nodded as if she'd come to a decision. 'Thing is, Fraser…I'm so confused. I swore I wouldn't ever fall for someone else and yet here I am, sitting in my car on a freezing winter's night, wanting you like I've never wanted anyone before. I don't need a man in my life. I don't want to feel less than… worthy all over again, not when I've finally clawed some self-respect back.'

He wondered why she'd decided to be so honest with him when she'd been reticent before, and hoped it was because she was starting to trust him. He tilted her chin so he could meet her gaze. 'You are worth so much.'

'I don't want anyone to have a hold over me, but the moment I see you I feel…captured. But not in a bad way, well…not much.' She laughed shyly as her hand fluttered across her face. 'I'm not making sense.'

She didn't want a relationship but she wanted him. His heart thudded a weird rhythm against his chest wall. 'There's a lot of stuff going on here…like this baby, like Ellen and Lily and our past. Your reluctance to trust, me not knowing how to navigate any of this and doing everything badly. But cut through all that and, well…I like you, Bri. I have no idea what the hell is going to happen between us and I'm probably going to regret saying this, because I know you're just going to walk away, but…I want you. That's the easiest part of it.'

'Is it?'

'You want to see?'

'I…' She tilted her head towards him, and he saw the need in her eyes, the tremble in her hands. 'Yes.'

He slipped his fingers into her silk-soft hair, then his mouth covered hers. He felt her initial uncertainty, then heard a guttural mewl of pleasure as she opened her mouth and it almost broke him.

The kiss started out gently, but she pulled him closer, angling her head and slipping her tongue into his mouth on a moan.

As the kiss deepened, he felt the kick in his gut and the tightening of his skin. Desire wound through him along with the sense that he'd both come home and yet was exploring an exotic foreign place. A need to commit every nuance, every taste, every sensation to memory because he didn't know if he'd ever get the chance to return.

Then he didn't think at all, just learned her again, getting lost in her taste and her moans and the caress of her skin against his. He wanted to drown in her. To anchor himself to her. Their gasps became frenzied. She grasped his face, kissing him hard and deep.

But when he tried to pull her over the gearstick she laughed and pulled away. 'Whoa.'

Her whole body was shaking and he ran his hands down her arms to steady her…or steady himself, he wasn't sure which. She bit her bottom lip and rested her forehead against his. 'We probably shouldn't have done that,' she said, breathless and wide-eyed.

'I can't get enough of you, Bri.' It was his truth and he knew it might scare her away, but he couldn't live without saying it, or without her knowing it. What she would do with that knowledge he didn't dare think about.

Her palms were on his chest as if she wanted to push him away but couldn't summon the strength to do it. Her eyes were still slick with desire, but her words were fierce. 'Now, yes. But what about in a year? Or three? I don't want to bring a baby into a minefield that's going to blow up any time. It's going to be difficult enough with shared parenting in two different houses.'

'So move in with us.'

'What? You're definitely staying here, then?' She

looked almost as surprised as he felt after the words had tumbled out. But he couldn't take them back. And, just as suddenly, the image of her all beautiful and pregnant and in his bed loomed into his head. Then a picture of a happy family…but she didn't want that. It was clear from her face. So why he kept on talking, he didn't know. Why they'd kissed, he didn't know…not any more. She'd been right. It just caused a lot more problems.

But, *man*, it had been one stellar kiss.

Was he going to stay here? 'It's a big house. We have space. A room for you, and another one we could turn into a nursery.'

Her expression softened but she kept on shaking her head. 'No. No way. I'm fine in my cottage. I have room for a little one. I'm going to change my study into a nursery.'

He felt himself free-falling from the passionate high to a slump of reality and he should have been glad she didn't want anything material from him, but a heavy weight settled in his chest. 'You seem to have it all planned out.'

'Not totally, but I've been looking online at babies' bedrooms and I'm getting some ideas.'

'Well, the offer is there. If you need help moving furniture or decorating, let me know. I'm a dab hand with a paintbrush.'

Bri rubbed the back of her neck and grimaced. 'I wish Ellen was here. She'd nudge me and tell me to pull my head in and take you up on the offer.'

'I wasn't suggesting you move in…with me. Like a relationship. Just that it would be more convenient.' Sheesh, he was making things worse, pedalling backwards from his off-the-cuff comment.

'Don't panic.' She patted his arm. 'But—and I mean this totally sincerely—I don't think Lily would cope with me being around twenty-four seven. I think she sees me as interfering. I'm expecting her to say something along the lines of, "You're not my mum, you can't tell me what to do."'

'She misses her mum. More than she lets on.'

Bri smiled sadly. 'I miss her too.'

'So do I.'

He knew Ellen would have encouraged him to have a relationship with Briana. *'Life's too short,'* she'd said in her more lucid moments. *'Promise me you'll find some-one and make a life. A proper life with a proper partner and lots of babies. Lily shouldn't be an only child like you were. She needs to learn how to share.'*

And, contrary to all he'd agreed, Lily hadn't shared him with anyone ever since. But now…? He had no choice but to share his life with this new baby, if not with Briana. 'I've been showing her old photographs again and we've been talking a lot about what Ellen was like before she got sick.'

'What does she remember?'

'Snapshots really—her sense of humour, her restless energy before the headaches started. We thought it was migraines, you remember? Then she was diagnosed with depression. She changed so much in a year. Lily tried to understand, she really did. But when you're a child, how can you be expected to understand or make allowances for the strange behaviour of the people who are supposed to protect you?

'Ellen became…unpredictable. Up one day, dancing and singing, and down the next, refusing to get out of bed. That's not good for a kid, they thrive on routine and predictability. As a result, Lily doesn't trust people eas-ily, expecting them to change their minds or be different tomorrow. So I'm glad she listened to you about inviting Jerome up. You're good for her.'

Her eyes brightened. 'I hope so. I wish I'd known how bad it was getting for you.'

'I wish I'd told you.' He wished they could get through an afternoon together without wanting to rip each other's clothes off. He wished they didn't use Lily as an excuse. He wished they weren't both so stupidly scared of taking a risk and seeing where this attraction might take them.

He opened the car door and climbed out into the cold night. 'So many wishes, Bri, and none of them are going to change a single thing.'

CHAPTER TWELVE

GIVEN IT WAS only the end of February, the sun was remarkably warm on Bri's face as she waltzed out of the designer clothes shop on Saturday morning with her new outfit in a smart brown paper bag.

Across the street, early snowdrops dotted the gardens with little pops of white and the sky was a cloudless dazzling blue. It was beautiful and fresh with a definite feeling that spring was just around the corner.

But Briana wasn't thinking about the colours or the flowers. She was thinking about that kiss in the car and the fact they hadn't discussed what that meant for them in the future.

Fraser seemed to be willing to talk about these things, but she still found it hard to be that open. Suggesting to Lily that a relationship was good when you were able to be truly honest with someone had made Bri think—could she ever be that honest? Had she ever felt comfortable enough with a man to truly voice her own needs and wants?

She'd managed it with Fraser when they'd been in bed. She'd told him she'd wanted his kiss. She'd said a few things the other day that made her cringe with embarrassment... *I feel captured. Not in a bad way...*

But it had felt good to put voice to the way she was

feeling and not have to pretend otherwise, even if she'd been surprised he hadn't run away right then.

But Bri didn't want to put a name to the emotions in her heart when she looked at him, when he kissed her or made her laugh. So how could she be truly honest with Fraser when she didn't want to be honest with herself?

She sighed and realised she'd stopped outside a nursery supplies shop. A beautiful carved wooden cot and soft patterned fabrics filled the window. A little row of pastel rainbow bunting hung above them and it was so lovely and whimsical it made her sigh.

She ran her hand over her belly and said silently, *That's what I'll do for you. Bunting and rainbows. In our house. Just you and me.*

And there was another thing: when Fraser had suggested she move into his house her mouth had said no but excitement had fizzed through her body at the thought of them all living together.

But the idea, while wildly tempting, was also ridiculous. She wouldn't be able to emotionlessly co-habit and co-parent like Ellen had done, when all she could think about was how good he made her feel. It would be torture to be around him the whole time. But she was going to have to get used to it. Somehow.

A sudden tap on her shoulder made her freeze. Her breath caught, her thoughts stopped. Panic crept through her veins. Tony? Was he here? Had he found her?

She slowly turned round and breathed out. She was so glad to see Fraser. So unbelievably relieved. 'Oh, Fraser. It's you. Hello.'

He frowned but pressed a kiss on her cheek as if it were the most natural thing in the world. 'You okay? You look very pale.'

'Sorry. Yes, I'm fine. I was miles away. You made me jump.'

He looked at her with concern. 'Do you need to sit down?'

'No. No. I'm fine Honestly.' She blinked and turned away from his piercing gaze. He knew she was not exactly being straight with him but at least he didn't ask why. 'What are you doing here?'

Stupid question, really. While Oakdale had a little corner shop, a newsagent and a post office, Bowness was their closest shopping centre.

'Stocking up on man food for Jerome.' He held up a bulging hessian shopping bag. 'That boy can pack away a decent amount. I've just dropped them off at the outdoors centre for a bush craft day. Starting with canoeing down the lake, then building their own shelter and cooking lunch on an open fire, then playing with knives or something this afternoon.' He winced. 'They tell me it's quite safe and even fun.'

'Good weather for it.' She laughed. 'What's Jerome like?'

'He's actually okay. Polite and well mannered. Very interested in Lily—not just in a guy way. He talks about how clever she is and her amazing grades at school last year. What a great actress in the school play, how funny. He's smitten. So is she.' He tapped his chest and pulled a sad face. 'And my heart is broken.'

Bria laughed. 'The joys of parenting, right? You'd better get over it or get used to it. You're going to have to be there for her tomorrow after they've said goodbye. She'll be in bits.'

'I know. I bought extra tissues and will make her favourite dinner.' He held up his shopping bag again. 'What are you doing here?'

'Looking for something to wear at Joe and Rose's wedding. I'm so honoured they invited me when I hardly know them.'

'It's Oakdale. You're part of the family.'

'I'm just not sure what kind of a wedding it'll be.'

His eyes narrowed and he scratched his chin. 'Hmm. One with vows...I think. They might mention something about till death us do part. And I'm sure there'll be speeches and possibly dancing.'

'Ha-ha.' She laughed. 'I mean, are we getting dressed up? Or will it be more casual? I'm not sure I've bought the right thing. They're your friends...can you tell me what you think?' She pulled the dress from the bag and showed him the fabric, a beautiful blue silk that reminded her of the lake on a calm, bright summer's day.

He shook his head. 'I don't know. I'd get a better idea if I saw it on.'

'Oh, well.' She stuffed it back into its bag. 'Then you'll have to wait until the wedding day.'

'Or you could try it on and show me.' He smiled, eyes glittering and teasing.

Was he flirting? The thought of parading around in her new dress, waiting for his opinion, made her heart thump. But she was probably reading far too much into it.

God. She was baffled by the push and pull of all this. Didn't know where she stood or what they were doing.

But he looked quite genuine. 'Come on, Bri. I've spent fifteen years giving my opinion on girls' outfits. I know not to say it makes your bum looks big and to take my cues from your excited or depressed expression. Although don't expect me to be too enthusiastic unless it's got a skirt down to the floor and a neckline around your throat. At least, that's what Lily would say.'

She relaxed a little. 'Well, you're going to be disappointed, then.'

'I doubt that very much.' Another rakish smile.

That was definitely flirting. His gaze caught hers and she didn't know where to look or what to say. Luckily, he filled the silence. 'What else have you got planned for the day?'

'Not a lot.'

'Me neither. I've got an empty nest, come play hooky with me. You can show me the dress. I'll fix us some lunch, I have more than enough food here.'

This was dangerous territory given their kiss the other day.

But here she was, asking for an opinion and being offered not only that but free food too. If she was going to have to get used to being around him on a personal as well as professional level, once the baby arrived, she may as well start now. Maybe, by the time the little one made an appearance, she'd be completely unaffected by him, just like Ellen had been.

She nodded. 'Okay. Just for an opinion on the dress.' She'd thrown up her breakfast and was now feeling quite hungry. 'And lunch.'

'Great, come up in about thirty minutes.' He grinned. 'We'll have to take Jasper out for a walk too, though.'

'Okay...' It was starting to sound wonderfully perfect. 'A walk and an opinion. And lunch.'

That was all. Nothing more. Nothing to see here.

Nothing to get excited about.

As if.

Fraser opened the door to a smiling, slightly breathless Briana. She was still wearing the bobble hat and jacket she'd had on earlier, but there was gloss on her lips that seemed to accentuate their plumpness and made him think about kissing her. He wondered how quickly they could get the pleasantries over and get her into his bed, given that was all he'd been thinking about since he'd seen her in town. Since before then, to be honest.

Given, too, that their kiss the other day hadn't led to a conversation about a relationship but had left the door wide open for exploration.

Jasper was weaving between his legs while simultaneously giving Briana soft pooch eyes and she laughed. 'Someone's keen for walkies. You want to go now? Have lunch later?'

Someone else was keen to stay in. But he knew he wouldn't get any peace unless Jasper was exercised. 'All right, Jasper. You win.' *This time.*

Briana started ahead of him down the path and waited at the gate. 'Since you're the new kid on the block, I'll show you one of my favourite walks.'

'Be my guest.' He shrugged on his thick coat, clipped Jasper's lead on and followed her cute backside through the village and up the steep incline behind Joe and Rose's house.

But, rather than the serene privacy Fraser had hoped for, the far side of the hill was filled with screeching people tobogganing, snowball fighting and building snowmen.

'It looks like the whole village is here.' He waved at Joe and Rose, who were clambering on a large wooden sledge, with Katy sandwiched between them.

'I'd forgotten this was the best sledging hill in the area.' Bri's cheeks were a delightful shade of blush. 'Tongues are going to wag about us walking here together.'

He laughed. 'Wait until they hear about the baby.'

She cradled her belly over her thick jacket. 'Do you think anyone's noticed?'

'You're not showing yet.'

'I kind of wish I were. I can't wait to get a bump.'

'You'll have some explaining to do. Correction…*we* will have some explaining to do.' He'd navigated it once, he could do it again. People would talk initially, then they'd get on with their lives. There were lots of unconventional families these days. The main thing was that the children were happy.

He thought about Lily and Jerome and hoped his daughter was having a good day.

'I don't care what people think.' Briana cradled her non-existent bump. 'I'm proud I'm going to be a mum.'

You are beautiful. The thought shimmered inside him, but he knew if he said it he'd frighten her off. 'You're going to be a fantastic mum, Briana.'

'Thank you.' She smiled, and he could see she was struggling to keep it from stretching into a grin. 'I hope so.'

He expected her to make some sort of quip about him not being father of the year or her expectations for how he'd be with their baby, but she didn't say anything. She just looked up at him, her eyes soft and misted, her hands on her belly.

His gaze connected with hers and the memories of their kiss, of her naked, of her stunning body tumbled into his head. And, *God*, he wanted to pull her into his arms right there, but there were so many people around it would engender questions from the whole village—and this was where things were so different from his situation with Ellen. He didn't know the answers to those questions so he swallowed the need, turned and trudged on through the snow.

Beyond the gentle slope was a cluster of trees and a group of teens having a snowball fight. As they neared it became obvious it had turned from a snowball fight to a fist one. The largest boy was bending over a kid on the ground and looking as if he was about to hit him.

Bri squinted and her eyes widened in horror, her hand gripping Fraser's sleeve. 'That's Lewis Parker. The boy who's been bullying Marco and a couple of others at school.'

'Right. This needs to stop.' Fraser marched towards the big kid, who was now rubbing snow into the other kid's face. 'Hey! Stop that, Lewis. Stop it.'

Bri was behind him and hissed, 'No, Fraser. Lewis is the boy on the ground.'

Being bullied himself. *Right. Interesting.* Fraser stopped and took in the scene. Lewis was curled in a ball with blood dripping from his nose. The burly guy was pumped and primed to lash out again.

'We've got to help him.' Bri ran forward but Fraser put his arm out to stop her. 'Do not get involved. Let me handle this.'

Her eyes blazed with indignation, her nostrils flaring. 'Fraser, I can—'

'No.' His body pulsed with adrenalin as he thrust Jasper's lead into her hand. 'Stay here.'

'Fraser!'

'No!' He didn't stop to look at her reaction, but he knew, just by her tone, she'd be foaming with anger. She probably thought he didn't think she could deal with this. He didn't care. He would not allow her to put herself or their child at risk.

He waded into the path of the bigger boy's fist and caught it as it propelled forward. 'I said stop.'

Jasper snarled and barked, tugging on his lead.

The older boy's lip curled. 'You can't tell me what to do.'

'Don't push me.' Fraser glared at him and lowered the kid's fist. 'Whatever is going on here won't be solved by a fight.'

The big kid looked at him as if to say, *No, but it would feel good.*

'I know the local police pretty well. If Lewis wants to press charges, he has two witnesses here, plus your rabble over there.' Fraser pointed to the two other kids who were standing a distance away. 'What's going on?'

The older boy looked at Lewis on the ground. 'He's annoying.'

'So? Walk away? That's what the better man does, right? You're older and bigger. Turn your back. Walk away.' Fraser opened his palms to the older teen. 'But, no, you hit him instead. Not good enough. Help him up.'

Burly boy snarled. 'What?'

'I said help him up.'

There was another staring standoff for one…two seconds and then the big kid put out his hand to help Lewis up. When he was upright Fraser addressed them both. 'Right. Explain.'

Silence.

So much testosterone and very little else.

Fraser turned to Lewis. 'If you want this sorted out you have to tell me.'

Lewis shook his head.

'I'm not going anywhere until one of you talks. You're both wet and it's freezing and pretty soon you'll have hypothermia, which is not fun.' Fraser patted his coat. 'I've got a warm jacket and all afternoon. As long as it takes.'

He caught Briana's eye. She was watching, bent over and calming Jasper. And, probably, taking emotional steps away from him because of the way he'd spoken to her. His stomach tightened. This was not how he'd anticipated their day turning out.

Lewis looked at the snow-covered ground. 'He wanted my money.'

Fraser looked at burly boy. 'Does he owe you money?'

A muffled *'No.'*

'Are you borrowing it or stealing it?'

Silence.

'Right.' Fraser nodded. 'I think I understand what's going on here. Did you take his money?'

'No.' Burly boy looked at his feet.

'Only because you didn't have time. You can apologise for hitting him.'

'What?' Burly boy's eyes grew huge.

'Apologise. Now.'

After a pause where no one spoke, Burly muttered something that sounded a bit like *Sorry.*

'It's not fun when someone older and bigger tells you what to do, right? Even worse when they're talking with their fists, which is the coward's way out.' Fraser turned to the other boys standing with their hands shoved deep into their pockets. 'You two are just as bad for not intervening. Is this fun to you?'

'No.' They both looked at the ground too.

'Lewis, are you okay?' Fraser assessed the kid's nose. 'It's not broken but it's going to be sore. How are you feeling?'

'I just want to go home.'

'That's fine.' He pointed at the big kid. 'If I ever see you treating another human being like that again there will be severe consequences, do you understand?'

Burly boy's eyes didn't leave his feet. 'Yes.'

'Oh, and I work at the school, so expect a meeting on

Monday.' He watched them slink away then turned back to Lewis. 'You sure you're okay?'

The boy rubbed his bloody nose and nodded. 'Yes.'

'Who was that?'

'Christian Holmes,' Briana said. 'Year twelve.'

He turned at the sound of her voice. Fraser was inordinately relieved she hadn't waded into this. She could have been injured. The baby could have been… He didn't want to even think about that. He cared for her, he realised. So much. Too much. Enough that he was going to get hurt along the way.

And, he thought blithely, it would be worth it. Because she was worth it.

So that made him a prize idiot.

He focused back on Lewis, 'How long has this been going on?'

A shrug.

Long enough that Lewis had been affected and was taking out his frustration and anger on younger kids. A spiral of hurt.

'I don't know what it's like to be a bully or bullied but I do know what it's like to feel helpless, Lewis,' Fraser said. 'I also know how to deal with bullies. In fact, we're running an anti-bullying workshop on Monday for the senior year groups. Hopefully it'll teach you some strategies for dealing with aggressive behaviour. In the meantime, keep away from him.'

'He's just going to stalk my phone and my social media and get all of his friends to do the same.'

There were so many ways to hurt someone these days. It wasn't just playground talk, fists behind the bike sheds. There was cyber-bullying too, which must seem endless when you couldn't get away from it. Then there was what

Briana had gone through. Living a long way from home, isolated, threatened and scared.

'Block him, block them all, Lewis. Do not give him the satisfaction of showing him that you're rattled. If you do, you give him all the power. Take it back for yourself.' He met the kid's gaze and saw a wealth of fear and anger and panic, but some relief too. 'It sucks, eh?'

'Yes.'

'So, I wonder if you can help me with the anti-bullying workshops?' At the boy's terrified expression Fraser clarified, 'I just need someone to help me put out the resources, the audio-visual stuff, that kind of thing. Nothing major.'

A shrug. 'I guess.'

'Brilliant. I'll send a note to your teacher to let them know you're helping me out.' Then he chose his words carefully. 'I know you want to make sure this doesn't happen to anyone else, Lewis.'

'No.' His cheeks turned the same colour as the blood on his face. And then Lewis half ran, half walked back up the hill. Fraser only hoped the boy had understood his message and by Monday would have given some serious thought to his own bullying ways.

They were left standing in the lee of the woods, an icy wind whipping round their ears. Fraser wasn't sure how to navigate this now. They'd been getting on so well and then this violent interlude had not only blown that up but had clearly affected Briana.

She was hunched over with her arms wrapped around her body as if protecting herself. His heart contracted at the sight of her. He ran his palms down her arms, unsure at what point it had become his mission to convince her that he was one of the good guys. But he wanted her to know that. To believe him. 'Hey, are you okay?'

She nodded. 'I was worried. I…I thought you were going to get hit.'

'I had it under control.' Fraser smiled at this revelation of concern, his heart still pumping with adrenalin. 'I shouldn't have snapped at you, but I was worried about the danger to you and the baby.'

'No, you shouldn't have.' Her eyes narrowed. 'I do not like being spoken to like that.'

'I know. I'm sorry.'

Her shoulders hitched. 'But at least you stopped the fighting.'

'I've a feeling Lily would have been mortified to see me getting involved.'

'Maybe she hasn't experienced bullying first-hand.' Bri swallowed, her face pale, and started to shiver. 'I really, really hope not.'

'The real work starts with the workshops, right? Giving people the tools to deal with someone like that.' He couldn't imagine how Bri must have felt at the hands of that douchebag ex-boyfriend. A physical and emotional threat that had scarred her.

Something feral uncurled inside him and, without second-guessing himself, he slid an arm around her waist and stepped closer to her. Wanting to protect her from any hurt or harm. Ever. 'I know we're not supposed to be saying this kind of thing, Briana, but I wouldn't have been responsible for my actions if that kid had hurt you.'

'Fraser…' She closed her eyes and leaned her head against his chest, as if she was struggling with something invisible. Then she sighed, and it sounded like frustration more than anything else. 'To be honest, I don't know what we're supposed to be saying or doing at all.'

He got it. There was something important going on between them and it scared the hell out of him. Worse, it felt that whatever it was—especially for her—was so fragile and fledgling that if he pushed her to talk, it would shatter.

He stroked her back, but she pulled away quickly, her hair whipping in the wind as she stood and stared at the spot where the boys had fought. He watched as she retreated into herself, pushing him away physically and emotionally, and wondered what she was thinking. Where she'd gone.

Australia.

He dropped his hand and started to hike back up the hill, putting some fun back into his voice. 'Come on, then. Let's go get some food, you must be starving.'

'I'm not really sure I could eat a thing,' she whispered, but he heard it.

The walk back to his house was quiet, punctuated only by the squeak of their boots on the fresh snow and the panting breath of his Old English sheepdog.

Fraser quickly fixed lunch while Bri sat with a cup of tea, then he served up, all the while the tight ball of tension in his chest seeming to get bigger and tighter. Everything had been going so well and now he felt as if they'd retreated into their own private worlds.

And he ached, more than anything, to be allowed into hers.

CHAPTER THIRTEEN

THEY ATE OUTSIDE in his cosy sheltered garden, a weak wintry sun and a gas heater overhead, with blankets on their laps. The food was good. The view, of Fraser, was amazing. Beyond him were snow-capped mountains, a breathtaking wide blue sky. Space.

It would have been wonderful were it not for this chasm of emotion and confusion between them. She'd been spooked by the fight and the aggression in those boys but, more, she'd been spooked by the way Fraser had looked at her when he'd shouted—as if she was worth saving, as if protecting her was his calling. And she didn't know how to handle that.

She didn't want to be protected, didn't need it. Didn't want any man to think he owned her. But Fraser wasn't like that. He'd been scared for her and the baby, that was all. She really, really needed to stop comparing him with Tony, because Fraser was kind, gentle, honest. A good man with a good heart. And great kisses.

And, wow, he'd looked fearless as he'd strode into the line of that boy's fist and caught it.

Eventually, she put her knife and fork down and smiled, wanting things to get back to how they'd been before they'd stumbled across the fight. 'It still feels super-weird having you here in Oakdale. Funny how things work out, eh? If you hadn't had Lily, what do you think you'd be doing?'

'Oh, I don't know. I can't imagine not having Lily. Travelling more, probably. Dating maybe.' He grinned as she rolled her eyes and laughed. 'What about you?' he asked. 'What were your plans before this little one rudely interrupted them?' His eyes dipped to her belly, hidden under a tartan blanket, and he smiled.

Which made her heart thrill. 'Oh, I was just pootling along.'

'You must have had some kind of plan? Coming back here? What next?'

'Once I came home, I had to heal, take stock of who I was, what the hell I'd been thinking, allowing myself to get into that situation with my ex.' She felt herself closing up at just the thought of him but she pushed herself to talk because that was what friends did: they talked about everything and nothing. 'I was just settling into a routine of work at the school, about to raise my head above the parapet and take a look around. Then…the rest is history. Now I'm going to retreat behind the parapet again and nurture our baby.'

His eyes slid up to meet hers. 'What had you been thinking? With Tony?'

This wasn't something she generally spoke about, choosing instead to keep it all locked away, hoping she could forget. But seeing that violence today had shaken something loose inside her. She needed to talk about it, finally, to exorcise it from her thoughts, from her bone and muscle memory—to rid her body of the darkness and fear. She did not want their baby to grow with all that spinning inside her. And maybe if she explained, Fraser would understand? Maybe she would too.

Goose-bumps prickled on her skin and it wasn't because of the cold weather. 'At first, I thought I was madly in love. He seemed like a really nice guy. He whisked me off my feet, treated me like a goddess and I enjoyed it. Revelled in his attention, in fact. It was a breath of fresh air after Ellen's death and all the grief and guilt. He suggested we go to his home town in Australia because his UK visa was coming to an end. I thought, *Why not? What did I have to lose?*' It had turned out she'd lost her self-respect, her passion for her job, for living.

'It was lovely at first. Hot. Sunny all the time. He bought me presents, took me sightseeing, refused to let me look for a job because I was supposed to be on an adventure, and he wanted to look after me. I was flattered, to be honest. All that attention…it wasn't something I'd ever been used to. I liked being in his spotlight. This handsome guy who adored me.'

She watched as Fraser's eyebrows rose and thought how ridiculous this must sound. How desperate. But Tony had helped her forget her unbearable guilt for a while. 'I got bored with him going out to work every day and leaving me on my own, so I got a part-time job at the local clinic. He wasn't happy about that. He liked the idea of having me to himself whatever time of day or night he chose.'

'Sounds like a real charmer.' Fraser shook his head.

'That was half the problem, though…he was very charming. At first.' She exhaled as a weight slid into her belly, the dread of those days edging back in. 'He took control of my bank account…which was my fault, I know now, but somehow he convinced me that it was a good idea to have him as a signatory. Then he controlled my spending. Monitored my emails and messages. He became super-picky about where I was, what I wore, who I was with. I didn't meet anyone apart from people at work and he wouldn't even let me socialise with them.

'We started to argue. Things started to spiral. Then… you know what happened.' She rubbed her wrist where Tony had twisted her arm until it had almost snapped. Even though the physical pain was gone, the emotional one lingered, making her keep her distance from everyone.

She looked across the table at this gorgeous man and wanted desperately to drop her guard once and for all. 'The worst thing is I let him do it. I should have walked away sooner or told someone else, but I was so ashamed. I couldn't admit to having let someone do that to me. To control me to that extent. I mean, was I so desperate to be loved that I gave him everything? All of me, my power, my agency and my life…literally?' And she was still giving him time and space in her thoughts. It had to stop. She had to move on before it ruined more of her life.

'How did you get out?' Fraser's hand slid over hers and their fingers intertwined. He was an anchor, a lifeline pulling her from her past and tethering her to the present.

'It ended up being so simple I couldn't believe I hadn't done it earlier. Tony liked to drink. One night I just kept plying him with whisky. He kept drinking. I pretended I was drinking too, but threw mine down the sink any time I had a chance. I was playful and put on an act, coaxing him into bed.' She shuddered at the way she'd used her body. The way he had. 'He fell into a deep sleep and I took my chance, grabbed a few bits of clothes, found my passport hidden in his work bag. And I got the hell out. I prayed that by the time he woke up and found me gone I'd be in Sydney already, or even on my way to England.'

'Did that plan work?'

'Yes. Although I couldn't relax until I was on the plane

out of Sydney. I walked the length of that aircraft economy section and checked he wasn't in one of the seats, spying on me. I was alone. Terrified and deliriously proud that I'd escaped, but the fear didn't leave me…not for a long time.'

'You're not concerned he'll come and find you?' His gentle, soft circles of reassurance spiralled through her skin.

'His visa ran out. He doesn't know my address here, only that I'm from the north of England somewhere. The chances of him coming back are very slim. The chances of him finding me are even slimmer. I'm good with that.'

'I'm not. I have a friend in the police force. I'll have a word with him.' Fraser's eyes were dark, his voice cracked and raw. 'If I get a whisper of that man entering the country, I'll be on him in a shot.'

She smiled at the determination in his face. The fact he wanted to fight for her made her chest flood with heat. 'I have no worries about him tracking me or stalking me here. Honestly. I've just got to stop looking over my shoulder.'

He gave her a small smile. 'You were a bit jumpy in town when I tapped your back.'

And she'd been unbelievably relieved when she'd seen Fraser standing there. 'I've a way to go, but I'm getting there.'

'But he still haunts you.'

'If I let him scare me then he's won. I'm so much better, I really am, but sometimes I get caught off guard.' She realised her leg was jittery. She needed to move, to get rid of this negative energy. She slid her hand out from under his, stood up and picked up the plates. 'I'm going to clear up.'

He followed her inside. The atmosphere between them

was back to being loaded again, but this time it was different. She felt as if she'd expunged her soul, let him see the very depths of her. She felt naked, exposed. She could feel his gaze on her and she was afraid of what she might see in his eyes when she turned round—thick rage at Tony that she couldn't handle, affection she didn't know what to do with, or pity. So she kept her back to him.

She knew he was closer when the little hairs on the back of her neck prickled.

She felt his hand on her waist, then he turned her round to face him. His fingertips grazed her cheek as his intense gaze pinned her in place. 'Thank you for letting me in. Now I understand why you're so adamant about being independent. Why you're so passionate about stopping bullies. And why you try to keep everyone just a little at arm's length.' He smiled gently. Softly.

Her heart squeezed. 'I don't know how to do this, Fraser. I know you're a good man. I know you won't do what Tony did. But I'm scared I've built up walls too high to come down.'

'It's okay.' His fingers stroked her back. 'It's okay, Bri.'

Every cell in her body yearned towards him. The arm's-length thing was definitely challenged when it came to Fraser. She put her hands on his chest, felt the steady thump of his heartbeat under her fingers. 'It's not okay. I need to forget it. Put it into the past. Be a different Briana. A better one.'

He frowned. 'Don't change. Please. Don't make yourself into anything other than who you are.'

'But that old Briana let him—'

'No.' He shook his head, stopping her words. 'You trusted him, because you're a good person who wouldn't imagine someone could behave like that. You travelled with him on an adventure because you see the positive in things, and the beauty in places and people and experiences. You had the strength to leave him, even though it was dangerous.

'And the truth is you wanted his attention because we all want that, Briana. We all want to be loved, be liked, to be cherished. There's nothing wrong in that. You deserve to expect that. To be treated properly, kindly and with respect. You deserve so much more. You deserve to be loved and honoured. You deserve the whole damned world, Briana Barclay.'

She closed her eyes, wishing he could be the guy to give it all to her. Wanting that more than anything. Knowing he could be if they both dropped their guard enough to let in the light that shimmered between them.

And knowing that if they couldn't she'd take this moment and hold it tight in her heart. Right now he believed in her. He wanted her. He knew her truth and saw someone strong, not weak. Someone who could trust and care deeply, not someone afraid of emotion and connection. She allowed herself to feel the heat his belief in her generated. To feel her power come back to her, to grasp the adventure again.

When his lips pressed against hers she let him in.

This kiss was different from any he'd ever had before.

He kissed her as if this was the first time, and the last. He kissed her to show her the strength of his belief in her and his promise.

She wove her arms around him and pressed herself against him. He felt her limbs soften, her curves fit perfectly into the hollows of his body. Felt the press of her breasts, the hitch of her breath. Heard the sigh in her throat. And, God, he wanted her so much he didn't know what to do with all the need, all the emotion clogging his chest.

As the kiss deepened he plundered her mouth and she put her hands either side of his face, anchoring him. Steadying.

He didn't want to be steady. He wanted to be rocked, to rock inside her.

He pulled away, breathing hard and fast, took her tight fists in his. 'Briana, I want you so badly I can't even find words to describe it.'

Her eyes were misty as she looked up at him. 'I need you. I need you inside me.'

He revelled in her words. That she could say them to him made him feel unleashed.

'You want to go upstairs?' He kissed a trail along her collar bone.

She smiled, all sex and teasing and hot. 'Yes, please.'

He picked her up and she giggled and screamed at him to put her down. But he carried her up to his room and placed her gently on his bed then stretched out along-side to face her.

'We have all afternoon,' he said as he ran lazy strokes over her arm. But it would never be enough time, he knew, and there would always be interruptions, a reason to stop when he didn't want to ever stop. He ran his palm over her shoulder, but she pulled him down for another kiss. This one was hungry and hot.

He slowly removed her clothes, teasing and tantalis-ing. And she removed his almost reverently. A slow un-dressing of their inhibitions and fears.

And, *God*, she was so beautiful it made his heart hurt. Soft silk skin, pale from winter's coverings. Swol-len breasts and darkened nipples that puckered when he sucked one into his mouth. She writhed against him, her hips so close to his erection he could have slid straight into her.

But he waited. It almost killed him, but he waited. Taking his time to stroke her, to kiss her throat, her breasts and lower.

His heart lurched at the sight of the slight swell of her belly. It was barely a bump, but it was there. A life. He placed his hands there, kissed the softness. *Our* child. His heart swelled at the thought, a tangle of panic and affection for this child. For this woman. 'My darling Briana. You are so beautiful.'

When he looked up he saw tears in her eyes, spilling onto her cheeks, and his gut tightened. 'Are you okay?'

She nodded, pulling him back to face her. 'I am more than okay. I've wanted this for so long.'

He pulled back and smiled. 'What do you mean? Weeks? Days?'

'Oh, come on. You must know I had a crush on you from that first night we ever met?'

'I had no idea.' Geez, things could have been so different. 'Really? On me?'

'Well, it wore off for a while.' She gave him a rueful smile. 'But…I think I'm crushing on you again, Fraser Moore.'

He laughed at her words and the wonder of how life had brought them to this amazing moment. 'Back at you, Briana Barclay.'

Then he kissed her and kissed her and kissed her. Kissed her cheeks, kissed the salty tears away, kissed her nose and her eyelids. Her mouth, her neck. He took his time.

He worked his way down her body, worshipping her with his mouth, his fingers, his tongue. Felt the slick wetness as he parted her legs and slipped his hand between her thighs. As he stroked her there she arched her back, and he watched the curve of her mouth, the slow smile on her lips that turned to the agony of desperation and the pure frenzy of release. Heard the half sob, half cry of his name and felt it deep in his soul, settling there like a promise. Watched it all as if this was a dream. A beautiful dream of touch and taste, of slickness and kissing. Of worship and prayer and vow.

He sure as hell didn't want to wake up.

Then she laughed. A beautiful sound fluttering in the still, pheromone-heavy air. 'Fraser, that was amazing.'

'*You* are amazing.' He kissed his way back to her mouth. 'You make me feel amazing.'

'Win-win.' She laughed. Mouths still together, she climbed on top of him, took hold of his erection and positioned him at her entrance. He could have thrust into her then, but he held back. This was Briana's call. He would follow. Follow her wherever she wanted to go. To the end of for ever.

She moaned his name as she sank over him, tight and hot, her fingernails tearing his skin where she gripped his shoulders. The pain was a thing of beauty, a scar of their lovemaking. A brand.

He was hers. That thought tore through the last shred of reserve he had and wound itself round his heart. He would stay right here for ever if he could. How could he leave her? Their baby?

He would stay.

For a moment she stilled, her gaze tangling with his and God knew what she saw there but she gasped and smiled as tears ran down her face, her palm on his cheek. She sank onto him again and again, taking him deeper until he couldn't hold back any longer.

He thrust hard and fast, gripping her hips, holding her

in place. But it wasn't enough. He flipped her onto her back, covering her with his body, sliding into her over and over. Then it wasn't a dream any more, it was real. So damned real it was like a fire burning in his soul, in his bones, on his skin.

His truth was in every look, every touch, every kiss. In the last deep thrust, and in the way he cried out her name.

He wanted more than all day, he wanted tomorrow, next week, next year. He wanted a lifetime. That thought had slid into his brain the moment he'd kissed her belly.

And glued itself to his heart.

CHAPTER FOURTEEN

BRIANA DIDN'T KNOW how long they lay there tangled in the sheets, unwilling to let go of each other, as if this was an end, not a beginning. As if the perfect, glittering spell would be shattered if either of them moved. She fluttered in and out of sleep, half scared of the emotions inside her, half clinging to them.

Her throat was tight and her cheeks still damp from tears. The way Fraser had looked at her, the intense light and comforting weight in her chest, the purity of his kisses…it had all been so much. Too much to feel.

She could love him, she knew. Could give her heart to him…was at serious risk of doing so. They were at a tipping point and she had to choose how this played out. For now she was in control, hanging on by a thread, but it wouldn't take much more of him for her to let go and fall.

Beside her, he lay with his eyes closed, his arm tucked round her body, holding her close against him. His breathing was calmer now and steady. Two things she most definitely wasn't.

She didn't want to wake him, so she lay as still as she could, trying to breathe through a sandpaper throat, and instead of looking inside herself she looked at her surroundings. His bedroom was bright and airy with exposed wooden beams, a luxurious en suite bathroom and a huge window with a view out to the mountains, even from the comfort of his large, luxurious wrought-iron bed.

There was space for a cot, she thought, over by the window. And a rocking chair for night feeding. More than enough space for two people's things. And even for three.

Then she shoved that thought away. She was getting ahead of herself. Thinking things she'd promised she wouldn't think. Impossible dreams. A cot for when it was his turn for the baby. Sure. If he was even still living here and not in London.

God, she wanted him to stay so badly, but couldn't ask him. Couldn't bear to face the rejection.

Her strength was in being on her own, not allowing herself to become embroiled or entangled. Or losing herself again.

She'd fought so hard to survive Tony and to escape intact. She'd spent years with him and he'd won her by stealth, stealing her bit by bit. In contrast, she'd been intimate with Fraser for barely a few weeks...with a large gap in between drinks, and she'd never felt so captured. So captivated by someone's words, kisses, touch. His smile. His laugh.

She'd told him everything and he thought he knew her. But he didn't. He thought she was strong, bold, courageous. He didn't know how scared she could be, how weak. How leaving Tony had taken every ounce of strength she'd had. How hard she'd fought. How few reserves she'd had left, but over the last few months she'd built them up. Impenetrable.

Or so she'd thought.

How at risk she was of losing it all again. How hard she was falling for him, making her vulnerable, making her second-guess her decisions. How broken she'd be if he couldn't feel these same things for her. And he hadn't before, so why would he now?

Her heart hurt at the light and dark. Something warm and beautiful could happen here and she so desperately wanted to reach out and grasp it but was terrified she'd get burned.

She lifted his arm and scooted off the bed. Wrapping herself in his fluffy white bathrobe, she walked over to the window and looked outside.

The light was fading. No beautiful sunset tonight, just a slow slip into darkness.

Her throat felt raw and tight. Her chest was like a vice. She couldn't breathe.

She glanced back at him, his careless slack-limbed pose. His beautiful mouth. That body. Her heart danced. One look at him and everything seemed brighter. But she couldn't rely on Fraser to make everything better. She had to do that for herself.

A bright bubbly tune blared into the silence, making her jump. On the nightstand Fraser's phone lit up.

He lazily rolled over and, not looking, patted around for his phone. His eyes were on Briana. A sexy smile. *Come back to bed* eyes.

And she was, oh, so tempted. It would be so easy to slip back in.

But he glanced at the screen and jerked up, holding the phone to his ear. 'Hey, Lily-Bee, yes, I know. Sorry, *just Lily.* It's a dad thing, okay? You'll always be my Lily-Bee. Good time?'

A pause as he listened.

'Excellent. I can't wait to hear all about it.' His mouth split into a grin. 'I'll set off in five.'

He lay back on the pillow, scuffed his palm over his

hair. 'I have to go pick them up.' He patted the space in the bed next to him. 'In five minutes.'

Bri looked at him. 'You'd better get dressed, then.'

'That'll take me about sixty seconds. Which leaves four minutes to play.' He reached out to her and she fought the pull, making herself stay by the window and drink him in.

Seeing she didn't move, he slid from the bed and crossed the room, wrapping her in his arms. His warm body enveloping her, holding her tight against his bare skin. His cheek against hers. 'You don't want to play?'

And, oh, she did. But she smiled, her eyes filling with tears, her throat hurting as she tightened the robe ties around the swell of her belly. She would tell him. Only... not yet. Not when he was heading off for Lily. His daughter needed him level-headed and calm. 'It's okay. I've had a lovely day, but now you have to go and be Dad again. I'll tidy up while you're gone and leave no trace.'

He tilted her chin so he could look at her. 'You never showed me the dress.'

She didn't have the heart or energy to parade in front of him for an opinion or feel his heated gaze on her body. She needed to extinguish the fire, not stoke it. 'Another time.'

'Okay. If you're sure?' He slipped a kiss onto her head, a glimmer of concern in his expression.

Then he was gone.

Much later the next day Briana saw Fraser's car drive past her cottage window en route to his home. From the station, no doubt. Dropping off Jerome.

She wondered how things had gone for the young couple. She hoped it had been wonderful and simple and not complicated and too emotional, the way Bri felt right now.

Whatever happened between herself and Fraser, she had to grow this relationship with Lily. It had been a solemn promise and she intended to make good on it.

She sent her goddaughter a quick text message.

Hey, how was the weekend?

A few minutes later a reply came.

Great, thanks.

She laughed. Teenagers weren't great on detail unless asked direct questions. She hesitated, because it was truly none of her business. But she wanted Lily to know her godmother was there for her whatever happened and however she was feeling.

She bit the bullet.

How was Jerome?

A smiley face covered in little hearts and a big red heart winged their way to Bri's phone. Okay. Now what? She really, really wanted details, but that would be too intrusive. Wow, this was hard to navigate.

She sent a heart back.

I'm so glad it went well.
Thanks for making me invite him. You're the best, Bri.

And another heart.

You're the best too.

Bri sent two hearts back as a solid warmth settled in her chest.

You're the best.

She hadn't been, but she was determined to be the best she could be now. If she couldn't have closeness with Fraser, she'd at least have a special connection with his daughter. With Ellen's daughter. And that meant everything to her, something to hold onto while her own world was starting to crumble.

She was taking steps away from him.

He saw it in the way she held herself, heard it in her tone and felt it in the way her body had stiffened as he'd held her that last time.

In the fact she hadn't replied to his texts with more than one-word answers for four days. She'd feigned busyness at work and locked herself in her clinic room.

The closer he got, the more she ran. And he didn't blame her one bit after what she'd been through, but he was damned if he was going to let her push him away without a fight.

And, hell, that was one big fat surprise. He'd never wanted a woman like this. Never given so much of himself.

He waited until after the outreach clinic and they were walking to their cars, falling into a conversation he knew she'd be comfortable with. 'The workshops went well, don't you think?'

'Great. Some of the kids are really starting to open up. I think we have a really good anti-bullying strategy in place now. A safe place for kids to come and a shared community direction on where we want to be.' She nodded, using all the right professional jargon that kept him at a safe distance. She looked pale and worn out as she added, 'How was Lily after Jerome went back to London? I messaged her and she said she was fine, but I'm thinking she might be glossing over it.'

He liked it that she had a relationship with Lily, that was something great that had come out of all this. 'She sobbed all evening and we went through two boxes of tissues. I almost rang you for fairy godmother advice, but she cheered up when I promised he could come back again at Easter.'

She rummaged in her handbag and zapped her remote key towards her car, its lights flashing orange in the dark night. Her eyes were skittish and her hands trembling. 'It's serious, then?'

'As serious as it can be at that age. But you know how these things can fizzle out as quickly as they flare.' The way it had between himself and Ellen, but with the additional gift of a baby. He'd put that baby first for the last fifteen years, but now it was time to give priority to his own needs. 'Thing is, I don't want to talk about Lily.'

'Oh?' Briana blinked at him and upped her walking pace.

He matched her step for step. 'Where are you running off to, Briana?'

'Home. It's late. I'm tired.' She turned to open the car door but paused to look right at him. 'I'm sorry, Fraser.'

He felt the kick to his gut like a punch. She wasn't apologising for racing home, or for the awkward, stilted conversations they'd been having.

'What's happening here, Bri?' He put his hand on the car roof so she couldn't climb straight in and drive away. 'We have epic sex…hell, it certainly blew me away. We connected. We did, didn't we? I'm not dreaming it? We have something? And now you refuse to speak to me.'

She shook her head dismissively. 'This is talking.'

'It's polite conversation that skirts around the freaking huge elephant in the room. Briana, I had a fantastic time on Saturday. I thought you did too.'

A pause. A reluctant nod in agreement. 'I did.'

She'd had a fantastic time…he hadn't imagined it. He wasn't in some deluded half-reality where this was one-sided.

'And now?' He didn't think he'd ever felt so disarmed. Raw. Putting himself on the line in a way he'd never done before. 'It seems we're pretty good together and we keep coming back for a repeat performance. So, I don't know about you, but I'm left wondering where we stand. What *this*…' he pointed first at his chest and then at Briana '…is.'

'It's…' She chewed her bottom lip. Her eyes briefly closed, then, 'Fraser, it's not anything. You and me. It's not going to happen. I don't want it. Can't you see? I don't want this.'

And yet he knew if he touched her, if he kissed her, she'd kiss him back. That she *did* want this. And more. 'Don't want it? Or just too damned scared to take it?'

'It's all too fast. I feel things when I'm with you, Fraser. I liked being numb. Cold. Pootling along. I liked being on my own, making my own decisions. Finding out who I am. And now…now I'm unsure. I'm dithering. I'm…' She shook her head. 'I'm losing myself—'

He took hold of her hand. It was cold. Shaking. But her fingers gripped his. Tight. 'You're scared, Briana. And that's okay. I'm not surprised. You've had a really tough time and this is intense. Hell…you know what? I'm scared too. I haven't dated anyone in years. I've barely thought about anyone other than my daughter for a decade and a half. I haven't chased something for myself. Haven't dared think about any kind of future with anyone.

'Apart from Lily, everyone I've ever cared for has left me. Everyone. I don't know how to do this happy families thing and I tried hard not to care for you. I tried to keep my distance. I tried not to fall, but here we are and in my head I have all these ideas. Images. Hopes.' Yes. He'd dared to hope. 'We have to face it. This thing…it's out of the blue, sure. There's the baby, which complicates everything, but…hell, Briana, we can work it out.'

She shook her head, tears shimmering in her eyes. 'I can't.'

'*We* can.' He put his hand on her cheek. Looked deeply into her beautiful blue eyes. 'I cared for Ellen. She was a wonderful friend and mother and I was devastated when she died. Imagine multiplying that caring by a thousand and learning to hope, but also being torn in half about what to do. Do I hold you close and let myself fall and who knows what might happen? You might die or leave… Or do I hold you at arm's length? That's easy and safe but it sure as hell isn't life-affirming. It's not living. I get you're scared. It's okay. We can be scared together. We'll be amazing. We'll work it out. Briana…' He hauled in oxygen and smiled. 'I—'

'No. No. No. Don't say it. Please. Don't.' She shook her head, eyes wide and wet. A vehement shake.

Love you.

There it was.

The feeling that had cracked his heart wide open. The tumbling sensation when he looked at her. The devastating need to protect her and the child inside her. His child. Their child. This conversation where his emotions poured out of him and he couldn't stop them.

He'd fallen in love with her.

And she was backtracking so fast he could almost see the vapour trails.

Her face crumpled. She pressed fingers to her lips as if holding her feelings in. Holding her words in.

Words he desperately wanted to hear. That she loved him back. That this could work. That they could make a life, the four of them. Create that picture he had in his head. Where he did the right things at the right time for once. Where he loved her and she loved him back.

That she wanted to try.

But despite whatever her heart felt, her head was telling her to run. She did not want this. Whether she did actually love him or not, she didn't want to. And there wasn't much he could do about that.

He loved her.

He was destined to be by her side for the next eighteen years and more. Co-parenting. Working together. Making decisions, swapping banal grey snippets of their lives. Instead of being a part of them. Instead of building a glorious golden future together. A future he hadn't ever envisioned and hadn't wanted, and now couldn't bear not having. He loved her and she refused to love him back.

His heart felt as if it was being cleaved into two pieces. Whatever happened, one half was hers and always would be. He might as well have cut it out and handed it to her on a plate.

He pulled himself together because she needed him to be okay about this. He wasn't going to push her into something she didn't want. Hell, that's what her ex had done.

But, then, what was he supposed to do now? Smile? Walk away? When his own hopes and dreams were fading and he couldn't grasp at them?

'We're not moving to London.'

'Oh?' Her eyes brightened just for a second.

'I want to be here for our child. I can't miss seeing them grow up. We're staying.'

'And what does Lily think of that?'

'She's not exactly thrilled but she understands.'

'I'm glad you're going to be here. For the baby… That's good. Thank you.' There was something in the silence she left hanging there. Tears welled in her eyes and he could see her summoning up all of her strength. 'Look, I'm tired. I have to go. I'm so sorry, Fraser. Honestly. I am. I just need to be on my own. It's for the best.'

'Best for who? You? You look devastated. Me? I'm—'

Broken.

'It's just not going to work.' She let go of his hand and looked meaningfully at him to move so she could climb into the car. There was nothing he could do but step away.

This was it. The end. In a dingy car park on a freezing winter's night.

He wished his chest was filled with the ice that was in the air, frosting the ground, frosting his damned feelings. Filling him up with cold and leaving no room for the bright heat and light he felt when he was with her.

But it wasn't. His chest was filled with Briana. Her smile, her scent. Her laugh. Her touch.

And now…her goodbye.

Briana climbed into the car and took a steadying breath. At least she tried to. Instead, her breath caught in her too-tight chest and stuttered, hiccupping out on a sob. Then another. And another. She thought her body would implode from the pressure she was exerting just to keep vaguely in control. Reality was she was falling utterly and completely apart.

He was right. She was scared. Terrified. Blindsided

by how much she felt for him. How much it hurt to turn away from what he was offering.

She knew he was still looking at her through the foggy window. Hoping she'd change her mind, but she wouldn't. It was for the best, it was. For all of them. This way they could all have a good life, survive. Thrive. Without the constrictions of emotions clouding everything. Without *needing*.

He loved her. At least, that's what she'd thought he'd been going to say. She'd had to stop him, right then, before the words had tumbled out. Panic had exploded inside her. Because she knew she'd have relented if those words had escaped his lips. Knew she'd have walked... run...straight back into his arms.

Knew she would have said it too. Because she did. Despite everything, she'd let him in. And it would be her downfall if she didn't stop it. She'd get carried away with dreams and drop her guard further.

This way was for the best.

It was.

Even though she was going to have to live alongside him for the next eighteen years.

She blinked hard, pressing her eyelids tight closed to stop the stream of tears. She had to be strong. Stronger than she'd ever been. Even though her heart was shattering.

Love.

She would shower their child with it and keep that part she had for Fraser locked away. She would be tortured every single minute she spent with him, and every moment she was away from him. But this was for the best.

She didn't know how long she sat there in her cold car with steamed-up windows, body racked with sadness. How many tears she shed, how many times she asked herself if she was doing the right thing. Whispering to her baby that everything would be just fine. Trying to convince herself.

But when her chest eventually stopped heaving and she could see enough through blurry eyes to drive she turned on the ignition and edged the car out onto the road. Towards her home.

To her future without Fraser.

She might have believed it was for the best, and she only hoped that at some point she'd actually feel it was.

CHAPTER FIFTEEN

WINTER HAD SLIPPED into a warm spring, and today was one of those bright sunshiny days that made your heart smile.

At least, there were plenty of smiles to go around here at the wedding reception, so Fraser imagined no one cared that the upturned curl on his mouth was fake. He was happy for Joe and Rose, of course. They were a special couple and their love and happiness was evident, touching everyone in the room.

Except him. He just felt hollow.

The speeches were finished and the tables cleared away. The happy couple was stepping off the dance floor to a round of applause after their first dance.

Which meant, if he was strategic, he could now slink away and no one would notice.

'Dad, can you at least look like you're enjoying yourself?' Lily nudged him. She looked adorable in a silver summer dress she'd ordered online. Probably trying to make herself look older, but all it did was accentuate her youth. She'd dropped the heavy make-up and was smiling real smiles a lot more. She fitted in well here with all these grinning guests. 'It's supposed to be a happy occasion. Duh?'

'Sorry.' He looked into his empty beer glass. 'I was

miles away. I have one of those faces that always looks miserable when I'm thinking.'

He'd been watching Briana across the room, laughing and chatting with Beth. Her hair was piled on top of her head in a messy bun with curls springing loose, framing her face. The blue silk dress was a perfect choice, tight fitting at the bust and flared around her hips. No one would have known she was pregnant.

But he did. He knew her. *Knew her.* Knew she wasn't happy. That she was living with her choice, but it hadn't brought her whatever it was she'd been hoping for. Not that that knowledge made him feel any better. He was living with her choice too.

Lily groaned. 'The resting bitch face excuse doesn't wash with me, Dad. Go ask her to dance.'

'Er...who?' He feigned nonchalance, even though his heart flared at the thought of her.

'You know who. Briana.' His daughter's elbow pressed into his ribs again. 'Go and dance with her.'

'Why?'

'Because she's standing on her own.'

Beth had just joined Alex on the dance floor and was beckoning to Briana to come too. She was shaking her head.

A glance towards him. A look away. A glance back.

He held her gaze as fire ignited inside him. He was angry she'd pushed him away and raging at himself for allowing himself to get into that situation in the first place. He should have resisted. Fought back. But it didn't matter, the love was ever present, a light always there, for her.

He forced himself to look back at Lily. 'I was thinking about going home.'

Lily glowered at him. 'Don't you dare. You're staying here and you're going to have fun.'

He remembered saying those words to Lily a few weeks ago. Oh, boy, had the tables turned.

'What's happened between you two? One minute you're all loved up and next minute you don't want to be in the same room together.' Lily did her exasperated eye-roll. 'This is so not going to work when she's had the baby.'

He rubbed his forehead. 'We decided not to pursue a relationship. That's okay. That's what happens, right?'

'With Mum, yes. But Briana's different. You're different with her. And a lot worse without her.'

'Gee, thanks. But the truth is she doesn't want me around.' He wasn't stupid or a glutton for punishment, and he sure as hell wasn't going to beg.

Lily grinned. 'Could have fooled me.'

'Why?'

'Woman's intuition. Also known as…she keeps looking over.' Lily's eyes settled on Briana. 'She looks sad. Lonely. Even with all those people around her.'

'I know.' His battered heart ached for her.

Lily turned to him, excitement in her eyes. 'So, do something about it. That baby is part of our lives and you're going to see Briana a lot. Are you going to spend the next eighteen years of your life being this grumpy?'

He slumped back in his chair. 'Probably.'

'Ask her out.'

'What?' Was this really his daughter talking?

'Oh, God.' She framed her face with her fingers and shook her head in frustration. 'Please, don't tell me I have to give you dating tips, too.'

'I think I can manage. If I ever decide to date again, which is unlikely.' Root canals had better outcomes.

'Decide now.' Lily groaned. 'You're both unhappy. You both like each other. What's the problem?'

'Why this sudden interest in my non-existent love life?'

'I've been doing a lot of thinking recently. You've spent a long time looking after me and now I'm going to look out for you. Especially as you're slipping into old age.' She winked. And giggled. 'Actually, I just remembered you do that weird dad dancing thing. That won't impress her. Go talk to her instead.'

She made it sound so easy. To a fifteen-year-old, it probably was. He put his arm round her and squished her close. 'Ah, Lily-Bee, I love you so much and I know you're only trying to help, but sometimes...' He sighed. 'Sometimes in life you have to admit defeat.' How many times did he need to admit his feelings to Briana and keep getting the same answer back? She didn't want him. She didn't want him. She didn't want him.

'Nothing I can do or say is going to change her mind and I wouldn't want to back her into a corner. That's not the kind of relationship I want. She has to *want* to be with me. She's an independent woman who makes her own choices and decisions. I have to honour them whether I like them or not. But, for the record, I don't like it. Not at all.'

And now he had to watch from the sidelines. He caught sight of her bump again as she twirled round, now on the dance floor, and his heart just about shattered all over again.

Whatever happened, he'd be fully involved in their child's life. He'd managed it with Lily and he'd manage it again. He'd be there for the first teeth, the first words, the first steps, only not in the way he'd hoped he could be. And perhaps he'd learn to quietly love Briana from a distance. Instead of this burning love close up.

'I think I'll head off. Are you okay to come home with Beth and Alex?'

'Of course.' Lily squeezed his arm. 'I wish I could make things better for you, Dad.'

He smiled. At least this part of his life was improving day by day. 'By saying that, Lily-Bee, you just made everything a whole lot better.'

Briana's heart sank as she looked over to where Fraser had been standing. He wasn't there any more. She scanned the dance floor. He wasn't there either. Or at the bar.

Maybe the toilet?

She watched as different people entered and exited. No. He'd disappeared.

He'd gone.

It's okay.

It wasn't okay. She wasn't okay. Her mouth hurt from the fake smile she'd worn all day. Her heart hurt.

She missed him. There hadn't been a moment since that day in the car park when she'd been relieved about putting a stop to things. She'd been trying to convince herself it was for the best, but her best since then had been the absolutely bloody awful worst.

Working with him was torture. That tiny little clinic area meant they had to negotiate their space and she'd barricaded him out with excuses. But she still breathed him in. Still ached for him. It physically hurt to see him. An awkward tension hung between them.

She'd thought she'd try to break the ice tonight. Somehow. Just try to be a friend at least. But she'd missed her chance. He'd gone. And it would never be the same anyway, not when she wanted to be with him.

She hurt all over again.

'Hey.' Lily came over and gave her a hug.

With a lump in her throat Briana wrapped her arms round her beautiful goddaughter. At least she had this gift in her life. 'You look lovely, Lily.'

'Thanks. So do you.' Lily smiled as she sat down at one of the huge round tables awash with crocheted wedding favours that Rose and Katy had made. 'That colour's nice on you and your bump is starting to show.'

Briana looked down and flattened the silk over her belly. Panic and wonder mixed inside her. 'Is it?'

'Only when you turn sideways. No one else would probably notice. But they will soon.'

'You okay with that?' Bri sat down next to her, hoping her baby's half-sister would grow to love this child.

A little shrug. 'I think so. Yes.'

'It's early days and a bit fresh for all of us. We've got a few more months to get used to the idea. But…if you ever want to come to a scan or anything let me know. Meet this little one before they're even born. Pretty cool, right?'

'A scan? Baby scan?' She looked horrified and delighted at the same time. 'I've seen them on the TV. You hear their heartbeat and see them, like, fully formed.'

'Yes. But no pressure.' And just to remove any pressure Bri changed the subject. 'That's a nice necklace.'

Lily fingered the little heart pendant at her neck. 'Jerome gave it to me.'

'Oh, the sweetheart. He has excellent taste.' At least one of them was having love-life success. 'Is he coming up again soon?'

'No.' The girl sat up straight. Businesslike. Growing up. 'Actually, we've broken up.'

'Oh, dear.' Fraser must have had a hard time navigating this. 'Are you okay about it?'

Lily nodded. She seemed perfectly fine about a break-up. Unlike Briana. 'It was my idea. I don't have time for anything long distance at the moment. Not with the play and everything.'

A break-up had been Briana's idea too but why? Why, when it made her feel like this? She was exhausted and she knew it wasn't just because of the baby. Grief made her weary. She had no energy, no enthusiasm. She just simply missed him. Her life had been so much better when he'd been in it.

She brought herself back to Lily. 'Ah, yes. The play.' Lily had been given a starring role in the school production. 'It must take up a lot of your time. Good call on the Jerome situation.'

'It was his idea I audition for it.'

'Do you miss him?'

As if you have part of you that's been cut off? Do you dream about him? Ache for him? Ache for what you could have had?

'Not really. It was one of those things that fizzles out. Plenty more fish in the sea.' Lily grinned slyly.

'Oh? Is there someone…?'

Lily looked at her through her long eyelashes and tapped her nose. *It's a secret.* 'Early days.'

This was good. Lily was sharing things about her life. 'Well, I'm here if you ever want a chat about anything.'

'Yeah. Thanks.' Lily frowned. 'Actually, my dad…'

Uh-oh. Truth time. Briana sat forward. 'Look, I don't know if he's told you…whatever we had…it's ended. But I'd really like for us all to work together when the baby comes.'

'Do you love him?'

'What?' Briana blinked. Maybe her relationship with Lily needed a few more boundaries.

Or maybe she should be proud Lily was a forthright and confident woman.

'Do you love my dad?' Lily repeated.

'I don't know.'

With all my heart, all my breath, with everything I have.

Bri felt her lip wobble. She couldn't lie to Lily and she couldn't lie to herself any more. 'Yes. Yes, I do.'

'Have you told him?'

'No.' That was met with an eye-roll that reminded Briana that she was opening her heart to a fifteen-year-old. 'It's not as simple as—'

'Right. I'm too young to understand. Okay.' Lily held her palms up. 'I know you love him and I'm pretty sure he loves you. I know he's miserable. And I'm pretty sure you are too. I know he isn't eating properly, and his face looks like the sun has gone in or something. He's told me he's going to be grumpy for the rest of his life. And that's just sad.'

Bri smiled. 'I hope he isn't. That would be terrible.'

'Especially for me.' Her goddaughter grinned. 'Look, I know it's a big thing that you weren't expecting. But you have to take a chance. Take a risk.'

'Wow, Lily.' Briana laughed. 'I don't know what to say.'

Lily leaned in and whispered, 'What would Ellen say?'

Bri gasped at the sharp sting in her chest. Beautiful Ellen, whose life was cruelly taken before it had really started. Ellen, who had told her over and over that Fraser was a good man. That he was a wonderful father. But, of course, Briana knew that and more. He was generous and funny and he hadn't pressured her into anything. In fact, he'd done exactly as she'd asked him to do and left her alone. She couldn't have asked for more.

And she loved him.

She knew what her best friend would encourage her to do, and now her best friend's daughter was saying it too. Two generations couldn't be wrong, surely? She cupped her goddaughter's chin. 'You're a chip off the old block, Lily Moore. You're pure Ellen.'

'And Fraser too.'

'And Fraser too.' His gentleness. His enthusiasm. His open honesty that was at once raw and yet freeing. He believed in her and made her believe it too. He hadn't been afraid to tell her what he wanted, and he'd taken a leap of faith regardless of the consequences. That kind of a man came along once in a lifetime. 'Ellen would say, *Hell, yes*. Go for it.'

'So, does it take a fifteen-year-old to bash your heads together? Talk to him. Talk to each other.'

'And say what?'

'Well, someone wise once told me that what makes you happy is being able to be truly honest with someone. Maybe you could start with that?'

Touché. 'But he's gone.'

'Actually, no. He's standing right there.' Lily pointed out of the French doors behind Briana to a private jetty that led down to the lake. He was alone, his back to her, silhouetted by fairy lights threaded through thick coils of rope fencing and a silvery full moon. In his suit he looked dangerous and magnificent, and the sight of him made her heart dance. Falling in love had been unexpected, unwanted. She'd come home with no plan, looking to hide away from her feelings and experiences and try to make something new for herself.

But it was Fraser who had made her see everything in

a new light; he'd helped create this new life inside her. He made her feel renewed and being in his arms made everything feel complete.

Could it be possible that maybe, just maybe, Fraser was her fresh start?

Fraser looked out across the lake breathing in the cool air that blew in from the mountains. In the distance he could hear music, laughter, chatter from the wedding party in the hotel.

He felt detached from it all. Untethered. Adrift.

It was cold, but he didn't care. The breeze reminded him he was alive, and he could breathe out here when he couldn't breathe watching Briana. Every glimpse of her made his chest constrict.

Boy, he had it bad.

'Fraser?'

He whirled round at the sound of her voice, his heart lifting and hurting at the same time. Her bun had come lose and curls hung round her cheeks. She was breathless, her cheeks flushed. She was beautiful. Perfect.

All he wanted to do was take her into his arms and kiss her until his thoughts blurred. But he just nodded, forcing himself to get used to being around her in this faux emotionless state—when in reality the emotion was just shoved down, pushed back, still bubbling under the surface. 'Hey, Bri. You okay?'

'Tired.' She gave a little shrug. 'But okay.'

Why was she here when she'd spent the last few weeks keeping her distance? His eyes dipped to her stomach and his own gut tightened in concern. 'Baby okay?'

'Yes. All is fine.' She suddenly looked nervous and pale. 'Look, Fraser...we need to talk.'

'Did Lily put you up to this?' He mimicked Lily's

voice. '"*Go talk to my dad. He's a sad sack who needs cheering up.*"'

Bri smiled softly. 'We chatted, yes.'

Ah. Then that explained it. A pity-party. *Great.* 'Take no notice. She's trying to help but probably making it worse.'

'Actually, she helped me clarify a few things.'

'How?' His chest tightened as he waited for more rejection.

'She asked me if I loved you.'

'Oh, God.' He wanted to shrivel up and die right there. 'Sorry.'

'No. No, it's good.' Bri held her palm up. 'She's amazing, Fraser, really. She's a beautiful, young woman and I'm so proud of her. She's not scared of emotions. She doesn't hide from them, she feels them keenly. Lets them work through her system. It's a good thing. And she's not scared to take risks.'

'Don't I know it.' He shook his head. Okay, so she'd come to talk about Lily. The little flicker of hope fizzled out. 'And?'

'And what?'

'The answer to her question.'

She took hold of his hand and looked up at him. Vulnerability and something else…fear, perhaps, or panic… flitted across her gaze. Then determination. Clarity. 'I told her that, yes, I do. I do love you.'

'The way I loved Ellen, right? Friends. Co-parents. That's…' He took his hand away from hers. 'Okay.'

He'd get used to it.

'Not like Ellen.' She stepped closer and took his hand again. 'Thing is…you were right. I am scared about making a commitment to you. I'm scared about planning a future with anyone. I told myself you didn't love me, couldn't love me, and I didn't want to hear it when you tried to say those precious words. I hid behind you planning to go back to London. Then when you decided to stay I had nothing to hide behind. I panicked. I'm scared about the way I feel because it's out of control. It's unpredictable. It's wild.'

She laughed. 'It's wonderful. I'm dizzy with it. Lost in it. Lost in you. And that's okay.' She breathed in and nodded, repeating slowly, 'That's okay. I was trying to hold tight onto who I am, who I wanted to be. But I realise now that being with you makes me feel stronger. Braver. More. So much more. You make me believe in myself more than I ever did before. You listen. You hear me. And I know *we* can work it out. I know we'll be a team. Together.'

He couldn't believe she was saying these things. Expecting that any minute there would be a 'but'.

She shook her head. 'I love you, Fraser. Like a friend, like a co-parent, yes. But I'm *in love* with you too. I didn't want to be, I fought against it. I raged against it. I didn't want to be trapped and I know you didn't want anything from me. You definitely didn't want a baby.'

'I do now.' His heart was racing. 'There's going to be more bumps on the road, I'm sure.'

'Then we'll face them together. Ever since that day in the car park I've felt as if a part of me was missing and I...' She took his hand and placed it over her belly. '*We* don't want to live another day without you.'

He blinked, still unable to compute. Had he fallen and hit his head? Was he back in his bed and dreaming? 'Are you saying...?'

'I love you. I want to be with you. I want...' she pointed to her chest and then his '...this.'

'I thought I'd lost you. You didn't want—' His

throat was too tight with emotion. His words stuck. He couldn't speak.

'Oh, God.' Her hand went to her mouth. 'Oh, no. I've read it wrong. You've changed your mind. You don't want it.'

'Don't want it?' In a panic he found the words pretty damned quick. If this was a dream he was not going to let it end. He laughed and pulled her close in case she totally got the wrong impression. 'I want you more than anything in the world, Briana Barclay. I want us. I want our family. I want…everything. A new start for all of us. I love you.'

'I love you too.' She slipped into his arms, her face bright with tears and smiles.

And then she kissed him.

EPILOGUE

Six months later...

'BE CAREFUL! WATCH IT! Whoa! Not there! There. Careful. Precious cargo.' Lily hovered around Fraser, shouting directions as he placed the baby car seat onto the bed.

Bri followed them in and sat down in the rocking chair, watching as father and daughter fussed. They seemed to be in a competition about who loved the baby the most.

She reckoned she won. She loved them all so much.

The bedroom was exactly how she'd envisaged it: the cot, the rocking chair, stacks of teeny baby clothes, even though they had a perfectly suitable nursery down the corridor. But she wanted to be on hand when the baby woke up, at least for the first few months. Her new husband agreed.

He grinned. 'I've got it, thanks, Lily.'

'Got *her*.' A Lily eye-roll, which took today's count to about number one hundred and thirty-four. 'I don't want you to drop her.'

Fraser laughed. 'I meant I'm in control of the car-seat manoeuvre. I've done this a few times.'

'But you haven't done it with this little one.' Lily unclipped the straps on the car seat and carefully picked up little Ellen Josephine Moore—Elle for short—who was making little gurgling sounds, and cradled her in her arms. 'I think she's hungry. Or does she need changing? How do we tell what her different cries mean? Can I change her?'

Bri smiled. It had been an intense labour and she was tired and wired. Excited and hopeful and teary. 'I think we'll learn as we go. Right now, I'd say she's just showing us how excited she is to be home. Just like I am.'

'This is where the fun starts.' Fraser took the squeaking little bundle from Lily and lifted her onto his shoulder, rocked from side to side, patting the tiny back and whispering, 'Hey, there, little Elle-Belle. This is our bedroom. This is your sister, Lily-Bee. She hates the Bee bit, but we say it to wind her up.'

'It works.' Lily snorted and stroked the baby's head, cooing soft words and giving her gentle kisses. 'Don't tell them, but I like it, really.'

'This is your mummy.' Fraser turned and bent to Briana, taking little Elle's hand and waving. He stopped, his beautiful smile turning to a look of concern. 'Oh. God, are you okay? You're crying.'

Briana sniffed and wiped her tears away. 'I'm absolutely fine. Absolutely, wonderfully, totally fine.'

He knelt down next to her and pressed his cheek to hers, protecting the baby on his chest. 'So why the tears?'

'It's so perfect.' She took them all in, her husband and her two beautiful daughters, unable to believe she could be this lucky. This *loved*. Unable to measure the love in her heart, because it was beyond anything she could ever have imagined.

The giving and taking, the wholeness, the care. The unity of it all. 'All of it. All of you. It's just perfect.'

* * * * *

REUNITED
WITH DOCTOR
DEVEREAUX

ALLIE KINCHELOE

MILLS & BOON

To my husband and family—
without your support, this book wouldn't exist.

CHAPTER ONE

AFTER EIGHT YEARS, three months, sixteen days, and—Camilla glanced up at the oversize clock on the wall of the law office—twenty-seven minutes, Danny Owens had walked back into her life. She swallowed hard.

Not that she was counting.

Counting would be stupid, considering that the last time they were together Danny had upended her entire future. So, no, she absolutely was *not* counting how long it had been since she'd seen the only man she'd ever loved. In fact, he was the last person she wanted to see, and her stomach churned as he knocked on the open office door.

Fleetingly, she thought it was good she hadn't eaten much today. If she had, the whirlwind in her stomach might have gotten the best of her.

Oh, she'd dreamed of the moment when she'd see him again, imagining how he would look and his expression when he first saw her face. Of the time when he'd come crawling back with an apology on his lips, begging her to forgive the stupidity of his actions.

But he never had.

Seeing him now, in this way, was so much harder than she'd expected, although she'd certainly never thought it would be easy. Maybe today she'd finally get some answers on why Danny had ended their relationship so abruptly. Maybe this was fate providing her with the closure denied her for the better part of a decade.

"Dr. Owens, thank you for coming in today." The estate attorney rose from his desk and offered a hand for Danny to shake. "Now that both you and Dr. Devereaux are here, we can begin." In a crisp dark suit, Danny showed little sign that he'd been traveling. He was immaculately groomed and held himself tall, with an authority to his presence that demanded attention. Six feet one inches of firm muscle? Oh, yes, he certainly commanded her attention. Awareness buzzed through her as her eyes roamed the once familiar angles of his body, taking in the changes his time in the Army had made to his physique. The masculinity he exuded had grown stronger with the years that had passed, and despite their painful history, a deep yearning rushed over Camilla when his gaze flicked in her direction.

Heart racing like she'd just run a full marathon, Camilla made eye contact with Danny only to have him look away like she was a total stranger. She watched him in profile as he shook hands with the lawyer and settled into the leather wingback chair next to her, never once glancing her way again. Well, if she'd needed further confirmation that she'd never meant as much to him as he had to her, she'd just gotten it.

If he could push her out of his mind so easily, then she would do the same. Danny Owens wasn't going to hurt her again, because she refused to give him that power. It had taken far too many years and prayers to fix what he had broken. Two could play this game. She straightened her posture and pushed away the burst of memories that threatened to overwhelm her. There was no time for a detour into melancholia, and certainly no time to let a shared past take her down the path to future heartache.

Letting stubbornness lift her chin, Camilla turned her focus to the attorney. "Are we ready to get started here?"

"Of course, Dr. Devereaux." The attorney shuffled a few files on his desk, opening one and putting on a pair of thick, black-rimmed reading glasses before looking up. He offered them each a sympathetic smile. "So, it can be a terrible thing, the reading of a will. Especially for someone as beloved to our town as Dr. Robert Owens."

"Yeah, yeah, we all know what a saint my father was," Danny drawled.

The gravelly quality to his voice had deepened since their last meeting. It sparked a curiosity about how else he might have changed over the years they'd been apart. No, no, no, that line of thought was forbidden. Camilla pinched her wrist. She could not go down that rabbit hole with Danny. It would only end badly for her. But keeping her mind on the conversation in front of her proved difficult as her thoughts wanted to drift off to the man sitting within arm's reach, the man she'd first given herself to, heart and soul.

"Your father was the best man I've ever known," she argued.

Robert Owens had been the only positive male role model she'd had. After bouncing from foster home to foster home for most of her formative years, she'd finally landed in a group home in Greenbriar, Kentucky. It was while attending the local high school that she'd met Danny. Then he'd brought her home to meet his parents, Robert and Linda, and his younger brother, Robby. For the first time in her life, she'd seen what a normal family dynamic looked like, warts and all.

Her early years had taught her that love was a fantasy only accessible to those with a tremendous amount of luck. And the one thing she'd most certainly never had?

Luck. But Danny's gentle touch and the way he and his family had treated her, like she truly mattered, had given her hope, and so she'd finally risked opening up enough to let someone in. To fall in love.

And just look where that got you, Camilla Ann.

"To you, maybe," Danny growled out, his clenched jaw showing his displeasure.

Finally looking at her, his brown eyes flashed with an anger she was all too familiar with. Those chocolate brown eyes had always mesmerized her, tempting her close with every sparkle, but the vibe he projected now silently screamed for her to keep her distance. A lot of feelings were displayed within the intensity of his gaze—anger, grief, frustration, but nothing loving. Nothing that showed their history mattered to him in the slightest. He closed his eyes in what would seem a long blink to anyone not watching him as carefully as Camilla was, and when he looked at her again, his face could have been chiseled from stone for all the emotion he showed.

"But then again, good ol' Dad never held your past transgressions against you like he did mine. He always loved you no matter what, didn't he?"

In some ways, she'd been expecting that comment. From the moment she'd met them, Danny and Robert had butted heads at nearly every step along the line. Yet she still gaped at him in shock. Somehow, she'd expected Danny to cool the animosity now that his father was gone, but the anger radiating off him remained raw and unfazed by time.

"Ahem. Perhaps we can stick to the topic that brought us here today," the attorney interjected before Camilla could form a rebuttal to Danny's accusation. "And that is the terms of Dr. Owens's will. I have a letter from him that he wished to have read aloud today. If you are ready?"

He paused, one bushy white eyebrow raised, until both Danny and Camilla acknowledged his question with a nod. Pulling a sheet of lined yellow paper out of the file, he cleared his throat and began to read.

"'Danny, Camilla, the two of you were my sole reasons for going on after Linda and Robby were taken from me too soon.'"

Danny stiffened next to her.

The lawyer paused for a second, but when Danny didn't speak, he continued reading. "'Have strength today, although I know how hard it is to say goodbye. Know that you were both deeply loved, and lean on each other as you grieve, but do not grieve for long. Life is far too short to spend time lost in the memories of the past.'"

Camilla could hear the words in Robert's deep baritone, as if he were sitting right there, speaking the words to them directly. Closing her eyes, she pictured his kind face. It was only a few days ago that she'd sat by his side, holding his hand while he took his final breaths. *Oh, Robert, how I will miss you!*

"'Danny, my dearest son, I may not have said it enough in life, but I couldn't help taking this last opportunity to tell you just how proud you have made me. Although I didn't agree with your decision to join the Army, you were right that it was your choice to make. Go forward in life with the fortitude your time in service has instilled in you. To you, my boy, I leave the lake house and all its contents. So many of my fondest memories of your childhood were made on the shores of that lake. It is my hope that someday, standing on the dock there and looking out over the water will fill you with as much peace as it did me.'"

The lawyer took a sip of water before continuing.

"'My cherished Camilla, you filled a void in my life only a daughter could, and these last months have only been possible as a result of your dedication to my care. I hope that you know how much you were loved and appreciated by this lonely old man. Take that knowledge into your future with an open heart. Be willing to take a chance when love comes your way again. To you, child of my heart, I leave the house on Maple Street and all its contents. Turn that house into the home it once was and is meant to be again. Fill it with children, laughter, and above all—love.'"

Danny scoffed, his mask of indifference slipping momentarily. "Of course, he leaves you my childhood home and I get a shack on the lake. Even in death, he's still punishing me for defying him."

"It's hardly a shack." She rolled her eyes at his grumbling. While the lake house was smaller than the house, Robert had renovated it a few years back to a high-quality standard. Given Danny's avoidance of Greenbriar, though, he probably had no clue what his father had done to it. If Danny wanted to sell it, then he'd have no problems getting a good price for it. But rather than continue to argue that point, she'd let him discover for himself what a gem he'd inherited.

"What about the medical practice?" Danny asked.

Holding her breath, Camilla awaited that answer. This was the part of Robert's estate she'd been waiting to hear about.

"I wasn't finished." The attorney waved the letter, his impatience with Danny's interruptions starting to show. He cleared his throat and continued to read. "'It is my last wish that the two of you will find your way back to each other, despite the years, despite the physical and emotional distances between you. Forgive an old man this last chance to meddle in the affairs of his loved ones, but I had to try. I conditionally leave Greenbriar Medical Clinic, both the building and the practice, to the both of you. You will run it together for the next six months and own it jointly at the end of that time. However, if you refuse to abide by the terms of this will, the clinic will be dissolved, liquidated, and any proceeds diverted to various military-connected charities, as well as the Greenbriar group home.'"

With her heart sinking all the way to her feet, Camilla stood and went to the window. She stared across the town square to the aging brick building that held the medical practice where she'd worked for most of her medical career. The sharp stab of what could only be labeled as betrayal cut through her. Day in and day out, she'd worked side by side with Robert. First as his employee, then later with the expectation that one day she would be a partner or take over when he retired. Robert had never said outright that he would leave the practice solely to her, but he'd strongly implied it.

Robert had known that she wanted—no, *needed*—to stay in Greenbriar, and their conversations had led her to believe that the clinic would be hers upon his death. He'd been more aware than anyone how badly Danny had destroyed her. His shoulder had been the one she'd cried on. They'd grieved together. He'd stood by her when she'd picked up the shattered pieces of her heart and stuck them back together with stubbornness and a little duct tape. Robert had been the only one who saw the depths of her pain. How could he put her future in the hands of a man who had already abandoned her once?

She took a deep breath and blinked away her fears. Now was not the time for that line of thinking. She had to find the strength that had carried her through those dark days and kept her moving forward. She would not let Danny Owens take away her future again.

Come on, Camilla. Pull it together. No tears. If you survived years of foster homes and having your heart marched across by Danny, you can handle six months working next to him.

She'd simply set a schedule where they didn't have to see each other on a daily basis and cross the days off on the calendar like she used to whenever she moved into a new home. But instead of counting up to see if any new home would break the record length of one hundred and forty-three days, she'd count down the one hundred and eighty days until Danny was gone from her life once more. She would get through this, like she'd gotten through every other hard time in her life, and when Danny left once again to go back to his, she'd continue on like he'd never shown his face here in her town.

"You're telling me that if I want to inherit my father's medical practice, I have to move back to a town that doesn't even qualify for a map dot for the next six months? I have commitments I can't fulfill if I'm stuck here in the middle of nowhere." Tight with anger, Danny's voice held a no-nonsense tone that demanded a reply.

"The terms of the will are set," the attorney confirmed. While he didn't cower at Danny's growling, the attorney looked uncomfortable. His eyes flicked toward the door as if he were getting ready to run out of his own office to avoid further confrontation.

"I'm not exactly jumping for joy at the thought of spending the next six months with you, either, Danny," Camilla said over her shoulder. Leaning her head against the window frame, she fought to regain her composure. She hugged her arms tight around her body, desperately trying to combat the creeping fear encasing her soul. The uncertainty of having her future in Danny's hands chilled her to the core, but she would not let him see how badly his presence upset her. "I've worked hard for this practice. I know the patients and their conditions. I have been on call for years so that your father could rest, and I took over entirely when his health deteriorated. I expected—"

"You expected him to just hand you the keys to a house and a profitable medical practice," Danny interrupted.

She spun around at the harsh accusation he threw at her. "I did no such thing!"

Hot stinging behind her eyelids reminded her of when she'd tripped and fallen flat on her face on her first day in a new school. That had been the last time she'd cried in public, too. She blinked hard, praying that the tears would stay where they belonged. She had come to this will reading with very little expectation, and for Danny to say otherwise was unfair.

"Come on, Camilla, what'd you think was gonna happen here today? You'd get everything even though he was *my* father?" Danny folded his arms over his chest and his suit jacket pulled tight across his broad shoulders. The straight set of his spine and the rigidity of his posture must have come from his time in the military, because the boy she'd loved had never been so solid. His sharp glare would wither a weaker person, but she had been through far too much in her life to shrink away from anything he could dish out. "Is it cutting to your core that you didn't get the lake house, too?"

"No," she asserted, standing up straight and facing him head-on. "I thought he'd leave me the practice and leave everything else to you. And if you truly think otherwise, then it's a good thing you and I didn't work out, because you clearly don't know me at all."

The thought that Robert would leave her everything had never even been a blip on her radar. The house was unexpected—very much welcome, but unexpected, nonetheless. She'd been renting the large, two-story home from Robert since he'd moved into the remodeled lakeside cottage when he'd gotten sick and stairs were too difficult for him to manage. That house was the only place she'd ever really considered a home and for Robert to have recognized that fact touched her heart, but she'd certainly never even hoped that he'd leave her anything more than the clinic she'd worked so hard for.

"Ahem. The letter continues, if I may," the attorney interjected, silencing any further argument. "'Here's where I'll say, quiet your protests. I know the two of you very well, so I'm sure you've both just had a moment. There may have been some yelling or even tears, but the time for that has gone. Find peace with my decision and know that it was made with your best interests at heart. Family is the most important thing in this life. Never forget that. And never forget just how much you were both loved. Now I'll say goodbye.'"

The attorney refolded the paper and laid it back on the file. Pulling his glasses off, he squeezed the bridge of his nose. His attitude screamed that he'd aged a decade in the reading of that letter. "Now, you can contest the will, but doing that will just take longer than the six months you two would need to work together."

"Does the six-month period have to begin immediately or can I have a few weeks to get things settled away from Greenbriar? I have commitments, a job. People are counting on me."

Camilla snorted. "Your father counted on you and you weren't here."

Danny closed his eyes and sucked in a deep breath, trying to calm the storm of emotions rushing over him. All he managed to do was get a lungful of Camilla's familiar, sweet perfume. The soft floral scent permeated his being and stoked memories of times best left forgotten.

As if he could ever forget her.

Trust his old man to take one more stab at righting what he'd seen as one of Danny's biggest mistakes. His father had never forgiven him for pushing Camilla away, but what Robert Owens hadn't known was that ending things with Camilla had been the only way Danny could think of to protect her.

And now, thanks to his father, he was tied back to the town he couldn't wait to leave, and had to spend the next six months working with *her*. The very idea of them working peacefully side by side for an extended period of time was laughable. He'd spent eight years in the Army, some of that time in a combat zone; he'd watched people he loved die right in front of him, and the idea of spending one hundred and eighty days at Camilla's side scared him more than anything ever had.

She'd been his everything once. They'd planned to conquer the world together, or at least this one little corner of it. They were going to get their bachelor's degrees together, then go to med school, and then come back to Greenbriar and take over his dad's medical practice. Only part of that plan materialized when they'd been unable to get into the same medical school. Despite that hiccup, they'd stayed as close as possible through medical schools on opposite ends of the country. Then, in the blink of an eye, everything had changed. His mother and brother had been killed in an accident and he'd been behind the wheel.

When Camilla had shown up in his hospital room, he'd sent her away, filled with self-loathing and guilt. Ending things with her had been the hardest thing he'd ever done. He'd broken her heart because he knew he was no good for her. He'd been no good to anyone at that point, even himself.

But in the process, he'd broken his own heart, too. And now they had to coexist in a work environment made hostile entirely through his own efforts.

Fantastic.

Danny had a strong suspicion that his dad had guessed how difficult it would be for him to work side by side with Camilla and had probably done it to push him out of his comfort zone. His dad had never given up hope that Danny would "come to his senses" and beg for Camilla's forgiveness. This stunt was just a last try to push them back together. Even in death, the old man wouldn't relent.

"Dad never told me how sick he was," he argued. If he had known, he would definitely have made more of an attempt to come home sooner, to rebuild those bridges he'd burned with such enthusiasm on his way out of town. At least the ones with his father… He should have made time to visit when he'd processed out of the Army, rather than going straight to Boston and jumping right into his job there as an attending in the emergency department. But his dad had kept his health struggles tightly under wraps and hadn't let a sliver of information come out that would have clued Danny in to the cancer poisoning his father's organs. He'd only found out two days ago, when his dad's oncologist had called to tell him that his father was at peace, his suffering now over, and it was time to come home to lay his body to rest.

He'd had two days to come to terms with his father's death and it still felt unreal. He kept expecting his dad to walk through the door, gruffly saying, "What kinda son makes a man fake his own death just to get him to visit?" Man, he wished it had all been a joke. What he wouldn't give to hug his old man just one more time. He squeezed his hand into a fist and resisted the urge to slam it into the wood paneling lining the office. He hadn't gotten to say goodbye.

"Well, if you'd visited him anytime in the last two years, you would have seen it for yourself." Even when she called him to task for his transgressions, Camilla's voice was low and even. Her unique ability to maintain this soft and steady tone had never failed to impress him. The coldness in her eyes told him she hadn't forgiven him—not for the words he'd hurled at her that still haunted his soul, or his absence since that fateful day. Some wounds not even time could heal.

Not that he blamed her. He knew he'd given her something she'd never had—love and acceptance—and then snatched it away from her in that hospital room. In one cruel moment, he'd stolen years of hard-won progress from her. Her background had taught her that "love" meant someone wanted something from you. It had taken a lot of time and coaxing for her to open up to him and he'd stomped all over her trust, even kicking dirt into the wounds. What he had done to her was unforgivable.

"Camilla, I…" He trailed off. Every word he thought of saying sat heavy on his tongue, refusing to roll off into another lie. He'd lied to her enough. If nothing else, she deserved his honesty today. "Okay, you're right. I was a lousy son."

He looked away, not wanting to see the judgment in her eyes. As a sixteen-year-old boy, he'd fallen head over heels with the beautiful girl from the group home whose mismatched clothes never fit properly, but who had so much sass that she kept him on his toes. He'd promised her the world. It was a resolution he'd been unable to keep, unfortunately.

After he'd broken so many promises to her, he couldn't bear to look her in the eye. Not coming home had made it easier to avoid Camilla. Staying away allowed him to minimize the drama he assumed he'd find if he set foot in Greenbriar. He'd created a cocoon around himself that kept everyone at a distance, even the people he saw on a daily basis. But in protecting himself, he'd missed his father's final days.

One thing he couldn't avoid, though, was the guilt. He hadn't been there when his father needed him. He was a doctor, after all, so he should have heard in his father's voice how sick he was. There should have been something audible that told him the man was dying, but even in their final conversation last week, his dad had sounded the same to him as he always had. He'd asked for Danny to come home like always, lectured him again about the choices he'd made that had carried Danny away from Greenbriar and Camilla, but he'd ended the call with the same brusque "Love you, son." Like every phone call they'd had in the last eight years.

Why hadn't his dad told him he was sick?

Why hadn't his dad given him the opportunity to truly make things right between them?

Why was Camilla even more beautiful than the day he'd broken off their three-year engagement?

Inhaling deeply, he shoved that thought back into the box of memories he kept locked away in the dark recesses of his mind. He couldn't relive the day he'd broken their hearts or revise the inner turmoil that he still struggled to shake.

He shifted his weight and let the pain of seeing her

again wash over him. Eight years and it still hurt. Today he savored that pain, though, because the angry ache pulled him into the present and gave him something to focus on. It was a welcome distraction from the crushing emotions threatening to pull him under.

"I think asking for a couple weeks to settle your current affairs out of town is a reasonable request, and I see no reason why that can't be accommodated." The attorney pulled a blank notepad out and grabbed a pen. "How does beginning on February first sound to the two of you? Then the six-month time frame can end on August first."

Camilla murmured her assent.

Danny nodded. He could only hope that the administration at the hospital where he worked would be willing to let him out of his contract this soon. Maybe when he explained the circumstances, they'd be understanding. He'd only been a civilian for three months and already he was going to have to ask for concessions from an administration who eyed him warily at best.

Danny blew out a breath. It wasn't like he had many options. His dad had backed him into a corner, and after all the pain he'd caused in the past, Danny couldn't take the clinic from Camilla now. He was sure his father had banked on the fact that he'd realize she was the one who'd be hurt if the clinic had to close and that there'd be enough lingering love, or guilt, left inside him to keep him from rejecting the terms of the will and forcing the sale of the clinic.

The attorney jotted down some notes on the yellow paper. "I'll get this formalized for you both to sign. There are also a few signatures I'll need for the transfer of property from each of you."

Before any of them said another word, the door opened and slammed hard into the wall. Danny jumped at the sudden noise, heart racing. He had to force himself to breathe when his brain clued him in that there was no immediate danger and he waited for the adrenaline spike to ease. Even after being stateside for well over a year now, sudden noises still threw him back to his time in the war zone and the fear he'd felt as bullets whizzed past his ear.

The young woman who had burst into the office spoke in a rush, the words tumbling past her lips with barely a pause for breath. "Dr. Devereaux, Caden's having a lot of trouble breathing. I didn't know if it was safe to drive him all the way out to the emergency room, and they said it would be forty-five minutes before the ambulance could get out here because there's a big accident up on the highway."

In her arms she carried a small boy, maybe four years old, who was wheezing loud enough that Danny could hear the gasps from across the room. His mind sought to diagnose, beginning with the thought of asthma.

Before he could put voice to that, though, Camilla was already ushering them back out the door. "Let's get him over to the office and get him a breathing treatment. Have you given him his inhaler today?"

Their voices faded as they walked away.

With a quick glance at the attorney, Danny followed them out of the office. His gaze moved over the downtown area as he crossed from the attorney's office. The sleepy Southern town was cold this time of year. Dreary and dull, with the only action being the old men driving around the square in their pickups. When it was warm, they'd take up residence on the stone wall in front of the courthouse with their chewing tobacco and empty bottles to spit in. There was no coffee shop on the corner to get a caffeine jolt, just a single diner where the old women of the town occupied half the booths and gossiped about the old men.

If it weren't for the movement of the trucks, someone might think the town had been abandoned years ago. None of the vehicles within sight were current models and several looked to be as old as the buildings surrounding the square, including Danny's father's medical practice.

Stepping through those clinic doors was like stepping back into his childhood, though, and took his thoughts from the town that never changed to the grief of a son now orphaned. The hideous faded floral wallpaper his mother had picked out when he was a child still graced the walls but was now faded, and memories of her excitement at finding what she'd considered the perfect pattern fluttered through his mind. Other than the shiny new computer sitting at the reception desk, everything was exactly as he remembered.

A large picture of his parents hung on the back wall. Their thirtieth anniversary, he recalled. They'd never made it to thirty-one. His mom had passed away three months later. His brother, too.

He still took the long way into Greenbriar to avoid driving that stretch of road. And now his dad was gone, too. He swallowed hard, trying to shake the feeling of being at home for the first time in so long. To shake away the guilt that had settled back on his shoulders when he'd passed the city limits sign.

The only way to get through this was to focus on all the things he'd hated about Greenbriar. He couldn't afford to get sucked into the nostalgia and any comfort he might find here. While he needed to call somewhat of a truce with Camilla, he also had to make sure that she knew reconciliation wasn't an option—not that he was too worried about that last. The ice daggers she'd been shooting from her eyes ever since he'd arrived had showed no sign of thawing.

But he had to remove any temptation.

It was going to be a balancing act, for sure. He'd have to be nice enough to maintain the peace, but enough of a jerk that she didn't soften toward him. He took a deep breath and fortified his resolve. He'd faced down insurgents with semiautomatic weapons; a petite doctor with skin as soft as velvet shouldn't be too hard.

Stepping into the hallway, he looked into the first exam room and quickly moved past it to the second. There he found Camilla with the young mother and child. Camilla was setting up a nebulizer.

"Are you giving him albuterol?" he asked. The standard medication used to treat an asthma attack, albuterol was often given via a nebulizer like the one Camilla had in her hands. It would have been his first step, too, if the kid's lungs sounded as bad as his breathing indicated.

She glanced up at him briefly before opening a small vial of medication and pouring it into a chamber on the tubing. She slipped the mask over the child's face and turned the machine on before giving him an answer. "You know that I am."

"Steroids, too?"

Camilla nodded. "That's the plan."

"I'd grab them for you, but I don't have access to the medication cabinet."

"It's fine," Camilla muttered to him. She laid a hand on the mother's arm. "I'm going to step out and talk to Dr. Owens in the hallway."

"Dr. Owens?" The young woman looked confused. "But I thought…"

"I'm his son Danny," he said, hoping to clarify things for her. She looked vaguely familiar, like most of the people in this town, but he couldn't seem to come up with her name.

"I'll be back in just a moment to check on Caden." Camilla smiled softly at the worried mother and then turned to him, and that softness disappeared into a harsh frown. "I'm going to fetch those steroids and get them into him. If you would…" She waved a hand toward his father's office across the hall.

He stepped through the open door. Another intense wave of grief rushed over him when he stood in front of the antique walnut desk his father had kept polished to a shine. He ran a finger across the dark, gleaming surface.

Why didn't you give me the chance to say goodbye to you, old man? Did you hate me that much?

"What are you doing here, Danny? I am perfectly capable of taking care of a child with asthma. I don't require the assistance of a big-city trauma surgeon." Camilla crossed her arms over her chest and his gaze flicked down to the hint of cleavage her blouse revealed. Immediately adjusting her clothing, she hissed out, "Keep your eyes on my face and your thoughts to a PG rating, please."

"Maybe I just wanted to check out my inheritance," he snapped, trying to regain the high ground with her. He knew he couldn't afford to let his guard down, but even so, the baldness of those words sat hard on his heart. Maybe it was the heartbreak he glimpsed in her eyes before she shut down and the emotionless facade of their teen years returned to her gaze. But it was too late by that point to retract the words; the harm had been done. "That came out badly."

He was the one who had hurt her. She had done nothing but love him and she certainly had the right to be suspicious of his motives now. He'd given her plenty of reason. He'd broken her heart because he knew he wasn't good enough for her. He'd been of no use to anyone, even himself. So, why was he acting so defensively toward her?

Guilt, maybe? His mom had always said, *A guilty conscious will stalk you for the rest of your life*. If this wasn't proof of that…

Tilting her head, Camilla scrutinized him. He tried not to let her see what he was feeling, but her time in foster care had made her an expert at decoding faces. She'd always been able to read him like a book, while he'd struggled to name a single emotion from her. She'd kept her feelings close to the chest, burying things so deep he wasn't sure she even processed them.

When they'd first started dating, he'd tried to get her to open up to him about her past, to discover details about her childhood, but she had shut that line of questioning down fast. Even when they'd been together long enough for her to trust him, there were things she still refused to share, topics that he couldn't touch without her walking away.

Camilla had a policy that the past was the past and it had no place in her present or future. Knowing that, his last words to her eight years ago had been cold, cruel, and designed to cut straight to her core—the only way he knew how to protect her from himself.

He still hated himself for using that knowledge to his advantage.

In doing so, he had put himself in the position of being her past, and despite being forced together for the foreseeable future, there had never been more distance between them.

CHAPTER TWO

"I HAVE A PATIENT. I don't have time for—" she motioned between them "—whatever you are trying to do here."

Danny stared at her, his gaze searching. "We need to bury the past if we are going to get through this ridiculous condition my father has put on us. You think you can do that? Or should we just tell that lawyer to prepare the clinic for sale?"

Camilla pressed a fist to her mouth. She'd poured her heart and soul into this clinic, yes, but Danny had grown up here. Yet he could talk so callously of disposing of it, like it meant absolutely nothing. Sadness settled over her, burdening her already grieving heart.

Did the man really not have any emotional connection to this town or this clinic?

Or me?

"No, I do not want to prepare the clinic for sale!" Her hands clenched at her sides and she fought down the urge to punch something. *Or someone.* She took a deep, calming breath before she continued her argument. "You may have another job to go back to, but this is it for me. I painted those exam rooms myself. I scrubbed down the wallpaper in the lobby when your father refused to let me replace it. I will not give this place up without a fight."

He lifted one shoulder in a casual shrug. "My mom

picked out that wallpaper. Dad was probably being sentimental about it."

"Well, then you'll forgive me for being sentimental about wanting to hang on to *my* clinic." Being in Danny's presence made her feel exposed in a way she hadn't felt in years. She'd thought she had prepared herself for the emotional uproar that seeing him again would evoke, but she wasn't ready. She had practiced things to say. She'd memorized a few witty lines that she might use as comebacks to his verbal attacks, but now that they were face-to-face, those rehearsed words refused to come. The words she did manage to eke out revealed a weakness that she hated letting him hear.

Oh, and he definitely heard the quiver in her voice, because his gaze softened and his hand twitched in her direction like he might reach for her. But he stayed himself before allowing that tiny movement to become a full-on action.

As a kid, she'd learned to have a thick skin. It was a talent she'd developed through years of foster care, along with the ability to suss out the tiniest of reactions in a person's expression—like that hint of indication he wanted to comfort her. She couldn't let her guard down around him again, though. With a deep, stabilizing breath, Camilla locked down her emotions. No one got past her defenses if she didn't allow them to, and that mantra had kept her safe. She'd learned early the importance of protecting herself, and that lesson had been reinforced incredibly painfully by the man standing in front of her.

"It's that important to you?" he asked. He ran his fingers through his short hair. With a huff of disbelief, he continued, "You could move anywhere. Start your own practice in the city where people wouldn't try to pay you with chickens."

She rolled her eyes at his snarky comment. "Greenbriar is a small town, but it's not so backwoods that anyone has ever attempted to pay me in livestock. You know I made promises to the people of this town, Danny. They paid to put me through medical school. They upheld their end of the bargain and I'm still trying to uphold mine."

She'd honored the commitment to come back to Greenbriar and practice after the town had collected money to provide a scholarship fund for her. The small town had embraced her like a long-lost daughter and given her a much-wanted sense of family and community. She would not turn her back on that, even if that meant she started her own practice from scratch in her living room.

Danny gave an almost imperceptible shake of his head. His lips—lips she'd once lived to kiss—narrowed to nothing more than a slash. "I doubt they intended you to devote your entire life to this one-horse town."

For Danny, Greenbriar had been a prison that stifled his adventurous soul. He'd loved every minute of getting out of town for college and medical school. Camilla, however, had longed to put down roots. His upbringing had given him a stability that allowed him to take risks, while hers had made her desperate for the security of the familiar.

"We have three horses now, I'll have you know." She tried to lighten the conversation since there was still a patient in the building who didn't need to be subjected to the verbal brawl that would inevitably result from the two of them hashing out their differences. "And I have a patient to check on."

As she stepped past Danny, he reached a hand out and let his fingers brush against her wrist. "We have to talk about this."

The skin he'd touched burned like fire had kissed it.

She couldn't stop the gasp that escaped her at the contact. Flexing the hand, she tried to shake away the red-hot desire that ghost of a touch had spurred. Her body still responded to Danny, desperately wanting his touch, even if her heart raced in fear of being shattered again and her brain argued that logically, getting involved with a man who had already left her once was an incredibly bad idea.

She set her jaw and drew on the memory of their last meeting to give her strength. The reminder of how Danny had tossed her out of his hospital room after pulling the engagement ring off her finger was enough to secure her resolve. Even years later, the words he'd spit out still haunted her, creating doubt in every relationship she'd had since. Oh, she'd tried to put them out of her mind and move on, but his dismissal had been so harsh and definite that she'd given up dating altogether for years. If a man who'd claimed she was the love of his life could toss her aside like a wet newspaper, how could she ever trust a stranger?

Camilla straightened her spine. "I have a patient," she reiterated, forcing herself to move away from him and take the few steps across the hall. She tapped lightly on the exam room door and let herself back in.

Hoping that the fragile state of her emotions wasn't showing, she washed her hands and tried to pull herself together. Her patient needed—deserved—a focused doctor and she was going to give him one. Danny Owens had taken a lot from her, but she would not relinquish her professionalism.

"How's it coming along?"

Caden's mother shook the little medication chamber and very little remained. "Looks like it's about done. His breathing doesn't sound quite as labored. At least not to me, but it could be wishful thinking."

Flipping the nebulizer off, Camilla eased the mask from Caden's face. His lips were still as blue as they were before starting the albuterol treatment.

Camilla clipped the pulse-ox monitor to his tiny index finger and put her stethoscope to use as she listened to the child's chest. With her eyes closed, she focused on the sound of his breathing. Even with the albuterol treatment, he wasn't moving air as much as she would like. The good news was that Caden's chest wasn't completely silent. He was still moving some air, just not enough. His oxygen levels had risen only a single point.

"How are you feeling, Caden?" she asked.

The preschooler's nostrils flared in time with his still-labored breathing, his abdominal muscles rising with each struggling breath. "Hurts," he said on a gasp, waving one hand at his chest.

"It hurts to breathe?" Camilla asked.

Caden only nodded.

"The steroids and albuterol should have started doing something," Danny said from the doorway.

"Thank you, Dr. Obvious," she muttered under her breath. It was as if Danny had forgotten that she also had a medical degree. She bit back the harsher retort tempting her tongue.

"Let's do another albuterol treatment."

Caden's mom cuddled the boy close and ran her hand up and down his back. "What if that doesn't work?"

Camilla smiled at the gentle gesture of comfort. "We are going to think positive. Caden is going to need to go to the hospital tonight, though. I think it's best we keep him monitored and on oxygen. Let's have him see a respiratory specialist, too."

The other woman nodded slowly.

Danny brought in the second dose of albuterol, handing it over without a word. He must have found his dad's keys to the medication locker, Camilla thought. She took the little vial from his outstretched hands carefully to avoid another brush of her skin against his.

She extended a hint of an olive branch. "Do you want to listen to his lungs and see if you agree with my plan, Dr. Owens?"

Danny took the stethoscope from around Camilla's neck gently. The sharing of the equipment held an intimacy Camilla had not expected. She readied the nebulizer for the second dose of medication and tried to still her shaking hands.

"Okay, Caden, one more round of this yucky medicine. And hopefully then you can breathe without hurting." She reaffixed the mask to his face and smoothed a hand over Caden's baby-soft hair. The urge for a child of her own rose up, as it did each time she had a very young patient.

Someday, she promised herself.

The second round of medication perked Caden up some. "Better," he said, still struggling to speak in words. Phrases seemed beyond him.

Danny leaned over him, listening again to his lungs. Camilla wanted to snatch her stethoscope back so that she could hear for herself what progress the medication had given him, but forced herself to wait. Professionals didn't snatch equipment away from their colleagues.

Finally, Danny handed the stethoscope over. "There's still significant intercostal and substernal retractions. Pan-expiratory and inspiratory wheezes strongly present, although diminished some from the level prior to albuterol administration." His tone was clipped, clinical. "I agree with your assessment that hospital monitoring tonight would be prudent."

"Thank you, Dr. Owens," she said as she took the

proffered equipment. She put the stethoscope to her ears and listened to Caden's heart and lungs. Given that he'd had two subsequent doses of albuterol, his elevated heart rate was expected. His lungs did sound quite a bit better than when he'd first arrived in her office, but there was far too much distress remaining for her to feel comfortable sending him home.

Draping the stethoscope around her neck, she told the boy's mother, "Definitely think it is the best thing for Caden if we send him over to Children's to be monitored overnight. I know it's a bit of a drive, but I don't think going home is the best course of action. He's going to need albuterol treatments all through the night. And I'd really like them to keep an eye on his O2 saturation, as well. I'm going to send all his information over to the hospital. You head on over there and they should, hopefully, have a room ready for you by the time you get there." She smiled at Caden. "And I'll come by first thing in the morning to check on you."

"Thanks, Dr. Devereaux. We'll see you in the morning." The mother helped the boy into his coat before they left the exam room with a final wave.

Camilla typed in all her care instructions so that they'd be available to the hospital staff when Caden arrived. Since she'd never sent Caden to Children's and had no record of hospital stays in his chart, she sent over all the pertinent details, as well, choosing to err on the side of caution and provide more information on the off chance it was needed.

With that done, Camilla walked out to the lobby and took down the sign she'd taped to the door stating she'd be at the attorney's office that afternoon. She replaced it with the regular after-hours sign with her phone number in bold print.

"You were really good with him," Danny said from behind her, causing her to jump as he startled her. He'd been so quiet that she'd thought he might have left.

"What did you expect? That I'd be cold and unfeeling? I'm afraid I reserve that demeanor for only very special people." She filled her voice with as much ice as she could muster and could barely contain her delight when the barb struck home.

"Ouch." Danny winced. "No, I just meant that I hadn't thought you would be that good with children."

"Keep digging, Danny, just keep digging."

Why wouldn't she be good with children? Just because she hadn't had a proper family didn't mean she hadn't had more than her share of experience taking care of children. A lot of the foster homes she'd been in had only wanted a teen girl to help look after the younger children. She'd changed as many diapers as any parent had. Anyway, he knew she wanted a family someday. Kids had always been part of her plan, a plan that once upon a time he had been on board with.

She looked at him, trying to gauge his frame of mind and the meaning behind his words in case she was simply reading too much into his words because of their past. Although his countenance had matured since their last meeting, there was still so much that was familiar to her in the lines of his face. His thick dark hair was clipped shorter now than he'd kept it in his premilitary days. There were new shadows darkening his eyes, but the curve of his lips remained the same. He seemed taller now than before, but she thought that might be attributed to the stiffness in his posture. The more she looked at him, though, the stronger the vibe between them got and she had to look away first.

"It was actually a compliment," he grumbled.

She stomped past him, tossing her reply over her shoulder. "It didn't sound like one."

She felt, rather than heard, him follow her back into the exam room. Ripping the paper covering off the exam table, she crumpled it into a ball and shoved it roughly in the trash. He had only been back in her life for one measly hour and already she was responding to his presence in more ways than she was comfortable with.

"Wish that was my head?" he asked quietly, tossing the used mask and tubing away.

"Maybe," she allowed, her lips turning up in the barest hint of a smile. She grabbed the disinfectant and started rubbing down the exam table.

Danny let out a quick bark of laughter. "No maybes about it. Don't think I don't remember that you clean when you're angry. You can be honest about the fact that you hate my guts and would rather kick me than look at me. It will make the next six months go a lot smoother if we can be honest with each other."

She paused her movements and looked up at him. "You want honesty?"

"Yes."

Raising an eyebrow at him, she sought confirmation. "Are you sure you can handle it?"

He stepped out of the room and she almost laughed at the absurdity of him asking for honesty and leaving before she could say anything else. She scrubbed at the table harder than necessary, trying to ease some of her frustration.

"I do want honesty from you. Even if it hurts. And I hope that I can be honest with you, as well." Danny stood in the door, broom and dustpan in hand. "I figure we can start this partnership by giving this office a good cleaning, and if you want, something of a remodel. It's stuck in decades past."

"It may be a little dated, but it is clean." She bristled at the implication that she'd allow the clinic to be less than hygienic. How low was his opinion of her if he could think she'd run a dirty medical practice?

"That's not what I meant." Danny held a hand up to stifle her objections. "Can we start again, please? I promise you, every word out of my mouth is not meant to be a criticism."

After examining the expression on his face and seeing only honesty, she nodded slowly.

"Okay, good. Here's the thing. I have a life away from Greenbriar. I never intended to move back here, but now I don't exactly have a choice."

"Not my problem."

He closed his eyes and she saw the frustration he was trying to squash. His next words were slow and followed the grinding of his teeth. "I'm trying here, Camilla. I think if we could maybe agree to some ground rules, it would help."

"Okay," she agreed cautiously. She was no longer confident in her ability to read him correctly. Instinctively, she wanted to believe him, but her instincts had failed her with Danny in the past.

"Earlier I was a little harsh with you about my father giving you so much. I had no right to complain about what he chose to do with his estate, and you were right that you've been the one here day in and day out. You cared for him when he refused to even tell me he was sick. You've put the work into this town and this practice. You've earned it in a way that I never wanted to do."

She nodded slowly. His expressions said he was genuine, but she wasn't sure where he was heading with this conversation.

"Okay, so I have to be here until August. We have to make this work for six months, right? Well, how would you like to buy out my half of this practice then?"

The offer to sell her his half of the clinic at the end of the six-month period had slipped out without a lot of thought. He pressed his lips together tightly, almost needing to drag the words back and consider that proposition for a moment. His parents had poured years of time and attention into building this medical practice with his dad as the town doctor and his mom working at his side as his nurse. His dad had been so proud of his work in the community and had always hoped Danny or Robby would come home to take over when he retired. Unfortunately, neither of his parents made it to retirement, so that part of the dream would never come true. Robby hadn't even made it out of college. Danny swallowed hard, shoving down the guilt and the grief.

If he sold out, it would be like trashing his parents' dream. So he had to ask himself, did he actually *want* to sell his father's practice?

Camilla pressed forward, leaving him no time to examine his initial idea of stepping away from the clinic. "And then what? You'll sell the lake house and leave town forever?"

"Hadn't thought that far ahead," he said with a shrug.

Maybe he'd keep the lake house as a vacation home. The idea of having a secluded spot where he could leave the city and reconnect with nature certainly appealed. Being on the lake was one of the few things he had missed about Greenbriar. He could go to the ocean, yes, but he'd always been more of a tranquil lake guy. And that cottage was the last physical connection he had with his parents—letting go of it wouldn't be an easy thing to do.

"Well, this is the first time you've been back to Greenbriar since you left, so it might be best if you just made a clean break." Camilla wrapped her arms around herself, tightly. Self-armoring for whatever she planned to say next? "We were never enough for you, were we?"

A fresh wave of guilt rushed up over him. Despite knowing his reasons for leaving her were solid, Danny knew she'd felt abandoned. He'd known she would feel that way before he ended their engagement, and while he stood by the decision being the right one, seeing just how deeply he'd wounded her in the process hurt. The pain he'd caused them both still left a raw, gaping wound on his soul.

Some nights he lay in the dark, staring up at the ceiling, and wondered what would have happened if he'd let her in back then. If he'd told her just how badly he was hurting, how her unwavering positivity felt like she was pushing him beneath the surface to drown in his own pain, would she have backed off a bit and stood by his side through it all? Camilla was one of the strongest women he'd ever met, but would she have been strong enough to weather all the nightmares he'd suffered? The flashbacks and the panic attacks that came with the terrible memories of what he'd done? Could she have looked him in the eye again, if he'd told her the complete truth?

Time had given him the distance and maturity to see that Camilla's gung ho peppiness had been a cover for her own fear and grief. Trying to explain everything to her now would only seem like excuses, though, wouldn't it? Was there anything he could say that would ease the pain she clearly still felt? Would she even believe him? He struggled to find the right words. "Camilla…"

"It's okay." The weak smile she flashed his direction said otherwise. "I don't want to bring up old grievances."

Grievances? That was how she was going to refer to their past?

"In the spirit of honesty, I think we need to." He swept the last of the dust from the floor into the dustpan and propped the broom against the wall. Turning to face her, he offered the closest thing to an apology that he could bring himself to utter. "I hurt you and there are still raw edges there that we need to smooth over so that we can both move on."

She snorted, a derisive little sound. "That's a pretty massive understatement. You more than hurt me. You ripped my heart out when you snatched my engagement ring off my finger. And when you told me that you'd never really loved me? That destroyed me."

"That wasn't…"

"I believe your exact words were, 'I don't know why you ever thought your love would be enough for me. You were simply the best option available.' So, go ahead. Explain to me what else you could have meant."

"I didn't mean to…" Sucking in a deep breath, he tried to think of a way to justify the choices he'd made that day in a way she'd understand. He knew Camilla well enough to know that telling her he'd broken up with her for her own good wouldn't go well. He finally settled on a somewhat sanitized version of the truth. "When I ended our engagement, I was miserable, and I wanted everyone around me to share in that misery. You were so…in my face with positivity, my own personal cheerleader, when what I needed was time to mourn the loss of—" he swallowed hard "—my mother, my brother, and in a way my father. All I really wanted was to regain control of my life. And I just couldn't, so I took it out on the people around me. You bore the brunt of my pain."

It was mostly true, anyway.

"Are you saying that you think I played a part in you dumping me?" Her eyes narrowed at him. "I certainly didn't ask to be thrown out of your life without any warning."

Danny sighed. He'd said more than he meant to and once again caused Camilla pain. This was exactly why he kept his distance from her. Everything he did, everything he said, somehow jabbed that knife right back into her heart. This right here was why he pushed people away.

If he didn't let anyone close, he couldn't hurt them.

"I know you had the best of intentions, and I know I should have just talked to you about how I was feeling. I'm the world's biggest jerk. At the time, though, that felt impossible, and I needed breathing room. But I was in the wrong headspace to have a rational conversation with you about you being so positive. I didn't need a cheerleader. I needed a shoulder to cry on. And I could only see one path through—being alone and focusing all my attention on myself. It was selfish, but it's the truth."

Every time he opened his mouth, more details than he wanted to share poured out. Why couldn't he stop this flood of soul-baring confessions?

"So you up and joined the Army." Camilla skipped over the emotional baggage to focus on his then hoped-for outcome. "Was it just to get away from me?"

"Not entirely. It was to get away from everything."

By joining the Army, he'd set off a bomb in his personal life. His dad had been against it from first mention, and Camilla's attitude toward him now was a direct repercussion of his actions back then. While he had regrets about how he'd handled it, he still stood firm that the decision was the right one. He'd ended things with her in a way that was definitive. If he'd let it drag on, or given her any hope of reconciliation, he'd have only tortured them both and it would have ended up hurting her more in the long run. And clearly, he'd hurt her plenty.

Even now, some days his mood was so dark that several members of staff at his current hospital had worried about his emotional well-being, and had recommended him to administration for counseling. Being forced to confront his own behavior like that had been an experience he could have done without, but it served as proof that he wasn't fit to be in a serious relationship. Reinforced his decision to end their engagement, too.

Camilla gently brought him back to the present conversation. "Your dad was proud of you, even if he didn't agree with your decision to enlist."

"Could've fooled me." A lump rose up in his throat. He pinched the bridge of his nose and tried hard to swallow.

"And now you are a trauma surgeon in Boston?"

The coaxing tone in her voice he remembered well. She'd always been able to pull him away when a conversation grew too intense. Even after everything he'd done to her, she was still looking out for him. Subconsciously, maybe, but she was. Camilla's kind heart and the way she looked after everyone around her was one of the things he had loved about her.

Nodding, he responded to her question. "Emergency attending. I hate the cold, but the pay is good."

The frigid air did a number on his temper, too. The bitterly cold days in the depth of winter were the days his mood was darkest. But he endured the miserable weather because it served a dual purpose for him—first as a penance for the pain he'd caused Camilla and second as a regular reminder that he was far too damaged to maintain a healthy relationship.

"I don't think I could live that far north. I'm a Southern girl at heart."

"I remember when you first moved here. Everyone teased you about your accent. I'm not sure how you moved further south and had a more Southern accent than any of the folks around here."

Camilla rolled her eyes at him. "I didn't sound more Southern, I sounded more country. There's a difference."

"Oh, yeah. And your accent still gets thicker when you're upset, you know." He smiled at the same old argument she'd been presenting for years. The familiar words comforted him, reminding him that they'd had a lot of good times, too. Remembered affection softened his voice on his reply. Her accent had slipped at other times of heightened emotion, too. He'd loved how thick her drawl would get when they'd slipped away during high school and summers during college to spend the evening stargazing out at the lake house.

"Well, you would know. You're the only one who insists on upsetting me every time we end up in the same room."

Danny puffed out a breath slowly. The sentimental moment had passed, too fleeting to hold on to, even if they'd been inclined to do so. For the briefest breath there, he'd allowed himself to consider the what-if, but too much hurt made it impossible. "I'm really not trying to upset you, Camilla. I just want to get on some sort of level ground so that we can move forward here."

"That will be hard when your very existence upsets me," she snapped.

He flinched at the harsh words.

Camilla covered her mouth and her eyes filled with instant regret. "I didn't mean that."

Even if she hadn't meant to snap at him just then, Camilla was not going to make any of this easy on him. That much was clear.

"I think this place is cleaned up enough and we should call it a night before either of us says something else we might regret." He grabbed the broom and took it to the utility closet at the end of the hall. He placed it inside and closed the door. Leaning his head against the cool wood, he tried to soothe the ache her words caused.

"Danny, I'm sorry. I owe you an apology for what I said. Despite all the pain and anger between us, I hope you know that I would never want anything bad to happen to you."

"No?" Being in Greenbriar was going to strip him bare and pull out all those emotions he'd been hiding for so long. "Because it sure sounded heartfelt."

Their eyes met and he wondered what was going through her mind. What was she thinking in that moment? He wished he was better at reading her now. He thought he caught hints of desire, frustration, and maybe even a little fear, but nothing concrete.

The desire was surprising, but he wasn't certain he'd read her right. It was nothing he was confident enough to take a risk on anyway. Things were awkward enough between them without him making an unwanted advance. And given that he had no intentions of starting anything long-term, it was best if he kept his distance. Keeping her at arm's length reduced the chances that he'd hurt her again.

"I'm not sure what came over me. Rest assured, it will not happen again." Camilla smoothed her clothing and her hair.

The alarm on her phone went off.

"Reminder that you have a hot date?"

"Something like that," she murmured.

"Camilla—"

"It will not happen again." He saw the shutters slam down in her eyes. "I can trust you to lock up for the night, right? I have somewhere I need to be. Will you let the attorney know that I'll stop by and sign whatever he needs signed tomorrow?"

At his nod, she spun on her heels and strode down the hall and out of his sight. He heard the ding of the bell as she went out the front door.

He scrubbed a hand over his face. This was going to be the longest six months of his life.

CHAPTER THREE

WHEN CAMILLA WALKED up to the clinic the next morning after checking on Caden at the hospital, she was surprised to see Danny reclining outside against the worn red brick. With the collar of his coat turned up against the crisp morning air and one foot crossed loosely over the other, he looked deceptively casual, but as someone who'd spent hours admiring his body, she saw through that facade.

His posture stiffened when he caught sight of her and he rose to his full height. The additional inches he had over her and the strength in his broad shoulders had made her feel protected. Butterflies fluttered around in her stomach at the memory of his touch.

"Good morning," she said as she took the key out of her pocket. A hint of pride washed over her when her shaking hands still managed to get the key into the lock on the first try. Letting him see how he still affected her was not on her to-do list for the day, especially after the bomb he'd dropped on her yesterday.

She had spent most of the previous evening trying to look at things from his point of view. She'd been trying to keep his spirits up back then and not let him see her own grief, but had it come across as way too much? In all honesty, it had been one of the hardest times of her life.

She'd been terrified that she was going to break down when he'd needed her to be strong. But in hindsight, she had to acknowledge that her over-the-top positivity could well have been suffocating.

"Why didn't you let yourself in?"

"Because I don't actually have keys." Resignation lined his voice and mingled with exhaustion.

"Right."

He'd so thoroughly distracted her that the thought of keys hadn't even crossed her mind. Between their argument and her rush to get to the tutoring session she had every Wednesday evening, she hadn't considered that Danny could need his own set.

Warm air pushed past as she opened the door and they stepped inside out of the winter wind. January and February would be the worst of the wintry weather in Greenbriar. They didn't get a lot of snow this far south, but frigid air and icy breezes were no strangers to the town.

Camilla unwound her scarf and hung it on the coatrack in the corner of the lobby. "Your dad's keys are probably at the lake house. Did you not see them?"

Danny shook his head and a grimace crossed his face. "I wasn't given the keys to the lake house, either."

She looked him up and down, closely scrutinizing his appearance. An uncharacteristic scruff darkened his normally clean-shaven jaw. Danny still wore the same dark suit he'd had on yesterday, minus the tie, and the rumpled fabric raised a lot more questions in her mind. Had he slept in his clothes last night? Or were the wrinkles from being left on some random woman's floor overnight?

Camilla tried her best to look nonchalant, but her heart ached at the thought of him in someone else's bed. She couldn't stop the question, needing to know the answer. "Where did you stay last night?"

"Why? You worried I found a pretty little shoulder to cry on?" The defensive tone contradicted the slight affront he tried to hide.

Interesting. So he was insulted that she thought he'd stayed with another woman. She wasn't sure if she should address it and confront the issue outright, or just let it go with the resolution to keep her distance from Danny Owens. It wasn't any of her business if he'd found someone to spend the night with. What did she care who he chose to spend his time with?

Yet she couldn't help but feel relieved that he'd been alone last night. They hadn't been a couple in years, so whose bed he slept in shouldn't matter to her, but it so did and that spark of jealousy frustrated her. She tried to pivot from accusation to concern, desperate to cover up her interest in his personal life. "I was actually worried you might have slept in your car, if you must know."

Before she could say anything else, Danny changed the subject. "So, before we got, uh…derailed last night, I'd brought up selling you my share of this clinic."

He sat on the edge of the front desk, managing to look both perfectly at home and completely out of place at the same time. Reconciling the man in front of her with the man she'd loved and lost might take some time. There was a different energy about him, a somberness to his gaze that held secrets. Secrets that she shouldn't want to expose to the light of day, and she shouldn't want to soothe those fine worry lines around his eyes, either.

Stop it, Camilla. He's off-limits.

"Were you serious?"

Knowing she shouldn't look a gift horse in the mouth, she still couldn't stop the question that slipped past her lips. If he sold her his half of the clinic, it would be hers exclusively. She could put her name in large letters on that front window and make all the decisions. It would check the box on one of her biggest dreams—to own her own medical practice.

"Yes, I'm one hundred percent serious about that. I admit last night I second-guessed it a bit, worried that I'd be dishonoring my father's memory or letting him down somehow. But you were right. This is your clinic, and other than my last name on the plaque, I have no claim here. You've put in the sweat equity and my father should have recognized that. We'll get the attorney to draw up the paperwork for you to buy me out when the time comes, if that's what you want, or we can sell it outright if you'd prefer."

"Just like that?" She searched his gaze, watching every micro-expression on his face. After his outburst at the will reading, something about Danny giving in this easily felt off. The Danny she'd known never backed down, so she'd geared up for battle on this, because she wasn't giving up her clinic without a fight. And having him step aside so reasonably just sanded the grit right off her.

Shrugging, he agreed, "Just like that. I figured we could spend some time fixing the place up—it will help it sell if you don't want to buy me out. We can alternate days working, or you can see the patients and I'll do the renovating. Minimize how much time we spend together whenever we can. I'd like to get out of this and back to my life with as little drama as possible."

And there was the angle she'd been looking for. She knew there had to be one.

"Get out of this…"

Of course, once again, Danny just wanted to run away from Greenbriar. Away from her… He didn't want to be tied down to this sleepy little community. That couldn't be plainer if he'd painted it on the water tower in hot pink spray paint like the love note he'd put there in their senior year of high school.

As a member of the town council, his father had been furious about the three-foot-high letters telling everyone in Greenbriar that Danny loved Camilla. As a seventeen-year-old girl, though, it had been the most romantic thing anyone had ever done for her.

It still was, if she was being honest.

Seeing him profess his love to the entire town like that had made things real for her. She'd naively thought Danny treasured her love like she'd treasured his; after all his painted words had proved it. Eagerly, she'd shown him that night how much his actions had meant to her. The paint proved more durable than their love, however, so while the now faded pink words still graced the side of the water tower, they no longer served as a romantic memento, but were a haunting reminder of heartbreak and love lost.

But words were just words, and they meant nothing if the person writing them wasn't sincere. Maybe he had been earnest in that moment, maybe he had loved her in some small way once upon a time, but his feelings had faded like the paint on the tower. She hadn't been able to give him what he needed.

No matter what she did, it never seemed enough. Her own parents had chosen drugs over her. She hadn't been able to keep a foster family. Or a fiancé… So many tears had been shed over people who'd probably never blinked an eye at never being near her again.

She looked away from Danny. Picking up the crispy brown fern behind the reception desk, she sighed. She must have forgotten to water the poor thing while trying to keep everyone in Greenbriar healthy and help Robert through his last days. She hugged it to her chest. Even plants refused to stick with her and chose to die instead.

She was never enough.

"Are you even listening to me?" Danny interrupted her thoughts as he stood up, came around the desk and invaded her personal space.

"Hmm." She jerked herself back to the present. There'd be time enough for self-pity when she was home alone with her dog. At least Fidget loved her unconditionally.

His brow wrinkled in concern. "Are you okay?"

Taking a step away from Danny, she answered his question. "Yes, I definitely want to buy you out. What are your terms?" Camilla blinked rapidly, trying to keep any tears from falling and ruining her mascara. She was stronger than this. She didn't cry over decade-old memories or dead plants.

Danny laid a hand on her shoulder, the weight comforting and confusing all at once. "Can I get you anything? Water? What do you want?"

She wanted to chastise him for wanting to run away again. She wanted to curse him for all the pain he'd caused her. She wanted to kiss him until he remembered how good they were together. Love him so deeply that he'd fall in love with her all over again, because the pain she still felt at his presence said she wasn't completely over him.

But life didn't work that way.

And she certainly wasn't telling him all that and exposing herself to further rejection. If she'd learned anything, it was that she couldn't trust Danny Owens with her heart.

"I just realized this plant is beyond help. I'm going to go dispose of it before our first patient arrives." She lifted the plant slightly to emphasize her words and hopefully draw his attention from her face long enough to pull herself together.

Danny's head tilted as he considered her answer, but he thankfully didn't call her on it. "You don't happen to know if my dad kept a spare key to the lake house anywhere here, do you? I'd really like to shower and change before the service."

Fumbling a little, she managed to get the key to the lake house off her key ring without upending the lifeless fern onto the carpet. Wordlessly, she handed it to him.

"Thanks. I'll see you at the funeral?"

Camilla nodded, not trusting herself to speak. Her emotions were getting the best of her in that moment. While she could control them if she stayed quiet, she wasn't sure she could say the same if she opened her mouth. Words might come out, or equally it could be sobs.

He strode out the door, the little bell chiming his departure gaily. And she sank down, her back against the wall, still cradling the lamented maidenhair.

"It's going to be a long six months," she said aloud. Looking up at the anniversary portrait of her late boss and his wife, she shook her head. "I don't know why you thought this was a good idea, Robert. Danny has made his position crystal clear, and no amount of wishing is going to change the course he's charted."

She drew in a deep breath. When she'd woken up that morning, she'd known she would have to face Danny again at the funeral, but he'd caught her unaware by showing up at the clinic before opening. That had thrown off her entire game plan for dealing with him. She'd expected to have the buffer of a crowd to soften the interactions between them.

She couldn't let him close enough to upend her foundation this time. The fact that she'd never seen their breakup coming had rocked her axis entirely. Usually a dying relationship showed some signs of withering first—unanswered calls, secrets, or lies, but theirs hadn't. At least, not anything visible to her. So when he'd ended things so swiftly, she'd been gobsmacked. Looking back now, she could see some of the cracks in their relationship; she could see how he had shut down and needed a different tactic from her, but the fact remained that he'd broken up with her without so much as a discussion. With how she'd prided herself on reading people, it had really shaken her confidence.

What was that old saying? Pride goeth before a fall?

Yeah. She'd certainly fallen. Danny's rejection had been a massive hit to her pride, but she wouldn't let him catch her off guard again. They'd get through Robert's funeral today and they'd meet to discuss a schedule for how to manage things at the clinic with minimal interaction. That was a discussion she was prepared for. After that, she saw no reason why they even had to be in the same room at the same time.

It was safer for her heart if she put some distance back between them.

The bell over the door chimed as her first patient of the day came through. She rose swiftly to greet them, tossing the dead plant into the trash can.

If only the memories of a lost love were so easily banished.

The funeral home had been bursting at the seams as everyone in Greenbriar came to pay their respects to his father—a cherished member of their community. With barely space to breathe, claustrophobia sent his heart racing and the dark edges of a panic attack were banging at his crumbling defenses long before the service was over. The only thing that had kept him from crossing over that fine line between okay and not was the soft hand Camilla had slipped into his when the pastor began to speak. He wasn't sure if she took his hand to comfort him or because she needed comfort herself, but he'd desperately needed that connection. Her touch kept him grounded until his father's casket was carried out to the waiting hearse. He'd followed closely behind and sucked in a deep breath as he stood next to the provided family car. The cold invaded his lungs and made his chest ache, but it staved off the emotional breakdown.

The processional made the slow trek from downtown Greenbriar out to the cemetery on the outskirts of town. Danny made the ride alone, having no other family to join him in the limousine. Camilla had declined to go with him, insisting on driving her own car. Only minimal road noise interrupted the quiet within the vehicle. Danny wasn't sure the silence was any better than the bustle of the crowded funeral home. It gave him far too much space to think before the long, black car drew to a stop near where his mother and brother had been buried and where his father was about to join them.

Icy air whistled through the trees and yet a crowd of black-clad people soon stood next to the open grave. Despite the bitter cold, the sun shone brilliantly across the headstones all around them. The day should have been damp and gray: it would have been more fitting for a day of mourning.

His father had arranged every detail. All Danny had needed to do was show up. From the music played at the funeral home to the hymn they'd just finished singing here at the graveside, his father had preplanned everything. Danny frowned; he should have had to do something, plan something. Wasn't that part of grieving for a lost loved one? The final decisions made for their remembrance?

"Dr. Robert Owens was one of the very best men I've known, and I know a lot of people," Reverend Fitch said, his breath coming in visible puffs. A few people snickered at his little joke, but it was true. The man had presided over his mother's and brother's funerals, as well as marrying most of Danny's classmates—at least the ones who'd stayed in Greenbriar. "A loving husband and devoted father, Robert was a real role model to the younger generations here in our town. While we hate to say goodbye to him, we know that he's now reunited in heaven with his beloved wife, Linda, and their treasured youngest son, Robby. Let us bow our heads in a final farewell."

All around, heads bowed. The only noise was the occasional ruffle of someone turning up a collar or the wind itself. Silence dwelled as an entire town bid adieu to one of their favorite people.

Slowly, one by one, heads rose and people came up to Danny, offering their condolences for his loss. Each mourner shared stories of how his father had saved their life, or provided financial support when they'd lost a job or a family member, or some other unforgettable act of kindness.

He'd known his father had held a prominent place in Greenbriar. That hadn't been a surprise, but he hadn't realized quite how many lives his father had touched so deeply. These people stood out in frigid weather to say goodbye, and their faces were lined with genuine grief. Like him, they were saying goodbye to someone they loved.

Glancing over at Camilla, he saw that she was also

receiving stories and condolences. But unlike the deferential way they spoke to him, they spoke to her like she was family. He got respectful handshakes and an occasional pat on the arm, while Camilla was swept into hugs and lingering embraces.

Hmm.

She'd cemented her place in the local society in a way that he—despite being Greenbriar born and bred—hadn't accomplished. Like his father, she was beloved by these people. They would grieve for her if she was gone, like they grieved now for his father.

Who would miss me?

The thought cut through him harsher than the wind whipping past the gravestones and he inhaled sharply, trying once again to bring oxygen into his suddenly suffocating lungs. As the last of the well-wishers made their way back to their warm cars and out of the cemetery, Danny couldn't help wondering if he'd have more than a handful of colleagues show up at his funeral. He had friends, of course, from his Army days, but they were scattered across the country. Now he had a few friendly coworkers whom he spent very little time with outside work.

Would anyone grieve for him?

He stood watching as they lowered his father's casket into the ground next to his mother's. With both of his parents and his only brother gone, he had no family left. The mother who'd held him tight and kissed his boo-boos, the brother he'd fought with and fought for over the years, both taken in a single moment. And now, the father who'd taught him what it meant to stand up straight and the importance of keeping your word, taken from him without the chance to say goodbye to him, either.

Kicking at a loose clod of dirt, he sank further into the

turmoil these thoughts created in his mind. The guilt that had forced his hand in pushing away Camilla had also driven him straight to the recruiter's office. Instead of taking one of the fellowships he'd been offered, Danny had joined the Army to get away from Greenbriar.

He'd skipped over any risks in favor of the adrenaline rush that came with being a trauma surgeon. But somewhere along the way, the Army had become more to him. It had given him a purpose. It had become a deeper calling, that desire to serve his country. What had been initially a penance for his failures to save his mom and brother had become his salvation, too. But his Army career had kept him on a lonely path.

Swallowing hard, he realized that he had no community, and he couldn't think of a single person who would be truly upset that they didn't get to say goodbye if he was gone.

But being alone was what he'd signed up for, wasn't it?

He'd chosen to be alone when he'd ended things with Camilla. He was toxic to those who got close to him, so he pushed them away. He couldn't be trusted with loved ones; they always ended up hurt because of him. That knowledge had kept him from letting anyone else get too close. He dated, sure, but whenever things started to become even slightly serious, he always walked away.

Look where that had gotten him—standing alone at his father's grave with no shoulder to cry on. No loved ones to go home with or turn to in the middle of the night when the grief became too much to bear alone. He'd kept everyone at arm's length and now he had to face up to the reality of that.

There was a quiver in his breath as he watched the shovels full of dirt cascade down almost in slow motion, marring the polished wood surface of the casket. With each layer of soil, his heart ached more and more as the finality of the situation really dug in. The last person in his life who loved him was now six feet under. He'd never felt more isolated than he did in that moment.

"Do you want me to send the car back? I can wait for you." Camilla stood next to him, watching as the dirt poured down over the no longer visible casket. "It's okay to cry, you know."

He sniffed. Cry? Here? No. His tears would only come when there would be no witnesses in case he became a blubbering baboon. "Was there anyone in town not here today?"

She let out a soft snort. "I don't think so. They even closed the diner."

"Have you ever wondered exactly who'd miss you if you died?" He looked over at her and then shook his head. Everyone in town loved her; of course she didn't worry about something like that. "Never mind. I saw how the people flocked to you today. You've really grown into your own here and they'd be lost without you."

She smiled at him. "I do know what that feels like, though. Until you came into my life, I knew that no one would miss me, and that was a fact, not a silly worry. For what it's worth, though, Danny, I'd miss you."

He rolled her words around in his mind, trying to decipher the truth. She hated him, didn't she? After all the pain he'd caused her, how could she claim that she'd miss him?

"Sure." He scoffed, unable to reconcile her statement with her recent actions. "You've spent the better half of the last two days yelling at me."

"Maybe I like having someone to argue with?" Her tone held a teasing note.

Danny reached for Camilla's hand. Her soft skin was

warm despite the chill in the air. Their fingers inter-twined like they'd done a billion times in the past. A new tension between them kept the simple gesture from feeling familiar, though.

"You've always been my favorite person to argue with," he said, tugging her closer, not wanting to let the connection between them lapse.

Camilla's lips parted and he caught the flash of pink as her tongue darted out to moisten her lips. His head bent toward hers, their mouths only a breath apart. Kissing Camilla would be an epically bad decision, but he wasn't sure he had the strength to stop himself from making it.

"Making up after a fight has never been so fun as when I was making up with you."

Camilla stiffened at his words. "This is a bad idea. We've had far more than a fight. Danny. We've practi-cally fought an emotional war. I can't…" Without another word, she spun and walked to her car. He recognized the angry set of her shoulders.

Maybe he'd taken the flirting a bit too far, since he didn't plan on following through with anything. It wouldn't be fair to her if he started something he had no intention of finishing. He wanted to put Greenbriar in his rearview as soon as the terms of the will had been fulfilled, didn't he?

But what he wanted most of all in that moment was to find a way to banish that deep-seated sense of being completely and utterly alone in the world.

And he had no idea where to start.

CHAPTER FOUR

"COME ON, FIDGET," Camilla said, trying desperately to distract her dog from the French fries someone had dropped on the sidewalk and left there. "Those are yucky. We don't eat yucky things."

But the little black-and-white mutt she'd adopted last summer most certainly did eat yucky things she found on the street. In fact, the yuckier the better in Fidget's opinion. Looking rather like a dirty mop, the shih tzu mix pranced along beside her with the French fry dangling from her mouth that she'd managed to snag before Camilla could pull her away.

"Oh, Camilla, dear!"

Camilla closed her eyes briefly before turning around with a forced smile plastered on her face. It was barely above freezing this morning and yet this was the third person to stop her for a chat. Was a peaceful walk with her dog really too much to ask for?

Apparently so.

"Hello, Mrs. Sutherland. How are you this morning?" Camilla glanced down the street toward her house. So close, yet it might as well be miles.

Wrapping her bright pink robe more tightly around herself against the early morning temperatures, Mrs.

Sutherland pursed her lips and said, "My gout is acting up, but that's not why I stopped you."

Camilla had never thought the woman had interrupted her walk for a medical reason. Mrs. Sutherland was far too much of a gossip for that. A quick glance at her watch showed that she had just over a half hour to get the dog home, settle her down for the day, and make it to work.

"Oh?" she asked, despite being absolutely certain that she knew what her elderly neighbor wanted to talk about. She tried to keep her tone conversational, but not too eager. Mrs. Sutherland could gossip for hours if she had a willing audience, but the elderly woman was also the first to call with a casserole if someone was ailing and she never failed to toss in a few bills whenever she saw a collection being taken for a family in need, despite her own fixed income.

"I wanted to know if Danny Owens was coming back to town." The rolled newspaper in her hand was waved around like a conductor might wave his baton while directing a symphony. The faded pink rollers in her hair bobbed along with every movement. "If anyone here knows, it would be you. Don't think I didn't know about the two of you sneaking into my shed together doing Lord knows what. Why, the two of you used to be thick as thieves! But I suppose that changed after... Well, it was a horrible thing, the way that boy just tap-danced across your heart like it was a slab of hardwood and skulked out of town like a thief in the night. Watching you put yourself back together after all that took so much strength. Have I ever told you how proud I am of you for doing that?"

Camilla shook her head.

"Well, I am. We all are. You were Robert's rock through it all. He'd never have made it as long as he did without you. Anyhow, what news comes from over that way?"

"All I know is that Danny is supposed to be here for the next six months." Camilla pressed her lips together tightly and held in the rest of what she wanted to say. Since Robert's funeral, it seemed as though every person in town had dredged up memories of Danny, when she'd rather those painful remnants stayed buried in the muck and mire with the rest of her past.

Mrs. Sutherland leaned in and fake-whispered, "I heard rumors… Well, you probably don't care to hear them. And you know how rumors go."

Rumors had been swirling since the funeral. Camilla tried really hard not to listen to what everyone was saying, especially when it involved her, but at the same time, she couldn't help being curious. Danny was her partner in the clinic now, after all. She had a need to know what was going on in his life, or so she told herself. And since their six months of working together at the clinic to satisfy the terms of the will officially started that day, she was having trouble getting Danny off her mind.

Had he returned to town? She certainly hadn't laid eyes on him since the day of the funeral. He'd left her a voice mail at the office saying he had to get back to Boston and they would discuss the practice when he returned, but nothing since. What if he left her hanging and she lost all that she had been working for?

After realizing that she'd stopped listening to Mrs. Sutherland's rambles and was quite possibly being rude to the older woman, Camilla wrapped up the conversation quickly. "I'm so sorry, ma'am, but I need to get Fidget here home so that I can get to work. I have patients soon."

Four houses down from Mrs. Sutherland, Camilla headed up the driveway to the large four-square she'd inherited. The pale green house had a stately beauty to it, with a wide porch spanning the front, and the currently empty window boxes that she'd fill with colorful flowers in the warmer months to come. As she unlocked the front door, she ran her fingers across the little brass numbers she'd put on the door herself and sent up a little thank-you to the man who'd left her the first home she'd ever truly known.

It was within these very walls that she'd learned what a true family could look like. Her heart and soul had been filled with love and acceptance under this roof. Robert had recognized that and chosen to honor her with the ownership of this house, surely knowing that it would be her forever home. She finally had the roots she'd been trying to grow for years.

Sadly, she had no one to share it with but a shaggy little stray prone to scavenging for scraps. Longing for companionship, she'd adopted the dog to stave off some of the loneliness. While it did help, nothing would really fill that particular void but a human family. Someday, Camilla promised herself, these walls would be filled with the love and laughter of a family again—her family. She picked Fidget up and gave the little dog a cuddle that was more for her own benefit than the dog's.

Fidget fussed about being put in her crate, but after getting a massive vet bill because the dog had eaten things she shouldn't and after nearly losing her, Camilla didn't fall for the tucked-tail routine anymore. "Quit pouting. You know it isn't going to work. The crate is for your safety, after all. Bye, Fidget. I'll see you at lunch, okay?"

Camilla checked the weather on her cell phone before making the decision to walk to work. Clear and cold, the app said. No inclement weather expected. So she set out on foot. It was only two and a half blocks from her front door to the clinic, and she hated to parallel park if she could at all avoid it.

What would she do if Danny didn't come back? Leaving Greenbriar wasn't an option, and the terms of the will wouldn't allow her to buy the building or the practice directly if Danny flaked on her. At the end of Baker Street, she paused. There was an old hardware store that had closed up last year when the owner retired and moved to Atlanta to be near his grandchildren. It had sat empty for months now. It was the only commercial property she knew of for sale in Greenbriar, and it would take a ton of effort to convert it to a medical clinic, but it might be her only option if push came to shove.

With a sigh, she continued her trek to the clinic. No use borrowing trouble and worrying about things that had yet to come. She'd see patients in her living room if she had to. She was a doctor, and a darn good one. She'd briefly thought about doing a surgical residency, and she'd done a rotation in the emergency room where the fast pace had nearly convinced her that specialty wasn't for her. Her heart, though, was truly in being a general practitioner. She loved developing that relationship with her young patients and watching them grow. Making elders' final years more comfortable was heartwarming, even as she knew her time with them drew to a close. She truly enjoyed seeing people of all stages in life and she loved spending the time with them that was needed to really get to the root of their troubles.

"Did I see you looking at the old hardware store?"

She looked over to see Danny pulling something— was that a wallpaper steamer?—from the bed of a pickup truck with Massachusetts license plates.

"Just looking at my options."

"You didn't think I was coming back, did you?" He

raised a single eyebrow and that simple action took her heart on a jog.

Why did her stupid, traitorous body insist on reacting to his every move? Even if she could recall exactly how amazing his hands had felt on her skin and how loved she'd felt when wrapped in his embrace. *Remember how it felt when he took his ring back?* That thought put her back into the right mindset to deal with Danny. It killed the little hint of interest that his silly eyebrow had sparked. It was just an eyebrow, for goodness' sake! What would she do if he flashed her some abs—strip like an exotic dancer?

When she replied to his question, the ice in her tone surprised even her. "Well, it wouldn't be the first time that you'd put Greenbriar in your rearview without a second glance."

Or me.

Silence hung between them thick with accusation. Danny's eyes glittered with anger, but Camilla refused to be cowed by it. Although she hadn't quite meant to be so cold, the sentiment behind her words held true.

Honestly, her pride wouldn't let her back down from this fight. She was a young, healthy, more than reasonably attractive woman—if she did say so herself—and she was no longer going to allow this man to make her feel badly about herself. She'd spent years questioning her self-worth both before and after Danny Owens had made his mark on her life. Only in the last few had she finally found a modicum of confidence and she refused to let him destroy it.

"Fair enough," he grumbled, dropping his gaze.

With his concession, Camilla opened the door and let them into the clinic. She took down the after-hours sign. Her hands shook as she tucked the sign into the drawer on the table by the door and hoped Danny didn't see what standing up to him had cost her.

Putting on a brave front, and standing up for herself, was self-preservation—a skill she'd learned early in life. But it never got easier. No matter how many times she had to do it, her nerves grew raw each time.

"Since the people here are probably more comfortable with you, I thought I'd let you see patients while I worked on bringing this place into the current century." He tapped on the wallpaper and said, "Starting with this lobby. I'll do one side at a time so that the patients won't be subjected to a construction zone."

"You decided this all on your own, did you?"

She crossed her arms over her chest. How dare he think he could just show up and make changes to her medical practice? Okay, half hers, but he had no interest in lingering in Greenbriar and running this practice. He'd said as much. And somehow that translated in his thick skull as "change whatever you like."

No. Absolutely not.

"Did you think that maybe this was a decision you should have run past me first as your *partner*?"

His lips tightened in silent acknowledgement of the truth in her question. "I was going to let you pick the paint or whatever after this. But this—" he waved a hand at the wallpaper "—has to go."

Temper settling slightly, she moved her head up and down in agreement. She'd hated that wallpaper at first sight and it wasn't one of those things that grew on you with time.

"That doesn't mean you make these decisions without me, even if you think for sure I will agree." A huff of frustration rushed over her lips. "I'm the one planning to stay here, Danny. If either of us should make decisions about the decor, it should be me."

He nodded solemnly and then his face softened into a smile. "All right, I'll paint it all teal. That's still your favorite color, isn't it?"

He'd remembered her favorite color after all these years? She swallowed hard at the lump in her throat. That once upon a time he had cared enough to learn things about her stabbed down to her very soul. She wasn't prepared for a reminder of when things had been good.

"I think a neutral would be better," she finally choked out before hurrying down the hallway to her office. She slammed the door and leaned against the cold wood, desperately fighting for a scrap of composure.

One hundred and eighty days to go. One hundred and eighty days of trying to stop her galloping heart from racing out of her chest every time Danny flashed her that crooked grin.

One hundred and eighty days of desperately trying to forget how the man she'd loved had thrown her away like a crumpled newspaper while not falling for him again or ruining all her plans for the future.

"What did I say?"

Danny watched as Camilla strode down the hall, knowing he'd upset her, but not entirely sure how. He ran the conversation through his head over and over. Line by line he analyzed his words and her reactions. She seemed most upset about him remembering her favorite color. How was that bad?

Women, he shook his head. He'd never understand them. Really, wouldn't it have been worse if he had forgotten how much she loved any shade of teal, from the palest of hues to the deep dark, almost black shades?

His Camilla would have loved the fact he'd remembered her favorite color. This version was nothing like the woman he'd loved. He hadn't had much time to really consider all the changes in Camilla while packing up his life in Boston and moving back to Greenbriar.

Or are you just too worried about what you might discover when you do think about it?

This Camilla had a softness to her that the old version had lacked. She'd embraced a new style, her clothing now classic but feminine. Her long hair she left down in soft waves, or pulled back in a clip when she was with a patient, rather than twisted up tight in a bun or a ponytail. The tomboy in secondhand duds he'd first fallen for was nowhere to be found, and in her place stood a strong, beautiful woman with scars on her soul. A core strength now emanated from her, one that he envied. She'd done a far better job putting herself back together than he had.

Even in the familiarity of her touch, there was a difference, a newness that intrigued him. She'd been the best friend he'd ever had, his first—and only—real love. After the accident where his mom and brother died, and he'd been laid up in the hospital, she had barely left his side. The idea that she wouldn't have been strong enough to handle his mental struggles he could see now was a fragile construct that wouldn't hold up to too much scrutiny.

But if that linchpin of all his decisions regarding their relationship wasn't solid, then what else had he lied to himself about?

Those thoughts were entirely too much to unpack in that moment. Truth be told, he wasn't ready for the emotional maelstrom they'd bring into his life.

Turning his attention outside those difficult thoughts to the outdated lobby, he decided where to start. He began by rearranging some of the chairs, moving more to the side with the reception desk and clearing out space around the opposite wall. By starting on that side, he wouldn't have to move the computer or the file cabinets yet.

He eyed the old metal file cabinets. A fresh coat of paint on them wouldn't hide the dents and dings of age. He wondered if Camilla would be open to digitizing all the files so they could get rid of those ancient things. His dad would have clung to his beloved paper records as if they were his lifeline in an ocean of lost information, but Camilla had surely worked with digital records and computerized patient information in med school and residency. He'd save that subject for a day when she didn't look like she wanted to rip his head off and use it as a bowling ball.

After filling the wallpaper steamer with water in the small kitchen, he moved back to the reception area. Deciding it best to start at the door and work his way around the room, he plugged the steamer up to heat. Before he got to work, though, he gave in to his nagging sense of wrongdoing and went to apologize to Camilla for upsetting her.

He was going to have to guard his words and maybe hold some things back to make it through the next several months with minimal drama. Camilla deserved that much consideration after what he'd put her through, so even though he still wasn't sure what he had done, he knew he had to concede that something had gone wrong and it was clearly his fault. Tapping lightly on her office door, he waited for her acknowledgment before opening it. "Hey, I am going to get started on getting this wallpaper off, but before I do, I wanted to apologize. I realize I upset you, and I'm sorry for that."

Camilla crossed her arms over her chest and stared at

him. Anger glittered in her eyes. She gave off the distinct impression that she didn't believe a word he was saying.

He took a steadying breath and tried again. "I mean that, Camilla. The last thing I want to do is hurt you more, although this likely won't be the last time I upset you given that we will be in close proximity until August."

"I'm putting in a supply order today. I have the list on my desk if you want to glance over it and make any additions."

He recognized the tactic. Camilla always changed the subject when the conversation got too personal for her to keep a tight rein on her emotions. Hopefully, that meant she was taking his apology to heart. Danny scuffed his foot across the carpet, staring at the slight color change as he shifted the pile with his sole. The carpet in this office could stand to be replaced, too, he thought idly.

"So, are we good?" he asked.

"I suppose we are until the next time you decide to make decisions without me," she snapped. "From office decor to marriage, you seem to think me incapable of making rational choices."

Closing his eyes, Danny leaned against the doorframe. Before he left Greenbriar, he'd have to address their past, but it couldn't be today. The mental fortitude required to do this discussion justice was just out of reach for him today.

"It was me. It was all me. You shouldn't take any of it personally." Anger at himself for making her feel so inadequate rose up sharp and fast. She was a beautiful, successful doctor who shouldn't be made to feel less than that for anyone, certainly not a broken man too stupid to see her strength. He was scum for putting her in that position.

"How could I not?" Camilla scoffed. "You told me— word for word—*I wasn't enough*. That I would *never* be enough. It took me years to work through the damage your rejection did to my self-worth. I blamed myself for so long, wondering what I'd done wrong, what I could have done differently that might have changed your mind about us. Worrying that there'd been another woman, that it was because of my background. To know that you moved on, when I never really could…" She broke off with what sounded suspiciously like a sob. Eyes closed, she took a deep breath, and when she opened them, the cold fury in her eyes sent a shiver down his spine. "But I guess I learned what I'd always really known, that men can't ever be trusted."

"I'm an idiot. It's the best explanation I've got right now." He pushed himself upright. The depth of the wounds he'd dealt her were far worse than he'd thought, but the full truth might hurt her even more and he wasn't ready to divulge just how messed up he had been. Still was, if he was being honest with himself. "I think maybe we should just leave the past in the past where it belongs, don't you?"

"Fine."

"I'm going to work on that wallpaper now."

"We need to have a plan in place for what we are going to do after you get the wallpaper off. You can't just jump right in and have my medical practice look like a work in progress."

"Fine. I'll take my wallpaper steamer and go home for the day. You can work in *our* practice while I relax on the dock."

As he slowly moved back to the front of the building, he thought he heard Camilla call him a coward. She was right—he was a coward. At least when it came to her and the mistakes he'd made with her.

At the time he'd broken off their engagement, Danny had been convinced that she was better off without him in her life. He'd justified that decision with the belief that she'd move on quickly, like the stories she'd told him of moving from foster family to foster family with no permanent attachments. He'd told himself that her love for him wasn't permanent. It would fade with time and she would find someone else, someone more worthy of her. But the pain in her eyes just now made him realize a hard truth about himself—all his rationalizations were built on falsehoods and weren't worth a dime. All of them, not just the notion that she wasn't strong enough to withstand the darkness within his soul.

His breath was ragged as he picked up the wallpaper steamer. What else had he deluded himself about?

CHAPTER FIVE

TGIF. CAMILLA SIGHED. Awkward didn't cover how their first month of working in the same office felt. The days had passed at an agonizing pace—slower than a turtle. They'd both tiptoed around the other, somehow avoiding any further arguments or hurt feelings, but the tension of working side by side for four weeks was taking its toll.

She sank into the chair at the reception desk and looked around at the bare walls, splotchy white mud patches against the aged gray of the drywall. Her three o'clock patient had called to reschedule and she found herself with a little downtime alone while Danny ran to the next town to pick up paint for the lobby. He was planning to paint this weekend when there wouldn't be patients trekking through the office and potentially through the wet paint. It was one of the few things they'd agreed on finally. It had taken them well over a week just to agree on a paint color and when it would be best to start on the wallpaper removal.

Leaning back, Camilla closed her eyes and tried to push all the conflict and concerns out of her mind. In less than an hour, the foster teen she was caring for over the weekend would be dropped off and she wanted to get herself completely together.

She had done respite care before, but had needed to

stop when Robert had gotten so ill. Given her past, she wished she could do more, but her job wouldn't allow her to foster full-time or adopt at the moment. But with Danny here now, he could be on call since he planned to be at the clinic to paint anyways. And that left her free to play a small part in helping some foster parents have a break, and allowed her to show a teen that someone indeed cared and that being in the foster system didn't guarantee a bleak outlook. She regularly went as a mentor to the group home where she'd spent her final two years of foster care. It was one of her tutoring kids who was spending the weekend with her, in fact. Her hopes were that she could serve as a role model. If she could touch just one life positively, the effort would be worth it.

The tiny bell over the door jingled and Camilla straightened up, forcing a smile to her face that she hoped didn't look too fake.

"Dr. D., guess who got a B+ on that science test you helped her study for?"

"The same girl who is referring to herself in third person?" Camilla's pleasure now was genuine as she smiled indulgently at Maddie, the fourteen-year-old she'd been tutoring through freshman biology.

The teen's face lit up and she laughed like Camilla's words were the funniest thing she'd ever heard. "Good one, Dr. D. And yeah, you're right. It is me, the one and only Maddie B with a B+ in bio!"

"I'm so proud of you! I knew you could do it. High five!"

Maddie came over and slapped her hand against Camilla's before she hopped up to sit cross-legged on the reception desk. "Mrs. Stone said she'll be here in a few for you to sign off on the paperwork for watching me this weekend. She's picking up a couple last-minute things before they go out of town."

"That's fine. I have one more patient scheduled for today and then we'll go back to my place. What sounds better—movie night or game night? Either way, I have popcorn and ice cream."

"Both?"

Laughter filled the reception area and covered up the tinkling of the bell over the door.

"Dang, Dr. D. Who is *that*?" Maddie grabbed a flyer for the state children's health insurance program and fanned herself with it, faking a swoon. "That your man?"

Camilla looked over to see Danny, his muscular arms laden with painting supplies. "That guy? Nah… That's Dr. Owens."

"Oh, I gotcha. He's the new partner you were telling me about." Maddie eyed Danny with an eagerness far too adult for her age. A heaviness settled over Camilla at the realization of all Maddie must have experienced. She'd have to have a talk with the young girl about men and sex, for sure.

Danny looked uncomfortable at being the subject of the girl's scrutiny. He set the paint supplies off in the corner before turning to face them. "Sorry to interrupt."

Maddie hopped off the desk and sashayed over to him, offering her hand. "I'm Maddie."

"Dr. Owens," Danny said, not offering his first name. He gave Maddie's hand a very brief shake and then put more distance between them.

He moved over to the reception desk and leaned on the wall near where Camilla sat. "I picked up all the paint and supplies. Figured I'd get started tonight. Was gonna ask if you wanted to help me, but I see you are otherwise occupied."

"I don't mind helping," Maddie offered. Her words had a flirty tone that set up an awkward mood. Although far too young to be hitting on a grown man, Maddie seemed unaware of the impropriety. "Whatever you need."

"We already have plans for a *girls-only* movie and game night, remember?" Camilla shut the idea down. She trusted *Danny* to not cross that line, but Maddie was a different story. Camilla had been in Maddie's shoes and she knew how appealing an adult male with a job could look, and when that man looked like Danny, well, it was just best for them all to keep a little distance between them.

"Sorry I'm running late," Alma Stone called out as she walked through the door, her three-year-old son trailing behind her. "I swear, time has just gotten away from me today. We are leaving for Dave's sister's wedding in less than an hour and I still need to put gas in the car and drop Bennie off to the sitter. I still don't understand why they had to have a fancy wedding that we couldn't bring the kids to, but it's my sister-in-law, so I can hardly skip it."

She stopped short. "Danny Owens? Is that you?"

"Hey, uh, Alma." Danny sounded uncertain about the name of their former classmate, but thankfully he'd gotten it right. Alma was touchy about being confused with her twin sister, Amy. "How have you been?"

"I was so sorry to hear about your dad. Such a fine man and gone too young. I hated to miss the service, but Bennie was running a temp. Just a little sniffle, thankfully, but I didn't want to take him out in that cold air and expose everyone in case it was more."

"It's fine, Alma." Danny offered a reassurance to the chattering woman.

"Well, thank you for saying that. You were always so kind. All us girls were so jealous when Camilla here was the one to win your affections—oh, shoot. I didn't mean to bring up bad memories." Alma winced.

In high school, Alma had been the girl who never stopped talking. That hadn't changed. Fortunately, she'd grown a bit of an awareness to the pain her chatterbox ways caused others. Sadly, sometimes only after the words had slipped through her open lips.

"We have had our issues in the past, of course, but we are in a good place now. Aren't we, Danny?" Camilla said lightly.

"Better than we've been in years," he said with an earnestness that couldn't be denied.

Camilla stood. She wanted to get Alma out of the office before her old classmate brought up more history that Camilla would rather Maddie not hear. She wanted to set a good example for Maddie and her own past had been a little rocky at times. "Do you have those papers for me, Alma? I have a patient due any second and you did say you were in a hurry, right?"

The other woman looked a little flustered but pulled some folded paperwork out of her purse. "And you are good with dropping Maddie at school on Monday? We are going to be in sometime real late on Sunday night and I wouldn't want to wake either of you up."

"I will drop her off at the front steps myself and make sure she walks in before I drive away," Camilla assured Alma. They'd had their differences, mostly due to Alma's constant blabbering, but Alma really was a dedicated foster mother who truly tried to make Maddie and the other kids she'd had over the years feel wanted and at home.

Alma took the signed papers from Camilla and stuffed them back into her purse. "Okay, Maddie, you be good while we are gone. Listen to Dr. Devereaux. I'll text you and check in, but you feel free to call or text me anytime you want, okay, sweetie?"

"Yes, ma'am." Maddie nodded dutifully.

Alma gave the girl a brief hug, which was still more touch than Maddie seemed to want from her foster mother. Camilla had shied away from physical touch for a large part of her life, feeling unwanted or unloved, too. It made her more determined to help Maddie see that she had people in her corner.

"Thank God she's gone," Maddie said the moment the door closed behind Alma's retreating form. She exaggerated a sigh as she flopped down into one of the chairs dramatically.

"She means well," Camilla argued. Far better than some of the families Camilla had been stuck with herself. "I know Alma tends to ramble on and on, but you have to know she cares. If I'm right, you'll have had far worse foster homes than with Alma and Dave."

"Whatever." Maddie shrugged and Camilla watched as the girl began to retreat into her shell again.

Danny laid a hand on Camilla's shoulder, drawing her attention. His voice was low, but the deep tones carried well. "Man, she reminds me of you. Back when we first met, you were so much like her."

Maddie tried to pretend she wasn't interested, but Camilla saw her visibly perk up at the comparison. She'd been working hard to get through to Maddie that she could make something out of herself, despite her origins, but it had been a struggle. Maddie wasn't willing to hear a lot of it. But maybe, oh, just maybe, if it came from Danny, the young girl might start to believe a bit.

"How do you mean?" Camilla asked, although she'd long made the connection herself. She turned mostly toward Danny, but kept Maddie within sight so that she could watch for her reactions.

"Her mannerisms, the way she was flirty with me but standoffish with Alma. And just now, the withdrawing into her own head when you called her out in the slightest." Danny squeezed her shoulder. "You were the same way. Hiding if you could, fighting if you couldn't. More interested in connecting with men than women. All the time hiding your lack of self-confidence behind a mask of indifference."

"I wasn't flirting with you," Maddie argued, but the red in her cheeks highlighted her embarrassment. "You old."

Danny laughed. "And sassy, did I forget to say sassy?"

"You sure he's not your man, Dr. D.? Because he sure seems all touchy-feely for someone you ain't hooking up with."

Camilla's own face heated. Danny's hand still lingered on her shoulder, a warm weight both soothing and disturbing. His fingers tightened just once before he released her, right as her last patient of the day walked in the door.

"Ah, Mr. Jenkins, here for your appointment?" Danny stepped up. "You'd be more comfortable with a male doctor, right?"

"I'm here to see you anyway, Danny."

The elderly man looked over at Camilla and winked. Why, what was that old man up to now? Mr. Jenkins was a real character, and she had a feeling that he was up to something. Mr. Jenkins had been a fixture in Greenbriar for as long as she'd lived in this town. Every day, he wore a flannel shirt with khaki pants. She thought he must have three or four dozen shirts, each with a different plaid. And he wore those shirts regardless of season.

It could be pushing a hundred degrees out and Mr. Jenkins would limp by, cane tapping against the sidewalk, his flannel sleeves buttoned firmly about his wrists.

"Patient thief," Camilla whispered under her breath to Danny as she held out the file. She didn't really mind, though. Given that Mr. Jenkins and Robert had been such close friends, she wasn't surprised that he wanted to see Danny instead of her. She thought it might be good for Danny to connect with his father's friend; maybe it would even help him remember who he used to be.

"You can start your weekend early. I'm sure you ladies have big plans that you can get an early start on," he said with a wide grin, taking Mr. Jenkins's chart from her. "Let's go to Exam One, just there on the right, sir."

She watched as Danny followed their patient to the exam room. In the doorway Danny turned and caught her staring.

"I'll see you Monday?" he asked, one eyebrow raised.

Camilla could only nod, heat flooding her cheeks once again. She could control herself better than this. She was a strong, confident physician. She had been running this medical practice alone for some time. Why was she blushing like a young girl in the midst of her first love?

"You got the hots for him then, huh? I seen how red your face got."

"Saw, not seen. You saw how red my face got. And I most certainly do not have the hots for him," Camilla denied. She was a grown woman. A professional. She did not lust after inappropriate men. "And this is a conversation we will not be having, not here, not anywhere."

"Whatever." Maddie rolled her eyes. "You lyin' to yourself if you say otherwise. And for what it's worth, Doc, I think he feels the same way 'bout you."

* * *

"What brings you in today, Mr. Jenkins?" Danny asked, eyes skimming over the man's file. Other than age, the man was fairly healthy. No chronic illnesses, only some pain that flared up in winter from an old injury. "If you want to roll up your sleeve, I'll get some vitals on you."

In the month he'd been here, Camilla had hardly let him near a patient without making him work hard for the chance. He'd had to resort to using his charm on the ladies and asking the older men if they'd prefer a male doctor just to have something to do. He hadn't touched a scalpel in weeks and had found himself missing the hustle and bustle of the ER in Boston.

No, he missed having people to talk to.

He'd channeled all his social needs into patient care. Which was a sad but true fact that he'd only become aware of since he came home to Greenbriar. He'd used his patients and coworkers in Boston as a weak replacement for a social life.

"I ain't sick." Mr. Jenkins sat on the end of the exam table and tapped his cane against Danny's knee. "I told you that I'm here to see you."

That wasn't an answer he'd expected to hear and it derailed the line of questions he'd been about to ask his patient, even if he had known the man most of his life.

"I'm sorry?"

"Your father was one of my closest friends." He raised an eyebrow, silently waiting for Danny's acknowledgment of his statement.

"I haven't forgotten." Danny wasn't sure where the old man was taking the conversation, but he remembered the days of sitting between his dad and Mr. Jenkins on the dock, fishing. They'd catch enough for dinner and then sit there gabbing like a cluster of church ladies on a Sunday evening and split a six-pack.

"You gonna break that girl's heart again?" Mr. Jenkins put the question forth with no pretense. No waffling, no beating around the bush. Right to the point.

Danny liked a straight shooter, but maybe not when they got up in his personal business. Whatever happened between him and Camilla shouldn't be anyone else's concern. His hand tightened around the stethoscope in his hand.

Gritting his teeth, he growled out, "Sir, with all due respect—"

"Don't you due respect me, boy. I bet I know what you're gonna say. That it's not my business, right? Well, you keep right on thinkin' that and I'll say what I come to say anyways. Your daddy, God rest him, isn't here to give you this talk, but you need to hear it, and I'm the one here to give it."

Danny took a step back. He wasn't a little boy being scolded for taking a swig of the man's beer anymore. This was his medical practice and, patient or not, Mr. Jenkins didn't have the right to walk in here and talk down to him like he was a child in need of discipline. Stubborn patients, he was used to, but nosy ones were a new one on him.

His spine stiffened and he stared down his patient. "If you aren't sick, then maybe we should call this a day."

Mr. Jenkins faked a cough. "I'm a paying patient. You want me to tell the state licensing board that you refused me treatment—or better yet, that lovely young woman out in the lobby?"

Danny met the old man's eyes and saw that he wasn't going to back down. And while he gave a brief thought to making a run for it, he sank down on the wheeled stool and waved a hand for him to speak his piece. The deciding factor had been simple—getting this conversation over with would be less drama than avoiding it.

"You didn't see what a mess you made of that girl. How broken she was when you sent her away and skipped town like someone lit your hind end on fire. We did." Mr. Jenkins took a deep breath, as if fortifying himself for what else he needed to say. "We patched her up and made her whole again. We were the ones standing by as she held this practice up alone for the last two years while your daddy was too sick to work. Like Atlas holding the weight of the world, that girl held up your daddy and this whole town on her petite little shoulders. She's got a strength to her that's come from clawing her way out of the pits of a broken heart."

Closing his eyes, Danny stifled a groan. How could he respond to that? He had no way to argue it. There was nothing he could deny in Mr. Jenkins's speech. He hadn't been home in years, because it was easier than risking bumping into Camilla. He'd missed his father's final moments as a result. He hadn't even known his father was sick until after he was gone and to hear, first from Camilla, and now from Mr. Jenkins, that he'd been sick for two years was almost too much to bear.

"And I'm here to tell you that this town will not allow you to break that girl again." Mr. Jenkins jabbed the tip of his cane into Danny's side to drive home his point. "You listening to me, boy?"

Danny nodded nice and slow, pushing the cane down gently. He got the gist of it—the whole town was on Camilla's side and he'd better not screw things up with her again.

"Now, nobody's gonna be unreasonable here. I saw the way the two of you were still looking at each other, and I ain't blind, despite pushing eighty. If you have honorable intentions and want to court the girl proper-like, and if she deigns to give your yellow-bellied butt a second chance, well, that's her business. But know we will all be watching you."

"Yellow-bellied?" Danny shook his head. What did this old man know about anything? Mr. Jenkins had no right to judge the choices he'd made. If only he could get someone to understand why he'd *had* to end things with Camilla... Why he'd had to leave town... If even one person was on his side, maybe the guilt wouldn't be quite as bad. "You don't know anything about me or why I made the choices I made."

"You think I don't know why you broke things off with that girl after the accident? You think I carry this cane for the fashion of it?" He twirled the wooden implement in the air to emphasize his words. "Naw, son. I've been in your shoes. I was the one behind the wheel when a car wreck shattered my thigh and, worse than that, took my only son from me."

That confession made Danny look at Mr. Jenkins with fresh eyes. The man had used a cane for as long as Danny had known him, but never once had he asked why. He never knew Mr. Jenkins had been in an accident, but before he could ask for any details, Mr. Jenkins continued his story.

"You think I wanted to come home to my sweet Mary Ellen as the man who couldn't protect our baby boy?" A haunted shadow in his eyes backed up the words. He shook his head and then tapped his finger against his temple. "The damage to my leg was nothing compared to the sinkhole that formed up here. The nightmares, the flashbacks. I didn't want to bring that mess back home to Mary Ellen and our baby girl."

Danny found himself intrigued by the man's story and the feelings so similar to his own. Mr. Jenkins's generation didn't talk about things like mental health issues usually, but his words resonated deep. While Danny had walked away from the accident that had killed two of the most important people in his life with comparatively little physical injury other than some shrapnel to one leg, mentally it was a completely different story. He'd felt less than whole, like damaged goods too far gone to contaminate Camilla.

Despite her childhood, Camilla had this goodness about her, this light, that made everyone around her feel better about themselves. He'd known that she would give and give to try to make him whole again, even if it took everything from her, and he had made the decision to spare her that. To not bring his mess back home to her, to borrow Mr. Jenkins's phrasing.

"But you did."

"God help me, I did." Mr. Jenkins stared over Danny's shoulder at an empty patch of wall. Pain left his aged face raw, decades after the time of his tale.

Danny felt that in the depths of his soul. Even after eight years, some days his pain was as raw as the day of the accident. Would he still feel it as keenly as Mr. Jenkins did when he reached eighty? His insides churned with that thought.

"It worked out for you, though, right?" he asked, trying to focus on the positive. Mr. and Mrs. Jenkins had always seemed so happy and in love from his point of view.

"Mary Ellen had the patience of a saint, I tell ya. She got me up when the nightmares got too bad, and she took our daughter to her mama's and came back to take care of me when the darkness pulled me under and I tried my best to drown myself in a fifth of whiskey. Even if I could have walked away from Mary Ellen, telling myself she'd be the better for it, I couldn't do that to my daughter. I'm ashamed to say that my wife had to do her grieving for our son alone because I couldn't be the shoulder for her to cry on. I was too lost in my own guilt and shame."

Danny buried his face in his hands. How many times had he been glad that there'd been no children thrown into the mix? Like Mr. Jenkins, if he and Camilla had had a child, he couldn't have walked away.

"Mary Ellen was stronger than I believed a woman could be and she stood by me through my worst, never once forsaking me. You were wrong if you thought Camilla wouldn't have done the same for you. You were wrong if you thought you were doing her a favor by pushing her away." Mr. Jenkins stood and put a wrinkled hand on Danny's shoulder. He squeezed tight in the way old men do. "And you are wrong now if you can't accept that some things in life we just can't change, no matter how hard we might wish or pray otherwise."

He paused before cracking a grin. "Other things, now, they just need a little sweet-talking."

After warning him off, was the old man actually encouraging him to try again with Camilla? Surely not? It was a moot point, anyway, because she'd never give him another chance. He'd hurt her far too much for that.

"She'd never forgive me for leaving her like I did." He didn't *deserve* her forgiveness.

With a shrug, Mr. Jenkins started out of the exam room. He stopped in the open doorway. "You might want to start with forgiving yourself first, son. Can't ask her to forgive what you can't."

Somehow, he'd ended up being the patient instead of the doctor today. The old man's footsteps and the soft tap of his cane receded and the tinkling of the front bell told

Danny he was alone with his thoughts. The magnitude of his poor decisions bombarded him. The worst part was that Mr. Jenkins was right. He was a coward. All those emotions he'd been shoving back for so long were fighting for release. The walls of the exam room felt like they were closing in on him.

Gasping, he tugged at the collar of his shirt. Coils of panic spun out around his heart, squeezing it until his chest hurt with the pain of just keeping his heart beating. He tried to get air into his lungs, falling to his knees on the cold tile of Exam One.

Closing his eyes, he breathed in through his nose, out through his mouth. Each breath grew easier and deeper until he felt strong enough to climb up off the floor. He touched the exam table, pulling a handful of the white paper into his hands and focused on the familiar sound of the crinkle. Every detail of the exam table got a once-over as he concentrated on the single object and pulled himself back to a calm state.

Once he was able, he quickly cleaned the exam room. Turning off all the lights, he locked the door. The painting would need to wait until the morning. He climbed into his truck and a familiar song came on that took him straight back to high school prom and Camilla dancing in his arms. Nope. Couldn't go there while he was driving.

Switching the radio off, he drove out to the lake house. Despite the chilly winter temperatures, he went straight out on the dock. Sinking down on the cold, weathered planks, he stared out over the water. There was no breeze tonight, keeping the cold from being unbearable. Wood smoke hung in the air, carrying over from one of the neighbors' chimneys, the scent another reminder of what he'd left behind here in Greenbriar.

He was supposed to be here for the short term. No

connections, no emotions, but somehow that didn't seem to be working out for him. Instead, he had people throwing his past up in his face, reminding him of all his deficiencies. Worse than that, though, was the temptation. Camilla's soft smiles and the way she leaned toward him subtly whenever they talked made him want things he definitely had no business wanting.

"Did you want to destroy me emotionally, Dad?" he asked the sky, bold with streaks of pink and orange. "Is that why you forced me back into Greenbriar and Camilla's life?"

A sob rose up from deep inside him, and for the first time in years, Danny cried. Not a few random tears trekking down a cheek to be swiped away with a single brush of the hand, but deep soul-wrenching cries filled with grief and a longing for what had been lost. The memories of all that had gone swam through the tears, leaving behind an ache that couldn't be filled. His mom. Robby. His dad.

Danny grieved, not only for his parents, but himself, too. The man he'd been before a drunk driver had crossed into his lane and shattered every vestige of the future he'd envisioned for himself. For so long he'd denied himself the ability to miss who he had been. Recently, however, he'd become aware that he no longer liked the man he saw in the mirror each day. He wanted to go back to being the happy-go-lucky guy who had the self-confidence to sweep his girl off her feet. Who had the confidence to risk loving someone and not let the fear that he was no good for them keep him from letting anyone close.

The wind picked up, swirling a pair of leaves around him before landing them in his lap. He wiped his face with the sleeve of his jacket and stared down at the leaves, stems twisted together so tight they'd carried on the breeze as a single entity.

His parents' marriage had been like that. They'd weathered all that they'd come up against, from miscarriages to failed adoptions—until death had finally separated them.

He wanted a love like that.

But loving someone meant taking a gamble. Chancing that his demons wouldn't overpower any love he had to offer. Putting a wager on his ability to protect the ones he loved, when he'd failed so miserably at that in the past. How could he take that risk?

CHAPTER SIX

As Camilla backed out of her driveway, Maddie sighed over in the passenger seat. Camilla spared a glance at the girl before returning her attention to the road.

"Why can't the weekends be longer, Dr. D.?"

"The older I get, the more I wonder the same thing myself." Camilla turned off her street onto the main road heading toward the new high school. The building that she and Danny had attended had been torn down a few years ago and an apartment complex now stood in its place. A lot of memories—good and bad—had happened in that old building. The grounds of the new apartment complex were haunted by teenage bullies, the ghosts of first loves, and the specters of adolescent heartbreak.

Maddie nibbled at her nails and sighed again. Although they'd had a lot of deep and productive conversations over the weekend, Camilla couldn't help but feel that the young girl had something else on her mind she wanted to discuss. Unfortunately, their time was nearly up, so Camilla couldn't take as long as she usually would to circle around the idea first.

"Wanna talk about it?" she coaxed, getting straight to the point.

"There's this boy…" Maddie let it trail off.

It's always a boy.

"And you like him?" Camilla gave a small, tight smile. Advice about boys wasn't really her wheelhouse, but Maddie was opening up to her. And that was a huge step.

"Well, yeah. He's a senior and he is *so* cute. I think he likes me, but I'm not sure. He kinda has a reputation for fighting and getting in trouble, but when he's with me, he's not like that."

Camilla started shaking her head. While a senior boy was a far more appropriate crush than a grown man like Danny, he was still not a good choice. Maddie really didn't need a boy who was going to lead her down the wrong path because he couldn't keep himself straight. "I don't think that's a good idea. You are far too young to be dating a senior, honey. It's very rare for a guy that much older to really want to date a freshman."

"What do you know?" Maddie scoffed. "You ain't got no man."

"I remember being a freshman and falling for a senior boy's lies." Camilla pulled into the still-empty parking lot of the insurance agency. She wanted to be able to make eye contact while they talked, and she couldn't do that while she was driving. She had to tiptoe up to this conversation or risk undoing months of trust-building with Maddie. "I was in your shoes. The cutest guy, a senior to my lowly freshman self. And by some miracle, he liked me." She swallowed as the humiliation of those memories filled her once more. "It was great, for a short while, but after he got what he wanted, he was gone. Then he told everyone in our school about it, and the truth merged with the exaggerations and the rumors. Before long, I was fighting about it on a daily basis and soon I lost my foster home. That's when I ended up in the group home here in Greenbriar. I didn't have the strength I do now, the emotional fortitude to stand up for what I believed in without throwing my fists around. I just desperately wanted someone to love me back, even if it was only for a short while."

Maddie bit her lip and looked away. "But how do you ever know if a boy really wants you or just…that?"

Camilla brushed a lock of Maddie's hair away from her face, hoping that by some miracle she was reaching her in a way that the girl would truly understand. "You make him work for it. If he really wants you, he will stick around and wait until you're old enough."

Maddie grinned. "How long did you make Dr. Hottie wait?"

Camilla snorted. "What makes you think—"

"Oh, come on." Maddie rolled her eyes. "I might be young, but I can sense the vibe between you guys. Plus… Everybody in town has been talking about the two of you. How you used to sneak around together…"

"Danny was my first love." *My only love…*

Looking off into the distance, Camilla tried not to drift too far into her memories. "He was the first boy willing to put in the work to really get to know me. We were friends for a while before I was willing to let him be more. And even once we started dating, it was quite a while before…that…happened. I was a few years older than you are now."

Maddie's forehead wrinkled as she seemed to be digesting Camilla's words. Camilla could almost visualize the thoughts running through the girl's head in that moment. *Does he really like me? Is he just using me?*

"Does that answer your question?" Camilla asked softly.

Maddie nodded. The serious expression she'd had a second ago was replaced by one filled with teasing mischief. "How long you gonna make him wait for it this time around?"

"Hush, you." Camilla put the car into gear and pulled back onto the highway. The kid had some nerve! "You need to worry about your school work, not my love life."

"I've known you a long time, Dr. D., and until he came around, I never once saw you blush. But you blush all the time when you talk about him. I just was thinking that if he still gets to you that much, maybe you ain't over him yet."

Camilla slowed the car to a stop in front of the high school. She looked over at Maddie and said, "I'll take that under advisement. Out you go. I'll see you Wednesday night for tutoring."

"I'll take that under advisement," Maddie mocked as she shut the door.

Camilla waited until the girl had crossed the threshold into the large brick building before driving away. She didn't need a fourteen-year-old girl to tell her she might not be over Danny. She huffed in frustration. She could love him with everything she had and it would never be enough if he didn't return the sentiment and share the same wants in life. She'd learned that the hard way when she'd poured every ounce of herself into their relationship and he'd ended things without even the hint of a warning. And she was no longer that teenaged girl fiercely longing for someone to hold her. Now she had enough self-respect to make the tough choices and delay a quick physical release if it didn't satisfy her emotional needs.

When she parked the car in front of the office, she realized she'd driven the entire way on autopilot. *That was safe, Camilla.*

She grabbed her purse and hurried through the crisp early March air. She kept close to the brick storefronts that lined the street, the buildings breaking some of the wind. She slowed when she reached the medical practice. The sign painted on the front window still read Dr. Robert Owens in large letters, with her name below it in a smaller print. She'd need to change that. Unlocking the door, she stepped inside, where the faintest hint of paint fumes still clung to the air. A lovely gray shade warmed the walls. Camilla gaped as she took it all in. The neutral paint brought such a crisp modern feel to the office, replacing the dated wallpaper with a timeless classic look.

Everything had been put back in its place, ready for patients bright and early this morning. The chairs were lined up along the wall, evenly spaced. Danny had even taken the time to fan the magazines out on the coffee tables.

It was perfect.

"So, how'd I do?"

Camilla jumped, her hand flying up to cover her heart that tried to jump out of her chest. She hadn't realized Danny was already in the office this morning. "Other than scaring the life outta me?"

"Didn't mean to startle you." Danny stood in the opening to the hallway, one hand propped casually on the wall. His faded blue jeans and paint-splattered T-shirt looked out of place in the setting, but oh-so-right on him. Snug denim hugged his thighs and the cotton of his T-shirt stretched tight across his broad shoulders. "What do you think?"

"It's amazing." Camilla spun slowly, letting it all sink in while hoping Danny hadn't caught her staring at his gorgeous form. "The color on the wall is better than I hoped. It's the perfect shade."

When she completed her revolution, Danny was no longer at the edge of the room but right beside her.

"So you like it?" he asked.

She nodded and swallowed hard at his sudden nearness. Knowing he was within arm's reach had her body in a state of wicked awareness. Physical release does not lead to emotional satisfaction—she repeated that mantra in her head as he moved even closer.

"Good." He reached out and touched her scarf with a single finger. "I can't believe you still have this. I would have thought you'd have thrown it in the fireplace."

"I thought about it. But it wasn't the scarf's fault that you bought it for me. Plus, I've always loved it." Every time she'd tried to get rid of the soft cashmere, she'd second-guessed herself. She'd bought other scarves, but none had ever managed to convince her to dispose of this one.

"Even when you hated me?" While his question was barely audible, there was something in his eyes that seemed to be screaming, "Please don't hate me!"

"I've never hated you," she confessed just as quietly. "Not even when my heart was breaking."

He grabbed both ends of the scarf and tugged her against his chest. Eyes searching, Danny stared down at her for a moment. She was completely unprepared for the feel of his touch. His arms slipped under her coat and held her tight, hands splayed on her back.

Camilla's heart skipped a beat as he lowered his head toward hers. Her hands came up to his chest, feeling the strength in his muscles beneath her fingertips.

The phone in her pocket rang, but they didn't immediately move apart. Slowly, Danny eased back the tiniest bit, barely enough to allow either of them to take a deep breath. They stared at each other. Danny's eyes were full of passion and wonder, and Camilla thought he must be seeing something similar in her own. She couldn't stop the flood of emotions overwhelming her senses in that moment, or that every single part of her was saying, "Kiss him."

Her phone rang again.

"You should answer that," he said, still holding her close.

Removing her hands from his chest to grab the interrupting device, she winced when she saw Alma's name on the screen. She'd forgotten she was supposed to update her when she dropped Maddie off at school. The woman would be frantic.

"Hi, Alma, yes, she's at school. I dropped her off on time. I just got a little distracted and forgot to let you know." Camilla's voice was shaky as she tried to reassure the nervous foster mother that her charge was safe and sound at school, where she belonged. All the while, Camilla remained wrapped up in her ex-fiancé's arms.

Alma fussed for a minute, but then ended the call, thankfully.

"Um…" Camilla bit her lip, not knowing what to do with Danny. His arms remained around her, but the moment had passed, and now things between them felt awkward again. She didn't know if she should step back or wait for him to. They stood that way for a bit, both seeming to want the other to make the decision.

Camilla put her hands up on his chest again, this time to keep him from tugging her closer. Having her hands on him was a temptation, though. Mixed with the familiarity of his embrace was a new vibe between them, something deep and thrilling that hadn't been there the first time around, but it served to make her hyperaware of each spot his body touched hers.

For years, she'd dreamed of the day when Danny would realize the mistake he'd made in letting her go

and come back to her, ready and willing to try again.
But now that the moment had possibly arrived, she discovered she had far more concerns than her fantasy had
ever allowed.

To make things even more confusing, Danny was
being so sweet and helpful. He'd made the changes to
the office so perfectly that it was as if she'd done every
bit of the work herself. And the way he held her had
brightened a part of her soul that had remained dim for
the better part of the last decade. Yet she couldn't help
being afraid of what the future would hold if she let her
guard down. What if she inadvertently did the opposite
of what he needed once more and he pushed her away
again? Could she handle losing him a second time?

"I don't think we should do this," she said finally.

"Yeah, you're probably right. I'm going to head out.
I've been here since yesterday getting this place ready
for business today. I could use a nap." He stepped back
and she watched as he put more than physical distance
between them. Barriers dropped down in his eyes as he
emotionally blocked himself off from her again.

"Bye," she said softly.

He strode out the door without grabbing his coat and
she couldn't help thinking he was running away from
her and that earth-shattering near kiss they'd just about
shared. An almost embrace that had the power to upend
her world. Maybe the potential of it had rocked his axis
as hard as it had rocked hers.

Sitting on the edge of the desk, Camilla brought a hand
up to her lips. Danny Owens could still shake her to the
very core. If she wasn't careful, she was at risk of falling head over heels in love with him again and handing
him the ability to destroy her once more.

The problem was, she wasn't sure she could stop it. Especially not when such a simple touch tempted her soul and being in his arms again had felt so much like coming home.

When Danny got to his truck, the realization that he was running away yet again hit him. He turned and leaned against his truck and stared back at the office. Mr. Jenkins's words tumbled forth into his mind, that he'd have to forgive himself first. One of the biggest things he'd struggled to get past was the guilt he carried from all the running away he'd done through the years. He'd run away from Camilla, and from his dad. He'd run at the first hint anyone was ever trying to get close enough to connect with him. He wasn't going to do it again. Wasn't going to pile more guilt onto his already overburdened shoulders.

Squaring his shoulders, he strode back to the office. Visions of how many ways this could go wrong flashed through his head, but he bounced them right back out. He only had headspace for positivity. He might not be able to get through all his past guilt just yet, but at least he could avoid adding to it.

Camilla jumped up from the desk when he walked back in the room.

"I think we need to talk about what just happened." He certainly didn't want to talk about it. Talking would acknowledge the elephant in the room put there by that spontaneous embrace, but he and Camilla were only just landing on solid ground and they had to rebuild their whole foundation. That meant putting it all out there, even if it was miserably uncomfortable. He wasn't running from her again. Not physically, not mentally.

She nodded and gave a weak smile. "That was… unexpected."

That was an understatement and a half. "For me, too."

"Then why?" A deep pink rose up in her cheeks. It made her look even more kissable.

He put his hands in his pockets to keep from reaching for her again. "I could say it was just nostalgia or a heat-of-the-moment thing. But I don't want to lie to you. While it was an impromptu gesture, the feelings that rose up made me wonder if we might still have something there to explore."

"Maybe trying again would be worth it, or maybe I'll get my heart shattered again. What if we are just toxic to each other and this will only end in pain for both of us?" She gave voice to some of her concerns.

He held a hand up and she stopped speaking in response. "I know we have a lot of things to work out. And I know I really don't deserve another chance with you. But maybe we could take some time to get to know each other again, see if there is more there than just a spark of leftover passion."

"Spark of leftover passion…" Camilla echoed his words, her tone suddenly tight and clipped. She sucked in a breath, as if fighting against herself before continuing. "I think we need to focus on the keyword in that sentence—*leftover*."

"Why are you pushing me away?" They were teetering on the edge of a precipice and one wrong move from either could send them both back into the abyss of anger and avoidance, but he couldn't help taking another step forward.

"I don't feel like I can trust you."

Defensiveness rose swift and sharp in his gut. "What

do you mean you don't trust me? Do you honestly think I'd ever intentionally hurt you?"

"You ended our relationship without so much as a conversation. I never got to find out what went wrong, whether things were fixable or not. Nothing. Just 'give me my ring back and get out of my life.' I thought we were fine—I mean, yeah, of course I knew your accident was going to change some things, but I didn't think we were at the point of breaking up forever. I trusted you, more than anyone in my life, ever, and when you threw us away—threw me away—like an empty pop can, then it broke my trust."

An emotional sound, somewhere between a sigh and a sob, escaped her, but she continued her speech. "It made me second-guess everything about myself. I couldn't trust my own judgment, because my judgment had told me you were trustworthy, that you cared about me, and look where that led me."

Reaching out, he cradled her hand within his. He wanted to wrap his arms around her, hold her in his arms and soothe away her concerns, but settled for holding her hand. While he might have lost her trust in one swift moment, it would take far longer than that to rebuild it. Patience would have to become his new best friend. "If it helps at all, I am truly sorry."

"Danny, I…" She trailed off and considered him carefully. He could see the warring emotions that crossed her face.

Before Camilla could answer, the office door opened and slammed back into the wall. A man in blue jean overalls and a dusty ball cap staggered in, his arm ripped open and blood pouring from the jagged wound. The blood on the carpet would never come out, but, thankfully, it needed to be replaced anyway.

"Doc, I think I'm gonna need a few stitches," the man said, wobbling backward and sitting down hard on the table by the door. Medication brochures fluttered to the floor from the impact. The man's face paled. "Boy, this room sure is spinning."

Camilla gaped at the man. "Mr. Hughes, what did you do?"

Danny jumped into action. Finally, a patient he could take point on. Helping the gentleman to his feet, he led him to the exam room. As he gloved up, he called out, "Camilla, I need an irrigation tray and some gauze. How'd this happen, sir?"

"My yard had just started to look shaggy and I was trying to get the first cut of the season in. I sneezed and ran my mower into the dang fence. Barbed wire snapped and got the best of me." He winced in pain as Danny probed the edge of the cut with a gloved fingertip.

Camilla brought the irrigation supplies in and got them set up next to the exam table. "What else do you need?"

"Gotta see what we are dealing with here." He put a gauze pad over the wound and smiled at his patient. "Hold that in place. Give me just a sec to talk to Dr. Devereaux in the hallway, okay?"

He motioned for her to step outside. When the door clicked behind them, he asked quietly, "Do you keep any blood products here?"

"No," she answered back, her voice low to match his own.

"Okay, go ahead and call for an ambulance. I'm going to patch him up as best I can, but this wound needs far more than simple stitches. I need to make sure that there's no nerve damage first and we just don't have the equipment here for that."

When she moved into her office, he hurried back to his patient. "Now, let's flush this out and see where it stands."

A few minutes later, Camilla knocked and came back into the exam room. She was handling this remarkably well given that she normally didn't see blood pouring out of a man in large quantities. This was well beyond her typical cases of strep throat and sinus infections. He had no doubts that if he hadn't been here, Camilla would have taken good care of this patient. If he knew one thing, it was that she was an excellent doctor.

While she was gone, he'd been able to clean the wound and wrap it tightly to slow the blood loss. "I was just explaining to Mr. Hughes here that we need to send him over to County to make sure there's no nerve damage and let them stitch him up."

"Right." She nodded in agreement. "You don't want me to sew you up, Mr. Hughes. I'm afraid I haven't done more than dermal adhesives or a few staples in years. This is a little beyond that."

"I could do it, but I want to have a neurologist take a look first," Danny felt the urge to add. He wanted Camilla to see him as a skilled trauma surgeon, to see that he hadn't wasted all the time they'd been apart, at least.

"Thanks, Docs. I'm feeling pretty woo…woozy," Mr. Hughes stuttered as he swayed on the table.

That ambulance couldn't get here fast enough to suit Danny. This patient needed far more care than they could give him here. They didn't have a surgical suite. Honestly, they didn't even have an X-ray machine, just one old ultrasound machine and an automated external defibrillator. None of which would do much if Mr. Hughes coded on that table.

"Why don't you just relax back here then. Best to lie down before you fall down, don't you think?" Camilla moved quickly to recline the table. She elevated Mr. Hughes's arm and kept talking to him in a soft, crooning voice.

"You sure are prettier than ol' Doc Owens," their light-headed patient muttered, flirting with Camilla.

"Why, thank you!" she replied with a smile, turning that Southern charm of hers on the man.

Her words were having a calming effect on the patient, so Danny didn't want to say anything to distract from that. But he did want to get his vitals. Danny stepped to the other side of the exam table and listened to the man's heart while Camilla kept his attention engaged. His vitals were far shakier than Danny would like to have heard.

"I need to ask you a very serious question, Mr. Hughes," Camilla drawled. "When did you last have a tetanus shot? You and I both know that barbed wire fence around your place has seen its share of rainy springs and has more than a touch of rust on it."

When Mr. Hughes said he couldn't recall, Danny slipped out of the room and retrieved the medication and a syringe. A tetanus booster was always a good idea when rusty metal was involved. He also grabbed an IV kit and a bag of saline. Without blood products, saline was the best alternative he had access to. He injected the vaccine into the man's deltoid muscle on the uninjured arm and set about getting intravenous access established.

"Danny," Camilla said quietly, drawing his attention from the IV he'd just got going. Her eyes flicked to the bandaged wound that was bleeding through the gauze already, even tightly packed and elevated.

He nodded at Camilla and stepped back to the supply closet. He grabbed more gauze pads and a suture kit. As much as he hated to close that wound without a neurologist to check for nerve damage, he had to get that bleeding stopped.

"Okay, Mr. Hughes, we got a slight change of plans here. Since this stubborn laceration of yours insists on bleeding still, I'm going to throw a few stitches in and see if we can't get that slowed down." He moved up next to Camilla, who was still holding the patient's arm in an elevated position. He carefully peeled the bandage back and held back a sigh of relief when blood didn't spurt out at him. He motioned for Camilla to move the limb down onto the irrigation tray. Flushing out the wound with saline again, he scanned the cut for the bleeders.

Finally, he saw the culprit. "Gotcha now, you little bugger." He carefully stitched the bleeding vessel. Stitches weren't always the best choice for that, but when the bleeding wouldn't stop, he didn't have much choice. With that done, he waited to see if there were more, but that seemed to be the biggest source of bleeding. He recleaned the wound carefully before putting in a line of careful sutures.

He once again checked Mr. Hughes's vitals and was pleased to see they were stable now, if a bit weak. His stitches were holding and the bleeding had stopped.

The front bell rang, and Danny couldn't help feeling a little annoyed that the paramedics were there now, after he'd already done the hard work in stabilizing the patient. He directed them to the exam room, rattling off the man's vitals and current condition to the first responders. They soon had the man on a stretcher, wheeled him out of the office and loaded into the back of the ambulance. Hopefully, the surgeon who looked at it wouldn't have to undo all the stitches, but at least the patient would live to reach the hospital.

As the ambulance drove away, their patient safely inside, Danny started feeling the adrenaline crash that always came with the end of a trauma. He flipped the Open sign to Closed, locked the door and carefully stepped around the bloody mess on the carpet. He went looking for Camilla.

She was still in the exam room, trying her best to clean up. He joined her efforts. Side by side, they scrubbed the exam room down in silence. When it was back in shape, they stepped into the hallway.

Camilla took one look at the trail of blood leading from the front door to the exam room and he thought she sighed heavily. But then she closed her eyes briefly and he watched as she visibly summoned that inner strength he so admired.

"Where do you think we should start out here?" She shot him a wry look. "I'm not sure a carpet cleaner will do much, but they rent them over at the grocery store."

Raising one eyebrow at her, he silently begged her to reconsider her statement. Those little rental cleaners would barely make a dent in this mess. They needed industrial-strength machines and chemicals. Or maybe just new flooring altogether.

"I think we need professionals," he finally said.

She pursed he lips. "Yeah, you're probably right on that. I'll call our guy, see how much it will cost to get an emergency clean done as soon as possible. We can't see patients until we get this taken care of."

"I already locked up."

"Good. Could you get the appointment book and reschedule the patients you can? Maybe we can do house calls for the others? Just until we can get the office usable again."

"On it." He went into the lobby, dodging the still-tacky blood on the carpet. He sat at the desk and pulled up the day's appointments and started making those calls. He pushed as many of them as he could back to next week and agreed to do a house call for one elderly woman who sounded like she was hacking up one of her lungs just to have a conversation.

"They are going to send a crew over in about an hour to start on the carpet. I warned them it was bad." Camilla sat on the edge of the desk next to him. "How's it coming with the rescheduling?"

"I'm done. There's only one that I think one of us should do a house call on. She might be more comfortable with you." He gave her the woman's name.

"Her lungs are so bad, but she's determined to stay in her home. I usually go by and check on her every Friday on my way home from work anyways. So I don't mind going out to do a house call for her. Could you stay here and let the carpet cleaners in? They're safe to leave in the building alone and will lock up after themselves. So you can go home after that."

He nodded slowly. "Are we going to talk about what happened earlier?"

"You were brilliant with Mr. Hughes. I'm so grateful that you were here, because I have to tell you, my heart froze at the sight of all that blood. I… Normally, I'd say that I am one hundred percent confident in my abilities as a physician, but my emergency rotation was a long time ago and I haven't had much opportunity—thankfully!—to keep those skills up. Mr. Hughes is lucky that we had a trauma doctor in the building. You saved his life. Can you believe he drove himself here? Stubborn old goat."

"That's not what I meant, and you know it." Danny had to squash the urge to preen like a peacock at her praise, though. She radiated positivity and he was a man starved of upbeat feedback. Having Camilla recognize his hard-won skills sent a balm of peace through him he hadn't expected.

"Oh, that." Camilla laid a hand on his arm. She met his gaze, her eyes filled with confusion and a hint of pink coloring her fair cheeks. "I'm not yet sure how I feel, Danny. I need time. It took me a long time to get over our breakup, and I can't just ignore that."

"I'm not asking you to," he argued gruffly.

"I'm going to go see that patient. I'll see you tomorrow." She squeezed his arm.

"I'll look forward to it." And he found that he really meant that. He'd taken a step forward with Camilla, he thought. And he'd helped save a man's life, while proving to Camilla that he was a competent surgeon.

Today had felt really good.

CHAPTER SEVEN

"REMIND ME AGAIN how we got roped into this?" Danny grumbled, but he hooked another balloon to the helium tank and filled it. He'd already filled a dozen, but there were several more waiting for his attention.

"Because Dave got called in to work unexpectedly and Alma needed help getting ready for Bennie's birthday party." Camilla rolled her eyes. "You know this."

"Correction then, how did *I* get roped into this?" He hooked the next balloon to the machine.

"Because Dave used to be one of your best friends and you are trying to rebuild your relationship with him?" She shrugged. "I don't know your reasons. I'm here because Alma asked me."

He snorted. "And when did you and Alma actually become friends? I know I was gone a long time, but that still surprised me."

"Because as an adult, I realized that Alma is just nervous and talks nonstop as a result. She really has a heart of gold and wouldn't intentionally hurt anyone. She just can't keep a secret to save her life and she has no filter to tell her when to stop talking."

"Hmm." He'd have to take her word for it. He looked around the gaily decorated yard. Crinkle paper party streamers covered in cartoon pirates hung from the fence posts and swayed in the breeze. He'd already set up a series of folding tables and then taped colorful paper tablecloths to each of them to keep them from blowing away in the spring breeze. He'd helped hang a piñata shaped like a pirate ship from a low-hanging limb of a maple tree. "And still, I ask, how did I get dragged into helping prepare for a kid's birthday party on such a beautiful Saturday in April? I could be out on the lake with a fishing pole in hand, enjoying this sunshine from a boat on the water."

"Clearly it was so that you could spend the day with me, of course." Camilla stepped closer, laying her palm on his arm. "And that will make it all worth it, right?"

Danny hissed in a breath as she ran her fingers along his forearm. "Yeah," he said, his voice higher and squeakier than he'd like. Camilla had been flirting with him for the last couple of weeks now, and he was finding her harder and harder to resist.

"I have balloons to fill with helium, woman. Stop trying to distract me." He pushed her back playfully. He kept his tone light. "Alma looks like she could use a hand over there. Go bother her."

"In a minute," Camilla said. "I was wondering if you would mind helping me with the Memorial Day festival at the end of next month. The clinic has staffed a first aid booth there for as long as I can remember."

"You need someone to help you hand out Band-Aids and sunscreen?" He shrugged. "Why not?"

"Great." Camilla beamed at him, making him glad he had said yes.

Over the next hour, he filled the remaining balloons, carried far more presents than one newly four-year-old boy needed to receive outside to the designated presents table, and taste-tested at least three different things for the women who had showed up early to the party. He was fairly sure they all knew their dishes were fine—after all, what Southern woman brought a dish she wasn't proud of out in public. From the way they'd been eyeing him, he was quite certain it was just an excuse to talk to him. He wasn't enjoying the extra attention. The party hadn't even started yet, and he was ready to get out of here.

Yet he stayed.

Because Camilla was there.

Danny found a shaded spot along the fence and sank down into the grass to relax for a bit. To get away from the overtly friendly women of this town. So far, he was the only male in attendance over the age of five. His gaze lingered on the deck where Camilla, Alma and the other women stood talking. Bennie and half a dozen other little ones ran around the yard wearing pirate hats, shouting things like "Ahoy, matey!" just before smacking each other with cardboard swords.

Alma's twin sister, Amy, strolled over with a bottle of water. She held it out to him. "You look like you might have worked up a thirst. Alma couldn't have pulled all this together without you."

"Thanks," he said, reaching up to take the proffered beverage.

Amy held on to it for a moment. "So I was thinking, if you are going to be in town for a bit…" Her words trailed off, but her intentions were crystal clear.

"I'm not sure how long I'll be here. And while I appreciate the, uh, invitation, I'm going to have to pass." He tried to think of a way to reject her politely. His eyes shifted behind her to where Camilla stood watching them. Even from a distance, he saw the stiffness in her posture.

"Man, is that the way the breeze is still blowing?"

Amy shook her head. "I thought the two of you had burnt out years ago."

"There's nothing between Camilla and me. But I'm only going to be in town until the start of August. It wouldn't be fair for you and me to start something up now." Danny stood up.

"But it could be fun," Amy said with a smirk, laying her palm on his forearm. Her touch did nothing for him.

"Sorry, it's still a no." He took a step back. "But really, I am flattered by the offer."

Amy looked mad enough to spit nails, so he thought it best to get as far away from her as he could. He stepped up on the deck and took a cookie off the tray there. The sugar cookie he chose was shaped like a skull wearing a red bandanna. Breaking a tiny piece off, he popped it into his mouth. The cookie was buttery and held a hint of vanilla.

"You aren't supposed to be eating those yet," Camilla scolded as she walked over.

"You gonna stop me?" he taunted. He bit another chunk out of the cookie skull.

"Not if you share." She reached out and grabbed a skull cookie of her own. Her pink lips closed over the red frosting bandanna.

"They're good, right?"

"Oh, yeah, they are." Camilla rubbed her thumb along his lower lip. "You have a bit of icing right there."

Danny went to speak, but his voice refused to come. She was trying to kill him. He was certain of it. His lip tingled from her touch and he desperately wanted to kiss her right there.

"Okay, now, you two," Alma called. "Don't melt my kid's cake, huh?"

"Sorry," Camilla said as she took a step back. The

bright blush in her face made him feel a little guilty for his part in the flirting, but she had instigated it.

"No, don't be sorry, honey," Amy added with a wry laugh. "If the rest of us had a shot, we'd be taking it, believe me."

Danny cringed inside, but did his best to keep his expression neutral. "When are we going to do cake or presents? I'm sure Bennie's beyond ready."

Alma shook her head at him, her face twisted with the effort of holding back a smile. "You aren't quite smooth enough to pull that change of subject off, Danny Owens, but since it is Bennie's big day, I'm gonna let it slide."

"Well, I think cake sounds like a brilliant idea," Dave said from behind Alma. He nodded at Danny. "I owe you a big thanks for helping to set all this up."

"It was no trouble." Danny shrugged. He didn't want any recognition.

Alma hugged her husband, then turned and shouted out to the kids, "Who thinks it's time for cake?"

Camilla locked her arm with Danny's and led him over to the side. Their part in making sure Bennie's party went well was now done. And she could enjoy herself a bit.

Honestly, it had taken her aback when she'd answered Alma's plea for help and found Danny already in the backyard, wrestling with a folding table. A kid's birthday party hadn't seemed like something he'd want to do, but he had really surprised her in the weeks since that almost kiss at the clinic.

"You want cake?"

"Nah, I'm good. But go grab some if you like."

Danny shook his head. "That cookie was enough for me. So, unless you want to share one, then I'm good."

"Better not." Her cheeks heated again at the reminder

of her brazen flirting. She wasn't sure what had come over her. She only knew she hadn't appreciated seeing Amy approach him like that.

"Too bad," he said. His dark eyes glittered dangerously. Camilla knew she could easily let herself fall back in love with him. Every moment they spent together made it harder to keep her hands to herself.

"Time for presents!" Alma called out, pulling their attention away from the tension between themselves. Maddie and her friend appeared from the corner of the deck where they'd sat whispering and giggling, to surround Bennie as he opened his gifts.

Bennie squealed happily. Soon bits of wrapping paper were flying left and right as the four-year-old tore into his birthday gifts. A gust of wind carried a piece of pastel blue tissue paper through the air toward them. Danny reached out and caught it, disposing of it properly.

Package after package was opened. The presents ranged from a couple of packages of toy cars up to a large block set. Finally, he got to the last present. That one was taller than him and wrapped in plain brown paper with a crudely tied bow around the middle. He ripped into it to find a stack of various sized boxes, a new package of markers and some colorful tapes.

"Oh, wow!" Bennie breathed. "I'm gonna build a rocket ship!"

"Go thank Dr. Owens," Alma said, her voice tight. Camilla worried that her friend was upset that Danny's simple gift had upstaged her much more expensive offerings.

Bennie ran over to Danny and flung himself into his knees. "Thank you, Dr. Owens."

Danny looked uncomfortable for a brief second before returning the little boy's hug. "You're very welcome, buddy."

"Come on! You can help me build it!" Bennie grabbed Danny's hand and pulled him across the yard and put him to work. The little one was like a tiny general ordering both Danny and his father around as a rocket ship was quickly constructed out of cardboard boxes and decorated with tape and markers.

Camilla bit her lip as she watched. The tension in Danny's frame eased and a smile graced his face. He was soon laughing with Dave and the little boys as they taped boxes together and decorated them.

Alma came up next to her and threw an arm over her shoulder. "It's not my place to say, but I want you to be careful. You've got those same stars in your eyes that you did back in high school. I don't want to see you get hurt again."

Camilla leaned her head against Alma's. "I know. Something about him draws me in like gravity, though."

"Camilla, he broke you. I…" Alma paused and Camilla wondered if her outspoken friend had actually chosen to not speak for once, but then Alma continued. "It took a long time for you to come out of the funk he threw you into. Going down that road again, is that the best idea?"

Camilla let out a long breath. "I appreciate the concern—"

"But you have already made your mind up to give him another shot." Alma gave her a squeeze. "I won't say anything else, then. And I honestly and truly hope that he's not gonna hurt you again. He seems different than I remember. You think he's changed?"

He had definitely changed. But she wasn't going to discuss the whys and hows with Alma, and certainly not in a yard full of people. Danny deserved far more privacy than that.

"Hmm." She made a noncommittal sound, hoping that would appease Alma for now.

Seeing Danny laughing, lying on the ground with a group of preschoolers piling on him like he was a mountain, made her smile, though. One day, he'd make a good father. He was great with kids when he let himself relax.

As the party wound down, people began to leave. She said goodbye to Alma and slipped out the gate.

"Camilla, wait," Danny called from behind her.

She paused and gave him time to catch up.

"Can I walk you home, Dr. Devereaux?"

"I think I'd like that, Dr. Owens."

"I have to admit, that was far more fun than I expected it to be," Danny said as they reached the sidewalk. "I didn't have high hopes for an afternoon spent at a children's birthday party."

"You looked like you were enjoying yourself." She sucked in a sharp breath when he interlaced their fingers as they walked down the sidewalk toward her house. Every touch of his hands brought with it a wealth of old memories and more than a little desire to make new ones. "I haven't seen you smile or laugh that much since you've been back."

"Greenbriar has been more relaxing than I expected it to be."

Camilla faked a gasp and looked around. "Shh… someone will hear you and think you actually like our town."

"We wouldn't want that, now, would we?" His deep voice held a hint of amusement. "I had a lot of fun playing with the boys. I never expected my box of boxes to go over so well. I remember when I was little, my mom and dad used to keep all the boxes that came through the clinic for us. Robby and I would build castles and forts and rocket ships that had medical labels on the side and sometimes we would pretend that was the name of our ship or the location of our castle."

Camilla steeled her nerves against the longing that rose up. She'd never had parents who would have thought to bring her boxes to play with. Her only memories of her biological parents were hazy and involved a lot of yelling. And the worst one of all, the sheer terror she'd felt when she woke up alone and they never came home. She'd never forget the look on the neighbor's face when she'd knocked on her door asking for food and if the neighbor had seen her parents. It was imprinted onto her mind, never to be erased.

"Well, Bennie sure enjoyed it." She forced a smile and a return to happier thoughts.

When they got to her house, Danny walked her up the steps.

"You should go," she said, her voice thick, and the words came out more like an appeal for him to stay than an order for him to leave.

He moved closer, though, pinning her against the front door. "Have I told you today how pretty you look in this color pink?"

"No." Her lips twitched with the effort of suppressing a giggle. Sometimes Danny made her feel like a teenager again, prone to blushing and giggles. What next, was she going to start doodling his name on her files at work?

"Well, you do." He brushed his lips against hers, ever so slightly. It was more of a tease than a kiss, a testing of the waters. When she didn't push him away, he kissed her again. His hands tangled in her hair and his lips moved over hers, soft at first, not tentative, but giving her time to pull back if she wanted to.

She wrapped her arms around his neck and returned

the kiss. Her legs felt a little weak and she clung to his shoulders to keep upright.

Then, as fast as it began, Danny ended the kiss. He took a step back and left her grabbing for the doorframe to make sure she stayed on her feet.

"So, uh… Thanks for helping me reconnect with Dave. I needed that more than I knew."

"You are very welcome," she whispered. Was he going to ignore the fact that he'd just rocked her entire world?

"I'll see you soon." Danny whistled as he walked away.

Camilla unlocked her door and leaned against the frame. She had to fight the urge to chase Danny down the street and snatch another kiss.

But what if he leaves again?

With one last, lingering look at Danny, she sighed. Stepping inside, she closed the door. Soon, she would have to really consider whether or not she could handle it if Danny left again.

But for today, she simply wanted to think of that kiss and the feel of Danny's hands on her body as he held her close.

CHAPTER EIGHT

CAMILLA WATCHED DANNY putter around her backyard like he was planning to be there forever. He'd practically jumped at the chance to do her yard work, and given how she'd nearly chopped her foot off last summer when she was mowing, she was hardly going to say no to the help. Being a homeowner was proving to require skills that she had yet to develop.

Thanks to Danny's attention, her front lawn had that manicured look that was usually only found in magazines, and now he'd turned his attention to her backyard. He had visions of turning it into some sort of lush oasis, and she'd loved the sketches he'd made, so she was letting him run with the idea.

Fidget had fallen head over heels for Danny. Camilla thought her pet might even like Danny more than her. Whenever he was around, she wasn't far away. While he worked in the yard, Fidget pranced along behind his every step, her little curly tail wagging nonstop.

Who knew Danny Owens was such a landscaper? Sighing, she gave up even pretending to look at her phone and set it on the porch rail. Danny was far more entertaining to watch than anything she could find on an app. The blue T-shirt he wore stretched tight across his broad shoulders, clinging to the firm muscles of his chest. He'd kept up with most of the physical training from his time as a soldier and it absolutely showed. The cargo shorts he wore were just tight enough on his behind to make watching him walk away a treat. When he bent over to pull some weeds out of one of the planter beds, she had to bite her lip to keep from moaning.

Still, he caught her looking. "Like what you see?"

Camilla did her best to prevent her cheeks from glowing incandescently at the grin on his face. "And if I do?"

His amused gaze met hers. "Good. Because I like looking at you, too."

She'd always had a thing for men who did things for her without being asked, and Danny was certainly filling that well for her. Each and every day, he showed her a little more of the man he was now. He gave her tidbits into his life, into the years they'd been apart, and she wanted more than tidbits. The problem with this was that the six-foot-one, gorgeously muscled man had a "look but don't touch" policy going on. They'd shared that single kiss the day of Bennie's birthday party last month and nothing since.

"Well, aren't the two of you just so incredibly sweet? It makes my teeth hurt even looking at you," Mrs. Sutherland called from where she stood in the open gateway.

"Close the gate!" Camilla cried.

But it was too late.

Fidget caught sight of the opening and bolted through the wide-open gate with glee. Nothing more than a black-and-white blur, she was gone before Camilla could get up out of her chair.

"Fidget!" she cried out, but her beloved pet didn't stop.

Danny hurried out the gate past Mrs. Sutherland after the little dog. He was around the corner and out of sight before Camilla even got off the porch.

On the verge of panic, she moved toward the gate but was blocked by her nosy neighbor.

"Camilla, dear, I stopped by—"

"I really don't have time at the moment." Patience was also in short supply. What kind of person opened a gate and just stood there with it open?

"I wanted to speak to you about that girl you've had over a few times, the one that Alma Stone's fostering. I think she's falling in with the wrong crowd. I do watch what's going on in this town, you know."

"I'd love to talk to you about Maddie another time, but right now, I need to find my dog." She did want to know if Maddie was going astray, but her immediate concern was for Fidget.

"Pshaw." Mrs. Sutherland waved a dismissive hand at her. She shook her head like Camilla was silly for even being concerned. "It'll come home when it's hungry. And besides, it's just a dog."

Just a dog?

"In case you've forgotten, Mrs. Sutherland, I have no family. That furry little dog is all I have and I love her very much." She glared at the woman as she stepped aside. Normally, she was far more respectful of her elders, but right now she simply wasn't capable of it.

"You're right," Mrs. Sutherland conceded, her face paling at the realization of what she'd done. "I apologize. I really didn't mean to let her out."

Camilla softened. The elderly woman really wasn't the malicious type. Gossipy, yes. A bit careless at times, but she wouldn't do something to hurt someone intentionally. "I know you didn't, but I need to find my dog. Can we talk later?"

"I'll sit on your porch and see if she comes home." Mrs. Sutherland offered. "Go on, find your little furry friend."

Camilla ran out the gate and stopped when she reached the street, trying to decide which way she should go to begin her search. With no way of knowing which way Danny or Fidget had gone, she was nearly paralyzed with fear. She couldn't lose her dog. She just couldn't.

Thankfully, Fidget was not a super-high-energy dog, despite her current display of athletics. A ten-minute spree around the yard once or twice a day suited the little dog, and it suited Camilla just fine, too. When she'd gone to the shelter in search of a pet, she'd been thinking of a cat, because she wasn't a jogger and didn't want a dog with massive exercise requirements. But when Camilla walked past Fidget's cage, heading toward the cat room at the back, the little dog had jumped up on her hind legs, waving, like she was saying, "Pick me!"

And that had been that—love at first sight. Instead of a cat, Camilla came home with a shih tzu who loved to eat trash and anything yucky off the ground, but also loved more than anything to spend a quiet evening curled up in her owner's lap. So, surely, she wouldn't be far away.

"Fidget!" she called, heading toward downtown, along their normal walking path. Maybe Fidget had followed their familiar route and was waiting for Camilla to catch up. She'd probably made it to the edge of the park at full sprint and then run out of energy.

Please let her be waiting for me up ahead.

She ran up the street, shouting her dog's name as she went. Each person that she passed, she stopped to ask if they'd seen a little black-and-white dog, but no one had seen her. Eyes scanning each yard, Camilla got closer and closer to downtown. With each empty yard, the pit in her stomach grew deeper. The alley behind the clinic was empty: no sign of her furbaby.

Walking around the end of the building, she searched

the square. Something black-and-white by the back tires of an old truck caught her eye and her heart lurched. Slowly, she moved in that direction. It wasn't moving. When she got closer, she could finally make out that it was a stuffed toy and not her sweet pup. "Where are you, Fidget?"

A sob rose in her throat at the thought she might never hold that furry little body again. Her rescue dog had become more than just a pet to Camilla and she wasn't sure how she'd go on if something happened to Fidget. Self-recrimination rose up within her. She hadn't done enough to protect Fidget. The gate shouldn't open so easily from the outside. She should have fixed it so that not just anyone could get into her backyard.

As the sun sank lower, Camilla's heart grew as heavy as her legs. The fading light left dappled shadows on the ground, creating harder conditions to see a multicolored dog. Her voice was hoarse from shouting out Fidget's name over and over.

What worried her most about her dog being out alone, besides the fear of the shih tzu getting hit by a car, was that Fidget had no sense whatsoever. If a coyote or a bigger dog came after her, she wouldn't back down from a fight. When it came to fight or flight, Fidget got in the fight line twice. She had no concept of being only eight pounds, and would bravely go after something four times her size.

A car slowed next to her. Alma rolled the window down. "I ran into Danny. He told me about your dog. Hop in and I'll drive us around slow and see if we can find her."

Blinking away tears at the kindness of the gesture, she climbed in the front seat next to Alma. "Thank you for this."

"Of course." Alma put the car in Drive again and they cruised slowly up and down the streets. Quietly at first, but before long, Alma's natural tendencies to talk became too much to contain, and the flow of words began. "It's the least I can do given all the help you have given Maddie in biology this year. You might not remember, but I didn't exactly ace science. I've always been more of a history buff."

"Anything for Maddie." Camilla sighed. "Mrs. Sutherland had actually come over to talk to me about her, but I put the conversation off to find my dog. She's worried about some of Maddie's friends or something."

"Oh? I have to admit, I've been worried, too. Dave and I try to give her structure—I think kids need structure, don't you?—but I worry that if we push her too far, she will hate us more than she already does. She's so angry, though."

"Mmm…" Camilla mumbled in agreement.

"If we thought she'd be okay with it, Dave and I would like to adopt her. Bennie loves her, and she's really good with him."

"Adopt?" Camilla whispered.

"Yes, is it a bad idea?" Alma slowed to a stop in front of Camilla's house. She flashed Camilla a look of remorse. "I'm sorry, I need to get home and get Bennie tucked in."

"Thank you for trying, at least," Camilla said earnestly. "It really means a lot that you would take time out of your evening to help me."

Reaching over, she took Alma's hand in hers. When she spoke, she chose her words carefully, not wanting what she said to sound at all discouraging or accusatory. "And if you are certain that you want to adopt, I think it could be a really great thing. Ask Maddie what she feels about it. But be absolutely certain of your decision before you speak to her. Not much is harder for a foster kid than the hope of a permanent home being snatched away because the parents changed their minds."

It hadn't happened to her, but she'd seen the disappointment and the anger more than once with her temporary foster siblings. She'd watched as the hope of adoption faded until they were as hard and jaded as she was. Adoption had never been an option for her. Her parents had hated her just enough to keep the potential that they might come back for her on the table, which meant no permanent placements.

Alma reassured her that they wouldn't change their minds, but that they would be careful how they broached the subject with Maddie. Camilla hoped Maddie would be open to what a great thing being adopted by the Stones could be for her. To have a stable, permanent family? Oh, what Camilla would have given for that at Maddie's age.

Camilla stepped out of the car and watched as Alma drove down the street.

Mrs. Sutherland sat in the rocker on the front porch. "Camilla, honey, there you are. I haven't seen any sign of your dog. I'm going to mosey on home now. Again, I'm sorry about letting your dog out. Stop by sometime this week and I'll share my concerns about that foster girl."

"Good night, Mrs. Sutherland," Camilla called over her shoulder as she looked under the bushes at the front of the house. She walked around the side, hoping maybe Fidget had come home but was hiding from Mrs. Sutherland. Sadly, there was no sign of her.

Or Danny.

Camilla let herself in the house and got a drink of water for her parched and achy throat. Where had she left her phone? Maybe it was still on the back porch…

Yes. She picked it up and saw eight missed calls from Danny. Hitting the button, she returned his call.

"Hey, babe," he said as he answered, and then she heard a clatter. "Hang on, I dropped you," he said, his voice sounding distant.

Smiling, she waited for him to pick the phone back up. She finished her water and placed the glass in the sink. Digging under the sink, she looked for a flashlight. There was one under there somewhere, she was sure of it. It was getting dark and she couldn't search for Fidget without light.

"Okay, sorry about that. I've got my hands full here and couldn't hold on to my phone and your squirming mutt at the same time. You could have told me she doesn't like to be carried."

"What?" A tear trekked down her cheek.

"Fidget. Did you know she isn't a fan of being carried?"

"Yes. You...you have her?"

"Yeah, I found her about twenty minutes ago. She was begging for pepperonis from some kids having a pizza party out at the skate park."

She'd been circling the kids, barking and sitting up on her hind legs so that she could beg like a lunatic for bits of pepperoni or pizza crust. The kids had found her hilarious and wanted to keep her. Two brothers had even convinced their mom to take the dog home with them. He'd never tell Camilla that they'd been discussing what they might name her dog.

Thankfully, Fidget had responded to him and come running over when he'd called her name or they might have had an issue. As it was, he'd had to endure a lecture about letting his dog run free and disappointing young children as a result of his irresponsibility. But, he'd chosen to be the bigger person and not cause a scene in front of a group of kids. Who just decided they would keep an obviously well-loved dog with a collar on like that anyway?

The little mutt in his arms wiggled and he almost dropped her. Again. "Hold still, Fidget," he grumbled. "She's determined to make me drop her. I swear."

"She likes to use her legs." Camilla's voice was thick with emotion. He wasn't used to hearing tears in her voice. Anger, yes. Uncertainty, sure. Pain, too often, unfortunately. But not this.

"Are you crying?"

"No," she said with a sob. Sniffles came through the line as she struggled to get herself under control. "Why would I be crying?"

"Babe…" The endearment slipped past his lips before he could stop it. What could he say that would make things better for her? He'd thought she'd be happy he found her dog. Were these happy tears? Impossible to tell over the phone.

"Where are you?"

"I'm at the end of the street. Fidget and I will see you in a minute, maybe two." Danny hung up the phone and roughly shoved it into the pocket of his shorts, all the while trying to maintain his hold on the shaggy little dog in his arms. Having made the mistake of letting her down once, he wasn't falling for that again. The yappy thing had run circles around him for five minutes, teasing him until he got his hands on her again.

Before they got halfway to the house, Camilla ran up to them. She snatched Fidget from his arms and hugged the little dog until it squeaked. Standing in the middle of the street, she held the dog close and just sobbed. The outpouring of emotion made quite the spectacle in the middle of the street. He thought it was a pretty sweet scene, though.

"Might wanna let her breathe. I didn't spend the last two hours looking for her just so you could squeeze her to death." He put an arm around Camilla's shoulders and turned her back toward her house. "Let's get you both home."

Camilla was crying so hard he doubted she'd have made it home without his assistance. Her face was buried in the dog's fur and she let him guide her completely down the street.

The trust she showed him in that moment humbled him. She was allowing him to direct her down a public street, trusting he'd protect her from any traffic. He hoped maybe one day she'd trust him like that in all aspects of her life.

When they got inside, she carried Fidget to the couch while he locked the door. She sat, never releasing the dog. Her sobs cut him to the core. Trying not to disturb her, Danny eased down next to her. Wrapping his arms around her gently, he did his best to comfort her.

"I could have lost her," she cried, still cradling the squirming dog like a baby.

"But you didn't." He brushed a lock of hair away from her tear-dampened face. Camilla never cried like this. She'd always been the strong one, the one people leaned on. To see her fall apart was hard. "She's right here. Safe and sound."

"I need you to put a lock on that gate as soon as you can. No one should be able to open it like that." There was a desperation in her eyes he couldn't deny. He could see that she needed this something fierce. Getting a lock on that gate was now *her* first priority. She begged, "Please, Danny."

"First thing in the morning. No, tomorrow's the festival. But I promise you, the first chance I get, I'll take a look and see what options we have." He'd have to try to squeeze in a trip to the hardware store this weekend. Even if it was a chain and padlock until he could find a more permanent solution for her.

She nodded at him. "I can't lose her again."

"You won't," he reassured her, even though it was a promise he couldn't be sure he could keep. But if there was something he could do to help make sure her dog didn't get lost again, he'd do it. "Has she run off like that before?"

Camilla swiped at her tears with the back of her sleeve. "Not like this. She normally runs circles around me just out of reach until she tires out."

Chuckling, he scratched the dog's ear. "She did that to me, too. After I got her, she wiggled so much that I had to sit her down so that I could readjust my grip. She got away from me and did loops around me for a good five minutes until I could get a hold of her again."

"She's a punk." Camilla smiled, giving the pup another squeeze.

"How long have you had her?"

"About a year." Camilla relaxed into his side, so much of the tension now gone from her body. "I meant to get a cat, but look at this face."

"You're really attached to her, huh?"

She nodded. "We are a package deal now."

"I see that. First pet?"

"Is it that obvious?" Her smile was shy when she looked up at him.

"Little bit, yeah." He shrugged.

"She's all I've got."

It made more sense now just why she'd gotten so upset about the dog's disappearance. With no family, and no serious relationships, the little mutt had become Camilla's family. She was such a loving person, and in the absence of a human to love, she'd focused all her attention on this furry rascal.

She had him now, too, a human in need of her loving attention. And he was going to make sure that from now on she knew she had someone in her corner. Some might say they'd had their chance, but since they'd crashed and burned, they should leave well enough alone. But the truth was, they'd been solid until he'd let his insecurities and the trauma of the accident come between them. Maybe this was their chance at finally being whole again.

His fingers tangled in her hair as they snuggled on her couch, just the two of them and her dog. The riot of emotions normally swirling through his brain was calm tonight. Between the two hours of walking, and even more so, having Camilla in his arms, his mind was blissfully quiet. He couldn't remember the last time he'd been so at peace.

"I always laughed at people who said their dogs or cats were their kids. Now look at me," Camilla said suddenly, snorting in amusement at herself. "I completely lost it when Fidget got out. I was rude to Mrs. Sutherland, and I'm never rude to my elders. Alma came seeking me out, and didn't even talk my ear off, so I must have looked pretty bad. It's been such a weird night, all because of an open gate."

Danny shrugged. "Mrs. Sutherland will get over herself soon enough. She likely just wanted to flap her lips a bit anyhow."

Camilla shifted so that she could stare at him, a wide

grin on her face. She shook her head, still smiling from ear to ear.

"What?" he asked, his lip curling up slightly in response to her smile.

"Did you hear what you just said?"

His forehead wrinkled as he thought about his words. "Oh, man. What have you and this town done to me? You'll have me saying *ain't* and *y'all* again before summer is out."

After years away from Greenbriar and the southern part of the country, he'd slowly eliminated some of those country colloquialisms from his speech. A few months back home and in Camilla's presence and the words rolled off his tongue like he'd never stopped using them.

"I think it's adorable," she drawled, exaggerating her own accent.

"You would."

Fidget jumped down, and for a minute, Camilla tensed up like she was going to follow her. But then she lay her head on his chest and sighed.

"Thank you again for finding her."

"Anything for you."

"It means the world to me. She's…she's my family. And I would be lost without her. Knowing that you spent your evening looking for her, on foot no less, shows me how invested you are in rebuilding my trust. If you hadn't helped me look for her tonight, you'd have ruined any chance of that."

"You needed me."

He was slightly stung at the implication he might not have helped her, but he knew he deserved it. He hadn't always put her needs before his own in the past. If he wanted Camilla back in his life, it was something that would have to change. Work and more work had been his entire existence for so long. His life had been so monotonous and he hadn't even noticed. Day in, day out, he'd let the busyness of the medical tent or emergency department distract him from anything more personal. But with Camilla, he wanted it all. He wanted the laughter and the arguments and even the tears.

Camilla's finger tapped on his nose. A lock of her hair fell down in front of her eyes and she brushed it away in annoyance.

"What?" he asked, blinking.

"Where'd you go?"

Shaking his head, he pulled her close once more and tried to explain away his lapse in attention. "Babe, if you said anything just then, I'm going to be honest, I wasn't listening. I was thinking about how different my life is here in Greenbriar, with you."

She huffed. "Good differences, I hope."

"Yeah." He gave her a squeeze, laughing when she grunted and slapped his stomach playfully. He pushed the envelope a little more and tickled her side.

"Don't…" she warned, raising up, her eyes glittering.

"Fine." He glanced at his watch and sighed. If he left right now and went straight home he could get a possible five hours of sleep at the most. "I should probably be getting home. It's late and I have to be at the clinic early to pack up supplies for the festival tomorrow. The town council want us set up and ready for potential patients by nine."

Some of the sparkle left her eyes when he mentioned leaving. "Okay," she said softly, but it was her tone that set him to aching.

He searched her face, seeing the disappointment etched there. He wanted to stay. Of course he did. But he wanted to do things right and that meant taking his time. Denying her had to be one of the hardest things he'd done in years, though.

Touching his thumb to her cheek, he gently smoothed it down to trace her lower lip. She had a mouth that was meant for kissing. "We don't need to rush this."

"I know." Eyes closed, Camilla leaned into his touch.

"You know, I don't have to leave just yet." He brushed his lips over hers. "I have time to at least give you a proper goodbye."

CHAPTER NINE

ON MEMORIAL DAY MORNING, Camilla sat on her back porch alone, enjoying the quiet of the early hours. She'd always been a morning person, up by sunrise without a complaint, so that she could have a few moments of alone time while in a crowded foster home or group home. Even once she'd moved out on her own, the habit of being an early riser lingered, and was perhaps too engrained in her personality to change now. Even if she and Danny had been up until the wee hours of the night talking.

The years that had passed when they were separated had shaped them into different people than the young couple who'd broken up that day in that hospital room. Camilla could certainly admit that she'd been changed by her experiences and she was learning a lot about the man Danny was now. The Danny she'd intended to marry had been light and carefree, not this serious, sometimes brooding man that she found equally intriguing.

In other ways, things remained as familiar as always. Danny remembered just how to make her laugh and even recognized when he'd pushed her a little too far. And each touch of his hand was both deliciously familiar and excitingly new all at once.

Every day, she knew she was falling deeper and deeper into love with him. And that honestly scared the snot out of her. He hadn't told her yet what his plans were come August 1. Would he stay? Would he go? One way meant the possibility of having nearly everything she'd ever wanted—her own medical practice and a loving partner to share her life with. The other? Well, she didn't want to think about what she'd do if Danny disappeared from her life again.

Finishing the last dregs of coffee from her mug, she called Fidget inside and shut the little dog in her crate for the day where she'd be safe. She had to get downtown. She needed to help Danny set up the first aid booth before the festivities got underway.

When Camilla made it downtown, all the vendors were already there and a small crowd was gathering. At the edge of the park, she could see the fireworks display being set up. The town always did a massive pyrotechnics display for Memorial Day. It was one of her favorite parts of the celebration.

The sweet scent of funnel cakes wafted over on the breeze and took her straight back to high school. One of her first dates with Danny had been to come to this festival. They'd shared a funnel cake that day, too. Wistfully, she let the memories of that day rush over her and she could almost feel the giddy hopefulness her younger self had felt when *the* Danny Owens—elite quarterback and star of the dreams of every girl at Greenbriar High School—had held her hand as they walked through the booths together. It was the day she'd started to fall in love with the handsome dark-haired boy who'd had no idea how harsh life could be, and the day he'd begun to show her that not everything in life had to be hard.

True love existed, she really believed that, because of Danny. He'd opened her eyes to possibilities she'd never thought achievable. It was because of him and his family that she'd found her calling as a doctor. She'd never have dreamed as big as medical school without them. She was a poor foster kid, and her ambitions had been much more modest and geared toward independence. They'd showed her that her situation didn't have to affect her future, and more than that, they'd proved how important the love of a family could be. Before Danny had snatched it all away and that family had shrunk to just her and Robert.

She shook herself to clear those negative thoughts that persisted on creeping in. Today was not a day to dwell on the past. She had far too much to do in the present.

When she got close to the first aid tent, she could see that Danny was already there. She stopped for a moment to watch as he worked. He had a pale blue T-shirt on with the Greenbriar Medical logo stretched snug across his broad chest and khaki cargo shorts. She'd noticed he had a thing about needing pockets now and he carried so many things in them that she teased him frequently about retroactively becoming a Boy Scout.

From her position, she could see that he had boxes of gauze, antiseptic and cold packs already set up under the counter. He was organizing the next large box of supplies when he looked up and they made eye contact. Nerves danced around in her stomach as their eyes met.

Pull it together, Camilla. You aren't sixteen with a crush anymore.

When she walked up to the booth, he came over to greet her. "Good morning," he said, wrapping his arms around her. "It looks like it's going to be a perfect day for the festival. Sunny, but not blazing hot. I grabbed far more supplies than I think we will need, but could you look through and see if there's anything I missed while I have time to run back to the clinic and grab things? I like to be prepared."

"Mmm." She snuggled into his arms, enjoying the security of his arms wrapped around her. So they'd only shared a few kisses and cuddles so far, but it had given her the time to work through what she loved about him. And the strength in his arms making her feel safe was only one of them, even as a small part of her persisted in warning her that getting too comfortable in his embrace would only lead to further heartache. "I think we have time to say a proper hello first, don't you?"

"A proper hello, huh?" He leaned down, smiling. His lips grazed against hers as he asked, "What's a proper hello to you?"

Sliding her arms up and around his neck, she initiated the kiss. Pressing herself against the firmness of Danny's chest, she sighed when he deepened the kiss. When his fingers rubbed in small circles over the small of her back, she settled further into his embrace. Nothing more than a scraped knee ever happened in Greenbriar anyway, so why did they need a fully staffed first aid booth?

A catcall from right behind her ruined the moment. She wanted to cry when the kiss ended abruptly. It had been such a perfect kiss, too. The interruption was almost a tragedy.

Pulling away with real reluctance, Camilla turned to see Maddie and Alma standing there with matching smirks on their faces. Alma raised one perfectly arched brow and shook her head in amusement. Camilla rolled her eyes and bit back a smile. Then she made the mistake of looking over at Maddie and the sparkle of amusement in the girl's irises was too much, and she felt the heat rising in her cheeks.

Camilla cleared her throat and had to force down the urge to apologize. What did she have to be sorry about? She was a grown woman. While it was a little display of PDA, they'd kept it PG-13 at most. They were barely even PG-13 in private these days.

"Good morning, ladies," Danny said from behind her, his tone casual and unbothered by the fact they'd just been caught practically making out. Even when they were teenagers, he'd never gotten flustered when someone busted them, though. He'd always been so cool and calm about it. "Are either of you in need of first aid?"

"No, I was actually hoping that Camilla could be Maddie's check-in person today?" Alma put a hand on Maddie's shoulder and Camilla couldn't help noticing that this time, the girl's posture didn't stiffen at the touch. "She wants to spend time out here with her friends and Bennie's just too small to be at the festival all day, especially in this heat. I don't want to treat her like a toddler, of course, but I'd feel better if she had someone here to come to every hour or so, to make sure everything is still okay."

Camilla had a no ready on her lips, because her focus needed to be on the first aid tent, but the pleading in Maddie's eyes stayed her refusal. Gosh, she was such a sucker for this kid and her sad eyes. Nodding slowly, Camilla agreed to be a sort of chaperone. "That's fine, but she will have to come to me, and if she doesn't check in, the best I can do is let you know, Alma, and you'll need to follow up."

"Thanks, Dr. D." Maddie rushed forward and hugged Camilla hard, nearly knocking her off her feet in her enthusiasm. "I promise I'll check in every hour on the dot."

"You better."

"You are the best!" Maddie said with a big grin. She looked a little shy and whispered to Camilla, "Alma and Dave said they want to adopt me. I won't screw that up."

"I know you won't." Camilla could tell Maddie didn't

want to make a big deal of her potential adoption, so she let the subject drop. Glancing down at her watch, Camilla said, "It's nine forty-five now, so I expect you to check in by eleven or I'm texting Alma at one minute past."

With a sassy salute, Maddie ran off to join a group of teens who had gathered around a booth with virtual reality headsets and games. Teenagers were the same no matter how many years had passed. They liked the newest technology and to avoid adults.

Camilla watched the group fondly. She could only hope they didn't get into as much trouble as she had at that age. At least in such a small town, someone would usually be keeping an eye on them and wouldn't let them get into too much mischief. Hopefully.

Alma reached out and laid a hand on Camilla's forearm. "Thank you, truly. I'm trying to give her a little more freedom, but not too much. As you know, it's a delicate balance with her."

"No problem," Camilla reassured her, although it was a distraction she didn't need that day. But it was a small enough favor that helped both Maddie and Alma, so she hadn't felt that she could refuse.

"You could have said no," Danny said as Alma walked away. He seemed to be reading her thoughts again.

"Could I, though?"

"I suppose you couldn't. I would have." He shrugged, but the grin he flashed her was not so nonchalant. "But no one expects me to be nice all the time. In fact, if I were nice all the time, people would start getting the wrong idea. They might start to think I liked them or something equally as horrid."

He faked a look of fear.

Rolling her eyes, Camilla sorted through the remaining boxes, double-checking what Danny had brought.

He'd overprepared, if anything. Danny had brought the basics, along with doses of epinephrine, pressure bandages, arm and leg splints, and their portable defibrillator and various other supplies. Last year, she'd only used antiseptic, a handful of adhesive bandages, and a couple of cold packs. Mostly she'd handed out bottled waters and made people sit in the shade for a bit until they'd cooled off.

"I think you brought our entire supply closet out here. I can't think of a single thing you missed." She nudged him. "You know you are in Greenbriar, right?"

"I wasn't sure what we would need and trust me when I say that I'd rather have too many supplies than not enough." Shadows darkened his eyes. Visibly, he withdrew to someplace she couldn't follow.

Concern welled up inside her. She stepped closer and touched his cheek. "You okay?"

"Hmm." He blinked rapidly as he returned to the present. "Sorry, got lost in my head there for a second."

Camilla wanted to ask. Maybe one day he would trust her enough to tell her about his darkest days. So far, most of their conversations had been light and fluffy; the deepest ones still didn't touch his time overseas or what he'd gone through over there. He'd never once talked to her about the day his mom and brother had died, either.

"How's this festival looking compared to the ones in the past?" Danny reclined against the counter. He stared out over the growing crowd.

She hopped up on the counter and sat next to him. Pointing at the VR booth they'd seen Maddie run toward, she said, "The tech booth is new this year. Mrs. Sutherland and her friends have had that quilting booth next to it since we were coming here as teens. Not sure what that pink glittery tent is on the far side of Mrs. Sutherland. I can't read the sign from this angle."

Danny shook his head. "I didn't know tents could sparkle, but that thing's blinding when the sun hits it just right. It reminds me of the way the sun shimmered on the sand in the desert."

All around them, townsfolk were coming out to shop at the various booths lining the street and leading into the park. Most of the town's older women clustered around the quilting booth, gossiping. When Mrs. Sutherland saw Camilla look her way, she held up her hand and tapped at her ring finger with a smile.

Nosy old busybody. She and Danny would move forward when and if they were both ready. Not based on the teasing or pushing of some old woman who probably didn't even remember what romance was.

"You know what I don't see?" Camilla searched the booths to be certain. "Pam's Popsicles."

"Oh, man." Danny straightened up, eyes scanning through the crowd and searching each of the booths and trailers. Disappointment lined his face. "That's such a bummer. It was one of the things I was looking forward to today. I was thinking it would be a good trip down memory lane for us. Do you remember? Our first kiss was Pam's Popsicles–flavored—Red, White and Blueberry, to be exact. Over by that big oak tree at the Maple Street entrance to the park."

"You remember that?" An affectionate rush of emotions swept over her. The little details that meant so much. Danny recalled them all and it made her all mushy and gushy about it.

"Remember it?" He picked up her hand and laced their fingers together. His palm was warm again hers. A simple act, hand-holding. But it was a connection, an intimacy, that she couldn't get enough of. "A couple summers ago I got a blueberry snow cone and it brought all the memories back, taking me in my mind to Greenbriar and that kiss. I almost broke down and called you that day, but I talked myself out of it, convinced that you wouldn't want to hear from me."

With her head leaned against his shoulder, Camilla sighed. How many times had she wished he would pick up the phone and call? Or prayed he'd be standing at the door when an unexpected knock came? "I wish you had. I've always wanted to hear from you. Of course, given how things ended, I could never be the one to make first contact. The scraps of my remaining pride wouldn't allow it."

"Camilla, I—"

Whatever words Danny had intended to utter were drowned out by a series of resounding booms. Before Camilla could look around to find the source, Danny had thrown her to the ground, his hard body landing on top of her. Pinned between the grass and Danny's chest, Camilla could barely breathe. The horrible sounds coming from the direction of the park sent a shiver of fear down Camilla's spine.

"Danny, I don't know what just happened." When the screams for help started, it galvanized her into action, though. "People are hurt. I need you with me."

Slowly, they rose to their feet, side by side. As she gazed out over the grassy area that had only minutes ago been filled with laughter and smiles, she recoiled in horror at the scene in front of her. Tears filled her eyes as she took it all in.

"Wh-what on earth?"

CHAPTER TEN

THE CARNAGE IN front of him matched his memories of war. All that was missing was the rapid sound of gunfire and the rotors of the chopper stirring up sand all around them. He stood, briefly frozen, watching as people started picking themselves up off the ground, tears and blood running down their faces.

"Danny…" Camilla's hand reached for his. There was an unusual sweatiness to her palm and a slight shake to her hand. "Where do we start?"

He focused on the hand holding his. Camilla need him to be strong today. With zero experience in field medicine, Camilla needed him alert so that he could guide her through whatever had just sent a rude awakening through their sleepy little town.

Resolve strengthened, he pulled her close, pressing a hard kiss to her mouth. Handing her some gloves, he pulled some on himself. "We get through this one patient at a time. Triage first. The minor stuff waits while we treat and assess worse injuries. Call 911 and tell them we need as many ambulances and medevac choppers as they can send."

Grabbing a couple of tarps, he carried them out and spread them in front of the tent. People were starting to make their way to them for help. "These tarps are for serious injuries only. If you just have minor cuts, I'm going to need you to step aside."

Two men carried a third man over and put him on the tarps, his entire front bloody. "The fireworks, they went off early. Rick said they saw a bunch of teenagers messing with them. They must have jacked the timer or something. Nothing was supposed to go off until at least eight o'clock. He went over to scare the kids off, but before he made it all the way, some of them started exploding. He caught something to the chest. Didn't see what."

"Rick? Just lay still as you can. I'm going to do what I can to fix you up." Danny moved quickly, using his pocketknife to slice the remnants of a cotton T-shirt away from the man's torso. He grabbed a stack of gauze pads and pressed them to the worst of the gaping wounds. Working fast, he pulled them away quickly and tried not to wince when he saw how bad the damage was. With no surgical equipment, no blood products, and no hospital close, this man's chances were slim. Danny packed the wound, taping it tightly and hoped that would slow the bleeding enough to allow the medevac chopper to arrive. He quickly bandaged the other wounds that were bleeding significantly. He asked the men who had carried Rick over to hold pressure on the wounds as best they could. "All right, Rick, that's all I can do right now. I'm going to see if any of your buddies need to be patched up."

Hurrying away felt like the coward's way out, but he'd seen enough similar injuries to know that Rick was about to ask him if he was going to make it. Scars already crisscrossed Danny's soul from all the lies he'd told to soldiers about how they were going to be just fine. He wasn't sure he had it in him to tell that lie again today.

Ripping his gloves off as he walked back to the tent, he tossed them in the small trash can he'd brought over from the clinic. It would never be big enough. Camilla had joked he'd brought the entire supply closet, but he was worried they wouldn't have enough to last them until backup arrived. He quickly poured sanitizer on his hands and grabbed fresh gloves and more gauze and bandages.

Sparing a quick glance at Camilla, he decided she didn't need him for the patient she had in front of her. Instead, he moved on to the teenager that Maddie and another boy were leading over.

"Dr. Owens, he needs help bad," Maddie said as they got close. Her words were rapid-fire, verging on panic as she blurted out everything she knew about her friend. "One of those fireworks shot him right in the chest. It didn't explode or nothing, but then another whacked him right upside his head! It took him clear off his feet and he hit that ground so hard. He don't seem to be breathing right and I don't know if his ear is still on his head."

Danny already had his stethoscope on the boy's chest. Breath sounds were diminished. The boy had air escaping into his chest cavity. He grabbed a pile of gauze and slapped it over the mangled remnants of the boy's ear and wrapped some tape around his head to keep it in place. Head wounds bled profusely. If the boy survived this, he'd carry the scars for the rest of his days.

"Let's sit him down over here. Keep him sitting up, though, okay?" He waved toward the tarps where Rick lay, his chest moving up and down in a ragged pattern. "I need to grab some supplies."

He really did not want to have to deal with a pneumothorax in the middle of Greenbriar's Memorial Day festival, but it didn't look like he had much choice. He hurried over to the first aid tent and riffled through the box of miscellaneous supplies. He had brought some empty needles, he was sure of it. Finally, he found the target of his search.

He hurried back over to the boy and checked his lungs one more time before he uncapped the needle, pulled the plunger free, and jabbed the needle between the boy's ribs. The sudden hiss of air and the boy's gasping breath told him he'd gotten it right. He taped the needle in place with gauze around it.

"Maddie, I need you to stay right here with your friend. If he stops breathing, if he starts breathing in a weird way or making any unusual noises, shout out for me or Camilla immediately, okay? Don't let him pull this out. If he does, he could die."

Maddie nodded, fear filling her eyes, but she sank down on the tarp next to her friend. Danny hated to walk away on that sort of statement, but he didn't have the time to coddle her, particularly when there was a good chance her buddy there had caused all this destruction.

As he began to approach a woman with some shrapnel lodged in her shoulder, Camilla called out for him and he ran over to her side. She was crouched next to a teenager, another from Maddie's crowd earlier. Camilla was holding his hands while he struggled against her.

"He's trying to pull the splinters out. But is that the best idea?" She looked at Danny for confirmation.

The boy had multiple chunks of wood lodged in his arm and one in his cheek. If Danny had to hazard a guess, one of the large mortars had hit a wooden booth and turned it into shrapnel.

"These three we can take out, shouldn't be any issue." Danny pointed at a few of the wood slivers. "But those are far too close to an artery for me to feel comfortable pulling them out here in the field."

He leaned over and made eye contact with the boy,

who couldn't have been more than sixteen. "Listen to me. I need you to lay still. I will take out the pieces that are safe to come out. But the others, they need to stay in until you are at the hospital. If you pull them out, and one of your arteries is damaged, you will bleed to death. We have no blood products, no surgical equipment here. There isn't a single thing we'd be able to do but watch you die. Do you hear me?"

The boy nodded ever so slowly, his body growing still as he stopped fighting against Camilla. His eyes filled with pain, tears, and more than a little fear. Danny shrugged off the guilt that came with being so blunt with an injured young boy, but he didn't have time to sugar-coat things to keep the kid from hurting himself even more than he already had.

"Okay, then. This is going to hurt. On the count of three… One…two…" *Yank.*

The kid whimpered but didn't cry out. He glared hard at Danny, but didn't try to speak.

"You mad that I didn't go on three?" Danny asked. "You would have tensed up and made it hurt more." *Yank.* "I know, you're even more mad now. But trust me, kid, it hurts worse when you—" *yank* "—know it's coming."

He spoke from personal experience on that one. Having the shrapnel pulled out of his leg from the day of the car accident was one of the worst medical procedures of his life. The doctor doing it had counted to three before he removed each and every single piece, and Danny had tensed up each and every time.

Ghostly wisps of a helicopter's whir tickled at his eardrums, so faint he thought he'd imagined it at first. Gradually, though, it grew louder and a medevac chopper dropped to the ground in the middle of the park, a short distance from the end of the line of booths.

"Finally," Camilla said with relief. "I've never been so happy to see a helicopter in my life."

He murmured an agreement as he taped gauze over the wounds he'd just pulled the wood slivers from. "That should help a little," he told their patient. "But don't touch the rest of them, okay?"

Sanitizing his hands yet again, he grabbed fresh gloves and moved out to meet the flight paramedics. He sent Rick with them first. They had him on a stretcher and were back in the helicopter taking off within minutes.

Hopefully, there were more on the way. More medical personnel, something. Camilla had looked so relieved to see that chopper. Hopefully, she wouldn't be disappointed at the size of the rescue crew.

"We need a doctor over here," someone shouted. "We can't move this guy and he's in bad shape."

He and Camilla both grabbed an armful of supplies and headed in that direction.

They found a man with the majority of a booth collapsed on him. His lower half was pinned beneath the wooden structure and his abdomen was flayed open. Danny had to bite back a curse. They were going to need another medevac chopper for sure.

He sank down on his knees and started assessing. Airway seemed clear as the man was able to breathe, although the breathing was ragged. Circulation was going to be a problem, with the amount of weight crushing the guy's lower extremities, though. He was going to be at real risk for crush syndrome. He pressed as much gauze as he had to the wound and secured it as best he could. It wasn't going to be more than a stopgap measure that would hopefully buy him some time to get him to hospital.

"Let's get an IV started," he said to Camilla. When he looked over at her, she'd already started to prep for that.

"I assumed you'd want that." She wiped the man's arm with an antiseptic wipe before inserting the IV needle in place, taking care not to jar him. She taped the cannula down and hung the IV bag of saline on the frame of the collapsed booth above his head.

The patient was in and out of consciousness, which was a bit of a worry. Danny wasn't sure if the man was bleeding beneath the wood that was piled on him or if it was merely pain taking him out.

"We need to stabilize him in the event of a spinal injury." He closed his eyes briefly and thought about what they could use. As a small-town clinic, they didn't keep that sort of equipment on hand. He needed a DIY replacement.

Quilts.

He hopped up and ran over to Mrs. Sutherland's booth. "I need all the quilts or blankets you can spare. And if you all could scrounge up some duct tape, that would be a huge help."

Mrs. Sutherland handed him a stack of quilts and the sparkly booth next to her pulled out a roll of shiny duct tape. He carried the armload of supplies back to his crush victim.

"Help me roll these into blocks to stabilize him with. Also, if someone could find us maybe a kid's sled or something long and flat that we can use as a makeshift backboard, that would be great."

He and Camilla quickly rolled the quilts and taped them tight to use as blocks to stabilize the patient so that they could hopefully move him. Someone ran up with a large sheet of plywood.

Danny and Camilla worked in sync, supporting the man with the rolled-up quilts and duct-taping them across him. Once they had done all they could with the quilts, they were ready to get the plywood in place.

"Okay, guys, Dr. Devereaux and I are going to gently raise him up just enough that you should be able to slide the plywood beneath him. Slow and easy, okay? On the count of three. One. Two. Three."

With the plywood in place, they eased him down onto the wood. Danny listened to his lungs again, but there was no change.

"Now we need to get this booth off him. Camilla, you and I will have to be ready to examine the lower limbs as soon as we pull him free. Watch for bleeders and fractures or dislocations."

Camilla nodded as a group of the townsfolk gathered around the damaged booth and readied themselves to lift it.

"On three." He counted down and when the booth rose, they tugged at the plywood, pulling the man free of his entrapment.

"You," Danny said, pointing at one of the men. "Run back to the first aid tent and grab the inflatable leg splints, all the ice packs you can hold, and the box labeled Miscellaneous."

Soon the man was back, nearly dropping the large armload of supplies onto the patient. Danny quickly grabbed the leg splints and tossed one to Camilla. "Check for fractures and distal pulses."

Camilla felt one leg while he palpated the other. The ankle was extremely deformed on his side and he could feel no pulse in the foot. He slipped the leg splint under the man's leg and then carefully tugged the foot back into the vicinity of straight. A faint pulse met him for the effort. He inflated the splint and looked over to see Camilla inflating hers, as well.

"No obvious deformities," she said. "Surprising, considering all that."

The whir of a helicopter overhead was a welcome sound. He joked, "Oh, now they show up. After we've done all the hard work."

Camilla snorted. "I bet they'll take all the credit, too."

The next few hours passed in a blur as they sent patient after patient to the hospital in ambulances, medevac choppers, and even the back seats of cars. As evening drew near, the line of people waiting for care had trickled down to a slow crawl. When they hadn't seen a patient in over twenty minutes, Danny finally thought it was safe to close the first aid tent up for the night.

Sinking down on a cooler, he opened a bottle of water and downed it in practically a single gulp. He could live the rest of his life without another day like this. Working trauma in a fully equipped medical center—that he could handle. But he'd left his days of field medicine behind when he left the Army. Or so he'd thought... The bottle in his hand started to shake as the adrenaline that had fueled him for hours wore off and all that remained were the unwanted aftereffects.

Camilla sank down on the cooler next to him, unusually quiet. She held an unopened bottle of water in her hands. Waves of exhaustion rolled off her and he felt each and every one in his own bones.

"You okay?"

She nodded slowly, but then contradicted herself. "No, I don't think I am. I'm going to have nightmares about this for weeks."

"Weeks if you are lucky. Years, more likely." Danny picked at the label on his water bottle, peeling the wrapper off slowly, as he talked to Camilla. Finally, he opened up to her a little. "Seeing people that you know with blood running down their faces, with their chests flayed open, and in obvious agony, it's not something you get over easily."

Choking back a sob, Camilla leaned her head against his shoulder. The heat of her tears soaked through his T-shirt. He slid his arm around her shoulder and just let her cry. Occasionally, he murmured a reassurance, but nothing he could say would ease the pain of seeing so many friends with traumatic injuries. He knew that from experience as deep as his soul.

He'd had the benefit of distance today. There were some familiar faces, yes, but he wasn't involved with these people on a daily basis like Camilla. It made it easier for him to push them into the role of patient and leave them there. For her, though, these people weren't just patients; they were her friends, the people she sat with at church on Sunday, and the foster kids she tutored in biology. They meant something to her, and that simple fact alone meant that staying objective and keeping a mental distance would have been impossible for her. He knew that pain. He'd had the same struggles while patching up his platoon. But worse than caring for his men had been the pain of trying to save his mom and brother and knowing he could do nothing. That had been what had broken him and sent him on that one-way ticket out of town.

He hugged her tighter, wishing he could shoulder the brunt of her pain. "It's going to be okay."

"Excuse me." A man cleared his throat. "Sorry to interrupt."

Danny looked up to see a uniformed police officer standing a few feet away. "What can I help you with?" he asked, hoping it wasn't medical care. He was wiped and Camilla was in no shape to treat any patients.

"I need to get statements from both of you for our in-

vestigation. Do you have a minute?" the officer asked.
"Maybe I could start with you, sir?"

"Yeah, I'll go first," Danny offered, glancing at Camilla, who was swiping roughly at her tear-stained face and trying to gather her composure. If treating neighbors had hurt her this badly, how would she react if she ever lost a loved one? Was it fair to her to have her fall in love with him again? Danny swallowed hard. What was he doing to her?

CHAPTER ELEVEN

"THIS ALL HAS to be a horrible dream, a nightmare, really," Camilla muttered to herself as she cleaned up the first aid tent. She boxed up the few supplies that remained to go back to the clinic. It all fit in a single cardboard box that she could carry with one hand. Fidget outweighed the box of leftover medical bits. A handful of colorful children's bandages, one box of antiseptic, bottles of sunscreen, and some packets of pain reliever were all that was left unused.

And she'd teased Danny that he'd overprepared.

Never again would she fault him for wanting to have more supplies than they ever expected to use. In fact, she'd probably bring all the supplies they possessed to any events they attended in the future.

But, oh, man, was she going to need to place a massive supply order the next day. She might have to run out and stock up with what limited supplies she could get at the drugstore just to see them through until her supplier could get the clinic replenished.

She carried the little box over to the clinic herself and set it on the floor of the mostly empty supply closet. Repeating to herself, "It's all gonna be okay, it's all gonna be okay," she tried hard not to burst into tears again. Hopefully, her little mantra would keep the nightmares away, because the horror and destruction of the past eight hours still dogged her every breath.

Camilla liked to think of herself as a levelheaded person, a strong and capable woman who kept her head in an emergency. But even the strongest had their limits and hers had been breached today. She wasn't prone to drama, but surely a few tears were warranted, given the day's events.

She took a moment to wash her face and hands before changing into the spare outfit she kept at the clinic. As a family practitioner, she'd learned to keep a change of clothes handy because if you didn't, it was guaranteed that a puking patient would make you wish you had. Her old clothes she tossed in the biohazard bag. She didn't want to know what was on them and she wasn't risking taking them home with her.

That done, she walked back over to the first aid tent, which was completely empty. Glancing around, she saw no sign of Danny, who'd been giving his statement. Where could he have gone?

No sign of Officer Shea, either. Figuring they'd eventually come here to look for her, she sat down and put her throbbing feet up. What a day!

While she waited, she pulled her phone out and called Alma to check on Maddie. Alma told her that Maddie was physically okay, but had cried herself to sleep over seeing her friends injured. Most of all, the girl had been worried that Alma and Dave wouldn't want to adopt her anymore. Camilla hadn't even thought about that being a possibility, but Alma had assured her that Maddie's choice of friends hadn't changed their minds about making her a permanent part of their family. Soon she would need to talk to Maddie about her the people she chose to spend her time with, but for now, sleep was the best thing for her. Alma and Camilla chatted a few more minutes about Maddie until Camilla saw Officer Shea walking up. She ended the call with a promise to check on Maddie the next day.

"Dr. Devereaux, is now a better time for your statement?" Officer Shea asked, pulling a small notebook and pen out of his uniform pocket.

"It's as good as it's going to get after the day I've had." She patted her hand on the wooden counter where she sat. "You don't mind if I sit, do you? It's been a long day and I am exhausted."

"Of course, no problem at all." Officer Shea flipped through his little book until he found a blank page and scrawled her name across the top in black ink. "I'd like to ask you a few questions about today, starting with, did you see what happened?"

Camilla recounted what she knew, which wasn't much.

Shea closed his notebook and shoved it roughly back into his pocket. "You've corroborated what I've been hearing. Teenagers messing with the dang fireworks. Serves 'em right if they have lasting scars, after they hurt half the town and traumatized the rest."

She raised an eyebrow at him and he colored under her scrutiny. That was a harsh statement to make, particularly in regards to young people.

"I mean, I don't wish none of them any permanent harm or nothing. But they should have a reminder of what they done wrong, don't ya think?" Shea held his ground on his opinion, even if he softened it slightly.

With a sigh, she nodded at him, too tired to argue that they were young and had made a stupid mistake. "Do you know where Dr. Owens went?"

"No, ma'am, I sure don't." Shea nodded and took a step back. "You have a good night, ma'am."

Ma'am? How old did he think she was? She was only a few years older than Officer Shea and he wanted to call her *ma'am*? She hopped down from the counter shaking her head. Sometimes Southern manners made her want to hurt someone.

She pulled her phone off and sent a text to Danny.

His reply came quickly.

I'm sorry, but I need some time.

Her heart raced as she processed those words. He needed time? Because of what had just happened? Because of her? Because he was leaving town again and never coming back?

She sucked in a deep breath and sent him a single word reply. If Danny was gone, then she might as well call it a night and go take care of Fidget. Her poor puppy was probably about to piddle all over her crate after this long.

As she walked home, she noticed the town was unusually quiet. Yards were empty, and so were the streets. She couldn't blame her neighbors for wanting to be safe and sound within the walls of their homes. That was certainly where she wanted to be, even if she didn't want to be alone.

When she walked up the drive to her house, some of the stress melted away, because she knew that in this house, she was safe. She spared a glance at the gate to the backyard to make sure it was latched before she went up on the porch. Another night like last night was beyond her current energy level and emotional capacity.

Fidget started barking as soon as she unlocked the front door. "I'm coming, Fidget," she called out. When she opened the crate, the little black-and-white dog darted out between her feet and started running in a circle around the kitchen, yapping her little head off.

Camilla didn't even bother shushing the dog, and let her get her energy out. Unlocking the back door, she let Fidget out and stepped out on the porch to sit and watch while her dog ran laps around the yard.

When Fidget had done her business and gotten tired, she came back up on the porch and hopped up in Camilla's lap. Camilla hugged the little dog close, burying her face in the mutt's shaggy fur. For years, she'd prided herself on her collected demeanor, the key to which was having a good purge every so often. Usually, that took the shape of a sad movie or book. Today, the explosion of fireworks and resulting trauma had forced that purge. Or rather, the aftermath had, because once the adrenaline had left, all that remained was a desperate need to cry.

"Oh, Fidget, I can't even tell you what a day I had." Tears fell unimpeded from her eyes and dampened the dog's fur. "I don't want to even speak of it out loud, it's so awful. And Danny may…he may not be coming back."

Flopping forward on the empty bed, Danny punched his pillow and bunched it up under his head. He'd taken the coward's way out in leaving without speaking to Camilla.

She'd texted him. A single word.

Goodbye.

It had a finality to it that sent an ache down through his core. Somehow, he'd ignored every light flashing a warning of dangerous roads ahead and had pushed forward until his lips were pressed firmly to Camilla's and her curves were against his body, tempting him to want things he had no business wanting. What had he been thinking?

He *knew* Camilla should have been off-limits. He'd left once to protect her from himself. Not much had changed, so why he thought another attempt at their doomed relationship had made sense was escaping him at the moment.

But a few months back, Old Man Jenkins had gotten him thinking about the what-ifs… And the sweet kisses he'd shared with Camilla had only doubled the ante on that gamble.

What if he'd never ended things with her? If he hadn't, they would have been long married by now. Maybe he'd have given in to her wishes to settle in Greenbriar. Or maybe he'd have gotten her to consider somewhere else. Maybe Boston, but Camilla was a Southern girl through and through, so most likely they'd have stayed somewhere in the South. They could have had children. It had been something they'd talked about—with plans to have both biological and adopted. A picture of a little girl, Camilla's mini-me, popped up in his mind and made him smile.

Those hypothetical children could still happen. It wasn't too late, at least not from a biological standpoint, but the worry that she would never really trust him enough to build a future with him, to have a family with him sat heavy on his heart.

What if he hurt her again? Worse than he had before.

And that was the biggest what-if, right there. And, to be truthful, the most probable outcome. He could see in her eyes that she was falling for him a bit more each day.

He sighed.

Nothing had really changed from eight years ago. He could end up hurting her again. Somehow that felt like fact. He had a lot of soul-searching to do if he was going to keep pursuing a relationship with her, starting with finding ways to make sure his darkness didn't seep into her light. He hadn't been able to protect his mother and Robby. He'd let them down when they needed him most. They'd died and no police report saying the drunk driver was at fault could completely absolve his guilt. He should have swerved.

He couldn't be trusted to love someone.

A man was meant to protect his family. Not get them killed.

He rolled to his back and grunted in frustration. But being alone was getting harder and harder with each day that passed. He didn't want to wake up to an empty house. The silence and isolation had long grown old. He wanted so much more.

But it wasn't just his own heart he'd be risking.

Physically at least, Camilla still wanted him as much as he wanted her. That much he could be sure of. Knowing that meant making some changes to his life that he wasn't certain he wanted to make. Namely, if he wanted to be with Camilla, it would mean staying in Greenbriar for good. She'd never leave this town now.

If he went to her house tonight, then that would be it.

A commitment that he had to be completely sure of.

With his mind racing, Danny gave up on the idea of sleep. He got out of bed and went to the kitchen table, where he pulled out his journal. He opened the leather cover and flipped to the first blank page. Putting thoughts on paper had been one of the strongest coping methods he'd found. The act of writing his stresses down acted as a purge, letting him see his situations more objectively.

He'd been journaling since his time in the hospital, handed his first notebook by the therapist assigned to his case. Through the years he'd filled a dozen or more notebooks of varying sizes, but the fact remained that it was a cathartic endeavor for him. He'd carried a notebook with him in the pocket of his ACUs through multiple deployments and field assignments.

The nib of his pen scratched against the paper as he got into the flow of writing, allowing his thoughts to pour out onto the page. Concern that, whatever she said, Camilla might never fully forgive him for the past ate up a large chunk of his writing. He filled multiple pages with his insecurities and worries before he'd expelled enough emotions that rational thought seemed possible. Then another tidbit of Mr. Jenkins's advice hit him—the need to forgive himself.

Danny sighed.

Slipping the cap on his pen, he left it across the page as a bookmark for when he revisited those thoughts with fresh eyes later. Getting that little bit of distance usually helped him gain a lot of perspective over the thoughts he'd inked and allowed him to make better decisions. But forgiveness still felt so far away.

He pushed up from the table and went outside to sit on the dock. With his feet dangling just above the water, he watched the bright colors of the sunset spread across the water.

His mother had always loved the sunsets over the lake. The place had been bought as a weekend getaway, but they'd spent most of the summers out here. He and Robby had shared the tiny loft while his mom and dad had the sole bedroom, but it hadn't felt crowded. Probably because they spent so much time outside, either on the dock or on the water.

Camilla had been a little slow to warm to his mom, but his mom had refused to give up. She'd taken to Camilla from the moment they met. When he'd proposed, his mom had cried big fat tears of joy. She'd have probably kicked his butt all over Greenbriar if she'd known how badly he'd ended up hurting Camilla.

But that was what he did. He hurt people.

Camilla was better off without him. And he was better off alone.

The decision should have made him feel lighter, like a burden had been lifted from his shoulders. Instead, it felt like an anchor had been dropped on his soul. As the night settled in and darkness replaced the cascade of colors, a darkness settled over Danny, as well.

He deserved this pain.

This was his true penance. It was the end of May. He had two more months to finish out the conditions attached to his father's will. Then he could leave for Boston on August 1 and never have to see Camilla's beautiful face again.

CHAPTER TWELVE

WHEN MORNING ROLLED around without a single word from Danny, Camilla's heart filled with dread. They still had two more months on the agreement before they could inherit the medical practice and she could buy him out.

She let out a shaky breath.

Those two months might as well be an eternity. Not that she'd have to worry about seeing him every day. He'd taken the easy way out once by leaving town and he probably had done so again.

She closed Fidget in her cage and walked to the clinic alone. Each step felt like trudging through waist-deep mud as she made her way toward the dream that would shortly be snatched away from her. When she got there, she lovingly traced her fingers over her name on the glass. What would take its place when the clinic closed? Or would it sit empty like the old hardware store?

When she went to unlock the door, the knob turned freely beneath her hand. A ripple of panic ran through her. Had she forgotten to lock it yesterday? Her mind had been such a mess that it was possible.

Cautiously, she opened the door and stepped inside.

Danny sat at the front desk, typing away at the computer. He looked up and some of the color drained from his face. He nodded and returned his eyes to the screen.

If that was how he wanted to play this, she could pretend nothing had happened, too. She tried to keep her chin up and refused to glance his way again as she moved past him to her office. Somehow, she resisted the urge to slam the door.

Sinking down into her chair, Camilla tried not to cry. Danny being here was wholly unexpected. She'd thought he'd have had his truck packed and been halfway back to Boston by now. Instead, he was here at work acting like he hadn't just ripped her heart out and stomped on it for the second time.

But this time was far crueler, as he had stuck around to witness her collapse.

Camilla swallowed hard.

She wouldn't give him the pleasure of seeing her crack. Straightening her posture, she rose to her feet and went to the supply closet. The clinic was in desperate need of supplies and she needed to take inventory first.

"Camilla," he said from behind her. "Can we talk?"

"What's to talk about?" She shrugged, refusing to turn and look at him. She'd always had a harder time hiding her true emotions from him. He could see through the facade she put up easier than anyone else. But Danny had wedged himself into her heart, getting closer to her than anyone else ever had. It was that closeness that let him read her so easily.

"I already made a supply list."

"I'll make my own."

Danny snorted. "You don't have to be so stubborn about this. Why make more work for yourself? Is it just to spite me? Well, honey, I'm still here. You are stuck with me for another two months whether you like it or not."

"Whether I like it or not?" She spun around, anger pulsing through her veins. "Let me tell you something.

I'm getting about tired of you coming into my life and using me for your own amusement and then tossing me aside when things get serious. I would never treat you the way you have treated me. Just because you're scared doesn't mean you can take that out on me."

"Scared?" Danny scoffed. "Who said I was scared?"

"No one had to say it. It's written on your every action. You are scared of commitment. You are scared to let anyone close. Scared to love."

"I'm not scared." His eyes flashed with anger, but beneath the anger, she saw the hurt her words had caused him.

"Okay, then. You're not scared. Then answer me this one thing…why are you running again?" Raising an eyebrow at him, she crossed her arms over her chest and tapped one toe on the floor impatiently. "I'm waiting."

Rather than answer, Danny spun and stomped away.

She called after him, "And you said you weren't running scared."

When she heard the clinic door slam shut behind him, she briefly worried she might have pushed him too far, and that she'd put her future at the clinic at risk, but she had to stand up for herself. The first time Danny had left her, she'd had no chance to tell him how she felt. This time was different. She wasn't going to take this without a fight.

Danny drove out to the lake house determined to get out of Greenbriar and away from Camilla as fast as possible. He didn't have to stick around and listen to her accusing him of things that just weren't true. They could just sell the practice outright. He'd planned to stay in town so that in two months they could divide the practice between them legally, but if she wanted to push him away, he'd go.

"Who does she think she is, calling me scared?" he muttered to himself as he packed. He started throwing his things into laundry baskets and anything else he could find that would hold his belongings. He loaded the back seat of his truck as he filled the containers. The sooner he could get out of town, the better he'd feel.

"Scared to love," he said with a snort of disbelief. "How can Camilla think I'm scared to love when I'm just trying to protect her."

He pulled an old family picture off the wall. His college-aged face stared back at him standing next to his parents and brother. Camilla had taken the photo out on the dock with the sunset behind them. It had been his mom's favorite photo of them.

Carrying the framed picture with him, he walked out onto the dock. That day had been one of the happiest he could remember. He'd proposed to Camilla that very evening, right on this very dock. He ran his finger over each smiling face in the photo.

Every person in that picture wore a genuine smile beamed straight at the woman holding the camera—Camilla. His parents had been enamored with her. Robby had the most massive crush on her from day one, but he'd soon gotten over that and considered her the sister he'd never had. They'd all have been so disappointed with him for running away from her again. His dad had been extremely vocal about it the first time. Now that Danny was trying to do it again, he could imagine the lectures his father would be giving him about not running scared from the love of his life.

"I'm not scared to love?"

What he'd meant as a statement to confirm his own thoughts came out as a question. He didn't want to hurt anyone else he loved. That didn't make him scared.

Or did it?

He closed his eyes and it was Camilla's face that flashed through his thoughts. She was the first person he thought of when he woke each morning, and the last person he thought of each night before he fell asleep.

So why was he running away from her?

She was right. He was running scared. He was the world's biggest idiot and he needed to find a way to fix this.

Now, how did he make it up to her?

He had some work to do.

And he knew just where to start.

CHAPTER THIRTEEN

WHEN THE GATE OPENED, Camilla looked over in panic. Seeing Danny cautiously step through the gate was not what she'd expected. Thankfully, he was careful not to let Fidget out.

"What all do you have there?" She tried to avoid just flat out asking him *why* he was there.

"I went to the store to get that length of chain and a padlock to secure your gate for you. I promised you that I'd secure it so that we didn't have any more escapees."

"We?" she asked, swallowing down her heart that had just filled with hope and lodged itself in her throat.

"I also brought you this." He slowly climbed the steps to the back porch and held something out to her. "I never imagined I'd show this to you, or even a therapist, to be honest. And maybe today isn't the best time. I'm not sure, but I do think you need to read it at some point. I don't expect you to dive in tonight and read every page before sunrise, though."

She took the leather-bound notebook from his outstretched hand. The patina on the leather said it had been well used. "A journal?"

"There are two inserts in there. One is my first journal that begins at the time I was in the hospital and goes through our breakup and my enlistment. The other is the most recent, covering the time I've been back in Greenbriar. The ones in the middle are probably not as beneficial, but maybe I'll show you those, as well, sometime if you are interested." He sat down next to her and took her hand in his. The porch light highlighted his solemn expression. She could see that whatever he was about to say was serious and truthful. "Someday, I want you to read this. It's not a graphic recollection of the accident or my time in the Army, nothing like that. It's more of an account of my thoughts and feelings."

"Are you sure you want me to read it?" Even as she asked, Camilla held her breath because she desperately wanted to understand where his mind was at, during the time of their breakup. She caressed the journal reverently, knowing that Danny had handed her a private piece of his soul and entrusted her with the knowledge contained within its pages. The trust he showed in allowing her access to it made her feel honored. He wasn't running away. In fact, he was finally opening up to her, which couldn't help but bring forth the slightest bit of optimism.

He nodded. Sighed loudly, and then nodded again, almost as if he was reassuring himself that it was okay. "Yeah, I think it's important for us moving forward that you do. Not going to say that it's not triggering a little anxiety, but yeah, I want you to read it."

"Thank you for trusting me enough to show me." She thought it important for her to acknowledge what a big step he'd taken in coming here. To reveal his innermost thoughts, particularly those from such a tumultuous time in his life, had to be hard. She scanned his face, reading his expression and looking at his body language. His knee bounced up and down quickly, an outward sign of his inward anxiety. "It means a lot to me," she said. "But if you need to change your mind, I do understand."

"No. You should read it."

"Not if it's going to upset you." As much as she was dying to open that front cover and absorb the words that would be written in Danny's familiar scrawl, she needed to determine that it wasn't going to hurt him more than it helped her.

He shrugged, but rather than looking at her, his gaze was focused out somewhere midway up her back fence. His expression remained blank, emotions locked away.

"Not if it's going to upset you," Camilla repeated.

Without looking at her, he said softly, "If I want you to trust me, I have to be willing to trust you. You can read it."

"I appreciate that. If it's anything like the emotional nightmare we just went through, and I can only imagine it was worse since you were dealing with losing your immediate family, then it's no wonder you were such a mess. My life wasn't in danger, I wasn't injured, and I'm certain that I'll have nightmares from the festival for a long time to come."

"And if you do, I'll be right here to walk you through them. I won't let you shoulder that burden alone." The conviction in his eyes spoke directly to her soul. "I'm done running."

She sighed. "I really wish I could believe that."

"Babe, if I have to spend the rest of my life making this up to you, I will. Camilla, I love you. I've always loved you. Even when I was too scared to let myself love anyone, you were the only woman I thought about."

In that moment, the way he looked at her…oh, it set her heart racing. Bottom line was that she loved this man, too. She'd loved him from the time she was a mere wisp of a girl on the cusp of womanhood and she'd love him until she left this world and could love no more.

* * *

"You want some coffee?"

Caffeine was much needed if they were going to have the type of discussion he expected them to be having from the seriousness of her expression. After his sudden epiphany, he knew what he wanted, and that was a future with Camilla.

"That would be great, thanks." Camilla moved past him, a wisp of her perfume carrying on the breeze that accompanied her through the doorway of his childhood home.

She moved into the kitchen area and took a seat at the table while he walked straight to the coffeepot. He'd just scooped the grounds into the basket when Camilla spoke.

"'Do I even want Camilla to forgive me?'" she quoted.

His hands shook as he started the coffee and turned to face her.

"When did you start…?" She trailed off, gesturing toward the journal.

"I know the entries should be dated, but that was right after we broke up." He shrugged. "The therapist I saw a few times suggested I start writing one."

He sank down into the chair across from hers, but kept his focus tightly on the polished wooden tabletop. It wasn't necessarily that he was embarrassed about keeping a journal, but the contents of it were so raw and personal that it felt like she'd ripped a Band-Aid off a gaping wound in his soul by reading even that one line aloud. Having her know that she was a topic of his thoughts, enough for him to write about her, bared him to her, exposed her to the kind of hurt he'd wanted to avoid passing on. By letting her know that he cared what she thought, he had opened himself up to the pain of rejection, as well. What had he written in the lines after the heart-baring truth she'd read back to him? He struggled to recall the free-flowing words he'd practically bled out onto the page. Most of what he'd said about her was positive, he thought, but the fear lingered that she'd read an intimate detail he wasn't fully ready to share.

Camilla's gentle fingers covered his hand, slowly, cautiously, like she thought he might reject her touch. "I'm glad you are seeing someone, or have seen someone at least."

He gave a slight nod. Camilla was so perceptive. He had always said she knew him better than he knew himself.

"Good. Does the journaling help?"

He nodded again.

"That's really good to hear. I'm so happy that you've found a way to cope. I've read studies about how many psychologists were using expressive writing as a type of ongoing therapy. If I remember correctly, they were looking at how it could be beneficial for other illnesses, as well, since that sort of private reflection allows them to sort through the personal grief of their reality and helps them to process it with deeper understanding. Is that how you are using it?"

"Yes." The curtness of his answer sat at odds with the soft tones Camilla had spoken in.

Her fingers moved across his, clasping their fingers together. "I'd ask why you were unsure you wanted to be forgiven by me, but if I had to hazard a guess, it's because you don't feel like you deserve to be. Maybe you haven't yet forgiven yourself?"

He couldn't even bring himself to nod that time as she cut straight to the core of his problem. Just like in the past, Camilla saw through him and knew exactly what he was thinking, what he was dealing with. That uncanny ability to see his truth, no matter his words or outward actions, had been a large part of why he'd pushed her away. She'd have absorbed so much of his pain, trying to help him, that she would have lost herself in the process.

She paused, giving him a chance to speak, but when he remained quiet, she continued, "This seems to be making you uncomfortable, but I'll just say, there's nothing to forgive."

Jerking, he brought his gaze up to meet hers. There was so much to forgive; how could she even think that? His brow wrinkled as he tried to come up with the right words to argue that statement.

With the bluntness he'd always loved, Camilla said, "Maybe I should phrase it this way—there's nothing left to forgive. How do you see us moving forward from here?"

Tightening his fingers around hers, he leaned forward and brushed his lips over the pulse point at her wrist. "I'm worried that what I want will be exactly what you don't need."

"I'm a big girl now, Danny, and I haven't needed you to protect me from anyone in a very long time."

But who will protect you from me? ran through Danny's thoughts, but he shoved that insecurity back and focused on the fact that the woman he still loved was in front of him, and willing to talk to him, even if he had messed up so badly in a thousand different ways. Since he'd ended their engagement, he'd been floating through life making no meaningful connections, allowing no one to get close. That was no way to live and he didn't want to do it anymore.

This wasn't a game. He couldn't press Pause or start over if he made a mistake. This wasn't casual dating, not for him. This was his entire future risked on convincing one beautiful woman to trust in his flawed and imperfect self.

Even a few short months ago, the idea of spending half a year in Greenbriar had felt like a heavy chain wrapped around his neck, choking the life from him, but now it symbolized a rebirth. In Greenbriar, and with Camilla, he could find the Danny that had been lost all those years ago and become the man he'd always intended to be.

He'd sure as heck never planned to become the grumpy old bachelor who people shied away from out of fear that he'd bite their heads off. Somehow, he'd always thought he'd be a lot like his dad, the type of man that people looked up to and came to whenever they had a problem, medical or not. He had a long way to go if he wanted to be that man, though. Maybe too far.

And he wanted to do it with Camilla at his side. He and Camilla were meant to be together. She was his future. That much he was sure of.

"Your forgiveness of all the pain I caused you is more proof of your strength. I'm here because of stubbornness. Camilla, you are the strongest woman I've ever known and I'm sorry I couldn't see that sooner."

"You know I need to read this right now." She waved the journal at him slightly.

"I didn't mean tonight…" He trailed off when he noticed the obstinate set to her jaw. Briefly, he considered arguing, but then she crossed her arms and stared until he backed down. Knowing better than to try to stop her when she'd put her mind to something, he shrugged and made the woman some coffee while she carried the journal off through the house.

When he followed a few minutes later with two mugs of steaming coffee, he found her snuggled up on the couch under a teal throw blanket with her nose buried in his journal. He sat the mug on the table next to her and she flashed a faint smile in his direction before her eyes focused back on the page.

He sank down on the opposite end of the couch and she tucked her feet under his thigh. Sipping at the steaming mug of black coffee, he reflected back on his last year. If anyone had asked him twelve months ago where he saw himself, the last place Danny would have said he would have been was cuddled up on the couch in his childhood home with the one who "got away." Never thought he'd truly consider this town his home. He'd spent so much of his youth counting down the days until he could get out of there that he'd never once imagined coming home to Greenbriar to stay.

Everyone who knew him would have put money on him staying in Boston or moving to another big city. They'd have said he liked shallow people and even shallower relationships. Some might have called him an adrenaline junkie or a rolling stone. And while that might have been true even a few months ago, now they would be all kinds of wrong. The things that man wanted no longer appealed. Thanks to Camilla, his entire plan for the future had shifted.

Danny was not only in his hometown, but planning to spend the rest of his life here. Assuming Camilla agreed to marry him. *Again.* While he'd occasionally fantasized occasionally about Camilla's return to his life, he'd always thought of her coming to him in whatever city he was living in at that time. Returning to Greenbriar had never factored into any of his fantasies.

But here he was and, excluding the unusual horrors from earlier in the week, he was happier than he'd been in years. And it was all thanks to the woman at his side, and her wonderful, forgiving heart.

Camilla adjusted her position and the movement sent the soft scent of her perfume wafting through the air to tickle at his nose. Every now and then, her breath would catch and that little noise would send his heart on a jog, as the irrational worry of that page being the one that sent her running for the hills crept into his mind. But she would simply pause to wipe away a few tears and continue reading.

When she got to the pages where he had been contemplating suicide, she sat up and hugged him so tight that he couldn't breathe. Her tears soaked his shirt, and in the quiet room, her sobs sounded painfully loud.

"Before you ask, I no longer feel that way and I haven't for a long time. That was years ago, before I joined the Army." He should have warned her about that part. Using his thumbs, he brushed the tears away from her cheeks. Hopefully, this would be the last of the pain he'd cause her from his actions over eight years ago. "You know I think I've seen you cry more this week than in the entire time I've known you?"

"Maybe I'm just finally opening up more myself." Camilla kissed his cheek, but bravely dove back in to her reading. The suicidal thoughts had been the worst of it, so the rest should be easier on her, he hoped. While she read, he kept himself busy with checking out all the changes she'd made to the house he'd grown up in. Somehow, she'd turned it into even more of a home. Within these walls, he didn't feel the creeping darkness. Even while she was reading the journal where he'd poured so many emotions out in his messy script, he didn't feel panicked or have the urge to snatch it from her hands. To say he had zero anxiety about her deep dive into his emotional past might be overselling it, but he wasn't on the verge of a panic attack at least.

When she turned the last page and flipped the journal closed, his breath came a bit easier. He waited impatiently after she finished reading, to hear her thoughts, her opinions, to see if it helped her with the whys behind his reasons for ending their engagement, to hear if she'd ever fully forgive him. With how entangled his reasons were, with his confused mindset at the time, it was important for her to know what kind of condition he was in. But for what seemed like an eternity, she sat holding his hand, staring down at their interlaced fingers.

Did she really forgive him? Did she hate him? Was she trying to think up a polite way to tell him to get out of her house and out of her life? His heart couldn't take much more waiting.

Finally, she looked up at him. Questions filled her eyes. Her fingers grazed along the line of his jaw, so light and tender. "So, when you said you were not cut out to be a husband…?"

"I could have married you and gone through the motions, but I was so lost in my head that I know for sure I'd have made us both miserable." Breathing deep and slow, he measured his words. This was a loaded topic and hard to vocalize. "I thought you were better off without me. At the time, I didn't see it as running away. I saw it as protecting you by removing a dangerous element from your life."

"You thought you were dangerous to me?" Shaking her head at him, she countered, "You were wrong. And I would have told you myself if I thought that I was better off without you."

He wasn't surprised by her statement. Not really. Camilla was a strong and proud woman who knew her own mind. Somehow, he'd lost sight of that fact and look

where it had landed them. He'd have to try harder to remember exactly who she was, going forward.

"I know that now." He grimaced, considering how
he wanted to approach the rest of this conversation. He
slouched back on the couch and blew out a breath. "Don't
hate me for saying this, but I wasn't sure you were strong
enough to face what I was dealing with."

She raised an eyebrow, calling him on the falsehood
he'd just blatantly spewed without thought. Silence hung
heavy between them until he revised his statement.

"Scratch that… Truthfully, I convinced myself that
you weren't strong enough, that I was toxic to you, and I
let those false assumptions lead me down the road to utter
stupidity." He reached out and let his fingertips touch her
cheek. Irritation still glittered in the depths of her blue
eyes. She was not going to make this easy on him. "It's
not an excuse, but an explanation that hopefully helps
you understand why I did what I did."

"You went so far down the road to stupidity that I think
you set up camp there." The ghostly hint of a smile landed
on her lips. He added another item to the list of things
he loved about her—the way she tried to hide her smile
when she was snarky, but was never really successful.

Her words were probably meant to lighten up the conversation that had moved deep into the heavy zone, but
he wasn't finished explaining how he'd gone so far off
course with her.

"You're right. Your strength is a force of nature. I
shouldn't have doubted you, because even after I destroyed all your hopes and dreams, you picked yourself
up. You made a life here without me. You kept standing
and you accomplished the plans you set in motion all
those years ago. You have a successful medical practice—
don't think I didn't hear that you kept it going alone while

Dad was sick. I was lost, though. The demons in my head outweighed my confidence in all aspects of my life. With all the negative thoughts, my insecurities became stronger than my common sense. And I wasn't strong enough at that moment to fight for us. I was exhausted from just fighting for myself. It wasn't until I came back here that I started seeing what I was missing out on with my self-imposed isolation."

"I know." She held the journal up and gave it a shake for emphasis. "This gave me so much insight. Reading firsthand what you were dealing with emotionally… Man, that was heartbreaking. You should be proud of how you fought those demons and didn't let them win."

Fidget ran over, and after a couple of false starts, managed to hop up on the couch next to them. She jumped in Danny's lap, sniffed his cheek and then snorted in his face. "Aww, come on, really, Fidget?" Despite his exasperation at the dog's unhygienic actions, she'd really grown on him. "What's next, sneezing in my eye?"

"She only snorts or sneezes in the faces of people she loves," Camilla said indulgently, rubbing the little dog's ear. "She's been kind of a mama's girl and doesn't like just anyone, you know."

"You think she'll like me as her daddy?" His heart pounded half out of his chest, but it was too late to take the words back now. He should have planned something romantic, taken her for a moonlit stroll, or out for a fancy dinner in the city. She deserved more than a blurted proposal via a dog, but it was too late to recall those words now.

Camilla gaped at him. For an unbearably long beat, she sat staring at him, completely motionless. Finally, she blinked rapidly before asking, "What are you saying, Danny?"

He stood and pulled the jeweler's box out of his pocket.

"Oh…" she breathed the single syllable. Her gaze darted from the black velvet box in his hand to his eyes and back. Tears welled up in her eyes, but the smile that graced her face was bright enough to power the town.

"Camilla Devereaux, I asked you this once before and your answer then was yes. I'm hoping you'll say yes again tonight. If you do, I promise I'll never give you reason to regret it." Dropping to one knee, Danny asked her the most important question a man could ask his woman. "Will you marry me?"

"Yes," she said, her voice solid and unwavering. She held her hand out for him to slip the ring on her finger. "I'd love nothing more than to marry you."

"This is going right back where it belongs," he said as he took the ring out of the box. The diamond slid onto her finger, a perfect fit, as it always had been. "I never should have taken it off your finger in the first place."

With that done, he pressed his lips to hers and poured all the love and desire he felt for her into that embrace. They clung together, entangled until they had to come up for air.

Emotion clogged his throat, making his voice gruff. "Hard to believe that only a few short months ago I thought you were out of my life for good. So much has changed."

"I know." She smiled, but then a seriousness passed over her expression. Far too weighty for minutes after a proposal.

"What's wrong?" His mind raced as he tried to problem-solve how she'd gone from tears of happiness to serious and morose in the space of seconds.

With a sigh, she gave him a sad little smile. "I suppose we will have to set up a visitation schedule for when you go back to Boston."

So that was the problem? She still thought he was leaving. Relief coursed through him when he knew it was something so easily remedied.

Tucking a lock of hair behind her ear, Danny said, "I have something for you. Don't move."

He ran out to his truck and came back with a folder. He handed it to her without another word.

When she opened it, she looked down at the legal papers inside and asked, "When do you leave?" Her voice sounded a little choked.

"That wasn't the reaction I expected."

"I appreciate the gesture. It means the world to me that you would just give me your half of the clinic."

"But…"

She sighed. "I wanted a real marriage where we were together every night. But I suppose I'll learn to like the long-distance thing as long as we are together."

"I never said I was going back to Boston."

"Aren't you?" Hope blossomed in her eyes.

"Nah. I have everything I need and I think it's time I put down some roots right here in Greenbriar. Have to admit, this place has grown on me." He grinned. "Besides, Greenbriar needs a trauma surgeon for the new medevac station that's going to be set up here in the fall. Boston would be a little too much of a commute."

Camilla closed her eyes and a single tear trekked down her cheek. When he wiped it away, she let out a little chuckle and shook her head. She bit her lower lip and tried to hide a smile. Unsuccessfully, yet again.

"Tell me what you're thinking?" he asked, curious to know what amused her about him staying in Greenbriar.

Her lips twitched before a full smile graced her face. "Just wondering if your dad was looking down right now saying 'I told you so' and grinning from ear to ear."

"As much effort as he put into orchestrating my reunion with you, Dr. Devereaux, I think you could put money on it." Danny pulled her in close, his chest shaking with laughter. With Camilla tucked safely in his arms, he let out a deep sigh and looked up.

"Thanks, Dad. This one time, I'm thankful you meddled in my life."

Five years later

"Everybody that comes to my princess tea party birthday is going to wear a pretty princess dress. Even you, Daddy!"

"A princess tea party?" Danny said, his voice filled with horror. "Are you sure you want a princess tea party for your birthday? We could do pirates or a bouncy house?"

Camilla struggled to hide her laughter. Their almost four-year-old daughter had wrapped Danny around her little finger within a minute of her birth, but having him wear a princess dress might stretch beyond the hold she had on her daddy.

"There will be no pirates at my party," Lindy insisted. "Only princesses."

The resignation in his voice was almost too much for Camilla. "But Daddy's not a princess, honey."

Lindy tilted her head and gave him the smile that usually got her way, and Camilla decided to step in before her husband ended up in a ball gown at the whim of his daughter. That little girl could talk him into about anything when she batted those eyelashes at him.

"If you are a princess, that makes Daddy a king. And kings can't be seen in a dress." She tapped Lindy on the nose playfully. "You wouldn't want a big ol' dragon to come in and think our kingdom had no king, would you?"

Their little girl considered Camilla's question carefully. Camilla could practically see the gears turning while Lindy considered that possibility and she really hoped she'd made things better, not worse. Danny might end up in a dragon costume instead of a frilly dress.

Finally, Lindy shook her head. "No, I don't want a dragon. Okay, Daddy, the king can wear pants, but everyone else has to wear a princess dress." She skipped off to chase Fidget around the yard.

Danny wrapped his arms around Camilla. "I'm so outnumbered here. Thank you for stepping in there. I thought for sure I was gonna get stuck agreeing to some fluffy pink concoction that would make me the laughingstock of the town."

Snuggling into his embrace, Camilla laughed. "It was purely self-preservation on my part. But if you are lucky, this one will be a boy and help balance out the numbers."

Danny leaned back so that their eyes met. "Are you…?"

She nodded. Her blood work had come back to confirm what her body and the two pink lines on the home test had already told her. Their second little one was on the way.

Things had never been more perfect for her. She had a thriving medical practice, a loving husband, one healthy child, and another on the way. It was all she'd ever dreamed of.

"I'm going to be a daddy again?" Danny asked, his hand coming to rest on her still-flat stomach.

She nodded again. "What do you think?"

"I have never been happier." A wide smile graced his handsome face. "I love you, Dr. Devereaux."

"And I love you, Dr. Owens."

* * * * *

MILLS & BOON

Coming next month

THE VET'S UNEXPECTED HERO
Traci Douglass

Lucy looked up at Jackson. "He's trained to be a therapy dog. He knows better than to jump up on people like that."

"Really. It's okay. I'm used to it. Like I said, some people find me irresistible." Jackson gave her a charmingly crooked, wry smile she felt all the way to her toes.

Oh boy. Not good. Not good at all.

Lucy needed something, anything, to distract herself from her unwanted awareness of this man. "Fine. Whatever. Good for you if people find you irresistible. I don't. I mean, there's nothing wrong with you, but—"

He crossed his arms, his smile widening as she babbled away like an idiot.

Her cheeks felt hotter than Hades now, and the more he teased her, the more frazzled she got.

Jackson studied her, his expression serious.

Flustered, Lucy forgot to be nervous and just laughed, easing some of her inner tension. She shrugged and stared down at her toes.

"Well, it was nice to meet you, Lucy Miller," he said, clasping his hands atop the table. Nice hands. Long, tapered fingers, well-kept nails. Strong hands. Capable hands. He was a paramedic, after all. He saved people. A small spark of warmth burst inside her. He'd certainly saved her just now, from dying from terminal embarrassment. "I wish I'd known earlier you were going to be here. I'd have brought a copy of the required binder with the emergency response team plan for you. I don't have a spare with me now, but if you give me your address, I'm happy to run one by your place on Big Pine Key tomorrow. It's my day off."

"Oh…uh…" Sitting beside him in the conference room was disturbing enough to her equilibrium. The thought of him at her compound had her quaking in her tennis shoes. "That's okay. Give it to Stacy and she can bring it to me. Or I can swing by the hospital and pick it up." She pulled a clean sheet of paper from her legal pad and picked up her red pen. "Just tell me what time would be best."

Jackson frowned. "It's really no problem, and it would be more convenient for me to drop it off. I'll be in your area anyway. Unless there's some reason you don't want me there?"

An awkward silence fell between them as they studied each other.

She couldn't help wondering what it might feel like to slide her fingers through his short black hair, learning its texture and temperament. The fluorescent overhead lights gleamed off his high cheekbones and there was a hint of dark stubble on his firm jaw. His lips were full and firm, with a slight tip to the outer corners that gave him a perpetual smirk, like everything amused him.

"Don't worry, I won't overstay my welcome. Promise. I'll Google your address," he said at last. Jackson stood and picked up his papers but didn't hold out his hand this time. The smile was there again though, still charming, too. "See you tomorrow, Lucy Miller."

Continue reading
THE VET'S UNEXPECTED HERO
Traci Douglass

Available next month
www.millsandboon.co.uk

LET'S TALK
Romance

For exclusive extracts, competitions
and special offers, find us online: